LUCKY BASTARD CLUB

30 MISSIONS

Michelle Lee

BLUE FORGE PRESS

Port Orchard ✹ Washington

For Lisa

I hope this honors your grandfather properly
and gives people more information on the fliers of WWII,
their heroics, and their sacrifices.
Thank you for asking me to do this.

Foreword

I wanted to start by saying that the Lucky Bastard Club is real. The novel is fiction based on fact, but the club exists. It's not an 'officially' recognized club. However, members of this unique group of people might think differently. To be a member of this elite group, you had to be a part of an aircrew that flew no fewer than thirty missions over Nazi-occupied areas and deliver explosive goodwill to Hitler and his merry crew. This story is told from a young man's perspective as he embarks on his journey through the military.

I've read many historical fiction novels and never once encountered this club. It's a shame, too. I urge anyone interested to do a little research and read the online articles about the Lucky Bastards. Their experiences speak volumes about a dark period in our history.

While the club was not officially recognized, the members still received a certificate after discharge declaring their accomplishments. Many of these members underplay what they experienced and chalked up the risk and dangers to nothing more than a day's work. It's so much more than that.

Dedication, bravery, and honor are but a few of the traits that these extraordinary men possessed. The Eighth Air Force pulled off some amazing feats during World War II. I hope to remember these men for the sacrifices and courage they brought to their missions and applaud them for surviving. Only one in three aircrewmen survived World War II, a shocking statistic to me. Over forty thousand airmen died in service.

No matter the war, branch, or duty, every veteran deserves our respect—my heartfelt thanks to all who served and are serving and those we lost.

LUCKY BASTARD CLUB

30 MISSIONS

Michelle Lee

PROLOGUE

Present Day

The morning activities hadn't started well for Lisa. The news Lisa watched talked of a storm moving in. Ordinarily, it wasn't a big deal; storms could be cathartic. Here in Florida, though, sometimes they say storm and mean hurricane. She had to spend an extra hour watching the depressing stories until they spoke of the weather again. It would only be a storm, as she knew storms were. It was hot and humid, so she guessed there would be lightning, rain, and maybe a little wind.

Lisa spent the whole morning making a donation pile, a dump pile, and a keep-and-take-home pile. All three of the piles were daunting in size already and only growing. Getting the keep and take-home items moved back home was a challenge she would try to solve on a different day. Right now, she focused on cleaning things up and possibly making a dump run before the storm hit.

The current room she was working on was her dad's bedroom, specifically the closet. How her dad had packed as much crap into the closet, she didn't know. Thankfully, she was down to the floor now. After she moved this big footlocker-type thing, it would go much smoother.

Lisa bent over, wiped the dust off an old wooden chest she'd dragged out of a closet, and then sat on it. The process of cleaning out a parent's house after death was complex, to say the least. Her father's entire life was in this house. Sorting through it when his passing was so fresh felt like it was opening wounds. There were so many memories made here, and no father to remember them with anymore. She fought back another wave of tears and shoved off the chest to distract herself. She wasn't a crier and she had things to do.

Lisa turned around and unclasped the lid, pulling it open. She didn't know what to expect anymore. Lisa had uncovered many hobbies her dad had: model trains, World War II research, sailing awards, and schematics for sailboats; it was a lot. She momentarily stared at the open chest in confusion before realizing what she was gazing upon in who knew how many years. It was her grandfather's World War II chest. She remembered her dad talking to her about it and the items inside. It had been years since she had thought about it.

She sank to the floor and closed the lid, staring at the faded green paint and white letters she missed when she came across the chest. Lisa gingerly reopened it and reached out to touch the items that were with her grandpa throughout the war while he was in Europe. Lisa carefully lifted the bomber jacket with a pinup girl on the back and smiled. She had a replica of the coat, but holding the original was astounding. It had held up well for being crammed into a chest for all these years.

She placed it carefully next to her and, piece by piece, rifled through the rest with the utmost care. Lisa set all the photographs in one pile, documents in another and handled each item of gear with tender care due to its age. It was all there, all his original war gear down to the safety kits. Some were in better shape than others, which was understandable, not just due to the age but because of where it was and the action it had seen.

Not wanting anything to happen to those, Lisa gently put them back in the chest, precisely where she found them, and looked at the two piles of documents and pictures. Not quite feeling up to seeing photos while her emotions were so raw, Lisa picked up the papers. She flipped through the pages of flights, awards, training schedules, and orders, skimming the information without reading anything and eventually found a stack of letters.

Lisa set the photos back in the chest on the top shelf and closed the lid. She then turned around, leaned against the chest and read some letters. The first correspondence appeared to be between her Nana and Grandpa, and Lisa read those, feeling a little like an intruder. She forgot about going through her dad's stuff and lost herself in letters between her grandparents. It was a step back in time and Lisa treasured the deeper look into their lives. Thankfully, there was nothing intimate, and she didn't read anything she didn't want to know.

She skimmed through letters that other family members had sent to her grandpa during his deployment. One of them was informing him of a death in the family. Lisa couldn't imagine getting a letter like that while being so far away and unable to do anything about it. She wondered how her grandpa felt while reading that, with him being in the war and immersed in a lot of bad things. She didn't know anything about his service other than he was a part of the Army Air Corps since the Air Force hadn't yet established itself.

A few minutes after she went through all the letters, she pulled out a typed document that was several pages long and had dated paragraphs. Lisa's jaw dropped as she saw the list of dates and understood that each of these paragraphs was a mission her grandpa had flown overseas during the war. Despite the mounting list of tasks she needed to complete before she flew home, she began reading.

She paid no attention to the storm brewing because it was Florida, and storms were something that just happened, and you'd better get used to them, or life would become a ball of anxiety and fear of hurricanes. Lisa had learned to tell the difference between them and the timing of when they would hit. After watching the news, she realized this was an ordinary storm. She didn't need to worry about the house getting ripped out of the ground during high winds.

Before she knew it, she was sucked into the world her grandpa lived during the war as she read the descriptions he'd written about his experiences. Her mind added what she knew of the man. A movie began to play in her mind. At that moment, her grandpa was alive again.

CHAPTER 1

1937, Milwaukee, Wisconsin

I stared out at Lake Michigan's cold, churning water and counted the days I had left to make my move. I turned eighteen in February. I was an adult, a man, and I had plans for my future that didn't match those of my parents. I supposed I wasn't the only person to want to go their own direction, and I was sure I wouldn't be the last.

My family had roots in Germany and owned a chemical company there. My father wanted me to be a part of that, and I disagreed. Suhm Company, Inc. wasn't for me. I was a Freemason as of recently, an amateur sailboat builder, a roller-skater, and about to be a soldier. I hoped.

The country was still in the Great Depression, jobs were scarce, and people were in bad health and malnourished due to food shortages, lack of medical care, and work. It was a hard time to be alive and I was lucky to have found something that allowed me to earn some money. I supposed it was because I was young and fit, though I wasn't about to look a gift horse in the mouth.

Tensions were building in Europe again and something told me the situation would escalate. I was born at the end of the First World War and remembered the mentality of people in the preceding years. The memories were vague, yet I distinctly remember the anger. Though it was valid, it's only a minuscule reason for wanting to join the military, the curiosity of what it would be like to be in a war. Mainly, I wanted to escape my home. Life there wasn't ideal. It was better than many others but wasn't good for me. My mom drank a lot and I seemed to be a target for her anger.

Sailing was great for getting away short term. The weather had to cooperate for it to work unless you wanted to die. Taking out the little boat I'd built in this would mean death for me. I was a man in the eyes of my country and they'd send me off to a war if one came up. However, I was eighteen and still a kid in many ways. Dying in icy water during a storm and drowning wasn't on my radar. I wanted to live and see the world.

I was good with my hands and my coordination was spot on. I could read and write plans for creating sailboats. I figured that with those skills, I could be useful in the military. I could find a career with the skills I learned in the Army; at least, that's what they liked to say. The military trained you and I didn't have to pay for college, ask my parents for money for school, or travel somewhere I didn't want to go. I could ask, but I would again hear the family business offer in Germany. That wasn't somewhere I wanted to go.

I was a fastidious reader of the newspapers and read them cover to cover every day. The editors often buried the world news in the middle or back of the papers, and things with Germany looked like it wouldn't be a good place to be, so why would I want to work in the family business over there? Learning the chemist trade didn't interest me either. Working with chemicals sounded droll.

I shrugged it off and watched the sunset reflect off the choppy lake waters. The wind was kicking up whitecaps, making it look like an ocean storm from my vantage point. It was one of the great things about the lake. It looked like an ocean, which was a fantastic thing to have in a landlocked state.

I'd walk home soon. The wind was biting cold and my jacket wasn't the warmest. I wasn't a bulky man and didn't retain heat well. One of the girls I'd danced with at the last Freemason mixer I'd attended called me lanky. To be fair, I towered over her as she wasn't tall and I stood at six foot four inches. By those standards, lanky would be an apt description.

The depression hadn't helped me with putting on weight, either. I didn't go hungry, but there wasn't a lot of extra to go around and build up muscle. I got more robust, but my body burned it up without extra food to maintain the weight. A lot of people around looked like me, only shorter.

Another gust of wind slammed into me like a knife trying to slice me open. Damn it. It was too early to go home, but I didn't think I had a choice. I pushed away from the tree, hunched into my coat, and headed home.

"No sailing for you today, eh, sonny?" an elderly man sitting on a bench asked me. "I've watched you out there before. Your boat's a beauty."

"Thank you, sir. It took me a while, but I poured my heart into making her," I told the gracious man. "I hope to get her out there again for another test run. I plan on entering a race with her."

"Ah, you made it? That's quite impressive, son," the man praised. "I'm no expert. I've just sat in this spot for more years than I can remember and watched the boats bob along out there. I've seen quite a few beauties and I have to admit that I admired yours. I remember it well because you are a tall lad and I thought you sailed well for someone so young. I do hope to see you out there competing. Congratulations on a job well done, young man." The older man pulled his coat tighter around him and shivered.

"Do you need help home, sir?" I offered. It was probably far too cold for him to be out in this kind of weather. "I'd be happy to walk you home if you do."

"Talented and polite," the man said as he smiled at me. "I'm fine, son. I only live a few minutes away, and I drove myself. My coat is a bit thicker than yours, but it is mighty cold out here. I do so enjoy watching the sunset on days when storms are brewing. It makes for a spectacular sight. It reminds me there's still a God out there and it eases my mind to think those sunsets are telling me He hasn't forgotten us."

It was a nice thought, though I wasn't sure I believed the sentiment. "Well, I thank you for your kind words and wish you a pleasant evening." I tipped my head at him in farewell and began the trek home.

I'd go to bed early and leave for my die-cutting job early in the morning. I made about forty-two cents an hour for labor and knew many would kill for the job. I didn't love it, nor did I hate it. The factory was bustling and I was getting paid. It was more than other men had. The work kept me busy, put money in my pocket and killed time until I enlisted—four more days.

April 16th, 1937
Whitefish Bay National Guard Armory

I took in a deep breath to calm my nerves and pushed open the door to the armory. The old red brick building was the start of my new beginning. Today was my enlistment day—

the date I'd been anticipating for a long while. I had an appointment for oh-eight hundred hours sharp and was five minutes early. To my surprise, I wasn't the first to arrive. I found five other men around my age standing awkwardly, not talking to each other.

I smirked and walked over to change that. "Gentlemen, hello, I'm Ralph. Are you all enlisting too?"

"Yeah," the shortest one of the men answered me. "Paul. Nice to meet you, Ralph. What's your interest?"

"I don't know yet." I shrugged my shoulders. "Maybe a flight crew. Being in the air sounds exciting. I can fix about anything, and I have good hand-eye coordination. I build boats, too. Sailboats. Do you sail?" I was merely going for a conversation to break the ice and get these guys to relax. If they were all tense, I was worried I'd be apprehensive too, for no reason other than they were.

"Nah." Paul shook his head. "I can't swim; got a big fear of water. Guess I'd better learn to get over that, huh?" Paul laughed nervously. "They'll probably make us do something in the water sometime in the next three years."

I saw a man in uniform headed our way and I automatically turned to face him and tucked my hands behind my back like I'd see other military people do. Paul followed my example; the other four men did the same moments later. I didn't know if it was right, but it's what I did.

"Welcome to Battery D, 121st Field Artillery, men. My name is Tech Sergeant Smith. We will start you with some intake forms in this line here," he pointed at a forty-five-degree angle to his right, "in alphabetical order. If you get through that, you'll move to medical, station number two. If they pass you there, you'll go to station three next for your eye exam. Are you seeing the pattern? If you pass all those, you'll get the required immunizations at our lovely station four. For those of you who don't know what that means, those are your shots. If you have a fear of needles, you'd better make your peace with it now. Do not lose the file they give you at station one, the intake. Where you go, the file goes. That file is in your hand at each station as you wait in alphabetical order. Make sure you know your alphabet."

It didn't take long for last names to get shared amongst the group and we lined ourselves up in front of the first station: intake. I was near the back of the line and got to stand there and try to wait with a semblance of patience. I wasn't as good at that as I'd like, and I fidgeted too much for my liking. Today was too important for me to botch.

I felt antsy because this was the first day of the new life that I had spent so much time envisioning for myself. I didn't know what that would look like since this was the beginning and it was nothing I had experience in. I supposed I'd built it up to some grand scheme in my mind and didn't consider the mechanics of everything, which wasn't like me. My usual was to plan everything out, map it, or draft it in the case of sailboats. Then, figure out where the best place to start was. I wanted change so badly that I overlooked the work that would need to go in to make my vision a reality. It was almost a rude awakening that made me feel inadequate.

Several things went through my mind as I stood there and waited and I found myself drifting off in thought to the sailboat I was working on. It was the only thing that kept me from dancing in line. I couldn't wait to test her seaworthiness and dreamed of sailing around the world on her. Gads! Imagine the excitement of that—nothing but myself and the unpredictable sea. The danger and the challenge thrilled me. I supposed being on a flight crew would be similar if that's where they put me.

"Suhm!" a deep voice barked. My thoughts consumed me so much that I practically jumped.

I bravely stepped forward and moved behind a curtained wall. "Ralph Suhm, sir," I answered as I stood ramrod straight. I wished they would tell me what to do.

"Sit." The burly man pointed to a chair. The man granted my unspoken wish.

The name patch on his uniform stated Nelson. I didn't know enough about the ranks to decipher the other patches, pins, and whatnot. I liked the looks of it all, though. Another thrill went through me to think I could have all that on my uniform someday. It was enough to distract me from what he was saying.

"Suhm! Focus!" Nelson snapped. "Do you have any special skills?" He impatiently tapped his pen against the open file on his desk.

"Sir, I can build sailboats and sail them, fix almost anything mechanical in front of me, and I have excellent hand-eye coordination. I'm not too shabby with painting, either. I don't suppose being good on roller skates has any bearing on anything I would do here, but there you have it. I'm willing to learn anything and eager to start," I succinctly replied. "If I get to request a position, I was thinking of something on a flight crew."

"Have you ever shot a gun?" Nelson asked, making a few notes and ignored my request.

"Yes, sir, a rifle," I responded. "I think I've got a pretty good eye."

"Not the first time I've heard that." Nelson slapped the file in front of him shut and handed it to me. "Take that to the next station. Keep your nose out of it. That file belongs to the government."

That was the rest of my day: station to station. Some guys seemed to have trouble with the medical exam due to malnourishment. For the vision exam, the same guys were less than stellar for the same reason. We all seemed to do okay on the physical test. The immunizations were when I found out I didn't want to be on a team with one of those guys who couldn't even take a shot to his rear. Then, we were declared fit for duty and told to report back the next day to start boot camp, even the guys who had issues with the stations. I guessed they needed people.

I could expect it to take ten weeks and I'd learn combat training and get taught discipline; they reiterated that several times. I would be physically tested, another reiteration, and become trained on various weapons.

Right after we finished the basic training, news spread of a woman pilot named Amelia Earhart, a pioneer for females in the aviation field. She was going to be the first female pilot to circumnavigate the world. Her plane was a Lockheed Model 10-E Electra, a twin-engine American-made all-metal plane. It was a nice-looking craft.

On July 2nd, somewhere over the mighty Pacific Ocean, Amelia Earhart and her co-pilot, Fred Noonan, went missing not long after they took off after refueling. The country was shocked and dismayed that it happened and speculation was rampant. Most presumed that she crashed and died over the water. They were so close to being finished and that was heartbreaking. I closed the newspaper and pondered the situation while I finished my lunch.

CHAPTER 2

1938

I sat back and let the waves of the lake rock the wooden boat. I'd finished her not too long ago and it was only around my third time taking her out. I named her Lady Luck. It was the second boat I'd created. She was a comet-class sailboat, a dinghy, which meant I built her for racing. I couldn't wait.

The dinghy weighed about two hundred and sixty pounds and she fit two people, but I'd be the only one sailing her. It was the perfect size for my tall frame. Lady Luck was about sixteen feet long and about five and a half feet wide with one mast and about one hundred and thirty-five square feet of sail. She was beautiful and I was proud.

I raced the one I made last year and did alright, but it was not great. I ended up selling that one. I learned areas I needed to improve in and put them all into the design and crafting of Lady Luck. From what I could see, I was successful and she rode the water smoothly.

After the last weekend of drill training for the guard, I was ready for the regatta. They ran us hard and I found it mentally challenging to hear the constant barking of orders. I didn't mind the discipline aspect of the military; it suited me. I struggled with the sergeants yelling in my ear and telling me I wasn't good enough. I knew it was to strengthen our minds and help us to get past the blocks that would come our way in life. It didn't mean I liked it.

The South Shore Yacht Club was hosting the regatta and the excitement was almost too much to bear. The few test runs I completed were with excellent results. Lady Luck was fast and beautiful with sleek lines. I sounded like a proud papa, and I wasn't ashamed to admit I felt like one, too.

The past year since I'd enlisted with the National Guard had its moments. I'd become proficient at shooting and could fix all the vehicles at my disposal. Physically, I was in the best shape of my life, but I still felt restless inside and needed more. They had me learning about the aircraft and I'd gone up in some smaller planes and enjoyed it. I was spot on when I said I'd learn new skills to make a career out of later in life.

I still lived at home with my parents and my sister Alicia. I was close with my sister, though I wanted to be away from my parents. Life on that front hadn't improved, yet my dad was excited about the upcoming regatta. The boats were one area I didn't disappoint him. He was boasting to his friends about Lady Luck and I think he even took some bets. I don't think my mom even cared in the slightest.

I caught the gust of wind right and swung the boat back toward shore to bring her in. I didn't want to. Being out on the water like this was peaceful and thrilling. It was a nice change from the die-cutting work, guard training, and relentless search for a woman to fill the empty places in my life. However, that part was the most fun.

I grinned to myself at the thought. I'd done much looking and relished every minute of it; no future Mrs. Ralph Suhm yet. It was easy to charm the ladies and I probably wasn't ready to settle down to a family life yet. That need for more excitement kept pulling at my soul. Tying myself to a woman now would only ensure she took the backseat to all my other hopes and dreams. That wouldn't be fair to her, whoever she may be.

I sailed up to the dock and climbed out of Lady Luck. I pulled her to shore, and a man standing there helped me get her out and loaded her up on the small trailer I'd built.

"Thanks, sir." I leaned over and shook his hand. "I appreciate the help with my girl."

"She's a fine-looking vessel. Is she yours?" the man asked me.

"Yes, sir, created with these two hands and I will sail her in the regatta," I announced happily. He nodded his appreciation and I went to get the truck to bring her home. She'd be back on the water in a couple of day's time, and the weather forecast called out good sailing conditions. Of course, the lake could be a fickle old girl and change in a heartbeat. Nevertheless, I was ready.

June 22nd, 1938, a day before the race, I was at a local club listening to the radio broadcast of the fight between Joe Louis and Max Schmeling in the heavyweight category. Joe, 'The Brown Bomber' Louis, was the reigning heavyweight champion, though people had been talking about this Max character being able to beat him because he had done it before. I didn't think it would happen and I put a few coins in the pot to bet on Joe. Max only managed to get two hits in on Joe and the fight was over in two minutes and forty seconds with Joe as the victor. The announcers and the crowd in the club went wild. I collected my winnings, grinned and went home.

I later learned that someone had dubbed the event the greatest match of all time because there were so many white people cheering for a black man fighting a white opponent. The club had been quite boisterous, though I didn't have anything to compare it to as that was my first boxing match. Probably not my last one; I'd had fun.

The day of the regatta arrived and I couldn't stand still. Anticipation raced through my body every step I took. It was unusual as that hadn't happened in the last race I participated in. It felt like a good day because those steps I took were light.

"Are you ready?" I called out to my dad. I'd attached the boat and trailer to the truck already. My dad would attend the festivities with me, along with my sister. I was sure my mom would be glued to a bottle of booze and not miss any of us.

"Almost," my dad answered. "Give your sister a minute to get down here."

I didn't want to wait; the lake called to me. I needed to register, check-in, and pin my number to my sail. Time was a-wasting! When we arrived at the lake, I popped out of the truck like I was on springs. I unloaded Lady Lucky and hopped on with a wave to my sister.

"See you!" I watched as my dad drove away to park, the engine purring like a kitten. I'd fixed her up the night before. When I brought the boat home, I noticed the engine misfiring a few days ago. Not anymore! That old girl sounded as good as new.

I climbed out of the boat, ensured she was tied up, and headed over to the registration table to sign in, get my number, and get my place in line before the start. I had a good feeling about the day. Ideal conditions and a beauty made with my two hands. *What more could a guy ask?*

"Ralph Suhm with Lady Luck," I told the woman behind the table.

"Looks like we have everything," the woman said with a smile. She handed me my number and checked my name off the list. "Here's where to take your place." She pointed to a map on the table. "It's nice to see an early riser. Good luck to you, sir."

I smiled warmly and took off at a jog back to the boat. With everything situated and my heart in my throat, I unmoored Lady Luck and lined up with the rest of the competition. I noticed that no one spoke many words between the competitors other than wishing them happy sailing. When the crack of the starting gun reached my ears, I set the sail, settled into a peaceful routine, and enjoyed the utter calmness of my soul as we sliced through the waters of Lake Michigan.

I didn't pay attention to the other craft around me other than to ensure our safety margins. Everything faded away until it was me, my focus, and the sound of the wind in my sails. Each turn was precise and I was in the lead before it dawned on me. *Woo-boy!* I thought. My excitement kicked up and I crossed the finish line like I owned it. It was a moment of pure bliss in my beautiful little boat. She performed well beyond my expectations.

I'd done it! I won the regatta for the comet class with Lady Luck. I could even hear my sister screaming joyfully from the shore, where she and my dad watched. He shook his fists in the air in a congratulatory dance. What a moment! It would live in my memory for the rest of my life.

I read the newspaper while I ate my lunch at work and shook

my head. Howard Hughes had made a record-breaking ninety-one-hour flight on one of his planes. What an impressive feat to have accomplished. It felt like something I could do sailing, but I couldn't imagine doing it in the air. I hoped that I would get to experience flying in a larger plane. Maybe someday.

Hitler was causing many problems in Europe, and I was grateful I never joined the family business. I didn't want to be a part of anything happening in Germany. It was a mess over there and people suffered from what I read in the tiny article.

Austria and Germany joined forces and were on a rampage of killing. The Nazi party murdered thousands of Jewish people. It was unbelievable. They rounded people up and sent them to what they called labor camps. I didn't know what that meant, but it didn't sound good.

"Can you believe this?" I asked the guy sitting next to me. I pointed at the buried news story.

"I don't pay any attention to the news," he responded. "I just do my job and go home to my family."

"You don't even listen to the news on the radio?" I wondered. I didn't understand not wanting to know what was happening around me. "How do you know what's happening in the world?"

"No, I don't. The world's affairs don't affect my life. I never hear anything good," the man grumbled and returned to eating.

Despite what the president said about remaining neutral, I didn't want to point out that it would affect him if we entered another war. It would affect everyone. I shrugged it off and went back to reading the papers. I lived my life the way I thought worked best for me.

In July, Howard Hughes, the man who had his fingers in everything from filmmaking, flying, business, investing, and charity, broke another world record. Again, I read the newspaper so I knew about it.

"Can you imagine flying around the world in ninety-one hours?" I asked the man to my right.

"I can't imagine even being on an airplane," the guy answered me. "My feet belong on the ground. What would happen if one of those things fell out of the sky?"

I could imagine it, yet I still wanted to be on an aircrew. "It would be bad if that happened, I agree. But ninety-one hours to fly around the globe? That's incredible. Though I don't imagine he got to see much since he was going for the record."

"I think if I can't drive there, God means me not to see it." The man shook his head. "I do agree that it's incredible. Good for him. Scary after that Earhart woman went missing. I think that would have put me off the idea."

"Seeing other countries is a dream of mine," I told the man in the spirit of a friendly conversation. I wanted to point out that God created man that made airplanes and one could translate that as God wanted us to explore His creation. I refrained.

"Good luck, pal. I hope that one day you can do that. Chasing dreams isn't bad." The man patted my shoulder. He went back to eating and I returned to the newspaper.

September brought disaster to the New England area of the States. A hurricane landed on Long Island with fierce winds and rain. It was front page news and I read about it with rapt attention. I'd never experienced a natural disaster like that.

We got big storms that blew in from Lake Michigan

and some frigid winters but I couldn't understand wind that could destroy so many homes. The newspaper said that over six hundred people had died and over fifty-seven thousand houses had gotten ruined.

The storm surge was terrible in Rhode Island and that was the area that most of the people perished in. I put the newspaper on the table and measured out ten inches in my hands.

"That's how much it rained during that hurricane," I told my friend Steve. He'd just started a job there and was on my shift.

"You could swim on the streets," Steve commented.

I rolled my eyes but nodded. "Look how many homes got destroyed." I pointed at the paper. "Can you imagine that many people were displaced? It must be horrible over there right now."

Steve glanced at the article in the newspaper and then finished his sandwich. "Guess we have a lot to be thankful for."

October blew in with cooler weather and I started to see more jackets and hats on the people around me. Gloves weren't necessary yet; however, it wouldn't be long until that time arrived either.

I settled at the bar counter and waited for my dinner to arrive. The establishment served a mean meatloaf dish, and I was hungrier than usual. The Guard drills the past weekend had exhausted me. I think I ran more miles over the weekend than I had my entire life. And I did it carrying a rucksack, guns, and wearing boots.

Then, the Guard taught us how to set traps for pursuing enemies, tactics for evasions, and setting explosives.

The sergeant said we would need to know these things if we found ourselves behind enemy lines and were trying to get to safety.

I wasn't one of the guys who complained about the training for war but I was probably the only guy on the squad that read the newspaper and kept informed about things happening in other parts of the world. The training we received directly correlated to that situation.

"You here to listen to the game?" An intoxicated man sat beside me.

"I figured I'd catch it while I ate my dinner," I acknowledged. "You here to listen?"

"I'm rooting for the Cubs." The guy smacked the counter. "Those Yankees have won enough of the series."

"They wouldn't be there if the team weren't any good," I pointed out. I didn't care either way. I didn't have money on the game like many men did. My eye wandered to a cigarette girl making her way through the crowd, trying to get some sales. She was a looker and I was looking.

The man began to ramble about some players, and I pretended to listen. I nodded my head every few minutes and hummed as if I agreed with him. I nodded to the man who put my plate of food before me and tuned everything out. Food was my focus.

Once the game began, that was more difficult to do as the crowd inside the bar grew until it was bursting at the seams. I didn't think one more person could fit and the noise level was out of this world. It was almost impossible to hear the radio broadcast. I stayed until the end, though, because it was fun to watch the crowd's reactions. The Yankees won and more than half the men let out a raucous cheer.

Money changed hands. Men grumbled while others

were exuberant and bought more drinks in celebration. It was true that baseball was America's pastime. I grinned and celebrated along with the guys around me before heading home for the night.

The Guard drills drove us hard on the training and after reading the news, I was glad. It seemed to me that they were teaching us life-saving skills. I couldn't believe the state of things happening there in Europe, yet a small part of me wished I was a part of everything going on. I didn't understand how it wasn't front-page news and concerning more people. The population here was more concerned with sports and entertainment.

I folded the newspaper and handed it to the guy next to me to read, finished my lunch and returned to work. The Freemasons were having another mixer that night and I hoped to fill my night dancing with pretty ladies. It was the night before Halloween and it should be fun.

There's going to be a new program on the radio," a gal named Sally told me after we danced. "It's supposed to start at seven. Do you want to listen with me?"

"Sure," I agreed. I didn't have anything else to do. I'd heard about the program and misunderstood what it was about. I'd mistakenly thought it was about the war going on over in Europe. When I heard about *War of the Worlds*, I finished reading an article about what Hitler was doing. It was only after I said something to a coworker that I understood it was about Martians invading Earth.

I hadn't read the novel, though I'd heard about it. Given what was happening in England, I found it ironic that the new program would be about invasions. Perhaps it was planned that way, or it was an odd coincidence.

Sally and I left the dance and went to a diner where we could join in with others to hear the program. I ordered us some milkshakes and pie to enjoy while we listened. The restaurant was surprisingly full. It could always be that way at that hour, I supposed. I wouldn't know since I didn't usually go.

"This is scary," Sally told me partway through the story. "Can I sit by you?"

"Of course." I patted the seat next to me. That was an opportunity I wouldn't pass. "It's not real." I enjoyed that she thought I could protect her.

"It sounds real," Sally said as she scooted as close to me as possible. I put my arm around her shoulders and tried to hide my smile.

It turned out she wasn't the only one who thought that it was real. People in the diner panicked, thinking an invasion was happening then. Chaos erupted. People began to call for the police and ran from the restaurant, screaming for their families. Paranoia took hold.

I was utterly bewildered. Sally wanted to leave, so I walked Sally home before the program was over and saw people on their porches with guns waiting to kill the invaders. Never before had I witnessed absolute hysteria on that scale. Not wanting an injury, I hurried home in disbelief.

The next day, all the news was about the invasion. It was my opinion that the focus should be on the real threat of Hilter and the happenings in Europe, not the mayhem a production of the novel caused. Some people took the performance so seriously that they ended their lives so they wouldn't get taken by the aliens. It was baffling.

Orson Welles became a household name after that.

The man was talented; he'd fooled half the country into thinking we were getting attacked by creatures from another planet. It was the most convincing performance I'd witnessed, though I knew it wasn't real.

November 1st, people were still talking about the non-existent attack. However, other exciting things were happening. The broadcast of a much-anticipated horse race was about to happen at Pimlico Race Course between War Admiral and Seabiscuit.

The human hearts loved the story of an underdog, and Seabiscuit fit that description. He was a horse from the west who hadn't done much of anything significant. War Admiral was the victor to those on the country's east coast. It was a battle of the coasts. Steve and I wanted to see what would happen.

The odds were in War Admiral's favor by a large margin. Given we were still in the depression and fighting our way out of it, I put money on Seabiscuit. Not a lot since I didn't have much to spare, but winning with Christmas coming up would be nice. It might also give people hope that they can beat the odds. The depression was hard on so many people.

I think the world came to a standstill when the race began. The announcers spoke every step, their voices carrying the excitement and drama of the horse race to people all over the country. Millions were tuned in. Horse racing and baseball were the sports of the time, and every person listening to that broadcast felt the thud of the horses' hooves on the track.

The announcers said the crowd was going wild and people were hanging from the rafters at the track. The facility was overflowing with spectators. Seabiscuit was not typically a great starter, while War Admiral was usually fast out of the gate. In the biggest surprise of the sport, Seabiscuit took off and the crowd's roar spurred him on to a four-length win, beating the previous track record.

Amidst the world stopping for the race, I collected my winnings, celebrated with the crowd and had a fantastic time until it was time for me to go home and sleep because I had to work in the morning. Steve and I parted ways, each of us counting our money.

Christmas arrived too soon. I had taken some of the winnings from the Seabiscuit race and saved it to do something special for my sister, Alicia. A new movie came out in time for the holiday. The Charles Dickens novel came to life, *A Christmas Carol.* It was a book she loved.

"Alicia, how about you and me go see a new film?" I asked my sister after dinner.

"Which one?" Alicia looked up from her book at me.

"*A Christmas Carol,*" I answered with a grin.

"Oh, yes! I'd love that," Alicia exclaimed. "Dad said we don't have any extra money for that."

"I have some," I confided in her. "It will be my present for you."

"Oh, Ralph!" Alicia threw her arms around my neck. "I can't wait."

It felt great to do something with Alicia that she loved. Spending time with her wasn't a hardship. The film was enjoyable, too. The actors did a marvelous job, and it was all Alicia could talk about until the new year arrived.

CHAPTER 3

1939

The year began with the sad news that the Earhart woman pilot was declared dead. It was disheartening, yet I also understood the reasoning behind it. They had been searching for the remains of the wreckage all over the Pacific in the area they presumed she had disappeared. There hadn't been any signs. It was like she vanished.

My thoughts on it were that they probably weren't looking in the right places. I knew how easily it was to get pushed off course in the water. I could only assume the same would be true for the sky. If Earhart were in bad weather or clouds and couldn't see, it would be hard to radio in a position. Or if her equipment went haywire on her.

There was a lot of speculation still, and people kept radioing in locations to look because they spotted something from the sea or the air. One person said they saw her on an island having lunch. I didn't find that credible. Regardless of what happened, the situation made me feel bad for the lady and those who loved her.

February brought the new John Wayne film to the theaters. *Stagecoach*, it was called. That was one that I was interested in seeing but didn't want to take my sister to. Instead, I asked

Steve while we were on our lunch break at work.

"Do you like the John Wayne movies?" I asked him.

"Who doesn't?" Steve replied with a smirk. "Are you going to see the new picture?"

"I was thinking about it. Want to go? I don't want to take my sister to that one," I explained. "I can always go alone, too, if you are busy."

"I'm not busy," Steve was quick to answer. "I think I have a few extra cents, too. When is it out?"

"The fifteenth," I told him, checking the date on the paper in front of me. "A couple of days from now."

"Shoot, I can do that." Steve nodded at me. "You've got a date." Steve winked at me when a few of the guys around us gave us disgusted looks.

I chuckled in response. "If I had a date, I wouldn't be asking you. And if I get one before then, you're out."

Steve laughed. "That just means I'd have to find one so we could double."

Neither of us found dates, but we went to the movie and had a great time. John Wayne was excellent, and there hadn't been a movie that had disappointed me yet. He did a fantastic job and the story kept us entertained.

New York had the first World's Fair and I badly wanted to attend, though I could not make it happen. There was talk about how they would show what the future would look like. Architects were building the city of the future, they said. The Ford Motor Company was going to have new vehicles, too. It sounded interesting to me and several men from work had plans to attend.

I'd also caught word that something called a ghost car would be on display. I wasn't sure what that meant, but the newspaper said it would be mostly invisible to the naked eye. I didn't know how they would make metal see-through but I wished again that I could attend.

Also, there was going to be a vehicle that was air-conditioned. I couldn't imagine that and dreamt of how nice it would be to have the inside cool on those blistering hot days when it felt like you couldn't breathe because the air was so humid and thick.

This year saw more regatta races, some of which I won; in others, I only placed or came in near the end. Lady Luck held her own, and everyone admired her lines in every race. My competition praised me because they hadn't grown accustomed to a kid with a handmade sailboat in the races. Every one of the competitions was worth the time and effort. There was nothing quite like the feeling of flying over the water, much less on something made with your own two hands.

The outcomes always depended on the weather and I was up against some sleek, lightweight vessels that were hard not to admire. They skimmed the water like a hot knife cutting through butter. Sometimes, I bested them; when I did, they were the first men to congratulate me.

A man probably in his sixties competed with me in the last race. He carried himself with a regal air and from the look of his boat, he came from money. Captain Tom is what the registration lady called him. He was in front of me in line.

"Next," the woman called out when Captain Tom finished.

"Ralph Sum, Lady Luck," I told her. She was no-nonsense with me, got me checked in, and handed me my number. She wasn't rude, but I was no Captain Tom either.

I walked back to my boat and pinned the number to my sail. Captain Tom walked up and motioned me onto the dock to speak with him. I quickly checked to ensure my boat hadn't touched his or caused damage and then climbed out.

"Lady Luck." Captain Tom looked her over critically. "I saw you race last year. It was your first race with her and you won, correct?"

"Yes, sir," I replied proudly. "You were there?" I wanted to feel elated that I beat a boat like his, but I couldn't boast that way. It wasn't my personality.

"I was." Captain Tom smiled at me. "I came in third. I also helped you take her out of the water before the race."

I thought back to that man and stared at him. "I apologize for not remembering, sir."

"I didn't expect you to, son," Captain Tom told me. "I mentioned it because I thought you would remember that better than you'd remember who was behind you. You sailed well, and you build beautiful boats. I'd be an interested buyer if you ever decide to sell Lady Luck. I also wish you luck today."

"I'll keep that in mind, sir." I smiled and shook his hand. "Happy sailing to you."

I didn't win that race, a fact that I wasn't upset about. I came in fifth, right behind Captain Tom, who had saluted me before I left. I didn't know if I would part with Lady Luck, yet I was thrilled that others saw the same beauty in her that I did.

"Ralph, did you see this?" Steve passed the newspaper back to me. "There's a flying boat."

"Yes. Yankee Clipper, they called it," I responded, pushing the newspaper back to him. I'd already read it cover to cover.

"It's going to carry mail overseas," Steve replied. "Why not people?"

"I'm sure that will be next. Pan American is a big business and carrying passengers is the natural progression of things." I shrugged. "You want to travel?"

"Who doesn't?" Steve answered. "I'd wait until things settle down first. Do you think you could build a flying boat?"

I thought about it before responding. I was sure I could, though I didn't think I would. I wouldn't know the first thing about piloting it and landing on water would be a challenge. I'd undoubtedly travel on one if given the opportunity.

"Maybe." I shrugged again. "Do you want to buy it if I do?"

"No." Steve laughed. "I couldn't afford that."

In early June, Steve and I were leaving work, and I had a newspaper tucked under my arm. Our lunch break today was a rushed thing because there were quotas that we had to meet and time ran short when some machines broke.

One of the managers asked me to assist in fixing it. I didn't know how much help I was, yet I tried. It put us behind schedule and I didn't get an opportunity to read the news. Now that the depression was ending, there was an upturn in the country's economy. More people were working, and things were looking up.

"Want to grab dinner?" I asked Steve.

"For sure. I'm hungry after how busy today was," Steve told me.

We walked to a club that played live music on the weekend. During the week, they served some excellent dinners and the atmosphere was relaxed and cheerful. They played the radio when a broadcast show was on, and some nights, there was dancing.

We found an open table and seated ourselves. I had barely sat the newspaper down when a waitress appeared with some menus. I ordered a soda and the steak they had on special. Steve ordered coffee and a plate of spaghetti.

"What's going on in the world now?" Steve asked after the waitress left.

"I don't know yet." I read the first three pages before our food arrived and filled Steve in while we ate. "The Baseball Hall of Fame is opening." I flipped the page and saw a small article tucked in the middle about a boat of Jewish refugees. The ship St. Louis carried nine hundred and seven people from Europe who were fleeing the hostilities. Officials turned the boat away in Cuba, and when they arrived in Florida, a denial for landing was issued there, too.

I showed the story to Steve, who skimmed it and pushed the paper back to me. He shook his head. "I thought we were the safe place for people to land."

"I guess it's because we are supposed to be neutral." I shrugged. It bothered me that those poor people would have to return to the horrors they fled from looking for safety. Chances are they'd get sent right back into it and end up dead. What a terrible fate.

"Ralph, you were right," Steve told me on our way to work one morning in July. "The Yankee Clipper is taking passengers to Britain."

"I don't know why anyone would want to go there," I told him. "Things are crazy over there. I'm guessing you listened to the news radio show this morning?"

"I did. I heard that many politicians would be making

the journey," Steve rambled.

"Good. Some should stay there," I retorted bitterly.

Steve laughed and clapped me on the back. "I suppose you are right."

"Alicia," I called up the stairs to my sister. My parents weren't home and I had the night free.

"What?" my sister said, coming to the top of the stairs.

"Want to go see *The Wizard of Oz?*" I grinned at her. She'd talked about the new film a couple of nights ago. It premiered in Los Angeles in mid-August and was now coming to theaters everywhere else.

"Do I?" Alicia exclaimed and bounced in place. "Let me get a sweater."

The film was in color and widely discussed amongst all age groups as the film to spend the money and see. I was busy the following weekend with Guard duties, so this was my chance to treat my sister to an outing. My parents were strict with her and even chaperoned, didn't allow her the same freedoms I had.

Alicia chatted about the film as we hopped into the truck and I drove to the theater. I bought her a box of candy and we found a couple of seats open in the crowded theater. I couldn't believe how many people were in attendance.

We settled in our seats and when the lights dimmed, the audience fell silent in anticipation of the highly acclaimed film. It was a musical and would be the first I had seen. I enjoyed music and the movies and looked forward to the evening with my sister.

As the movie played in vivid color, I must admit that it captured my attention as raptly as it did the rest of the people. I wondered if perhaps some of the content wasn't too frightening for children. The story was fantastical in genre, and the flying monkeys even made Alicia jump. Regardless, the movie was excellent and Alicia couldn't stop singing the rainbow song all night.

Steve joined me at a bar two nights later to watch the first televised baseball game. The Cincinnati Reds played against the Brooklyn Dodgers at Ebbets Field in New York. My money was on Cincinnati; Steve went for Brooklyn.

Very few locations had televisions, and we lucked out to find one near us that did. The place was bursting with people for that very reason. A camera on the field looked down the first base line, and then another showed the home plate. Watching the players live from a long distance away was something else.

The game was a doubleheader and the Reds won the first and the Dodgers won the second. Neither Steve nor I were losers. We had a gas. I hoped to see more games in the future. It was exciting to watch the famed players.

September 1st came and World War II officially began overseas. The papers, radio, and television all broadcast the news. Roosevelt again declared the United States was neutral. So did Norway, Finland, Sweden, and Switzerland.

On Guard weekends, they had enhanced their drills and training in combat, weaponry, evasion, and warfare. We did some wargame-type activities and the physical training became much more challenging.

Some squads talked about going overseas to assist. However, I suspected it was all talk. Several of us figured that our neutrality would end at some point, yet none of us knew when that would happen.

The news didn't last long. Soon enough, reporters buried it among the other news deemed inconsequential and people went back to watching Hollywood and sports.

A funny new movie about a politician fighting corruption came to the theaters, and I took a lovely lady I met at a mixer. It was ironic, considering what was happening in the world overseas from us. Mary was her name and I soon found out that she was one of the people that didn't pay attention to the world either.

Mary didn't understand the humor of the movie. I found it quite enjoyable and to make it up to Mary, I took her dancing at a club afterward and she forgave me. We had fun at the club. Nevertheless, it became clear that I wanted more from a woman than someone superficial.

It seemed like everything went crazy for a spell. Guard training was intense now that Europe declared war on Fascist Italy and Nazi Germany after the Polish invasion. The United States had declared neutrality and ceased trade with belligerent countries engaged in the war, though I didn't understand how we could take that stand when so many people were getting slaughtered. It was sickening.

Regardless, the National Guard felt like it was preparing us for war. In the recesses of my mind, I did see it going that way. It was my gut feeling that the politicians and people of this country wouldn't intervene unless what happened to the unfortunate souls in Poland happened over here.

In November, politicians released Al Capone from prison due

to failing health caused by complications of Syphilis. He was getting sent to Baltimore to a mental hospital there. That story was on the front page of the newspaper.

I didn't understand how this was crucial front-page news. I carried on with my life. Work and Guard took up most of my time. I didn't sail in the winter but started building a new boat. I hadn't gotten far with it due to lack of time, but I'd finish it eventually.

The world was changing faster than I could keep up with at times. It was dizzying and worrisome. The feelings all these events evoked in me were growing stronger and I started to believe that I was supposed to be a part of things. The direction I needed to go wasn't entirely clear, though a picture was forming. Life had something in store for me and I'd better get ready.

CHAPTER 4

1940

The start of the year already had my head spinning. Germans were bombing merchant ships in the Atlantic and English Channel. The Germans had essentially shut down the supply chain of goods to the United Kingdom. The whole thing caused bacon, butter, and sugar rationing. The radio broadcast said they were issuing ration booklets with coupons, and you had to stand in line at certain stores to turn the coupons in for the goods. I'd already heard about the fuel rationing, which could be considered a luxury to need fuel. Food, however, was a basic need.

The Winter Olympics scheduled for February were canceled last year due to complications with Germany and the war. Alicia was disappointed by that, as I'm sure the athletes and so many others were.

More stories were starting to appear in the newspapers or pop up in the news broadcast on the radio, though they still seemed more of an afterthought than something that America needed to be concerned about. There were times when the apathy was appalling.

"Hey, Ralph." Steve interrupted my reading. "You are a Freemason, correct?"

"Yes." I looked up at him after putting my finger on the spot I had been reading. "Why?"

"How do I join? I hear some pretty ladies attend their mixers and dance." Steve grinned at me.

"I can't deny that." I chuckled. "I don't want to share with you, though. You are better looking than me."

"That's true." Steve laughed. "You are only one man. You can't dance with all of them."

"Watch me," I challenged Steve. "You need a sponsor, you have to believe in God, and you need to do good for others. The members have to vote you in after they decide if your morals match theirs."

"Who sponsored you?" Steve wondered.

"The father of a girl I took on a date," I supplied. "His vehicle broke down and I fixed it for him. After that, he asked me many questions and then followed up with whether I wanted to join a group where I could make lifelong friends. As badly as I wanted to leave home and experience life, the answer was an easy yes. I'll ask if someone is willing to sponsor you at the next meeting of minds."

"Swell." Steve grinned. "I appreciate it."

April came, and Booker T. Washington, one of the leaders of the African-American community and a well-known advisor to several presidents, became the first African-American to grace the front of a postage stamp. I had to hand it to the man; he'd made his way from the bottom to the top and that couldn't have been an easy climb.

Steve and I went to a club to listen to the New York Rangers win the Stanley Cup. While the crowd wasn't as wild as they were for baseball, it came pretty close. Ice hockey was a much more physical sport than baseball, and the announcers liked to describe each brutal hit with painful accuracy. I winced more than once.

Three days later, the Cleveland Indians defeated the Chicago White Sox. I didn't get to go to a club to listen to that game, but it was playing on the radio at work, where I pulled a double-shift. I got a little excited and almost hurt myself on the machine I was using. Luckily, my supervisor didn't notice and I didn't get in trouble.

At the end of April, I was ready for Guard weekend simply to end the long shifts I'd been working. We were short some people at work due to retirement and the company was running lean, even though we were doing good business. I was exhausted by the time lunch rolled around.

"Ralph." Steve nudged me with his elbow. "Have you read the paper yet?"

"Not yet," I replied. "My eyes won't focus right now."

"A dance hall in Natchez, Mississippi, caught on fire. It was called Rhythm Club. One hundred ninety-eight people died." Steve read and whistled through his teeth. "That's a lot of people! Imagine if that were here. That could have been you or me with as much as we go dancing."

"Gad! Imagine how terrifying that would be," I breathed out. It almost made me want to skip the Freemason mixer a couple of nights from now.

May 9th came around and my time in the National Guard ended, though I had a period where the government could recall me into service should the United States come to war. It was my opinion we were headed in that direction regardless. My mind settled on the certainty that I'd get called.

I couldn't believe that three years had passed already. It felt like a blink of an eye and then gone. It was bittersweet, but I was still on reserve, and Europe was in chaos from what I had read in the newspapers. Instinct still told me that America would join the fray despite what politicians said. There had to be behind-the-scenes stuff going on.

My father threw a small dinner party for me on the night of my discharge with some friends and family. I believed he thought I would be more agreeable to joining the family business, though my mind hadn't budged on that decision.

The very next day, the Germans began a battle with France. The German forces invaded France and defeated them, advancing Hitler's reign of terror over Europe. There was talk about it on the radio broadcast of the news, and it shocked me that America was still doing nothing. It worried me because if no one stopped Hitler, where would he end? Would he take over our country, too? How was no one thinking about that?

I didn't want that to happen. No one would like that. The man was evil personified from what I'd read and heard. It wasn't like I had a choice in the matter. Regardless, I had to believe that I wasn't the only one who thought that way, despite America focusing on movie stars and sports. With Hitler at the head of the table, that nonsense would come to a screeching halt.

Yet a few days later, the news was all about a new stocking for women made of nylon. It was all the rage and stores sold out as soon as they opened. I had to shake my head and wonder where our great country was heading. Technology was great. I wouldn't complain about that; I only cared about priorities.

Roosevelt had to be pulling strings that no one knew about. The man went before Congress and asked for an astronomical budget of nine hundred million dollars to finance America making fifty thousand airplanes a year.

Why did he need fifty thousand airplanes a year if he planned to remain neutral? I wondered. I tapped the newspaper and shook my head. To me, it sounded like he was preparing for war. It was a suspicion I couldn't shake. I couldn't claim the intelligence that Roosevelt must have to be where he is, nor was I an idiot. I didn't see how others didn't draw the same conclusion. The signs were all there.

The end of May told the world that Hitler opened a new extermination camp in Poland called Auschwitz-Birkenau. I shuddered at the thought of how many people could potentially perish there. I didn't understand Hitler's vehement hatred of the Jewish people. I didn't think I would ever understand hatred toward anyone because of their race.

"Paris got bombed," Steve informed me. He'd started reading the newspapers like me and tuning in when they did news broadcasts on the radio. Neither of our families had televisions yet. I'd hoped to save enough money to buy one for my family, but I wasn't quite there yet.

I'd been working extra hours and taking second shifts voluntarily when I could. It wasn't quite enough, though I was trying. I had a small amount of side work for some people who needed vehicle maintenance, which would also help.

"I heard," I replied. "The Luftwaffe, if I remember right. I'd hate to think of the Eiffel Tower getting destroyed. It seems like a wonder, and I hope to see it someday."

"Phew! I don't know if I could. Being that high up would scare me," Steve admitted. "Mike is going to a dance tonight. Did he tell you?"

Mike was another friend of ours from school. I didn't

see him as often as Steve did, but when we got together, we always had fun. I was sorry I would miss it. I volunteered to work the second shift tonight. It was a shame; dancing would help me relieve some of the stress that had built.

"I can't, I'll be working." I groaned. "Sounds like it would be a gas."

"You know Mike." Steve shook his head. "That makes three nights this week you've pulled doubles. Aren't you tired?"

"Sure am," I confirmed. "I want to get a television for Alicia." Steve clapped me on the back and we headed to our separate stations.

"Listen to this." I read to Steve, "Roosevelt signs a Naval expansion act into law to increase the Navy's tonnage by eleven percent."

"What does that mean?" Steve asked.

"It means giving the Navy more ships," I spelled out for Steve. "Roosevelt doesn't believe Hitler has no aspirations for the western hemisphere. That's my take on it. He already advocated for more airplanes and now more ships."

"Seems obvious," Steve agreed. "What do you think, Frank?"

"I think you kids worry too much," Frank answered with a sneer. "Leave the country running to the professionals while we do the grunt work."

That was the problem. Those of us working didn't seem to have a say in elections for local officials to stand up for the little people.

July entered like a lion, with Roosevelt winning the nomination for an unprecedented third term. He would be the first president to hold that honor if elected. Everything I saw of Roosevelt was that the man was preparing us for war in a way that didn't panic all the workers. Roosevelt was getting us set up for success and he had my vote.

Hitler invaded Britain and bombed it, and suddenly, things were looking a lot different to the people of the United States. I heard more talk about the atrocities happening overseas and a shift started happening among us common working folk as we realized that could be us. How would we react to what these people faced?

Then, on August 31, I heard the government called for the US National Guard to get assembled. Infantry units were being activated and ordered to federal service. They were going to Fort Sill and Louisiana for training. I hadn't received orders yet, but I knew they were coming. It was a matter of time.

Shortly after I was discharged, on September 16th, the United States created a draft. They called it the Selective Training and Service Act of 1940. The act meant that men between the ages of twenty-one and forty-five had to register for the draft. It was the first peacetime draft in our country's history. To me, this screamed war was coming. Why weren't the people preparing? I wasn't a doomsday person; I was a proactive person.

I was still on the call list, so I didn't have to re-register. The selection happened by lottery, and if the government called your registration number, the individual would be required to serve at least one year in the military. I found that interesting since the Guard service term was three years.

The escalating war in Europe was beginning to make people in America uncomfortable. Several felt as if our country wouldn't be able to hold its own against the Axis powers should we come under attack. America didn't have the numbers after the First World War.

The draft made many breathe easier, though it also made people uneasy. No matter how you looked at it was a scary prospect regardless of who you were. Locally, some prominent families that believed their sons were above serving in the military caused a stink. Personally, I thought their kids could use the discipline.

November 5th, 1940, Roosevelt won by a landslide, his third term as president. The first and only president to hold office that long. The man had to do something right in that Oval Office to get the people to believe in him enough to put him back there again. I voted for him.

The very next day, Agatha Christie published her first book in the United States. And the day after that, November 7, the Tacoma Narrows Bridge in Washington State collapsed. It was the third longest suspension bridge in the world, and the crew that built it dubbed the bridge the Galloping Gertie. The area of the Puget Sound the bridge spans experiences high winds and on the 7th, the wind won. The bridge danced and then collapsed. I'd have been terrified to my soul witnessing that.

That was the ominous sign, that bridge. It had absolutely nothing to do with me, yet that was also the day I received orders that I'd gotten activated. I was getting sent to live on base, and after the new year, I'd move to New Jersey. I was now officially on active duty for the United States Army Air Corps 567th Bombardment Squad in Milwaukee, Wisconsin, soon to be Fort Dix, New Jersey.

My family vacationed there in the summer, so it

wasn't any place I wasn't familiar with, but I'd gotten my wishes. I wouldn't be living under my parents' roof. My time here in Milwaukee, Wisconsin, was now numbered. I would also be part of a flight crew. Things were looking up.

"Hiya, Ralph," Mike called out to me. He patted the empty stool next to him at the diner's bar. "Have a seat. What's been going on?"

"Nothing but work," I replied as I sat down. "I've pulled so many shifts since discharge, I think I forgot what the outside looked like. How is life treating you?"

"I followed your footsteps and enlisted." Mike grinned at me. "I go in a couple of weeks for the training."

"You had to register," I told him with a frown. "Did they call your number?"

Mike nodded. "I'm actually looking forward to it. It's the Navy for me."

I raised my eyebrows at that. "Did you learn how to swim?"

"I did." Mike nodded. "I won't win any races but I don't think I'll drown either."

"Good for you." I thumped Mike on the back. "Get ready for a lot of physical work and even more browbeating."

"That part is true then?" Mike sounded concerned. "They yell at you?"

"They do." I laughed. "It's to make you stronger though. It grated on my nerves but I am better for it. I received orders, too. I'm moving to base quarters and Jersey at the new year."

"You've done three years already. Let's eat," Mike replied with a frown. "I'm buying."

"I have money," I argued. I wasn't sure what made

Mike unhappy about my news and I didn't want to press the issue.

"I know. Steve said you were saving to buy a television for your house. Have you done that yet?"

"No. This next payday, I should have enough." I sighed. "It'll be my Christmas present for the whole family."

"You are a good man, Ralph." Mike shook his head. "I don't think I could do that. I'd be buying a car or a house."

"That's on my list, too," I confided in him. "I have the old truck. Did you notice the temperature drop outside?"

"Did I ever?" Mike raised his eyebrows. "Think we'll get snow?"

"I don't know." I shrugged. "I do know that it's time to dig out the gloves. My fingers froze."

Later that night, while I was at home listening to the radio, I heard a blizzard hit the Midwest. I wasn't surprised, though I was shocked that the snow didn't reach us. The news was saying that people had already died from the adverse weather. That was unfortunate. Mother Nature was fickle.

"Do you mind if I sit here?" I asked a lovely lady who was in the theater.

"Not at all," she told me as she plucked a piece of candy from her box.

"My name is Ralph," I offered up, hoping she would tell me her name.

"Alyse," she said with a polite smile.

She wasn't very talkative; however, we were here to watch a movie. *One Night in the Tropics* was the title. It was supposed to have two comedians in it. I figured that a comedy would be a nice change of pace.

The film was a riot. I laughed so hard my stomach hurt.

Abbot and Costello were the comedians and I'd love to see more pictures with them in it. It made for a wonderful evening, even if I were there alone.

"Maybe I'll see you around," I told the woman named Alyse as I stood up to exit. I gave her my most charming smile.

"Maybe." She shrugged. That was the first woman I'd been unable to charm from the start.

"Ralph!" Alicia cried out when I struggled through the front door with an awkward-sized box that was too heavy to carry by myself. No wonder the salesman at the store helped me load it in the truck.

Alicia ran over to help me and we muscled the new television into the living room, where we gently set it down. Alicia stepped back and stared at the box with her mouth open. I grinned despite my efforts to keep my face neutral.

"Did you buy a television?" Alicia whispered in awe.

"I did." I broke out into a huge smile. "It's my Christmas present for the family before I leave for Jersey."

"Mom isn't going to be happy," Alicia whispered again. "She thinks it will ruin my mind."

"Mom isn't ever happy, so don't worry about it," I whispered back. "Now you can watch programs, and Dad can watch horse races and baseball games."

It was mid-December and I'd be leaving in a little over a couple of weeks. I wouldn't get to see my sister anymore, and since I'd moved on base, my time around her was limited. I wanted the rest of her childhood to be as good as possible. I didn't think a television would make that happen, but it would bring some enjoyment to the house.

Alicia helped me and we got the television set up before my father returned home and we surprised him. He was more pleased than I thought he would be and was impressed that I had bought it with the money I had earned.

That night, he took us out to dinner as a family. My mother drank too much wine and made some rude comments, which was typical. Other than that, we had fun and on the way back home, I stopped at a newsstand to grab a newspaper.

"Oh, look," Alicia said, holding a comic book. "I've been hearing so much about this at school. It's you," Alicia joked.

The cover showed a man in uniform, and it was *Captain America*. "I'm no hero. I'm only your brother." I bought the comic book for her and we went home.

We watched the news broadcast on the television that night and saw that Roosevelt had a plan to send aid to Great Britain. My opinion of the man became more favorable, not that it was poor initially, but because I thought we should help with the war effort.

I was on base and getting put through some rigorous physical training when one of the sergeants stopped us so we could listen to the fireside chat with Roosevelt. We all stood there and listened as our president declared that the United States needed to become the greatest arsenal of democracy.

I exchanged a few pointed looks with some guys around me who thought the same way I did. We were preparing for war and the president was trying to keep that fact quiet. I didn't know why. Each of his public moves told me that this was what our future held.

France and London were getting bombed. Innocent people died for no reason other than their religious beliefs or bloodlines. Mussolini and Hitler were insane and tensions in

Asia were growing. You didn't need to be intelligent to know where things were heading.

I spent New Year's Eve with Steve since Mike had shipped out to the East Coast for his training. We went to a Freemason party now that they accepted Steve for membership. It was my last hurrah here in Wisconsin and I wanted to send the night off with a bang.

We danced until our feet wouldn't hold us up anymore. We drank champagne like water, and we may have snuck some women out of sight to steal some kisses, which wasn't easy since I was so tall. I didn't quite steal them; they were freely offered and by more than one dance partner. I was as charming as I'd ever been.

The night was a success and we watched some fireworks set off on the lake and each of us received our midnight kiss. I took it as a good sign and looked forward to what the new year would bring me—every year needed to start with a kiss.

CHAPTER 5

1941

The Army sent me to Texas, not New Jersey, for intensive training for the Army Air Corps. Jersey would be after the training. It was my first time seeing a B-24 Liberator up close. My time here would be spent intimately learning every aspect of the plane. I got hands-on experience with the engines and mechanical parts of the aircraft. I didn't go up in one but tore the engines apart and learned each component.

The Liberator was quite the plane. It had a wingspan of one hundred ten feet, was sixty-seven feet long, and boasted a height of eighteen feet. It had four engines that had twelve hundred horsepower each. That kind of power would allow us to travel about two hundred ninety miles per hour. With nothing in the machine, it weighed in at thirty-six thousand pounds. Fully loaded, that changed to sixty-five thousand pounds. Thirty thousand pounds it carried, with a payload of five thousand pounds of bombs.

The racks that held the bombs had a design that would accommodate different sizes, which was news to me. I didn't think I was aware that bombs came in various sizes. It made sense and I didn't know why the knowledge surprised me. The standard bomb was two hundred fifty pounds. The next size was a five-hundred-pound bomb, then a mind-blowing thousand-pound whopper.

I also learned about the different types of payloads: general-purpose ordinance, incendiary, and fragmentation. The instructors told us the most common type used would be the general-purpose bombs. I didn't believe that for one minute. Each target would be different and might call for another kind of ordinance. I let it go without saying anything because maybe there was new blood in the group and they didn't know.

The Liberator's armament had ten .50-caliber machine guns. The nose, top, bottom, and tail turrets each had two guns on the mounts. The waist positions had only one each. The plane was heavily armed and with accurate shooting, it would be deadly.

It took ten crew members to operate the B-24—a pilot, copilot, navigator, bombardier, and six gunners. I'd have nine other guys with me when I was assigned a team. We'd have to communicate well to make us successful and keep us in the air.

The nose gunner would be in the front of the plane. Behind him would be the bombardier, the navigator, the pilot, and the copilot. Next up would be the top-turret gunner, which was almost in the middle of the plane but not entirely. The bomb bay was in the middle. Behind the bomb bay would be the bottom ball-turret gunner, followed by the left and right waist gunners. The end of the plane would be the tail-turret gunner.

Each position and person on the crew had more training than their position. That was another thing I hadn't realized. It made sense because if one went down, someone needed to be able to step in if needed. The pilot was the airplane commander, pilot, and navigation specialist. The copilot's primary duty was assistant airplane commander, with the secondary duty as airplane engineering officer and assistant pilot. The Air Corps added the extra duties of fire officer, navigation specialist, and gunfire control officer. It was a lot of responsibility to be those two people.

The Navigator's principal duty was to be a navigator. However, he must also be qualified as a nose turret gunner. His added duties would be assistant bombardier, oxygen and equipment officer, and first aid specialist.

The bombardier's principal duty was just that, though he also needed to be qualified as a nose turret gunner. The added responsibilities for that position were an airplane armament officer and navigation specialist.

The aerial engineer would be the top turret gunner, though that was his secondary duty. His added duties would be that he needed to be qualified for copilot duties, parachute officer, first aid specialist, and assistant radio operator. Something about that position intrigued me, though it was daunting.

The radio operators would be the waist gunners as their secondary duty. They would also be assistant airplane engineers and first aid specialists and needed to be qualified to be top turret gunners.

The nose turret gunner had a secondary duty as a turret specialist. His added duty would be assistant to the armament officer. I imagined the man in the nose of that plane had to have a certain mindset to be front and center with enemies flying at you and guns blazing.

The belly turret gunner was the ball turret. His secondary duty was as a turret specialist. The instructor hadn't explained what that meant but I was sure I'd learn.

Finally, the tail turret gunner also had a secondary duty of turret specialist. His added duty was assistant to the parachute officer. I found that strange since the positions weren't close to each other.

It was during this training that I honed my mechanical skills on ground vehicles, as well as learned airplane mechanics. The instructors taught us weapons mechanics like how to repair a .50-caliber mounted gun, hydraulics, and how to patch a line to the landing gear quickly. Then came the parachute training.

I went up in a B-17 and learned how to jump out of one. I can't say it was one of my favorite things to do. The first time is one you always remember, though. That leap of faith is terrifying, from something solid under your feet to plummeting through the air, hoping and praying that the parachute opened correctly. Then there is immediate relief when that crazy free fall halts and you float down to the ground.

The thrill and fear weren't anything like sailing. I didn't know how soldiers over in Europe did this as they tried to evade getting shot out of the sky. It was terrifying without dodging bullets. The more we practiced that, the easier it got, but that first step was the most difficult. That part didn't change.

We learned how to check the parachutes for damage, test the cords, pack them properly and trust your flying crew. We had to load each other's chutes on one of the training days, then use it and pray they paid good attention while doing it. Since there was so much cross-training that needed to happen, there wasn't anyone who didn't participate in all of the training.

Then they put us in a dummy version of the turrets

and taught us the basics of using the mounted guns and how to fire without shooting your plane up mid-air. Gads, there was a lot to learn about being on a plane. It was a far cry from high school. I didn't fully realize how hard flying was when I figured it would be similar to sailing.

I enjoyed it. I truly did. In some ways, it made me feel like I was sailing, only it was a lot noisier and I'd splat if we crashed instead of in a boat where I only had to fall a couple of feet and get tossed around by cold water. There were more parts to worry about, too.

This aircrew and I had nineteen weeks of specialized training to qualify as a Liberator crewmember. Once we navigated through all that additional training, the Army sent me back to Fort Dix, where each person would get assigned to a specific crew and learn which of the eight non-pilot positions we would receive. Texas mainly was book learning and the ins and outs of each position; aside from the pilots, their training was on flying. The training, drills, and daily grind differed from when I was in the Guard. However, they put me to good use, fixing ground vehicles and miscellaneous aircraft engines.

I didn't know what was happening in the world for the first few months. My training was intense and all-encompassing. The extent of our knowledge was that things were becoming more tense. Roosevelt signed the Lend-Lease into law on March 11th, which allowed the United States to send military equipment to the Allies. That was the first news shared with the training class. All signs were pointing toward America going to war.

Our country was still neutral, yet at the end of March, German, Italian, and Danish ships that found themselves anchored in United States waters were put into protective custody. I felt disconnected from everything and missed my time reading the newspapers.

I learned how to fly and got some hours under my belt behind the wheel, so to speak. I don't think it was my strong suit, but whatever position they had in store for me after completing the training, the possibility existed that I would need to know how to pilot an aircraft.

May 1st came and the United States began to sell war bonds. The funds from the sales went into the military to help with equipment production. It amazed me that people bought these war bonds and still didn't understand that we were heading into war. Sure, the United States hadn't declared it, but the level of ignorance about the happenings was astounding. I honestly didn't believe myself more intelligent than the average person, yet I saw the writing on the wall.

On May 15th, our training was finally complete. We were all sitting around listening to the announcers talk about Joe DiMaggio of the New York Yankees going up against the pitcher Eddie Smith of the Chicago White Sox. It was a divided camp on whether DiMaggio would get hits with that pitcher. I didn't bet on it because I didn't know enough about the statistics since the Army sequestered us for training.

Fort Dix, New Jersey, was my new home. I was getting settled into the barracks and assigned to a team to begin training for our positions and work with the team. My position was going to be the aerial engineer, top turret gunner. It was a good thing I learned the basics of piloting since an added duty would be copilot should something happen to the one on my crew. That made me a little nervous, yet the position intrigued me the most.

It wasn't even June yet and the weather was already turning hot. A bell rang with the announcement for all soldiers to gather for a radio broadcast from our president, Franklin Roosevelt. I wondered if this was it. If this was the call to war, I knew that would come.

Men gathered around radios all over the base to catch the fireside chat. Roosevelt spoke at length about the Nazi regime and their plans for world domination and how we couldn't let that happen. He painted the same picture that had formed in my mind over the years about how Hilter's reign would progress, and if we didn't do anything to help stop him, we would be next.

It took a while to get to the point of the chat, but each word he used to get there fired up the men on the ground around me. Though I heard them, I paid more attention to their reactions than Roosevelt's words. He declared the United States in a state of an "unlimited national emergency."

There were a lot of fancy words in there for him to say we needed to build up our defenses and our equipment because we wouldn't stand idly by while Hitler tried to take over the world. We could come to aid Britain in her battle. It wasn't a declaration of war but a notice that we would act.

I found myself excited the same way the men around me were. Every man at Fort Dix wanted to help remove the threat of Hitler from the world. There was a better-than-good chance we would get our shot.

June 20th saw a change to the Air Corps. We officially became the Army Air Force. It came with the understanding that the Air Force would not separate from the Army during the war. The air and ground would all remain under the Army's command. It didn't change anything for us. I focused on the crew assignments instead.

Walter Rogers was our pilot. Our copilot was Jack Carlson. The navigator was Phil Hausman. Paul Jones was the bombardier. Frank Ribbits was our radio operator and waist gunner, along with Henry Cutty, and Mike Warren was the belly gunner. Sonny Young was our tail gunner, and Robert Merrill was the nose gunner, with me as the top turret gunner. That was our crew of ten. We spent a little time together to try and get acquainted. We decided to use our surnames instead of our ranks when we weren't in front of senior officers.

In an unprecedented move, the Army had over two hundred staff sergeant pilots. There weren't enough men with college degrees to fill the aviation cadet requirements, so Congress authorized an enlisted pilot program to help fill the need. Walter Rogers was one of those men. It was one of the first things he told us after suggesting we discard the ranks in informal settings.

We had training with groups of people in the same position as we were, and then we had training where we worked as a team, which is where bonding time came into play. We needed to trust each other and for that to happen, we had to prove to each other that we were worthy of that trust.

The plane configuration had the pilot sitting in the left seat of the cockpit. It was his responsibility to take charge of the crew. He was the commander and we all listened and took his direction, even while we weren't in the air.

Rogers's job was to fly the plane to its target and return to base or find a safe landing place if trouble arose. Part of the job of flying was to keep the formation tight and the plane in place within the formation. On large missions that could take a while, they warned us.

The copilot occupied the right seat in the cockpit and was the pilot's executive officer. In this case, he was a quiet man, Carlson. He split duties with Rogers during the hours in formation flying and would only take over in the event that Rogers got hit or killed. Carlson's responsibilities as copilot would be performing all the checklists with responses from the pilot, himself, and me and filing them.

Jones would be our bombardier, and he wasn't quiet. He was, in fact, the polar opposite of Carlson. Jones and Rogers had to know each other's jobs and cooperate during bomb runs when Jones would take control of the plane through the auto-pilot, which connected directly to the bombsight. The Pilot Directional Indicator, PDI, transmitted the desired course change to the pilot via an instrument. Jones's job required accuracy of altitude, airspeed, ballistics for each bomb type, wind, and air density. All of that would only come into play if we were designated lead crew. Otherwise, all Jones had to do was toggle the control for the drop when the lead plane released its payload. He had to learn the hard stuff before they taught him the toggle.

Our navigator, Hausman, was friendly and easy to get along with. He had to use dead reckoning, which calculates airspeed and time elapsed between checkpoints to compute our position. Hausman would have to combine that with pilotage, which meant using visible landmarks, radio, and celestial navigation. I was happy that wasn't my job.

Hausman would sit just forward of the cockpit in a little dome to take his readings, or what they called "shoot his fixes." They threw a curve ball at him with the celestial navigation. While on missions, he would use the pilotage method. The relief on his face was comical.

Then there was me, the aerial engineer, or flight engineer and top turret gunner. The instructors told me I had the most stressful job of all the positions because it would require that I know more about the plane than anyone else. I had to admit, it made me sweat a little. I thought Hausman's job was hard.

I would be the one that Rogers would turn to in the event of an emergency. I would have to assist in monitoring the engine's performance and track the fuel burnt. The top turret gunner position would allow me to watch all four of the engines during flight and give me a panoramic view of the airspace around us.

Given my mechanical skills, I understood why I was assigned to this position, though I didn't once think it would turn out to be this heavy of a duty. The constant training made much more sense to me now and I vowed to memorize every piece of the B-24. It might keep the crew alive if an emergency popped up.

The radioman, Ribbits, would be in the plane's upper fuselage, not far from the top turret. His job when not manning the waist gun would be to sit and listen to the static of the radio and give position reports every few minutes. He'd help Hausman take fixes and inform headquarters of targets attacked and the results. Likewise, he'd radio if we were under attack.

When we were lead crew, it would be a dedicated position for Ribbits. When we were in formation, he'd only be at the radio if we had to break formation for any reason. During formation were the times he would be on the gun while in hostile territory.

The gunners, myself included, would do specific training on our positions, which were turret or flexible. The waist gunners were flexible, and there was a school for that, the Flexible Training School. We had to learn the mechanics of the guns, how to assemble and disassemble them, even blindfolded. To help with the aim, we had to skeet shoot from moving platforms. It was a progression from small arms to automatic weapons to heavy machine guns and we practiced from actual turrets.

Some clever person mounted them on vehicles and we went on wild rides and had to hit our targets. Those sessions were inventive and sometimes fun. I supposed it wouldn't be as entertaining if someone fired at us while practicing.

We each learned every turret position. That included how to swing the massive guns and sight them in. The last step would be learning to shoot while flying. They would anchor a target to a plane and tow it. First, we had to master all the rest. It sounded easy in theory, even to myself, though I quickly learned otherwise.

The nose gunner, Merrill, had the scariest view, in my opinion. He saw the bombs falling and sat right behind the glass, giving him a bird's eye view of the action. The instructors told us it would be cold, cramped, and not a good time. Merrill would have an electric suit he would wear to help keep him warm but the instructor told us that they didn't work all that well.

Warren, the smallest of our crew, was the ball turret gunner. I thanked my lucky stars that it wasn't me because there was no way my frame would fit in that space. The first time I tried, it made the crew laugh so hard that their stomachs hurt. They likened me to a clown trying to get into an overstuffed clown car.

The ball turret gunner had no extra space for a

parachute. On take-off and landing, he wouldn't be in the position. On the B-24, the turret position pulled back into the plane for take-off and landing. They warned us of frostbite in these turrets and said we could expect temperatures as low as minus fifty degrees when we reached altitude.

The tail gunner would be Young. He was a serious man that I had yet to see let his guard down. His view of the formation behind us would be critical for watching for signs of enemy aircraft and announcing their positions.

Young would have two guns, his turret rotated, and his turret was also cramped. He wasn't much larger than Warren, but it was enough to make a difference in the space. One fun fact we didn't know was there were these funnels in the plane. They were attached to a hose that exited out the side of the aircraft. They were for urination on long flights.

One instructor told a story that had us torn between laughter and disgust. Apparently, it had happened that crew members had to use the hoses and the liquid entered the slipstream along the sides of the plane. It would hit the turret and enter in through the gaps between the turret and the body of the plane.

Young didn't say anything after that story but gave each of us a look that shook us in our socks if we dared to even think about using the hoses. It honestly sounded like something I would have done to a friend while I was in elementary school. The hoses were great in theory until you realized you would be peeing on your crewmate.

After hearing that, the waist gunners were happy with their positions. Their position was arguably one of the most dangerous positions compared to the others. They were more likely to catch flak, and the window was open for them to shoot and frostbite was a genuine concern.

After they told us the ins and outs of each position, the good and the bad, they discussed the exit points of the Liberator should we have to bail out. Those were the nose, wheel bay, forward bomb bay, rear bomb bay, and the rear hatch. They repeatedly tested us on those, threw scenarios that I hoped never to encounter, and we had to choose which exit would be the best option and why.

Japanese aircraft attacked the United States gunboat Tutuila on July 30th. The Captain anchored it in the Yangtze River in China. Despite our declaration of neutrality, Japan began to get aggressive. The next day, they apologized for it and it seemed like a game to me.

The move had our military forces on edge and it felt like war was inching closer to our doorstep. It sure incited many people on base and ruffled feathers of command. More than one crew wanted to put their training to the test.

The new fighter, the P-38, was just introduced to the fleet. The whole crew had the same idea of sending those planes over to bomb one of the Japanese boats and act surprised that it happened and apologize for it after the fact. Was it a petty thought? Probably. We didn't see it that way, though.

The P-38 had twin engines and a small one-person cockpit. They called it a fighter-bomber and a night fighter. They told us it could zip around at three hundred sixty miles per hour. It was lightening! It's not a plane I would be on if they ever deployed us, but it was fun to think of the speeds you could achieve. I wasn't going to be a pilot anyway.

"Suhm, did you hear the news?" Jones asked me as he plopped down beside me on the grass.

I'd just done a three-mile run and was trying to catch my breath. I shook my head at Jones and waited for him to spill the beans. The humidity was so high the air felt thick, and I struggled to breathe after the run. It was almost choking me.

"They changed the draft," Jones finally said. "Instead of a year, it's now thirty months."

"Wow," I managed to huff out. It didn't affect me one way or another since I was activated. I'd had to agree to thirty missions if deployed or three years, whichever was soonest. I hadn't joined because of the Selective Service Act.

"I figure there will be some mighty unhappy people about that," Jones mused.

"What's your time?" I asked once my breathing slowed down.

"Thirty missions or three years, whichever comes first," Jones offered freely.

"Same as me then." I nodded my head. "I'm okay with it. I don't have anyone waiting for me at home. I'm sure my old boss gave my civilian job to someone who needed it more than I did."

A new radio broadcast came on the radio at the end of August. It was supposed to be a comedy, and a few other guys and I were looking forward to hearing it. We listened in the mess hall with a large group of other men.

The show starts with a man named Gildersleeve moving to another town to care for his niece and nephew after his sister and brother-in-law died. It was entertaining and more than a few of us laughed during the episode.

A few days later, we had the news about the USS Greer getting fired up by a German submarine, and we were still a neutral power in the war. People like us were getting more tense as the activity to engage with the United States became more hostile and aggressive.

We didn't like sitting around doing nothing about helping fellow Americans who were under attack. It wasn't right. We didn't get deployed and continued the incredibly intensive training on the Liberator that we'd been doing since we arrived.

When I had a day off, I went into town and found a Freemason Lodge to establish myself with since I would be here in Jersey for the foreseeable future. I was lucky and found one that would take me on without going through the sponsor process again.

Even better, the lodge had a mixer planned that night and I would definitely be in attendance. I needed to let loose and have some fun to clear my head. I only had a few hours to kill before it started, so I set out to get some food first.

When I returned to the Freemason Lodge, a large group of people were gathered, and the music hadn't started yet. It was mingling time, and a few drinks were getting poured. I wandered through the groups, introduced myself and gave a little background on me. I found that I liked these guys better than the last lodge. It was a greater variety of people.

Oh boy, when the dancing started, I couldn't stop. I had a different lady in front of me each dance and I gave it my all. I earned a few kisses, spread my charms, and had a gas. It was a dance until you drop, and I almost did. I was exhausted by the time it was over. The good thing was my head was clear and I felt great.

We had a day pass from training on October 6th, and some of the crew and I found ourselves at a local bar to listen to the baseball game. I didn't have any extra money to bet, but Jones and Hausman did and they bet on the Dodgers to beat the Yankees. Myself, I would have bet the other way.

"Yankees can't win again," Jones argued when I spoke my mind. "The Dodgers have a great team and they deserve the win."

"It's not about who deserves it." I laughed. "It's about who plays better. The Yankees are the stronger team."

"Suhm is right." Rogers joined the conversation. "They've been unbeatable in the World Series."

"It's just time for someone else to hold the title," Hausman stated. "They make mistakes and I think the Dodgers want it more."

"Maybe." I shrugged and shook my head. "It won't happen."

The game started and the bar got rowdy. Sure enough, the Yankees took the 9th World Series and the Dodgers lost again. Hausman and Jones grumbled about the loss the entire way back to base to the amusement of Rogers and me.

The United States sent American forces to help defend Iceland as British troops were taking heavy casualties in the war. To top it off, America had a new fighter plane that joined our forces. At the end of October, our ship, the USS Reuben, was sunk by a torpedo fired on it by the German submarine U-552. It killed more than one hundred of our men.

The same day, work on Mount Rushmore ceased. It was as if those heads on that mountain were ready to speak and tell us they didn't die for us to sit here and do nothing while our men were getting attacked.

There was a lot of outrage over the loss of the men

and the ship. Our government was angry and my bones told me they were ready to react. I knew it wasn't only Fort Dix raring to go and get even.

Winston Churchill, the Prime Minister of Great Britain, spoke out on November 10th and declared his intent to side with the United States should we choose to go to war with Japan. With those words, I felt like Churchill painted a target on us like we were taunting Japan.

Four days later, a 5.4 magnitude earthquake hit California and caused damage out west. Hausman said the world was telling us to prepare to have things shaken up. I don't know if I believed in that kind of thing, like signs from higher powers. Yet there was a clear indication that things were changing and something was coming our way.

Overseas was still filled with strife and atrocities that we heard about on base more than the general population. Some of it was so bad it didn't seem real. Maybe it was propaganda to incite people over here, the same way Hitler was controlling the information disseminated from Europe. The thought was probably wishful thinking on my part.

Our guys heard talk about a type of new gas being used on prisoners of war overseas. There was a lot of talk about the camp called Auschwitz that opened last year and most of the terrible things we got news about involved that place.

Entire communities of Jewish people were getting exterminated and it was unfathomable to most of the people around me. America wasn't perfect; we had racial issues here. I hadn't heard anything like what was happening over there. I didn't understand what was so different about Jewish people that made them a target. I didn't know what made their blood dirty.

The war was in the papers daily, yet people continued their lives as if nothing were happening. Sports, movies, mixers, fairs, radio programs, and general growth went on rapidly in the United States.

On November 27th, all United States forces deployed in Asia, the Pacific, and Germany received notification that the government placed them all on war alert. Someone in Washington, DC, had received a warning about something; I felt sure of that deep in my bones.

The notice put us all on edge here in Fort Dix. I imagined men in other bases throughout the country felt the same way. We all knew war was imminent and all we were doing was playing the waiting game.

One day, we were out shopping for Christmas gifts to send home, and I found a comic book about a female superhero called *Wonder Woman*. I bought one to send home for Alicia. She loved Captain America, though her reading tastes weren't typically comic books.

December 7th came and everything changed in a heartbeat. An alarm rang out in the early afternoon that scrambled all the troops at Fort Dix to battle stations. Suddenly, we were on high alert and no one seemed to know why. The talk started spreading about us getting bombed and the guys on the gun batteries began looking toward the sky, ready to shoot planes down. After a couple of hours, details surfaced. Pearl Harbor in Hawaii had been bombed early in the morning by the Japanese. They decimated the Pacific fleet, killing thousands of servicemen and civilians.

December 8th, Roosevelt took to the radio waves and declared war on Japan. There was no more neutrality. The Japanese awoke the sleeping giant and turned her into a beast. The United States received a violent shove into war. My heart sank at the number of lives lost in the Pacific. I wondered when we'd get sent because it was evident that it would happen.

December 11th, Roosevelt once again announced to the world that the United States had declared war on Germany and Italy after they declared war on us. December 12th, Hungary and Romania joined the bandwagon of countries wanting to kill us. They declared war on the United States.

In December, we had massive numbers of people skipping the draft, going directly to military enlistment places, and joining. Our infantry divisions exploded with men wanting to join the ground forces and Navy. Where we were struggling to find men before, Pearl Harbor took care of that issue.

CHAPTER 6

1942

The crew hadn't received orders yet. However, several other units were shipping out by the thousands, mainly infantry, though a few aircrews left. I continued attending Freemason mixers when I could, looking for some normalcy while paying close attention to world events. I was going to attend one tonight.

It was New Year's Day, and before I left for the mixer, there was an announcement that world politicians had signed the proposed Declaration by the United Nations. China, the United Kingdom, the United States, the Soviet Union and twenty-two other nations agreed not to make any separate peace with any Axis Powers.

There it was. War was on our doorstep. I wanted to do a little dance because I'd been right, but it also wasn't something to want to be right about. It felt awful to know that at any moment, we could be the recipient of the same bombs that were destroying London and Paris.

I went to the mixer that night to bring in the New Year in a positive way. To my utter surprise, I ran into Alyse there. She seemed interested in the same things I was, and we danced well together. She even liked to roller skate. It was my second time meeting her. It was the first time we talked, but I was afraid of getting involved due to the world circumstances.

"What brings you to New Jersey?" I asked her after dancing several songs with her.

"My family has a house here," Alyse answered matter of factly. "I take it your station is here now."

"It is," I confirmed. "Fort Dix. We are waiting to see if we will get sent overseas."

"Is that what you want?" she asked me astutely. Her gaze searched my face for an answer.

"I do." I nodded and took a drink of the punch I'd grabbed for both of us from the refreshment table. "I feel like I need to be over there making a difference. I also have a desire for travel. I think I'm one of those people who have a restless soul."

"So you aren't a man set on marrying and settling down with a family," Alyse remarked casually.

I found the statement left me with a feeling of wrongness. "Not necessarily," I countered. "I think I want that, just not right now. It hardly seems fair to fall in love and then have to leave and have no set date to return home or possibly die in battle."

Our troops were getting killed over there and the carefree attitudes of the soldiers around me had taken a turn. There were a lot more grave and serious faces as people received news that someone they knew had gotten killed in action. I tried to imagine a new wife receiving that news of her husband and it bothered me.

Ships sunk, planes got shot down, and ground troops were taking heavy fire or getting captured. It wasn't something the soldiers were taking lightly. A sense of patriotism rose among the forces, yet the fear of getting sent still mixed with the excitement of wanting to receive orders to ship out. It was a paradox and I wanted to go.

"Well, it's good to know that now." Alyse interrupted my thoughts. "It means maybe I shouldn't get serious about you."

"Ms. Alyse, I would never mislead someone of your beauty." I bowed and grinned charmingly at her. I did like this woman, but my heart was still not ready for serious commitment. "However, I can lead you into another dance and maybe steal a kiss or two."

Alyse didn't protest and followed me back to the dance floor. The New Year began with a joyful night of dancing and my kiss. We parted ways at the end with no promises to each other nor a date set up since no one knew what would happen in the near future.

A blimp base began recruiting men not far from Fort Dix in Lakehurst and we lost a couple of guys to the new location as they got transferred. I didn't think I'd enjoy being on a blimp. The bombers were more my speed, and our training picked up tenfold.

The flight training increased, as did the hands-on training with the guns. Not only that, but they also added bomb training to the mix, which instructors put on the schedule for next month. Every member of our crew had to participate. The instructors would test us frequently.

We spent a fair amount of time starting the planes, which involved the pilot, copilot, myself, and whoever needed to be certified as a copilot and my backup. We took turns with the rest of the crew watching to see how the process would begin.

Instructor Wilson told me this would be a primary part

of my duty as the engineer, so they began with me. I would walk to each engine and hand rotate the propellers several times to ensure the pooled oil moved around or vented.

The copilot would be the one to actually start the engines, which Carlson would do with onboard batteries or an external battery cart that I would wheel out if that were what was needed. We had to learn both ways.

The crew had to start the engines on the Liberator in a particular order. From the pilot's perspective, the numbers were: the left port engine was number one, followed by number two, and the number three engine was the inboard engine on the starboard (right) side, followed by number four.

The starting sequence was engine number three always started first. That engine powered the aircraft's hydraulic pump, which I knew from the mechanical training. Engine number four was next, followed by number two, and then last, number one.

That order was so that I, the engineer, wouldn't have to walk through or toward a moving propeller while standing there with a fire extinguisher in case one caught fire while starting. There was a hydraulic pump in the aft bomb bay with an electric motor known to arc, causing explosions or fires on start.

Another fact we learned was that the Liberator was known for having a fuel leak in the bomb bay area, which was why the bomb bay doors were never fully closed so that the area would receive ventilation and minimize the risk of fires or explosions.

After I rotated all the propellors, I shouted an all-clear response to Carlson. After visually checking to see no personnel were in the engine area, he yelled the all-clear in response. Carlson began starting engines in the sequence taught to us while I stood near the whooshing propellors with a fire extinguisher ready to fire at the first sign of a spark.

We went through the procedure countless times until all personnel had it memorized and it became routine. We worked like a well-oiled machine and didn't have the problems we witnessed with other crews. I felt lucky.

America had a new flying machine, the Sikorsky R-4 helicopter. It was a two-seater, had three blades that rotated over the body and was powered by a radial engine. It took its first flight on January 14th and performed beautifully. Information released said it would have an altitude of twelve thousand feet. The Sikorsky airspeed could go to approximately ninety miles per hour and fly for one hundred hours without major incident.

I didn't get to see the initial flight, which was disappointing. A few crews at Fort Dix would be flying the machines. I thought it would be fun to ride in one, though I didn't get an opportunity. It was a bit on the small side for me to want to be one of the two people on board. I was comfortable with the Liberator and its size.

Almost two weeks after that, Thailand declared war on America and the United Kingdom. I didn't know what we did to them, or if it was just choosing a side they thought would win. Regardless, every day in the news was another battle or a strategic move to help us advance our war efforts.

Women were joining the workforce in droves because factories needed help now that so many men were serving their country during the war. The whole family unit seemed to be changing, and women were doing things that were ordinarily men's jobs. What secretly thrilled me was that they were doing it well, as well as men. Many didn't share the same view as me and weren't happy about wives, sisters, mothers, or any woman working the way they were, and they began to regret their decision to enlist after Pearl Harbor. It was nonsense to me.

I was of the small percentage that saw it as an advancement for our country and that we were united in fighting a war and keeping our freedoms safe. We were working together. I bowed out of several arguments about it because it wasn't worth the breath it took to state my case.

February rolled in with no care that time seemed to be slipping away. On the 8th, daylight savings time went into effect. It wasn't a practice I was fond of because it confused me for about a week after it began. Adjusting to the time change, I felt more tired and worn out than usual.

On the 9th, the SS Normandie that docked in New York caught on fire while undergoing troopship conversions, and she capsized. A lot of people were talking about that. The small blessing was it happened somewhere where she could be pulled out and repaired.

An executive order was signed that called for any people deemed a threat to be gathered and relocated further inland. Over one hundred twenty thousand Japanese Americans were detained and placed in these camps. The coasts were considered military zones. The order gave power to have civilians moved away from these areas. However, the only civilians who moved were of Japanese descent, even if they were born here and citizens of the United States.

I wasn't sure how I felt about that. It seemed no better than what the Nazis were doing to the Jewish people. I understood why they did it after Pearl Harbor and learned that a Japanese had been hiding and spying under their noses.

Around the same time, word spread to a few bases that a Harvard chemist invented a substance called napalm that could be useful for wartime and military purposes. It would stick to the skin and burn entirely through to the bone. It was gruesome and terrifying to think about but brilliant as a defensive weapon.

Someone on the West Coast in southern California spotted and reported something suspicious. Los Angeles was forced into blackout conditions and the government sent out raid wardens. They made their way through the city, looking for any activity that could be deemed dangerous to citizens and the country.

Soldiers fired battery guns out to where the sighting occurred over the water. No planes fell, and no one found anything. Yet five people died due to the activity.

"What do you think it was?" Hausman asked me as I folded the newspaper that someone left on the table.

"A weather balloon, probably," I guessed. "People are paranoid after Pearl Harbor. It's not bad because it makes people more aware of their surroundings and diligent about reporting things. The downside is it can cause deaths that didn't need to happen." I tapped the paper and shook my head.

"The Battle of Los Angeles," Hausman read under my tapping finger. "Right before the spectacle of the Academy Awards tonight. Have you seen any of the films that are up for awards?"

"I did," I confirmed. "I saw *How Green Was My Valley* with a girl I met at a mixer. It was good. She was over the moon about it, so that one will probably win."

"I didn't see it." Hausman frowned. "I haven't had any dates either. How are you finding these women?"

"My charming personality draws them to me," I joked smugly.

"Right." Hausman smirked. "I bet it's that you tower over everyone and stand out. They can't miss seeing you that way."

I couldn't argue that. "Join a local club," I suggested. "You can't expect to meet women at bars only. The ones there aren't the ones you want a future with anyway."

"I don't want a future. I want a right now." Hausman grinned and waggled his eyebrows. "I need to sow some oats."

The next day at breakfast, Rogers plopped down a newspaper before me. "I know you read these, and I picked it up for you after someone left it behind."

"Thanks." I opened the paper and read that the film I guessed would win won the Best Picture award. "Hausman, look, that film did win."

"Should have bet on it," Hausman retorted.

"You don't have to bet on everything." I elbowed him.

"You do if you want money to spend," Hausman groused.

"Ready for today's training?" Rogers interrupted. "Bombs today."

I remembered and nodded in response. I wanted to finish the paper before we had to leave. I read a lot of political articles and got through it all with barely a moment to spare before it was time to report to training.

"Gentlemen, these are five-hundred-pound bombs," the sergeant told us. "Currently, it's the most common load for a

Liberator. They can carry ten."

"Is it live?" Jones wondered.

"Not for training purposes," the sergeant told us. "They will be actual bombs when it comes time to test."

I swallowed a lump of fear. I'd have to get used to it because the Army wouldn't send us on missions with training shells. Each of us had heard stories about training going wrong and someone set off an explosive where people got severely hurt or died. Sitting in front of that many explosives on a metal tube was unnerving at best.

"The other common load the B-24s carry is five of the thousand-pound bombs," the sergeant continued. "While the ground crew will be loading your payloads, you will be expected to know how to prepare these in case of failure or other mishap. You must also know how to defuse them if you can't drop your payload. Is that understood?"

"Yes, sir," the crew chorused in synchronization.

"Good. Let's proceed." The sergeant held out fuses we each took. "This is the bomb shackle. Each of you should already be aware of where and what it is."

I nodded because we knew. It was a long piece of metal attached to the plane that had raised arms that held the bombs in place when loaded on the plane. It had three points on it. The two on the ends held the bomb by releasable hooks, and the third held what I assumed was the fuse the sergeant handed us. I was wrong.

"This one here," the sergeant held the point I thought was for a fuse, "is for the arming wire. This fuse will be the most common type of bomb fuse. You will insert the long wire into the fuse. When the bomb gets released from your plane, it will hold the arming wire and get pulled out of the fuse as the bomb drops. This action will trigger the arming vane." He pointed to the propeller on the nose. "It will cause the fuse to spin approximately two hundred sixty turns before it falls away. This count arms the bomb and happens once it's free of the aircraft. Understood?"

"Yes, sir," we responded as one.

"This is what today's focus will be," the sergeant continued. "For obvious reasons, you don't want this wire coming out while you are in flight and not dropping your payload. We will go over a different fuse type next week. Expect a test on what you learn here today."

The entire crew got down to business learning how to insert the fuse, check the bomb shackle, check each point, and ensure you set your wire correctly. We did this for four hours and then came the test.

The next day, when we were doing a test flight, there was an announcement that another of our ships had come under attack. Japanese fighters hit the USS Langley, which carried a load of P-40. It took heavy damage and the crew had to scuttle the ship to keep it out of the hands of the Japanese.

The news hit hard as America needed those planes to be delivered so that troops had them. They were in desperate need of the aircraft overseas. Having to scuttle a ship wasn't a good option either since we needed machines and equipment.

It resulted in the crew working extra hard to pass the exams and training so we could get out there and help the war along. It seemed like every day, things were getting more intense.

"Suhm!" Ribbits called out to me. "Did you hear there was a second attempt at Pearl Harbor?"

I all but halted in my tracks. We were out on a long-distance run and I was in the lead, only because my stride was longer than the rest of theirs. I turned and looked at Ribbits as he huffed his way up to me.

"It's true." He paused with his hands on his knees. "Two of those flying boats tried to attack and weren't successful."

"That's what you should have led with." I shook my head at Ribbits. "The unsuccessful part. Why on earth would they think they could get away with it a second time?"

"That was my response, too," Ribbits replied as he caught his breath. "Get running." He elbowed me. "I just stopped you to say I could catch you."

I laughed and resumed my run, quickly pulling ahead of Ribbits. I was the first to finish and sat down with the newspaper someone discarded to read through the news while I waited for the others. Plus, seeing their expressions when they reached me and I sat calmly with my ankle over my knee reading a newspaper was humorous.

Those of us on the East Coast now had orders to black-out at night. All windows darkened, so no light showed, no driving after a specific time and if you did, it needed to be with no lights on. Woo-boy, we did some training on driving in the dark, and what an adventure it was!

On March 9th, we had a base announcement about changes to the Army command. They now divided us into three separate divisions: Army Ground Forces, Army Air Forces, and Services of Supply. The one thing that didn't change for us was that Henry H. Arnold was still commander general of the USAAF. That was good news for us, in my opinion.

I saw Alyse a couple of times again at mixers and

spent time talking with her instead of only dancing and stealing kisses. I was interested, yet still hesitant to take it further due to the war. That didn't stop me from enjoying my time with her when I ran into her at the mixers. She was a doll.

"Did you see the paper this morning?" Rogers asked me before training.

"I read the whole thing," I confirmed. "Which part has you upset?"

"They are interring Germans and Italians now as well as the Japanese," Rogers stated with a flat look on his face. "People that were legitimately born here. Our nation's leaders didn't found this country on those principles."

"We both know that," I replied quietly because our views weren't popular. "Just as we know, it's wartime, and paranoia runs deep. Locking people up is how they are dealing with the fear. It's not right, and all we can do about it is do our job and hopefully deploy overseas to help the end of the war come faster."

"I know, Suhm. I just got word that some of my friends suffered the relocation," Rogers grumbled. "Every single one of them was born here, raised here, and never once set foot outside the country. Hell, they've never been out of the county."

That made me pause and think about my friends who had different backgrounds. I wondered if they were facing the same situation. It struck me that these things I read in the newspaper are disturbing enough from that viewpoint, but when it hit close to home and happened to someone you knew, it took on a more sinister meaning.

"Have you asked around to see if anyone can do anything to help it?" I finally asked Rogers.

"Discreetly, yes. One guy seemed to think it might get

him and his family out if my friend enlisted. I don't know, though," Rogers answered. "I can't think about it now. I wrote a letter to him suggesting it, but is sending him off to war better than being interred and relatively safe?"

"Good question," I mused thoughtfully. "Hopefully, our country isn't doing the same thing the Nazis are. If they are, he's better off in war."

"Hot damn!" Jones shouted, startling me from the letter I had written to my sister. "Suhm, you've gotta read this!"

I hadn't yet read the newspaper this morning, and we hadn't turned the radio on either. "What now?" I muttered darkly.

"There was a joint raid on some French city called St. Nazaire," Jones told me as he ran over with the newspaper clutched in his hand. "This is brilliant. Look!"

Jones shoved the paper under my face and I frowned at him before uncrumpling it and reading the article. It was one of those tiny articles buried, but I had to agree with Jones. The Brits pulled off a fantastic mission.

They repurposed an old ship of ours, lined the hull with explosives and cemented them in, then ran the boat into the dry dock of the German-occupied town. It cut the Germans off from repairing damaged ships. Lives were lost, yet it also hindered the Nazis in a big way. It forced the Germans to bring their ships through the English Channel, where the Brits could sink them.

"It's a well-thought-out strategy," I told Jones after finishing the article. "There's hope for an end to the war after all if people keep thinking like that."

"I still want a piece of the action," Jones replied with a smirk.

"We'll get our chance," I told him, positive that I was right.

"Cripes," I mumbled. "One of the U-boats got as close to us as North Carolina. U-85, it says." There wasn't anyone in particular I was talking to. We were all sitting around a table chatting after dinner. "The USS Roper sunk it. Good thing. Can you imagine the coast of North Carolina getting shot up?"

"It would ruin Nags Head and Cape Hatteras." Carlson interrupted my thoughts.

"Are those important places?" I asked. I'd never been to North Carolina and knew little about the state.

"A lot of wealthy people in that area," Carlson answered with a wry look. "Having their dunes littered with artillery shells wouldn't do. It's not proper."

That got a laugh out of the crew. I put the paper away and looked at the guys. "Who wants to play a friendly game of basketball?"

"Pick a better game," Hausman told me. "You are too tall to play basketball with and expect to win."

A week later we heard about Doolittle's Raid. Lt. Colonel James Doolittle led a bombing mission against Japan with seventy-nine airmen of the air force and sixteen B-25 land-based bombers. Thirteen of the aircraft flew over Tokyo to bomb places that would help their war efforts, like oil storage, factories, and military targets. The other three planes went to Yokohama, Nagoya, and Kobe to do the same.

It was an impressive mission and I had to say that it bolstered our enthusiasm to help the war and get revenge for Pearl Harbor. All but one plane ran out of fuel, which was scarier because they had to land in Japanese-controlled China.

We received unofficial word that sympathetic Chinese

farmers helped our men out and got seventy-one of our guys back to free China, where they could catch a boat or plane back to their base. Japanese forces captured the remaining eight men. Japan executed four for their crimes, and the other four became prisoners.

After we learned of the mission, the crew had a long talk about how we would handle landing in enemy territory and how we would, if possible, survive injuries or capture. There was a lot of speculation, though it was one of those things you rarely think about, even though the odds were pretty good that it could happen.

May 15th brought a surprising change to the army with the new law that Roosevelt signed. The Women's Auxiliary Army Corps came to life. The army was officially recruiting women. I had such mixed feelings about it that I couldn't wrap my mind around the fact.

"Women have no place here," Cutty spouted. "How can we do our jobs when we are worried about their safety?"

"The women won't be fighting," Rogers stated. "Sadly, war is good for the economy because it creates jobs. The more women they have doing clerical work, cooking, medical, even driving, the more men they can send out to the front lines."

I had to admit it wasn't a perspective I'd thought about since my views aligned with Cutty's. However, Rogers had a point and I was progressive enough to see that side of things. I wasn't against women working, but having them on the battlefield was a different story.

"The army already employs nurses," Jones pointed out. "This isn't that much more of a stretch. It gives me a reason to see medical and check out the new nurses."

Warren threw his towel at Jones and shook his head at the antics. He didn't say much most of the time and it made me happy when he joined in. We needed to be close-knit for our crew to be successful.

Soon, the US began to ration sugar, and I wondered if we would fall into the same situation that Europe found itself in, with shortages of everything. It was a scary thought and I hoped my sister was faring well back home.

I wrote letters to her, Steve, and a few other friends. I got replies, though they didn't come often. Alicia only spoke of films she wanted to see or new fashions she wanted to try. It was strange to be reduced to conversations about nothing when I was used to talking to her about various subjects. I wondered why they didn't share things, like if they had enough sugar to bake the things they needed.

"Would you look at that?" Young surprised me by speaking out.

"What?" I asked, looking around.

"Rhetorical, sorry," Young told me. He was sitting in front of the radio, listening to it quietly. "The Navy is accepting negroes now. First women, then negroes. It's about time."

I raised my eyebrows at the news but more so at Young's comment. His tone was even enough that I had a hard time figuring out if he was happy or not, despite the added comment about it being time. He usually sat with Merrill, Carlson, and Warren. Those were the quiet guys of our crew and they were hard to read.

"It's not like we don't need help and they bleed the same color we do," I responded. I had a few African-American friends at home. I saw nothing wrong with them having the same rights as we did. "Are you ready for more bomb training today?"

Young nodded, turned the radio off and stood up. "The more we know, the better off we are."

"Today we are going over the acid fuse," the sergeant told us. "If you screw this up, you can bet it will cost the lives of your crew and your plane. What makes these so dangerous is the tiny glass container of nitric acid with a plate between the nitric acid and the mercury. If your bomb isn't fastened correctly and falls off the shackle, it could cause the glass to break and detonate the bomb. It doesn't have to be armed for this to happen. Do you understand?"

"Yes, sir," we answered as a group.

It was a terrifying thought. I pictured dodging flak or evasive maneuvers before we got to a target and one of the shackles took a hit or something. The force of the plane landing on the runway could make that bomb detonate if that little glass broke. What a way to end your time in war.

"You can't remove this fuse after you install it. If you cannot deliver your payload on the target, you must find somewhere else to drop the bombs. I can't stress this enough, men. Details matter."

We were eating a meal at the mess hall when we heard about the battle at Midway with the Japanese and the cheer that went up around the base when they announced we defeated them was the morale booster that the troops needed to reinvigorate the desire to join the fight, especially after the training on acid fuses.

There were four Japanese aircraft carriers against our

three, the same four that were part of the attack on Pearl Harbor. We sunk all of them. What did they think would happen after they bombed us while we slept? Gads, the victory was sweet. It stirred me up something fierce.

We lost our carrier, Yorktown, and the destroyer Hammann. The other two carriers remained fully intact. Talk about fancy flying by the pilots. We had Catalinas, Avengers, Dauntless, Wildcats, Vindicators, Buffalos, B-17s, and Marauders. With those fighters and bombers, there was no way they would beat us. Midway proved a point to the Japanese, and they delivered the message loudly.

Two weeks later, we heard some sharp-eyed soldiers spotted a Japanese submarine at the mouth of the Columbia, a large river on the west coast of Oregon. They came at us again, looking for retribution for their defeat in the Pacific. They fired on Fort Stevens, a base that had been there since the Civil War. They fired seventeen shells at the base, and only one came close to the battery. The nerve of these guys was something else.

The base called the location to air support, and the soldiers identified the sub as I-25. A Hudson bomber found the target, but the sub escaped by submerging.

We all waited in anticipation as the US began their air raids. The 8th Air Force had their first mission in Europe over the Netherlands. Six light bombers targeted four Luftwaffe airfields; the Brits joined us with six of their light bombers. They knew we were coming and fought back. There was talk about superb flying by one of our pilots that has us rooting for them. What a way to spend the 4th of July.

The bombings were our area and we listened to the

radio every day to hear what was happening in Europe now that we were doing air raids. Reports came in mixed, and we heard that our planes were significantly damaged. In my heart, I knew that the Axis powers chose the wrong country to make an enemy out of because we wouldn't take it sitting down.

"Well, I'll be damned, fellas." Ribbits walked into the barracks. "The Navy is accepting women. They created a women's reserve like the Army."

"I'm sure you're already damned," I retorted, "but not because women joined the Navy."

Cutty barked out a laugh. "I'll second that, Suhm. Soon, they'll have women flying the planes for us. Better watch out, Rogers."

"There are no live bands anywhere," a bar owner told the crew. "There's a music strike going on. It's something about royalty payments or nonsense like that. You'll have to dance to the jukebox if you want to dance. Music is music."

It wasn't the same. A live band drew people into the establishment so they could watch them play. It made the dancing more fun. "Beggars can't be choosers," I told the guys. Getting the whole crew out had taken me a ton of effort.

"We're already here," Jones pointed out. "And there are women over there just waiting for a group of fine-looking gents like us."

I think a couple of our guys were married already, but I wasn't sure because they didn't talk about their lives much. I supposed they were the ones who sat at the bar instead of trying to entice the ladies onto the dance floor. Regardless, I wasn't going to waste a night out.

"Why on earth are they playing a Christmas song on the radio in August?" Hausman groused.

"It's to promote a movie that will be out, isn't it?" I asked. I'd read something about it in the paper. It was odd to hear Christmas music in the middle of summer; I'd give Hausman that.

"What do you think about that blimp?" Jones plopped down next to me.

We'd just finished more training on bombs with proximity fuses that used radio waves, most effectively used in fragmentation bombs. I swear I would have dreams about fuses chasing me if I could get some sleep. We were all sitting on the ground outside listening to a radio we'd stretched the cord on to sit in the hot sun.

"The one that went down in California?" I asked to be sure which one he was talking about.

"Yeah, that one," Ribbits piped up. "Creepy."

"Do you believe in ghosts, Ribbits?" Hausman asked.

"No," Ribbits sneered. "That's foolish."

"Then explain how no one found any bodies or signs of the crew at all," Hausman provoked Ribbits.

"It's a mystery." Ribbits shrugged. "Maybe they all jumped."

I rolled my eyes and couldn't help but wonder what had happened to the crew. The blimp went down near San Francisco and with no trace of the crew. It baffled people all over the country, myself included.

The 8th, the unit I was in, made their first independent raid on occupied France. Every guy on the team was on the edge of their seat, waiting for word on the crews. Eighteen B-17s were targeting the marshaling yards in Rouen-Sotteville. It wouldn't be the last time.

The mission was successful in that all planes returned to the base and dropped their payloads without issue. Thankfully, the government hadn't rationed alcohol and my friends and I went out to celebrate the successes of the 8th. We hoped to bring more wins to the group when it was our turn.

"I told you!" Cutty shouted. "Women are joining the Air Force. They are going to fly planes now."

I chuckled at the righteous look on Cutty's face. "Is there a problem with that?"

"What if they get hurt?" Jones added cautiously.

"They can get hurt crossing a street," Rogers challenged them. "I'm not worried about it and neither should you be."

"Are you afraid they are going to outclass you?" I joked. "Because that already happened."

Cutty scowled and waved his hands at us. "The lot of you is no good."

"Yes!" Hausman shouted.

We were in physical training and had just finished combat fighting while we listened to the World Series on the radio. The Yankees, the reigning champs, were playing the St. Louis Cardinals. It was the series' last game, and the Cardinals were taking the title.

"Yankees lose!" Hausman did a boxing jab dance.

"Are you anti-Yankees?" I asked him.

"It's nice to have someone else win." Hausman

stopped his dance and looked at me. "I also just won a bunch of money."

"Wow, how do you not see another plane coming at you?" Jones shook his head as we listened to the radio broadcast of the news.

It was late October, and the nights had significantly cooled off, so we were holed up in our bunker, playing a game of cards while we listened.

"It's easier than you think," Rogers replied. "You know the variables."

"I do," Jones agreed. "It's just crazy to think a DC-3 didn't see a bomber. That composer guy died. The one who did all the music for the movies."

"We heard the same as you did." Cutty scowled and threw some cards down. "Let's make sure we don't make the mistake of missing something and having it happen to us. Formation flying is already on the scary side."

"Whoa, Suhm, look at you." Cutty whistled at me as I smoothed my uniform.

"I've got a date." I winked. "Don't wait up."

"Where are you taking her?" Jones raised his eyebrows and grinned at me.

"To see the new film *Casablanca* and to dinner," I supplied. "Wish me luck."

"You don't need it." Hausman smirked. "You seem to have a way with the ladies."

"Looks like our driving is going to be limited while we are on leave." I tapped the newspaper. "The government is rationing gasoline now."

"Right in time for Christmas," grumbled Ribbits unhappily.

"Don't worry." Jones laughed. "Santa doesn't need gasoline to deliver presents."

A week later, the USS New Jersey battleship launched from Philadelphia. Luckily, we could watch the launch from a bar with a television. The entire crew wasn't there, but most of us were. It gave us a sense of pride since our station was in New Jersey. Though I didn't want to be on her, she was a fine-looking ship. I wanted to be in the sky.

A couple of weeks after the USS New Jersey launched, the Allies publicly acknowledged the Holocaust for the first time. It was sobering for many people. I was happy that the atrocities were getting their deserved attention. Maybe we could put an end to the senseless murders carried out in the name of a madman.

We all made it through Christmas and all the way to New Year's Eve. The year had been fast-paced for the most part and we all looked forward to when we could do our duties for the war. It was easy to admit impatience in that arena.

All of us were on base since we didn't have leave for the holiday and for the first time ever, the ball over Times Square didn't drop. Instead, the country fell into a hushed moment of silence to honor those who perished in the war. There was no kiss for me and I hoped it wasn't a bad omen.

CHAPTER 7

1943

The war dominated the newspaper, television, and radio from the start of January. It was ironic how much information was out there now. I don't believe all of it was true because speculation ran rampant. However, the Holocaust was now front and center.

Mid-January began the Casablanca Conference. Roosevelt and Churchill met in the city of Casablanca, Morocco, to discuss strategy for dealing with the Axis powers and what they deemed unconditional surrender.

I was of the opinion that Hitler didn't understand the word surrender and there was no point in discussing it. Hitler needed to die once and for all to stop the insanity he inflicted on the countries that he stepped foot in.

The entire world became consumed with war, yet we still sat at Fort Dix waiting for orders to deploy. Other than relentless training on bombs, proving we knew how to arm and disarm, if possible, fly, shoot guns while flying, and fix machines and equipment, we weren't doing much.

On January 29th, the marines joined the women's

movement and established a women's Marine Corps reserve, much to the consternation of the men, especially those who were married. None of them wanted their women close to the military other than to see them off to war and welcome them home. Thankfully, not all the men I knew felt that way and I couldn't help but wonder if I would feel the same way they did if I were married.

A couple of weeks later, we were leaving another bomb training class when the news broke that the United Stated had secured Guadalcanal and drove the Japanese out. Cheers went up around the base and we jabbed our fists into the air with a victory shout. Wins hadn't been easy to come by lately.

"Shoe rationing?" Merrill interrupted our idle chit-chat. He was sitting in front of the radio, listening to it at low volume. "Why are we rationing shoes?"

We each shut our mouths and turned to look at Merrill as if he had grown an extra head. None of us could answer his questions, nor was he even looking at us for a response. He hunched forward with his ear practically glued to the radio.

"Oh, my," Merrill breathed out. "They are only going to allow three pairs of rubber-soled or leather shoes to each person now, and they must use a ration coupon to purchase. The military is the reason for it. I'm the reason my family can't have shoes."

I don't think that Merrill was aware he was speaking. I truly believed he thought he was thinking to himself. None of us wanted to interrupt him or poke fun at him, either. The reality was each of us was thinking about what a shoe shortage meant for our families.

Our jovial attitudes sobered up quickly. I realized that

the world was rapidly becoming a foreign place for many people and nothing about life would be the same. Change was frightening for many, especially on the tail of the depression ending and for those that lived through the first World War. I was scared to wonder what would happen next.

The next day, we learned about the censors. It was as if fate tempted me to wonder more so it could toss another curveball at me. I had a date with Alyse in a few days to see the newly released movie *The Outlaw*.

"Good thing that film was out before the war office censored it," Cutty pointed out as I griped.

I couldn't argue that. Sometimes, I just needed the reminder that there were still things to be thankful for, even as things deteriorated.

The newspaper said that a man in India named Mahatma Gandhi practiced peaceful protests, usually by fasting. He was arrested and imprisoned due to the unrest caused by the Indian National Congress in 1942. The Brits were holding him and his protest was for being detained without charges. It lasted twenty-one days. I was astounded.

"Can you imagine not eating for almost a month?" I asked Jones as he was putting food in his mouth.

"I can't imagine a few hours without eating," Jones deadpanned. "I might perish. Are you talking about that Indian fella, Gandhi, or whatever his name is?"

"You knew about him?" I allowed the surprise to color my tone.

"He has a history of fasting as a weapon," Jones told me. "The guy was a lawyer or something to that effect over there in India."

"Call me gobsmacked," I replied and folded

the newspaper.

"I call you a lot of things, Suhm," Jones said, smirking at me and finishing his meal.

"Did you hear about the Navy battle?" Alyse asked me at dinner. "It was all over the news."

"No, I didn't," I responded. "Fill me in. I was in training all of today. I think it was the last of the fuses, finally."

"That sounds exciting," Alyse teased. "Over in the south Pacific, the Bismarck Sea, I think, we worked with Australia and sunk a convoy of Japanese ships." She paused to think for a moment and an odd look came over her face. "This part bothers me," she told me in a lowered voice. "I don't think I'm supposed to know it, but I overheard my father talking to one of his military buddies. Everyone shot up the survivors that were in the water."

I bit my tongue until I could gather my thoughts. While I hadn't seen action yet, I'd heard plenty of stories, good and bad. I decided that blunt honesty was probably the better course for me to take. Alyse didn't seem like a 'soften the edges and put sugar on it' type.

"War is murder," I finally said. "No matter how you look at it."

"I know." Alyse nodded, her eyes shining with tears. "Try and look at it from my point of view. I don't favor the Nazis or the Japanese or question why we are killing them, especially after Pearl Harbor. We don't have to be cruel, though. We aren't Nazis. Those guys were already dead. They were floating in the water, dead bodies already around them, probably attracting sharks. The likeliness of them making their way to land was slim. We didn't need to shoot them in the water."

I couldn't deny that Alyse had a point and a good one. We didn't need to be cruel. I hadn't heard anything about the strafing of the survivors, though I had heard about the sinking of a convoy. I hadn't known where or who it was. I couldn't speak for those who did it either.

"What bothers me the most is that I know you are going to Europe," Alyse continued. "I know you must do things I can't begin to understand. You'll see things I never will. You have a good heart, Ralph. I'm worried what those things will do to you. Enough about that. Tell me the exciting things you learned about fuses today."

I swallowed what I had prepared to say in defense of soldiers and forced a smile at the woman I suspected I was falling in love with. "I learned about contact fuses and that some bombs have two fuses on them instead of one. That's all I'm allowed to say without compromising the security of our nation." I winked to show her I was joking. "How about some pie?"

"In other news," Jones imitated the radio broadcaster's voice, "Nazis are killing all the Jews in Greece now."

We'd just heard about that a few hours ago and it bothered many people. They didn't even bother to call it a labor camp. They called Treblinka an extermination camp. Since they publicly acknowledged the Holocaust, we'd heard a lot about it. None of the camps were good.

There were Jewish people on the base with us. Some of them had family in Europe, and I wasn't sure where. Things became more real as the war started touching people closer to home. I elbowed Jones to hush him since his voice carried.

"I know you aren't making fun of the situation," I cautioned my crew mate, "but others don't know you. I don't want a fight to start over someone not understanding you are upset about it."

"Suhm is right," Rogers added. "Someone is always listening and what they hear might not be what was said."

"Who wants to make a bet on the Academy Awards tonight?" Hausman asked to change the subject. "Suhm was right last year. Shall we hear his prediction and make a wager on it?"

I huffed out a laugh and rolled my eyes. "If you had a date, you might get to see a movie and decide for yourself. I'm not a connoisseur or critic."

"You've got enough dates for all of us," Ribbits whined. "It wouldn't hurt you to share."

"It wouldn't hurt you to shower." Jones laughed at his rebuttal.

"I say that *Mrs. Miniver* will win." Rogers interrupted what was sure to be a loud argument.

"I didn't see it." I shrugged. "My money is on Rogers."

It wasn't often that Rogers bet, other than in card games, so that caught the attention of the others. It turned out he was right.

I quietly folded my newspaper and pushed it to the side of the diner table. I was meeting a lady I met at a mixer for dinner. I hadn't yet decided if I wanted to be exclusive with Alyse or not, though I reluctantly admitted to myself that it was what I wanted. This date was a test to see how I felt with another woman.

"Hi, Ralph," Betty said as she slipped into the booth. "Sorry, I am late."

"It's okay. It allowed me time to catch up on the newspaper reading," I accepted her apology.

"That doesn't sound fun," Betty pouted. "There's nothing good to read in there."

"I like to keep up on events," I stated, annoyed with the pout. "Being in the military, I think it's important to know what's going on out there in case I end up there."

"I see." Betty nodded absently. It was apparent she wasn't paying attention to what I said. "What's good here? I've never been to a diner before."

Betty couldn't hold a flame to Alyse. "Have you heard the latest on the Holocaust?" I asked, ignoring her question.

"I don't believe in the Holocaust. I think it's something made up." Betty tapped the menu. "I think I'll have a salad."

A gust of wind not strong enough to fill a sail could have knocked me over. "How can you not believe in the Holocaust? It's been going on for years. Jewish people are getting massacred for no reason. How would you feel if that were your family? Or if you had family in Warsaw where they rounded up the last of the Jews to send them to an extermination camp after they tried to fight to save themselves?"

"I'm not Jewish, I'm Protestant," Betty claimed. "It's not something I need to worry about."

I don't know what prompted me to ask for this date with this shallow woman. "You should care because those people are human. Excuse me for being rude, but I'm not feeling well. I think the coffee I drank earlier isn't agreeing with my stomach." I dropped some money on the table. "Please, feel free to order your salad. I'll still pay for it."

"Oh, you poor dear." Betty slid out of the booth. "No need to buy me a salad. I prefer to eat somewhere else anyway. I do hope you feel better. Maybe we can see each other on a different day."

"Sure," I lied. I practically ran out the door, leaving my money on the table. The guys on base were going to love hearing about this.

"Did you hear what the Army is doing?" Jones asked me the first thing in the morning, the day after the disaster date.

"I just woke up," I replied. "No, I haven't heard. Either tell me or stop talking."

"You are grouchy." Jones smirked. "I take it the date didn't go well."

"It was terrible. Betty would be perfect for you." I smirked right back at him. "She doesn't have any brain cells."

"I'm not picky," Jones replied with a shrug. "Anyway, do you know what ENIAC is?"

"No, I can't say I do," I told Jones as I walked to the counter to get some coffee.

"It's a machine the Army is going to build with the University of Pennsylvania," Jones stated, following me. "It's going to do calculations, so humans won't have to do as much math."

I laughed. "I'm sure it will do more than that."

"That's good enough for me. I hate math," Jones quipped. "Now, tell me about this lady."

"Can you think about anything else, Jones?" Rogers walked up to us. "Suhm, the first crew of the 8th to make all their missions and return intact, the Memphis Belle B-17, has returned to the United States. Remember how we were talking about making it home if we went? That's the news I needed. I can get us through if we get orders."

"Rogers, that makes me happy to hear that." I thumped him on the back. "You have my full confidence. You lead and I'll follow."

"Look!" Cutty ran into the yard waving a magazine. "Women are going to make us useless."

I snatched the magazine from Cutty's waving arm. It was a copy of the Saturday Evening Post featuring a woman in a worker's uniform with a tool in her lap and a sandwich in her hand. "The last I checked, they still need us for reproduction. Women in the workforce don't make us useless. They support us and what we are doing here."

I smacked Cutty in the head with the magazine. The cover was certainly a conversation piece and the woman's arms portrayed on the cover were strong. I wouldn't say I liked the idea of women in the military fighting because, in my limited view, seeing a woman on a battlefield would distract me because I'd be worried about her safety. I knew my view was sexist but it was how I felt.

On the other hand, I saw nothing wrong with women working in factories doing the same jobs we'd done prior to joining the military. Even after we returned home, I didn't see a reason why a woman couldn't work and earn her own money.

"You would be okay with that doll you've been seeing going to work in a factory run by men, with a predominantly female workforce using tools that men struggle with sometimes and pulling long hours, being out alone after dark, and not at home with the children?" Cutty retorted in astonishment.

"That's right," I returned. I honestly hadn't thought about it in the way Cutty presented it. Maybe I'd have some misgivings, but I don't think I would say she couldn't do it. Alyse wouldn't stand for me telling her what to do anyway. She was a strong-willed woman, a fact that I quite admired.

I'd had a lot of dates with Alyse. Far more than I did any other lady. A subtle shift had happened inside me and the thought of having a wife wasn't so terrible. The idea of getting deployed and not having someone on the home front waiting for me was bothersome. If I married and she had to work, I'd understand that.

June 6th brought another first for the United States. The very first All Girls Professional Baseball League played their first game. The American pastime saw a reduction in men players due to the war, so they recruited women to carry on the tradition of the sport. It was a clever plan to keep the sport alive.

"You wouldn't go see women playing baseball?" I asked Hausman, who had been grumbling about it. "I would. I think it would be fun."

"Are they naked?" Jones interrupted. "I'd buy a ticket to see that."

"It wouldn't be a family sport if they were naked, you idiot." Ribbits smacked him in the back of the head. "However, I agree, I'd pay to see that too."

"They are wearing these tiny little dresses," Cutty pointed out. "And look at this picture; some of them are dolls. It could be fun." Cutty shrugged.

"Is it dangerous for us to be out on the town with race riots going on?" Alyse asked me as we walked to the pier.

"They are happening in Detroit." I shrugged. "I don't see any unrest here. I won't let anything hurt you."

"So gallant." Alyse smiled at me and took my offered arm. "It's sad. People are dying over race, the same that is happening in Europe. It's a senseless death."

"That it is," I agreed. "Not to mention the amount of damage to the city it's causing. They should have joined the infantry and fought for a cause if they wanted to fight."

Alyse laughed and I smiled. She was radiant when she smiled like that. I felt swept along happy currents when I was with her. I loved that we could talk intelligently about current events and that she wasn't afraid to voice an opinion.

"Where are we going?" Alyse wondered.

"I thought we could take a stroll down the pier," I suggested. "Does that sound agreeable to you? We can go skating afterward if you'd like. I have until tomorrow afternoon. We can be out all night if you'd like."

"I don't think my father would like that as much as I would," Alyse teased me.

Little did she know I'd already talked to her father. "You are probably right, dear." Alyse was an intelligent woman—funny, sharp, and fun. I started making plans in my head a few weeks ago and finally decided to ask her to marry me.

We wandered down the pier and when I found a spot with fewer people, I stopped her and leaned her against the railing to kiss her softly. Alyse smiled and before she could wrap her arms around my neck, I dropped to a knee.

"Alyse, I fell in love with you somewhere on these many dates. I know the timing isn't great with me being enlisted and likely to get sent overseas, but I was wondering if you'd like to marry me?" I asked and presented her with the ring I'd bought. "You'd make my life happy and complete if you said yes."

Alyse stared at me in complete shock for a good minute before she physically jolted and threw her arms around my neck. "Oh, Ralph! Yes!"

I slipped the ring on her finger. Walking on clouds, we went skating and out to dinner. Then I took her home, where she presented the ring to her parents. We got our blood tests the next day, applied for a license, and we would set the date once we received it.

"Damn," Rogers breathed out. "The Allies invaded Sicily."

"Why is that upsetting?" I asked him. "Mussolini is in bed with Hitler."

"I know." Rogers sighed. "It's just thinking about how much history is in that country. I'm going to feel awful if we have to be the ones to bomb it. I've always wanted to go there."

"It's France for me," I admitted. "I've always wanted to see the Eiffel Tower. And we are already dropping bombs there. I know what you mean, though. It's not a good feeling."

"Let's talk about something happier." Rogers shook his head. "Are you ready?"

"I am." I grinned like a fool. "I can't believe I'm getting married. I'm one of those who told myself I enjoyed being single, and here I am."

"I'm going to do the same thing when I get home," Rogers confided.

"I wanted a reason to make sure I returned home," I confessed. "I think the Army will send us over there this year."

"You really think so?" Rogers frowned.

"You don't? Look at how many crews got shot down. A new crew is getting sent every week. It's a matter of time," I calculated. "We've received all the training we could possibly get and passed all the tests."

"I know. I was hoping for one more trip home before it happens," Rogers told me. "I'd like to see my parents."

"Just make sure you are at the church on time." I elbowed him.

I married Alyse on July 15th. It wasn't a big to-do, but it was a good time. The crew, as well as Alyse's parents, were there to witness the occasion. My father drove out with Alicia since my mother said she didn't feel well, and we had a small family reunion.

After the wedding, we went to a bar to celebrate the nuptials and Alyse threw her little bouquet to Alicia, who couldn't have been happier. Alyse's parents brought a small cake, and we did the cutting tradition. To my great amusement, Alyse smashed it into my face.

We stayed the night at a hotel and immensely enjoyed our first night as a married couple. In between the consummation parts, we talked about the state of the world and where we thought we would like to settle down.

We both agreed the vacation spot in Surf City was a nice place to stay, so we talked about saving up to buy our own place and then talked about what would happen if I got sent overseas. We both knew the reality of the situation and that it would probably happen sooner rather than later.

Once the serious talks were out of the way, we returned to the fun of the wedding night and slept in late the following day. We had breakfast with my father and Alicia, and they got to know Alyse better.

"How's it feel to have a ball and chain?" Jones teased me when I returned. "You look tired. Did you get any sleep at all, or did you both sit up reading newspapers all night?"

I chuckled and shoved against Jones's shoulder. "Don't worry, some day a woman will want to take your pants off. Don't be scared."

"Suhm," Rogers called out to me. "It happened. The Allies bombed Rome."

"That happened fast," I remarked. "Maybe it means that we won't have to do that."

Rogers nodded sadly. "I hope not."

"Why don't you come and see *Stormy Weather* with me and Alyse next week?" I offered.

"Sure, why not? I'll be your third wheel." Rogers laughed. "Or Jones can be my date since he can't get one for himself."

Jones rolled his eyes. "I don't know what you are talking about. I was just asked on a date by this pilot guy."

"I heard rumors that Mussolini got arrested," I said quietly to Rogers. "Have you heard anything?"

"Just the same rumors you did," Rogers confirmed. "Do you think the war will end soon?"

"No." I shook my head. "Hitler is still on the loose. If the rumors are true, that's just one less dog we have to put in a kennel."

We listened closely to the radio and read the newspapers diligently, though no mention of Mussolini happened for another few weeks. But we did hear about a mission the Army called Operation Tidal Wave, where one hundred seventy-seven B-24 bombers flew in a formation to bomb Romania. That happened the same day that race riots broke out in Harlem, which was closer to us than Detroit.

That gave the crew something to talk about for a few days and we all wondered if this race issue here in the United States would continue or fall silent. I didn't think it would quietly go away. There appeared to be some injustice happening and I vowed to pay more attention to local news than war news.

Then, in a surprise announcement, we heard word that Rome declared itself an open city. They promised to demilitarize themselves if the Allies would stop bombing them. Italy was desperate. I didn't blame them. I wouldn't want my country destroyed like that either, and much like we were learning with Germans, not all Italians were on the side of Mussolini.

"Have you ever been to Texas?" Ribbits asked me as I read an article about a fire at the Gulf Hotel in Houston, Texas. The week before, there had been a trainwreck in New York, the Lackawanna Limited. A passenger train hit a freight train going seventy miles per hour—total devastation.

"Only for training," I replied and continued to read. Ribbits sometimes read over my shoulder and most of the time, I didn't mind.

"Fifty-five people dead." Ribbits whistled. "I can't imagine dying like that."

"Have you imagined dying at all?" Hausman asked. "I have, but only because a war is going on."

I thought about it for a minute and shook my head. "I haven't thought about it all in that regard. I think about it when I'm sailing sometimes."

"Hey!" Rogers shouted. "Radio broadcast coming on. Some announcement. Come on!" He waved his arms to get us to follow him.

I put the paper down and followed my leader to the mess hall. A group had gathered there and we waited until the announcer said that Eisenhower would be addressing us. I glanced over at Rogers and he shrugged. I knew it couldn't be a declaration that the war was over.

"Italy has surrendered to the Allies," Eisenhower announced.

I spared another look at Rogers and he had raised eyebrows. The hair on my arms stood up as if warning me about impending danger, and then, just as swiftly, it passed.

The World Series game was on the bar's television, and a few crew members were with Alyse and me to watch it happen. It was between the Yankees and the Cardinals again. Fists were thumping against the bar tops with each play. People were shouting at the television while announcers on the radio voiced each player's move.

"People really get worked up about baseball," Alyse whispered into my ear.

"Do they ever," I agreed.

It was down to the last play and every person in the bar had quieted while they watched and listened to the radio simultaneously. The Yankees had it in the bag. The bar erupted with cheers and the usual money-changing hands. Alyse witnessed it all with me, and I liked that. She didn't shy away from things as some women did.

The next day, there was an announcement of a broadcasting company formed for television called America Broadcasting Corporation, or ABC for short. They'd be showing programs on their channel—exciting times in this new modern world of technology.

"Orders," Rogers announced, his face pale and tense. "We are getting sent overseas." He held the papers out and since I was the closest, I looked.

"Just you?" I asked.

"No, they will be handing you yours. Get ready," Rogers told us.

Sure enough, each of us received the same orders Rogers had; the time had arrived. We each received three weeks' leave to do what we needed at home and, as they said, get our affairs in order in case we didn't come back.

"It's really happening," Alyse said stoically. She gave the orders back to me.

I had to hand it to her; she handled it like a champ. I expected tears and dramatics and received none of that. I'd already called to tell my parents and Alicia and now I was at Alyse's parent's house, where I delivered the news.

"I'd like to take you to look at a house tomorrow if that's okay." I reached for my wife's hand.

"Of course." She nodded. Her movements and voice held a subdued tone and I understood why. Our marriage had just started and the scenarios we discussed were now happening.

"Would you like to watch the game with me, son?" Marvin, Alyse's dad, asked me. "It's the Lions against the Giants."

"Sure, sir," I accepted and sat down, pulling Alyse beside me. The only sign she was distressed was the way she clutched at my hand. The game turned out to be a scoreless tie for the NFL. It's anticlimactic if you ask me.

I took Alyse to Surf City, where I'd found a house for a reasonable price and we met with the man selling it. He showed us the house and allowed us to walk around by ourselves, talking about it. Alyse finally agreed that she liked it.

"My father has sent me some money to put down on the house as a wedding gift," I told Alyse before we walked back out to talk to the man about purchasing the house. "I will take out a loan for the rest."

"If you think that is what is best," Alyse hesitated to say. "That means you have to come home. I want you to promise me that you will come home. You have to because I am pregnant."

The words I'd been about to say flew out of my head as I digested her words. "Pregnant?" I echoed, fear tinging my voice. "A baby?"

"Yes, Ralph, a baby. You will be a father, so I will need you to come home from Europe," Alyse repeated. "Will you do that for me?"

I looked down at her stomach and back at her face. I didn't know if I should be happy or terrified. Honestly, I was both. "I'll come back," I promised. "Let's go buy a house."

I'd managed to get all the paperwork done for a loan and find furniture and household items. Some of the crew helped me move all the stuff into the house. Alyse's mom was going to help her get settled after I left. The last two items were a radio and television.

We'd had all the serious talks and several more intimate moments, and then we watched the news the night before I had to head back to base. We'd watched as a reporter talked about how the owner of the Philadelphia Phillies got permanently banned from baseball for betting on his own team.

I didn't see the problem with it. If the guy knew they were good, why not bet on his team? It would be worse if he bet against them; their morale would drop, affecting their game. After the news, we spent the night wrapped around each other and the following day was a quiet and somber goodbye.

Alyse would be allowed to be at the dock when we left but not while loading. It was our moment alone together for me to carry while overseas. We promised to write and I gave her one last bittersweet kiss before I had to go.

CHAPTER 8

December 4th, 1943

The Queen Mary loomed before me on the New York Harbor; massive cold gray steel cocooned in the blanket of fog gave the old girl an ominous look. For safety reasons, Alyse couldn't join me on the pier as we loaded up that night. I glanced around me and couldn't believe the number of troops boarding. Thousands upon thousands of men lined up to make the climb to the deck of the famed Gray Ghost. The crew and I stood there waiting our turn, no one speaking. I think reality had kicked in for each and every one of us. The air crackled with nervous energy.

The old girl received a new paint job to camouflage gray from her stately black and white to help protect her from the enemy. The drab color didn't detract from the impressiveness of the vessel. Even at this late hour of the night, I could see her size and that she was still beautiful after her makeover. Shipbuilders retrofitted the grand lady to carry a gigantic amount of troops across the Atlantic instead of wealthy people seeking adventure. In her regular state of ferrying passengers, I imagined she was a splendor unlike anything I'd seen before.

We weren't setting out tonight; we were only loading

all the troops that received orders to deploy. Never before had I seen so many people in one place; it was a wonder that the ship didn't sink under all the weight of the bodies. Some areas were standing room only. There had to be over ten thousand men on this ship. My crew was assigned a room, and all ten of us crammed in together in the confined space. It was a good thing we were used to being around each other.

We all spent the night onboard. I don't reckon many of the guys got much sleep—the chock-full rooms filled with amazed whispers and nervous tones that filtered to the passageways. The guys were talking about all the stories they'd heard from other people, chatting about friends or family stationed in Europe. Being a part of the varied military groups from all walks of life was quite something. Gads, some of the horror stories we heard in the passageways terrified me, while others revitalized the need I had to help and be a part of something great.

One marine guy said that three-quarters of the men on this ship wouldn't make it home. That statement drove home what was on the line and how serious it was for our crew. The fear I felt was a fraction of the excitement, though I was sure that would change once I was there.

The mood shifted a little when people began to fall asleep. I was one of the luckier ones since I shared a cabin with my crew. I didn't envy the guys who had to sleep on deck. It was December, and the weather was not the best.

"Suhm, you awake?" Rogers whispered down to me. He was on the bunk above mine.

"I am. I'm feeling overwhelmed and can't decide if it's a good feeling or one of dread," I said in a hushed tone.

"Some of those stories were hairy," Rogers decided.

"I can't stop thinking about them."

"Me too," I confided. "That comment about most people not making it home hit me hard. I don't want to lose any of our crew."

"None of us want that," Rogers agreed quickly. "That's why we are going to be better than they expect. They won't send us out right away. We'll have to do more training."

"Ironic since that's all we've been doing," I grumbled. "Alyse is pregnant," I added as an afterthought because that thought hadn't left my mind either.

"Suhm, that's the best news I've heard in a long time," Rogers stated. I could tell he was grinning. "That gives us even more reason to make sure we make it back."

We both fell asleep after that and were woken up early with all the ruckus of the rest of our shipmates in the passageways looking for food and probably coffee. I wanted to be on deck when we left to see if I could spot Alyse. One last sight of her wouldn't hurt. Rogers and I were the last out of the cabin, and it was begrudging that it happened.

At ten in the morning, the Queen Mary's deck was chock full of soldiers as we watched the New York Harbor fade away into the fog. It was at that particular moment that sadness gripped me with the unknown. I wasn't able to see Alyse because the fog was so thick. The best I saw was vague shapes of people watching us leave. Rogers stood next to me the entire time.

"I could turn out to be one of the men that don't make it back," I told Rogers. No one knew what would happen once we arrived. I wasn't trying to predict anything. It was more like giving voice to something we'd heard several times for me to face it.

After a glimpse around me, I saw more than one man with a tear in his eye. Once the fog swallowed the giant ship whole, New York was nothing more than a misty gray blur. Perhaps they all thought the same thing I did.

"It could be any of us," Rogers finally answered. "But remember, we will do what we need to do to be better. Better than the enemy, better than we were before, and better the next day. Let's go find the rest of our guys." His positivity kept me from panicking.

Melancholy rolled through the masses as easily felt as the waves under the massive ship as we searched—more than once, I thought about Alyse and the unborn child she carried. I would be a dad when I returned if I did. Would I be a good one? I liked to think so, but I could end up detached like my father. Or worse, I could end up like my mother.

We found Merrill, Carlson, Young, and Warren near the bow, their eyes still fastened on where the New York Harbor would be. Their expressions were haunting as the reality of what we were heading into sunk into all of us. Rogers clapped each of them on the back and said quiet words to each of them before we turned to look for the others.

The boat drill broke our moods at precisely eleven o'clock. The siren shattered the dampened air and made more than one soldier jump. The boat drill would be the ongoing routine that those of us on Queen Mary would experience. We were now on the lookout for U-boats or other vessels that would try to attack and sink us. I was at home on the water but had never had an enemy pursue me. Quite a few men appeared uncomfortable on the water, and when they looked down, they turned a little green.

"You sail?" Warren asked me weakly. "How do you not

get sick?"

"The same way you got used to being in the air." I shrugged. "Look at the horizon," I suggested. "It's a straight line and will dull the motion sickness a little. Get used to the view and in your peripheral vision, look for things without changing where you look. It will be easy to spot things that seem out of place once you get used to it. If we are near land, watch the land. You want to focus on something fixed."

I noticed that Carlson and Young listened raptly to my suggestions, taking every word to heart. I was glad that my time sailing came in handy for the others. It gave me a good feeling to be able to help my crew with something so simple. Rogers, Jones, and Hausman seemed to do okay on the water. Ribbits, Cutty, and Merrill were somewhere in the middle of all of us.

Besides the daily boat drill, there wasn't much to do except wait and take turns on patrol. We played cards with other crews, had chats, made friends, and did patrol. The first two days of the journey were easy sailing and calm seas, something that most of our crew were thankful for as they adjusted. After that initial break-in period, the Queen Mary turned into a tiny overloaded canoe in rapids. She pitched and tossed us around like we were nothing. It even made me a touch sick and turned my equilibrium on its ear.

I felt awful for those poor souls who had to sleep on deck. They were a mess of seasickness and had to worry about getting swept overboard. I couldn't imagine traveling like that; that's what happened when I sailed, except for the sleeping on deck part. My biggest worry about Queen Mary was getting tossed out of my bunk. It happened to other guys and they sustained some injuries and lost teeth. Imagine arriving at a war already injured from the crossing. It was irony at its finest.

For the most part, the crossing was uneventful, yet it took longer than expected. "Wasn't the point of taking the Queen was that she was fast, and we would get there in three days?" Ribbits asked.

It was day four, and we seemed to be in cooler water temperatures as if we'd turned north at some point. I couldn't say I knew the route the captain would take to get to our stop. I figured it was the bad weather we encountered and we rerouted to go around it. I told Ribbits as much that seemed to appease him.

The food was ridiculously horrible. Something that each of our crew commented on daily and sometimes colorfully. We feasted on kidneys, something I can't say I was fond of, bread, which was hard and somewhat stale, butter, and coffee, which was too weak to be anything other than brown water. When I saw the food the first morning on the ship, I couldn't eat it.

"Suhm, you are going to have to eat at some point on the journey," Jones pointed out after he gagged down his first bite.

"I know, but that point isn't today. I'll be fine," I replied, sipping the tea-like coffee.

Young copied me and didn't eat either. After that first day, to sustain myself, I had to, and my stomach didn't thank me. My small saving grace was I didn't suffer seasickness on top of the food. Hopefully, we'd have better food once we arrived.

I assumed the captain zigzagged our route to avoid the

submarines, and I didn't know how many other guys noticed the change in direction, but I did. Sailing created a few helpful skills, even on a ship as large as this one.

"Look!" Jones yelled, drawing the attention of several men. He was pointing to the sky and grinning like a fool. "A blimp!"

A Navy PBY wasn't far behind and I pointed to that. "Must be scouting for subs," I guessed. The PBY was a flying boat, which intrigued me since I was part of both worlds. It made me feel better knowing we had backup in the vast ocean and it wasn't just boat drills and patrols keeping us safe.

"I wish there were room to do some sort of physical exercise," Rogers grumbled. "These quarters are so cramped that I am beginning to feel claustrophobic. There's less room on this ship than inside the B-24."

"I agree. My only solution is to use the side of a wall or the ship and do raised push-ups or jog in place. I've done squats to keep my joints from stiffening up on me," I told Rogers. "Every little bit helps. Just don't stand too close to someone doing jumping jacks, or you'll likely get an elbow to the head. I learned that lesson yesterday."

Rogers belted out a laugh before telling me to join him in jogging in place so he didn't feel foolish. It wasn't long before the guys in our proximity copied our moves. It appeared we weren't the only ones feeling cooped up and caged.

CHAPTER 9

December 10th, 1943

Y ou know what would be funny?" Hausman asked the four of us standing near the railing for fresh air. "If someone caught sight of us and saw only all the green-looking faces and thought we were a seafaring ship of aliens."

"Hilarious," Jones retorted, having one of the green faces.

"Poor sport." Ribbits elbowed him. "It would be funny. I think I've gotten used to it now, but I have to say I'm ready to be off the ship."

I agreed with that. There wasn't much in the way of scenery, just the bobbing horizon, the clouds, and the green faces of the sick men that Hausman pointed out. I think a few of the men constantly tried to repaint the side of Queen Mary, poor fellows. However, it was also why so many coveted a spot along the railing. Our crew took turns here to get the fresh air and not have to stand where someone was throwing the contents of his stomach up every ten minutes.

When land appeared on the horizon, a new excitement surrounded the ship. It meant our crossing was almost over and we would be off the boat and back with our feet planted on the earth, even for me, who loved to be on the water. I'd never been on a boat this long before and it made me rethink sailing around the world.

"Where is that?" Jones pointed at the land. "I mean, what country," he corrected himself before one of the guys could give him a hard time.

"Scotland, I hope," I answered. "If it's not, we are off course and only stopping to resupply."

"I hope it's Scotland," Jones groaned weakly.

"We all do," Rogers added. "We aren't close enough to tell yet. Still a couple of hours to go, at least."

To be a few steps ahead of the game, we cleaned our cabin, made sure we packed all our gear into our rucksacks and had them sitting on our bunks. Rogers decided we should leave it in better shape than when we boarded.

"Care to inspect?" Cutty smarted off to Rogers.

"You missed a spot." Rogers pointed to a rumpled blanket with a completely straight face.

It was only when we all burst out laughing that Cutty realized that Rogers was only messing with him. We had to take our fun where we could get it.

The ship's horn bellowed in the air, letting us know we'd arrived at our destination's port. The night was falling and we learned we wouldn't depart the boat until morning. It was disappointing news, though we had all raced topside to see where we were landing. By the time the ship docked, it was too dark to see anything other than vague shapes of buildings we couldn't identify. We all had to stay on board for safety reasons, so we didn't see any of the town we docked in. All I knew was that it was Greenock, Scotland.

Greenock was where the Royal Air Force had a station. It didn't exist until 1940 because they needed a maintenance base for flying boats like the P-38. I overheard some of the fellows that would be staying there talking about it. It told me what the buildings were we'd seen. "I guess a blitz happened here in 1941," I told the guys. "Other than that, Greenock is a fishing community from the looks of the coastline. I only spotted one or two sailboats."

"To play devil's advocate," Carlson piped up, "this isn't the time to be leisurely sailing through these waters. There might be more, but put away in storage where they can remain safe."

I couldn't fault him for correcting me because I hadn't considered his point. "Fair enough."

We were about twenty-five miles from Glasgow and wouldn't be traveling through it to get to our destination either. I'd hoped to see some of it since this was my first time out of the States. The best I could do was stare out at the harbor with the moon's light as my flashlight.

Back in our cabin, while I should have slept that night, I lay awake listening to the chatter around me in the passageway. One of the crew members mentioned an incident that happened during our crossing. The Queen Mary was halfway to our destination when the captain caught wind that six submarines were on our tail. My heart did a little stutter to learn that we'd been that close to death and hadn't known one lick about it.

"Suhm," Rogers whispered down to me. "Did you hear that?"

"Sure did," I replied as quietly. "A touch on the unnerving side of things if you ask me."

"Makes me not want to get on a boat again," Rogers admitted. "Think of what would have happened if six submarines unleashed their torpedoes at us."

"We wouldn't be having this conversation." I sighed. "Lady Luck was with us on that voyage."

"We need more than luck," Rogers commented. "We need an angel."

I remembered all our changing directions, and it made sense then. Those submarines chased us practically to Iceland, thirteen hundred miles off course. It was by the grace of Queen Mary and her great speed that kept us alive. And it was that thought that finally allowed me to rest.

In the morning, feeling weary and bedraggled, Rogers and I shared what we learned about the subs chasing us. The crew shared looks of fear and several glances back at the looming Queen Mary. Rogers and I shared a look that spoke of luck and angels.

We all stood on land for the first time in a week. Some of the guys had shaky legs, making me laugh. My sailing background had gotten me used to sea legs, though that was the first week-long journey I'd experienced. I looked back at the regal Queen and shook my head at the size difference of the boats that brought us to shore. I silently thanked her before moving on. I saw each of our guys give a nod of respect to the ship before we turned. The thought of the subs chasing us etched the respect for the vessel on their faces.

We could see the mountainous area surrounding us and the rolling green hills, some capped with snow, in the light of day. It was pretty when you looked past the hollowed-out shells of buildings leveled by bombs. Here was my first up-close, personal, and authentic look at the casualties of war. It was one thing to see cities after being bombed in a newspaper, a flat black and white photo on paper. In person, it was astonishing. The destruction was massive.

The blackened stones of the rubble told a story of how

hot the bombs were, leaving no room for doubt about what would happen to a person in that building. The collapsed structures spoke of how heavy the impact was and the metal fragments showed how far-reaching it could be. *I'd be one of the people doing this*, I thought to myself.

The crew's expressions around me showed their thoughts weren't far from mine. It was my first inkling that war would change my thoughts. I hadn't given it much thought until now. Seeing the devastation of what we would be doing was a rude awakening.

We marched past several bombed-out buildings on streets with craters, some that might have even been homes, before we came to what the Scottish called a train station. It was tiny compared to what I was used to stateside. Their train cars were half our size and looked not quite sturdy. I could definitely say that I was experiencing new things. Not what I expected when my younger mind wanted to help, travel, and see the world.

"Will you fit on the train, Suhm?" Hausman joked.

"Funny," I grumbled. I wasn't sure how to process the emotions of what I'd seen already. It appeared Carlson and Young were struggling the same way I was.

"He's joking to hide the other thoughts," Rogers said quietly in my ear. I nodded my understanding and climbed aboard the tiny railway car. Hausman had a point. I barely fit.

Once the train got underway, I realized that this contraption maxed out at probably a mean fifteen miles per hour. Not exactly speedy. "I feel like I could run faster than the little engine," I commented to no one. We passed through many towns, some that had been the recipients of bombs and others that looked like they could use a good meal or two. It emphasized to me how good we had it at home.

I saw women and children sifting through the rubble. They could be looking for loved ones, their belongings, or food. Emaciation was evident in a way I didn't understand or had experienced. The world was color, yet looking at them, I saw it as black and white, as though I was looking at a photograph. The color leached out of these people by war.

After that, I spent most of my time napping on the train. I don't know how since I was worried the train would fall apart under me. Yet my eyes closed and I was out for the count for a while. My body needed the rest, was all I could think. Most of the crew was asleep save for a couple of our guys who stared blankly out the windows. The trip took about twelve hours and I was happy to step my feet off that rattle-trap when we arrived in the small town of Stone.

It looked old, like it had seen its share of history. Streets of cobblestone and buildings crafted of red brick and stone. Master masons had left their mark in this place; of that, I was sure. The stonework was incredible. The town had a small canal with long boats that taxied people about from place to place.

"It's like a fairytale village," Jones said reverently. "I feel like the villain stepping foot into their idyllic world."

I shot Jones a questioning look even though I sort of understood how he felt. I didn't think the town looked idyllic, as he put it, but it bore the look of an old world with a few modern touches. I could see how it might look like a fairytale in the spring with blooming flowers, as Jones stated.

We weren't staying here in Stone, though, just passing through. We traveled approximately three miles to a camp called Howard Hall. It took me more than a few questions to people staying there to figure out what Howard Hall was about in the scheme of things. The Army camps here were designated the Army Air Force Reinforcement Depot. After the United States joined the war in 1941, it was given to the troops for housing while they trained.

It wouldn't be our permanent base. It was another temporary stop. Every day, all we did was details. That was a fancy way of saying that we were each given a job to do, and that was all we did. I felt like a monkey performing in a circus. I don't know why we were here and doing chores. I was so sick of it that I was ready to kill someone. That wasn't what I signed up to do with my time. Perhaps that was a selfish statement to make. However, I knew more than one person that felt this way.

"When are we leaving?" Cutty walked up to Rogers and me. "I'm so tired of this. I didn't travel all the way over the Atlantic with subs on our ass to come to this place and put away supplies."

"I don't have any answers yet," Rogers said placatingly. "We are all frustrated and have to do things we don't want to do. I think we are waiting for the training class ahead of us to finish and then we'll move to the training base."

"Training for what?" Cutty screeched. "We just did how many years of training back at Fort Dix?"

"We are in a combat zone now," I reminded Cutty, though I agreed with him. "Sure, they trained us for combat but we were in a place where there was no risk of getting a bomb dropped on our head."

That wasn't entirely true since that happened at Pearl Harbor, but after that, all the bases were on alert, and the waterways were getting patrolled.

"We'll get there," Rogers promised.

CHAPTER 10

December 22nd, 1943

I posted my first letter home to Alice from England. I told her about the journey, what the Queen Mary was like, how horrible the food was, and how many seasick men there were. Then, I did my best to describe Greenock, Scotland, and my first sightings of a bombed city. I don't think I'd ever be able to do it justice with words. Some horrors needed witnessing to understand them.

Phew! We got word no sooner than I sealed the letter and dropped it in the mailbag. We were finally leaving Howard Hall for a combat training school, as Rogers suspected. It's mandatory and lasts for about two months. Several of the guys were to the bursting point of frustration with training. Not that I blamed them because I felt the same way. My own words about not training in a combat zone came back to haunt me and I forced myself to calm down.

More than a few of us had difficulty understanding some of the dialects and thick accents. Some were way worse than others. So, as we marched to the next post, we didn't catch everything the locals said as we went by. I had a sneaking feeling that all were not well wishes.

"What do you think this training will be?" Merrill

asked me.

I believed the first three days would be the hardest as those were the lecture days. I tended to find lectures tedious and much preferred hands-on. I think I learned better that way, and with all the training I've had on combat drills, it shouldn't be too much trouble. Then again, I could be wrong.

"I honestly don't know what to expect," I told Merrill. "We've done combat drills countless times. I don't know what they can show us that we didn't know." I probably stuck my foot in my mouth with those comments, though I did wonder how much we didn't know.

We arrived at the new post about an hour later, frozen and hungry. We were at a place called Shillington now. When we leave here, we'll go to our permanent base, and I can't even say how much I was looking forward to that. I was ready to take to the skies and fight for the cause. At least, that's what I told myself. I think that is what we all said to ourselves.

We were handed our assigned quarters and went to set our stuff down and put our lockers at the foot of our cots. We arranged our things inside them and waited slightly impatiently for whatever came next.

"Do you think we'll do any flying here?" Young asked the group.

"Not likely," Rogers answered slowly. "I think this will be more about what to expect when we hit the sky, what to do if we are shot down or have an emergency landing, and what route we are to take if we land in enemy territory. It's nothing more than a guess. Since I didn't see a runway, I assume no flying yet."

"Suhm did this at Howard Hall before we left, but now would be a good time to write a letter to anyone expecting to hear from you. Let them know you arrived at a training school and will be here for a couple of months," Hausman suggested a way to break the tedium of waiting.

My mind wandered while the other guys did as Hausman offered up. I kicked back on the cot and closed my eyes. Having seen bombed areas now changed my perspective slightly on war. Not much, though, because I still wanted to fight. Not physically. I didn't think infantry was for me. Those fellows are in the thick of things constantly and in my mind, I could help them better from the air.

Regardless, this schooling was supposed to prepare us for combat with guns, mounted guns on a moving aircraft. We did that at Fort Dix with the guns mounted on vehicles. I doubted the guns shot differently over here than they did back home. However, I reminded myself we weren't in a combat zone there. By the end of this training, we were supposed to be ready to join the fighting if called. I'd been willing and waiting.

"Suhm!" Jones called out to me. "Let's eat. I'm starving!"

I had no idea how long I'd been laying there. I swung my legs off the cot and stood up to stretch. Jones smirked at me as my fingers grazed the ceiling. I rolled my eyes. Some of these guys loved to poke fun at the others and were always looking for new material—regular comedians.

The food I'd hoped would be better wasn't all that great. It wasn't as awful as it was on the Queen Mary, though it still wasn't good. Maybe the food in all of England was like that. I was used to American food, after all. Rationing and being short of supplies was a way of life over here. I was learning to adjust, and cooks had to get creative with their recipes to make enough food for everyone and to compensate for what they didn't have.

"Coming," I replied and followed Jones to the mess hall.

I was in a mood today because I hadn't received one piece of mail since leaving New York, which was depressing. Despite me having written to everyone I promised to write to. I watched the other guys eagerly open letters at mail calls and pore over them. Hopefully, I'd receive some soon. I'd like to know how Alyse was doing with the pregnancy.

I haven't seen battle yet and it still hit me that even the small things we found insignificant back home mattered a lot more over here, like mail. At home, it was usually bills. Here it meant someone was thinking of you and I imagined for those on the front lines, hearing from loved ones could mentally help when dealing with so much death.

"There they are." Jones pointed to the crew standing in line. "Hurry up before we starve."

CHAPTER 11

December 25th, 1943

Christmas. I sincerely hoped never to celebrate this holiday on foreign soil again. I didn't know what I would do at home with Alyse, yet I was sure it would be a better day than I had experienced here in England during a war.

The saving grace was the crew. We all wished we were somewhere else and with home at least five hours behind us, it was Christmas for me before it was Alyse. I wondered what she was doing and if she missed me. I missed our spirited conversations and the quiet way she cared for me.

"Homesick?" Cutty asked me before dinner.

"Yes, actually," I admitted. "Holidays away from loved ones are hard. I think I'm more aware of the distance this time. At home, I could get in a car and drive home if it bothered me that much. I can't do that here."

"That's the same thing I thought," Cutty agreed. "I miss the traditions and even the blasted Christmas tree my mom always made us put up. My oldest brother has little kids, and my dad would read them Christmas stories and tell them about Santa and how fast he travels the world to deliver presents after all the kids are asleep. It was nothing more than a ploy to get them to sleep so the adults could have a few hours to themselves."

I didn't have any memories like that, but Alicia and I would drink cocoa, stay up until midnight, and then sneak to bed before my parents woke up. It wasn't anything significant, but it was a tradition for us and I found that I missed it and looked forward to creating a tradition with my child.

"Come on." Cutty stood up. "Let's go see what mess is in store today."

I followed him to the mess hall and saw several of the crew sitting and chatting. The line wasn't open yet, but it was a gathering place and that's where we met some other fellows that we found things in common with and started to build a friendship.

"Hey, guys." Ribbits beckoned us over. "We were talking about things we'd be doing if we were at home."

"That's funny." Cutty grinned. "We were doing the same thing."

"We could build a snowman," Carlson suggested. "I'd do that at home. We had contests to see who could make the ugliest one."

"What about you, Suhm?" Rogers looked at me. "You are not very cheery today."

"I know." I shrugged. "My mind is all over the place. I never wanted to be married until this year. It took them so long to call us to duty that I can't say I thought about spending my first Christmas overseas in a war zone instead of with my new pregnant wife. What a way to start a marriage."

"It's not anything you had control over, Suhm," Warren reminded me. "You didn't plan for any of it to happen this way."

"I know," I agreed. "I can't help remembering why I

didn't want to get married, though. Other than settling down, which I didn't think I was ready for. I didn't believe it was fair to enter into a marriage knowing I'd get called to duty. Yet I did it anyway and now I feel guilty for it."

"It's a burden we all bear," Young stated morosely. "You aren't the only one that feels that way."

I knew that, and I wasn't looking for pity. Before I could comment, the cook called out that the mess was open. We all stood as a unit and formed a line behind others that beat us to the punch. It didn't smell terrible however, it wasn't what I was used to either.

I ate a turkey hash dinner at two o'clock in the afternoon—a tad on the early side for my tastes. At home, we would have dinner around four o'clock. The entire experience was dull and uneventful, food included, and I'd admit, lonely. Even with the crew around me because it wasn't what I wanted.

After I ate, I spent the rest of the day walking around the countryside. There was a light smattering of snow on the ground but more was falling.There were a few rolling hills, cottages showing their age, and beautiful stonework. But there were no Santa's, joyful Christmas decorations, or jubilant celebrations. It made me homesick in a way I didn't expect. I'd been so ready to leave and join the troops here I never once thought about how I would feel while over here. It was a strange battle to have going on inside me.

It would be remiss if I didn't mention that the crew felt the same way I did; they only handled it better. They found a reason to celebrate with each other while I moped around the countryside. I went back to camp and went to bed early.

I passed the week with heavy arms training and nights playing cards with the other fellows at the camp to pass the time. Blackjack and poker were the games. I had fun and it got heated sometimes when guys lost, but it never came to blows. It also cemented some new friendships outside the crew.

The winnings were handy to have while waiting for pay, which still hadn't happened. We weren't doing anything other than training, constantly training. Frustrations mounted and we all needed time away to decompress.

While at Fort Dix, we didn't consider how hard life would be overseas. I think we all dreamed of being heroes, saving people, and seeing other countries while getting paid. We didn't consider food shortages, clothing shortages, cold and dreary weather, relentless training exercises, and not getting paid or having any of those things we dreamed of actually happening.

Not to mention, I don't think any of the Brits wanted us here. The few times we saw the locals in the short time we'd been here, we received scowling looks and muttered words in accents so thick we had no idea what they were saying.

It was fine. I had plenty of charm and the locals would warm up to us if I had any say in the matter. We were fighting for the same side and we wanted the bombings in their cities to stop as much as they did. We wanted their food supplies to be there for their families. We weren't different from them; we just spoke different dialects.

CHAPTER 12

December 31st, 1943

New Year's Eve came with a change of scenery for the ten of us. We lucky fellows got invited to a party that fifteen pretty ladies were throwing. Of course, not one of us was about to say no to spending time with single ladies who were easy on the eyes, particularly when the women outnumbered us. Plus, they were out in the woods by themselves with no officers. It was the perfect setup. Even Merrill, Carlson, Young, and Warren were going.

"Can you believe our luck?" Jones crowed. "There are more dolls than there are guys. That means I get the extra."

"I don't think that's how that works." I laughed, feeling lighthearted for a change.

"You don't get a choice," Cutty interrupted. "You are married."

"Being married doesn't mean I can't have a good time," I argued with a scowl.

"That depends on your definition of a good time." Jones chuckled. "And your morals."

"Come on, guys." Rogers laughed. "Let's not question our engineer's morals. We need him."

"Teacher's pet," Ribbits muttered and elbowed me in

the side.

"Not likely." Rogers smacked Ribbits on the back of the head. "We all need a break and this party presented itself at the perfect time."

The invitation was what we needed to break up the monotony, frustration, and boredom. One of the women, Marigold, told us they had beer and food. That meant Jones and I went to procure the hard stuff because a New Year's Eve party needed that, also. The weather was frigid cold and our excuse for drinking was fortification. We managed to rustle up some music, too.

"Is it too much?" I asked, looking at the multiple bottles of liquor.

"Not at all." Hausman picked up some of the bottles to inspect them. "It's damn cold out there and if we drink all this, we won't feel a lick of it. The rest of us, except Suhm, might lose some morals along the way, but I'm okay with where mine are."

I laughed and swatted at Hausman. "It's a party and it's New Year's Eve. We all need to get a kiss, and I am not kissing any of your ugly mugs. A kiss is how you are supposed to start the year off for good luck. I didn't get a kiss last year and ended up in training all year with you guys. Maybe a kiss will help us get out there."

"I think that's a story you tell yourself so you can kiss all the ladies. You do have a reputation as a ladies man, Suhm," Rogers joked. "However, I agree with Suhm. I'm not kissing any of you fools. The liquid courage will work to my benefit."

I felt a twinge of guilt about Alyse. She should have been the one I was kissing, but fate's hand had me here and Alyse in America. I didn't want to break tradition and bring on any bad luck by not starting the year with a kiss, though I promised myself it wouldn't be any more than a friendly kiss.

The ladies lived about fifteen miles from the combat school in an area near Kings Langley. The town itself wasn't remarkable, though they took their church very seriously. I was sure our party wouldn't be to their liking and we'd violate all sorts of church rules. It was a quiet place and I wondered if we'd get in trouble for making a racket at our party. I hoped not. Our command wouldn't be happy with us.

Town officials told us we had to vacate the area by four thirty in the afternoon. Given the ratio of women to men, I doubted that would happen. We all agreed to the rules like the good boys we were supposed to be and made our way to the waiting ladies for a night of entertainment and fun.

"Let the party begin," Jones called out and waved some whiskey bottles in the air.

Ribbits bowed to a lady, pulled her into the building, and began dancing even though no music was playing. Several giggles rang out as the crew paired off with a lady or two while I set up the record player.

"What's your name?" a pretty dark-haired woman asked me.

"Ralph," I offered up. "Would you care for a dance?"

"I'd love it." she smiled. Her accent wasn't too thick and it only increased her charm. "My name is Lucinda."

It was well past our curfew time and we were in full swing of dancing, chatting, eating, and drinking. By ten o'clock that night, we were well fortified against the cold. I didn't feel anything other than friendly. I was sure I might regret things come tomorrow, but it wasn't tomorrow and I still had fun to have today.

I learned that these girls out here ran a searchlight and

they are a part of what is known as the A.T.S. I had to ask Lucinda to explain it since I didn't know what that was. Things got confusing with the alcohol at play, but she mustered through an explanation that I probably wouldn't remember. It made her feel good to tell me, and in that moment, that was what mattered.

Lucinda said the A.T.S., she pronounced it ats, was the Auxiliary Territorial Service, a branch of the women's British Army. They all volunteered to be here and had a couple of barracks, a dayroom, and a mess hall, and their duty was twenty-four hours a day. Lucinda was proud that she received two-thirds of the pay of what a man in the service did and was happy to perform her duty. She mentioned they did get lonely out there.

"Well, Lucinda, we are sure glad you invited us out here," I drawled and pulled her in for another dance. "We're here to take your loneliness away. We can dance the night away."

"Oh, Ralph, you're a charmer," Lucinda drunkenly replied, nestling herself into my chest.

I had another pang of guilt because of my pregnant Alyse back home, but I wasn't doing anything wrong. Dancing was a far better way to spend a holiday away from home than being sad and lonely. A soldier had to do everything he could to remain sane. That was something I'd heard Jones say.

I didn't even know what the other guys were up to because my mind was nothing but a haze and the music distracted me from everything but dancing. I did tell Lucinda I was married. I remembered that much. She was disappointed but told me she respected me for telling her.

The fellows and I didn't leave until two-thirty in the morning, and we had to sneak back to our temporary base. It wasn't as easy as it sounded: ten drunk men hiding from patrols in the area, ready to shoot any intruders dead on the spot. I think we got lucky because we weren't quiet.

When we arrived, we each stumbled to our assigned cots, smelling like a distillery and passed out until they woke us in the morning for the drills. With our heads pounding and sweat smelling like booze, drills were painful and I don't know how we made it through without losing the contents of our stomachs. They set us free for the day after we finished. All ten of us men showered and returned to the A.T.S. camp in the woods and helped the ladies clean the mess we left, which was no small feat.

"Ralph, do you think you lads could come back for another party sometime?" a dark-haired beauty named Beverly asked as she sat next to Lucinda. Her eyes kept darting to whoever was next to me.

"I think we can make that happen." I smiled and winked at the two women. I found in groups like this that the females tended to talk to me first. Perhaps it was my charm, though I was inclined to believe it was my towering height.

Once the space was clean, we sat around for a few minutes and rehashed the fun we'd had the night before. It looked like Hausman found himself a girl. It was fun to think our actions had put him in front of the woman he'd marry.

It proved my point: the new year needed to start with a kiss. We were off to a good start. If Hausman could land a woman, we could get through whatever was in store for us.

CHAPTER 13

January 2nd, 1944

The air split with a howling sound that had me roll right off my cot to the floor in confusion. "Air raid!" I shouted to the guys who slept like the dead. I didn't know how anyone could sleep through that racket. I found my footing and yanked on my shoes. I didn't grab clothes or anything. I flew into motion.

With my ears ringing, I grabbed people who weren't getting up and shoved them at the door so we could get to the bomb shelter. My heart thudded painfully against my ribs as each second ticked by that we weren't underground. I was experiencing my first-ever air raid. It wasn't at the top of my list of fun things to do. It was nerve-wracking. Adrenaline pumped through my body faster than it could process it and my limbs vibrated with nervous energy.

"Jerries overhead!" Jones screamed as we ran. I don't know how the planes didn't spot a bunch of men wearing white undershirts and boxer shorts in the black of the night. We were beacons of light, perfect targets. The thundering sounds of the planes made us all hunch over until we got to the shelter and jumped in, slamming the door behind us.

I sat there on my heels in a room full of men in their

underwear, shivering, waiting for the sounds of bombs dropping. The atmosphere was tense and in the frigid air, I was surprised that our coiled leg muscles didn't cramp up painfully. There was no sound other than what was happening outside. I couldn't even hear the others breathing.

We huddled closely together to try and keep warm while we waited for the ground to shake and the sound of explosions to fill the air. The noise never came that I expected. We heard the rattling of mounted guns and we murmured about other crews trying to get to shelters and that we hoped they weren't getting shot at.

If they weren't, that meant the people in town were the targets and that didn't make us feel better. Those people weren't soldiers. They were farmers, workers, and business owners, all trying to live their lives during the war and take care of their families.

Our breaths puffed out and in the dim light of the few flashlights in the shelter, it looked like eerie ghosts hovering in front of us. I wasn't keen on experiencing another air raid and logic dictated that we would.

"I'm going to sleep in full clothing after this," Cutty said with his teeth chattering. "We stood out like candle flames in the dark. Why didn't they cut us down?"

"Don't question that," another guy from a different crew answered. "Be thankful they didn't."

"We are," I replied before Cutty could say anything. I wondered the same thing Cutty did and he didn't deserve reprimanding for the thought.

"How did some of you sleep through that siren?" Hausman wondered. "I swear my ears are going to bleed. That thing is so piercing."

"When you grow up with loud siblings, you learn to

sleep through everything." Young chuckled. "Suhm was on top of it, though. I thought he was going to throw me right through the door."

"Don't think I didn't try," I told them. "My blood was pumping through me so fast I could have thrown an elephant."

"I remember my first one," the guy who'd spoken harshly to Cutty said. "I thought I was going to wet myself. One of the other guys vomited on the way to the shelter. It's scary every time, not just the first one. Imagine being one of the civilians and weaponless. At least we have crates with guns to help us should we get attacked."

It was a sobering thought and we listened to the heavy rattle of mounted machine guns. After an hour, the air fell silent. Hausman poked his head out of the shelter and got the all-clear for us to go back to sleep. I didn't believe it would happen, yet it did.

The adrenaline that kept me going disappeared suddenly and it was lights out. I thought I'd dream or have a nightmare. Instead, I slept more soundly than I had since being over here. Overall, it was a strange experience, and I developed a new respect for the people who lived here and had to deal with that all the time.

I woke before our morning bells and went to the mess hall to rustle up some coffee. That's where I learned that the Jerrie's mission had been releasing paratroopers and attempting to land to help take out our bases. Would we have even had time to open the crate and arm ourselves if enemy ground troops found the shelter and opened the doors? I shuddered at the thought.

"Thanks to the Limeys, those bastards never stood a chance," a pilot named Jackson informed everyone with a satisfied look on his face. "That was the gunfire you heard. They took those Jerries out."

The realities of war were beginning to sink in, though we hadn't experienced anything other than the air raid yet. I remembered the visuals of the bombed cities I'd seen and had the repeating thought that I'd be one of the people causing that destruction. I wasn't sure how to feel about it yet. It was becoming apparent there wasn't room for fear in war. Hesitation could get you killed.

"You're up early," Rogers said from behind me. "Couldn't sleep?"

"Opposite, actually," I told him. "I feel more rested than I have since we left the States. I slept soundly. I was just listening to that pilot talk about the raid. I guess paratroopers tried to land and the Brits got to them before they could get to us."

Rogers looked as shaken as I felt. "That's a scary thought."

"That's going to be us up there, Rogers," I reminded him. "If you are religious, I think now is the time to get good with God."

CHAPTER 14

January 5th, 1944

Woo-hoo! I did a little quick-step dance where no one could see me. I'd gotten my first forty-eight pass. The whole crew did, though we each had separate plans. I had wanted to see something of England since I had time to explore, but the problem was I had no money. God damn! What a situation to be stuck in. There'd been no word on when we would get paid. I tucked the pass into my pocket and wandered around until I saw one of my pals and borrowed a pound from him.

I set out and went to a nearby town called Aylesbury. It was another historic town, like so much of England seemed to be, with a mix of architectural styles, some of which appeared French. I was no expert in the subject. However, it was getting easier to decipher the style of buildings, structures, and the time frames of their construction.

I wandered in and out of the shops and didn't talk much to anyone. I received a lot of curious looks that I didn't understand since I wasn't the only man walking around town in an Army uniform. I didn't let it bother me and went to a pub to grab lunch.

"Aye! You're a bloody big bloke!" the pub worker

declared when I walked in. "We don't get many your size."

That explained the curious looks. I wasn't much taller than the others and wasn't burly. I was taller than most of the folks in this town, though. I wasn't going to hunch over to make them more comfortable. They'd have to get used to me. I ate my lunch unapologetically and continued my exploration.

I went through some old churches in the area and looked at some royal buildings from ages ago. I am interested in history, though I wasn't in the mood to delve deep into it today. Most of it was violent and I wanted to not think about war. I wasn't sure what I wanted and wandered aimlessly, taking in the scenery and talking with the locals who dared speak.

Before night came, I found myself a room to rent and then returned to the town to find some dinner. It was easy to spot the places that hadn't been hit as hard by the rationing happening, and I wondered if that had something to do with all the local farms around the area.

I didn't know how to ask, or if I would start trouble if I did, so I kept my mouth shut. I asked about the dishes and what the server recommended. I tried a sheep dish and it wasn't bad. My stomach tolerated it and I was famished. I ate the whole thing faster than I should have, and I think one of the workers took pity on me because they brought me a small shepherd's pie after that. I enjoyed that more than the dish I had just eaten.

I spent some time talking with folks who sat at the bar and learned things to see outside of Aylesbury if I got the chance. I committed them to memory and told them of life back in the States and what it was like over there. I tried describing the cities and only got stared at in confusion. The American lifestyle was something unheard of here. They couldn't fathom people having televisions in their homes when so many didn't even have a telephone.

I spoke fascinating tales of sailing and Lake Michigan to the townspeople. I talked about the boats I'd built and sketched out what they looked like on some napkins so they understood my terminology. It was a different way of life here and I thoroughly enjoyed myself and talking with these people.

I wasn't far from London proper and these farms were working farms, with some of the farmers here talking with me. I'd bet my right arm they had to supply food to the city. Maybe some underground action was happening, like their version of a black market.

I smiled to myself as I left and found a busy pub not far from my room and chose that place to have a nightcap and maybe catch some music. The beer was warmer than I was used to and it took me a couple of tries to get a taste for it.

There weren't as many willing people to talk to at the pub, and there was no live music, though there was a record playing. No one danced. They sat at their tables, huddled together, conversing with their group, or hunched over their drink alone. After a couple of beers, I headed back to my room.

My room had cost me eight shillings and sixpence. I still tried to wrap my head around the money system. The money difference was confusing and difficult to get used to. Twelve pence equaled one shilling; a pound was twenty shillings. Regardless, it felt like a good deal to me since the one room had three beds and came with breakfast to boot. It was a nice change from an Army cot with twenty other men in a room.

The bathroom was a shared room and once it was

free, I took my turn and luxuriated in a shower with no one else around me. I went back to my room and began a letter to Alicia. I told her about the town, the people who thought me odd because I was tall, and all the training we were doing. I left out the air raid.

I then wrote a letter to Alyse and told her the same, but this time, I included the air raid and my feelings on the situation. I asked how the pregnancy was going and if she was doing alright. I admitted that I missed her and wasn't used to having at least some money in my pocket as my job had paid regularly.

After that, I wrote a short letter to my parents and told them I was alive and well. I wrote about the town like in Alicia's letter and touched on the training. With all that done, I settled into the bed and stretched out as much as possible.

I slept well that night with a belly full of ale and food and a nice bed in a room to myself. I did not sleep as well as after the air raid, but it came close. I'd have to go back to the base tomorrow, but in the meantime, I planned to spend my time wandering around this lovely little town more.

CHAPTER 15

January 14th, 1944

Another leave pass today. "Anyone want to go to London?" I asked the crew. I wasn't opposed to going by myself. I only asked to be polite. We didn't always have to do things as a crew. I merely wanted a change of scenery from the base.

"Not me. I'm going to hang around here and sleep," Rogers replied as he kicked back in his cot.

"I'm going to meet up with Beverly." Hausman winked.

The rest was a chorus of nays, so I bid them farewell. I hopped on the train and went to London for the first time. I wanted to take in the sights. I didn't know what to expect, but bombs had decimated large parts of London. There were entire streets that barely anything stood on. Blackened rock, rubble, and people wearing threadbare clothes as they searched for belongings in the remains.

"Are you looking for something I might be able to help you find?" I asked one lady. She hunched forward with a holey blanket over her shoulders that couldn't provide much in the way of warmth. Her hair was stringy and not clean and her hands stained with blood, as if she had fought someone. She looked to be in her fifties, and her dress appeared almost that old. Dirt caked her clothes and her bones protruded from her arms and face.

She hissed at me in response and mumbled something that sounded like mind my own business, though I think she threw some curse words in for good measure. Only then did I understand that maybe that wasn't where she lived and she was just looking for things she could take and use. A wave of sadness swept over me for people who had to live that way.

Golly, London had taken a beating. I didn't think I was aware that it was this bad. London was nothing like Aylesbury, yet they weren't that far apart. It seemed worlds different not only in appearance but in atmosphere. London had historical buildings everywhere, but there was also a modern element. People moved faster, seemed more hurried, and there was a lot of gray. Aylesbury had some color to it.

Not only that, London was expensive. I asked a few people questions about things to see here if you were visiting for the first time, and some of the blokes had accents so thick I couldn't understand what they said. Not one word. I imagined there were places in England that had a different way of speaking as the southern parts of the United States did.

I nodded my thanks and kept walking until I found a subway station. I figured that would be a better way to get around, but gads, these subways in London are a worse tangle than New York! I couldn't believe it. There were throngs of people rushing about, no one making eye contact, arrows and signs pointing in all directions, and a map that had me utterly turned around.

I didn't have a long pass this time, only one day, and I spent five pounds and hardly did a thing except eat, get a room, and take the subway and busses. Sure, I saw some stuff from the bus window, though it wasn't the same as boots on the ground. London was one of those places where you needed at least a two-day pass and fifty pounds to boot. Everything costs money.

Plus, with all the bombed-out streets, it didn't seem like a great place to spend much time. I halfway expected another air raid and I tried to find shelters near wherever I was in case it happened. I enjoyed seeing the Royal guard in front of the palace as I took a bus there. They stood as still as statues in their fancy red uniforms guarding the palace. I wondered how quickly they would react to a threat. I knew my legs got stiff when I stood still for a long time.

London was one of the largest cities in the world. It was plain to see it was one of the Luftwaffe's favorite places to destroy. It was a shame, too. Some of those ruined structures were hundreds of years old and once had great figures who lived and worked in them. Something that stood the test of time until a maniacal ruler flattened it with explosives.

I felt sad seeing all the displaced people with no homes after the bombs fell. There was one street I walked down with some young kids, teenagers perhaps, that sat atop the rubble. I asked them if they needed something and prepared to give them money or my coat. They told me they sat there on their house every day in case their parents were looking for them. I don't think I'll ever forget the moment I realized that their parents probably died during the bombing. All I could do was caution them to be careful.

Seeing as many Americans as I did surprised me, though I supposed it made sense after we joined the war. If I remember correctly, we also sent people there before Pearl

Harbor to help them fly planes. And it sure looked like the British girls loved the American soldier. I can't count how many times I saw two girls hanging on the arms of one soldier. It was just another one of those things that made me smile and shake my head. To be fair, we were just as enamored with the British girls as they were with us. It was that thrill of something different and unknown.

I wrote another letter to Alyse and Alicia that night and told them about what I'd seen in London. There wasn't much to say, and I tried to make it as descriptive as possible. A writer, I was not. I told Alyse how expensive the place was and that I enjoyed Aylesbury more than London.

I was flat broke after catching the train back to my base the next day. It was an expensive trip, and now I'll have to live on what I make playing poker and blackjack. Hopefully, we could get a good game going with one of the other crews. I didn't always win, though I always had fun trying.

CHAPTER 16

January 19th, 1944

The long training days, practicing gun tactics, and proving we know what we are doing are tedious. I'm more than ready to get out there and do something. The days all bleed together until we get our next passes, and then it's trying to find money to go out and do something fun.

Hausman and his girlfriend, Jones, and I went to Aylesbury on another two-day pass. Each of us had ten shillings. It didn't even take us an hour before we were broke and decided to return to camp. This fame and fortune was what it was like to be a soldier. It was grueling at times. Not to mention depressing.

On our way, we ran into one of our buddies, Scott, who was out enjoying his pass. He was half-drunk and convinced us to go to London with him, that he'd foot the bill. Why not? It wasn't like we had anything to lose. I already knew I couldn't afford London; if he was paying, I might see something other than a bus and subway.

At first, each Hausman and I did the obligatory try and talk him out of it, but of course, we wound up on the train with him at eleven at night, which is the outcome we all wanted. That is, after we almost didn't make it on the train at all because we tangled with half the Scottish Army.

"You hear that shit?" Hausman said to me, furious. "Hear how they talk around my girlfriend?" He wasn't happy with the lewd talk. It wasn't my favorite and I tended to tune it out.

"They aren't talking to her," I pointed out. There were only four of us, the girlfriend and countless more Scotsmen. If we got into a tussle, we wouldn't come out on the other side unscathed.

"Doesn't mean they don't need to show respect," Hausman grumbled. "She's a lady."

I didn't point out that she was at a party when they'd met. We'd all received an invitation to the festivities, where things got a little out of hand with some of the guys, not that anything bad happened. However, it wouldn't shock me if I learned that one of the guys became an unsuspecting father.

"It's okay," Beverly loudly whispered to us. Her eyes were wide with fear and it was apparent she didn't want to make a big deal out of it.

"Feckin' Limey bastards," one of the Scotsmen yelled at us.

"Excuse me?" I let my temper take over. "We aren't Limey bastards. If you are going to insult us, get it right. We're bloody Americans."

It was looking like we were going to fight. The Scotsman could take us since they drastically outnumbered us, but we'd bash a few skulls in on the way down. Every one of those men was foul-mouthed and drunk. I agreed with Hausman that it wasn't right, but we couldn't change their personalities.

I squared up, ready to brawl, when one of the Scots began to laugh. "Americans!"

I narrowed my eyes, resigned to a fight, when they all clapped each other on the back and left us alone. I looked over at my crew who were preparing to get rowdy and shrugged. It appeared the Scots didn't like the Brits. That was interesting to learn.

"Let's go." Beverly pulled Hausman on the train after her and we followed. I felt on alert after the near fight and only relaxed when we arrived in London at twelve forty-five in the morning. I should have been exhausted and I wasn't. We hopped off the train at Baker Street and hailed a cab. That was probably the only street I knew. Our first order of business was to secure a room.

"No soap, guys," I stated tiredly after hitting a dozen places. London was all booked up. I couldn't believe our luck. "There's nothing."

We wandered around longer and finally ended up at the Red Cross at the Rainbow Corners joint. It was the most well-known club in the European Theater. The club was open twenty-four hours a day for American servicemen. I hadn't made it there on my first trip to London, though I had heard about it. I think every enlisted person knew about it.

The place was hoppin'. There was a G.I. playing boogie-woogie music, and no empty seats were available. I did the only thing I could do. I got on the dance floor and danced my heart out with whoever was available. This club was why Americans probably had the reputation they did with the Brits. If you wanted a good time, you could get one here.

The musician fellow had talent and could play any song with only one hand. I was sure of it. The music swept me away. The noise in the club was deafening, and the booze was flowing. There could have been air raid sirens and we wouldn't have heard them. It was the best time I'd had in a long while. I felt carefree and invigorated. When a party left a table near me, I ran over and grabbed it to rest for a minute. Our crew even cleared it for the waitress, who was too busy to notice.

It was a darkened atmosphere, with low lights over the tables around the perimeter and little low-flame oil lamps on the other tables. The windows were, of course, blacked out per regulation. There were officers huddled around some of the tables at opposite ends of the club and you could tell they were talking business by the severe looks on their faces. I didn't know how they heard each other.

Others, it was apparent they were there to enjoy the pleasure of the female company, which there was no shortage of in the club. The atmosphere was light-hearted and fun despite the devastation outside the doors and on the streets. It was a jolly fun time, and I'd happily return if given the opportunity.

I had to tell more than one pretty lady I was married when they tried to tug me into a dark corner for some personal time. Thankfully, none of them took offense to it and they moved on to dance with another man.

Staying there all night wasn't an option, so we left as a group at three in the morning and went somewhere else to have breakfast. It was a given that we wouldn't get any sleep and no rooms were available anyway. What was left for us to do? We ate a lot.

The five of us ate from three in the morning until six. "Where do you put it all, Ralph?" Beverly asked me as we finally left the restaurant. Which probably made the waitresses happy to see us go.

"Hollow leg," I responded. "These guys kept up with me." I wasn't the only one who put away the massive amounts of ordered food.

I was mostly sober by the time we came across an Army store and went inside to take a look. I found a fancy pair of wings that were handmade with silver thread. They were a piece of art and I had to get them. I couldn't pass those up. I'd kick myself forever if I did. At the very least, they would be an excellent reminder of the sleepless nights we shared in London.

The train back to Aylesbury we needed to catch didn't leave until the evening. We spent the rest of the day wandering around London. We found a theater showing a movie that looked interesting, so we watched that. I couldn't even remember what it was; I was so tired I swayed on my feet. After that, we went to another dance. I embarrassed myself by falling asleep. The guys ribbed me about it all the way back to Aylesbury to finish out our pass. My saving grace was I only paid for my wings. Then, I slept for twenty-four hours.

CHAPTER 17

January 26th, 1944

Finally, I took to the skies today for something other than a turn around the base. It was our first time, and man, did it ever feel good to be doing what we came to do, for practice at least. The weather was cold and even colder up in the air, but we had blue skies and I was thankful for it.

We got a good taste for what it would feel like on a mission, and oh boy, those Liberators had a lot of air leaks around the turrets. I felt terrible for the other guys, and especially Young, if someone used the pee funnels. I think my hands went numb after twenty minutes. I wouldn't trade the experience for anything, though.

We practiced the bomb drops without any bombs to ensure we had a good feel for how the plane operated at different altitudes. We all knew it would be different when we were fully loaded and someone was shooting at us.

Jones was at the front of the plane in the nose turret. He practiced both roles, bombardier and nose gunner. Hausman was behind him doing navigation. Then, it was Rogers and Carlson with me right behind them. Ribbits was behind me doing waist gunner and radioman. Behind the wings was Warren working the ball turret. When Ribbits and

Cutty weren't doing secondary duties, they would be behind Warren. That left Young squished up into the tail turret.

The instructor ran scenarios while we flew and had us running all over the plane to perform whatever duties we needed to accomplish the task. It showed our crew's closeness and knowledge of each position the instructor asked us to work. I tested on engine failures and Rogers had to feather them so we could identify the sounds from inside the plane. It also taught him how to fly defensively with engines out of commission.

The instructor also went out of his way to cause mental strain on all of us to see how we reacted and test our problem-solving skills. It was a good thing we all worked well together. He laid the pressure on thick and simulated several failures that I, as the engineer, had to communicate, fix, and get back to my position.

There were moments when my body didn't know whether to freeze or sweat. I think my sweat froze at times. We were running fools up there and I could easily see how people failed training and never got to fly.

Then, I tested my flight knowledge. I had to fly the plane and show I was ready if something happened to Rogers and Carlson. I could only say that I hoped that never happened. I passed the flying portion of the training but it wasn't anything I wanted to do if I didn't have to.

I began to wonder if this entire flight was a test for me. It sunk in how important the engineer's role was to the crew and the mission's success. Even one small failure on my part could have downed the plane for the whole crew. It was an incredible responsibility.

Then came the firing practice. The ground crew hadn't loaded us with live rounds and the instructor would pick a spot in the sky, call out the direction and order us to start firing. He would shout out imaginary obstacles and test our reflexes under duress.

The whole crew was beyond happy to have that plane land and be done with those tests. It was hard to say how we did because the instructor had a great poker face and I made a mental note not to play cards with him if the opportunity ever arose.

We went through the landing checklist, with each of us calling out every task we had to complete and announcing when we finished it. The instructor then came over to check and if we missed something, which we didn't. He prepared to educate us, as he said.

It seemed like things were going to start changing for us now. Holy smokes, was I ready for it, too. The crew's faces mirrored my own sentiments. Our flight time accumulated each time we went up, but flights longer than twenty minutes were a treasure when not under the duress of a test. We were up for a couple of hours today. When we landed and were finally released, I received word that my name was put on the 1-A form, meaning I was ready and available for unrestricted service.

"Well, Suhm," Rogers said as he walked up to me, "the Army cleared you for business. Did you like flying the plane?"

"I think if I were allowed to fly in a non-war situation and a smaller plane, I might enjoy it more. I don't envy you, Rogers," I replied honestly. "You've got a hell of a job managing that beast. She wasn't even loaded and I could feel how heavy we were in the sky. It's unnerving when you think about it, even more so when you think about it when undergoing a test."

Rogers tipped his head back and laughed. "My job is no harder than yours. One mistake by either of us could spell disaster for the crew."

"Do you think they'll send us out?" I asked hopefully. "Without the instructor?"

"I don't know." Rogers glanced behind us. "I think if he goes with us again, it won't be as a test as it was today. I think it would be only for observation and critique after the fact unless something came up that would jeopardize the plane or us."

"Let's hope that neither of those things happens," I stated. "I know we'll be under more pressure and stress on missions. I can admit to the instructor rattling me today. I felt like I didn't know which direction I was going. It was madness."

"War is madness," Rogers told me and pursed his lips. "We'll look back on today and wish things were as simple as they were today."

The plain truth in that statement was frightening.

CHAPTER 18

January 27th, 1944

Load 'em up!" Rogers shouted at me. "We're flying today! Coast to coast."

"What?" I looked up from my letter, startled. I'd been sitting under the plane after doing some routine training with myself and decided to write to Alyse. "That will finish out our required flying hours, won't it?" I could only hope.

"Sure will!" Rogers grinned. "How's that for something? Means we'll get sent to our permanent base."

"Hallelujah!" I jumped up and began loading the necessary gear and doing preflight checks. It was the best thing he could have said to me.

I'd be correct in my thinking that things would change. This flight was it. This flight was our last training flight, the big one. The guys were rushing all around me, each doing their part of the preflight with serious yet eager looks on their faces. We'd worked our tails off to get to this point.

I was the mechanic, engineer, and mid-top gun turret. Tools were prepped and ready to go, and the guns were oiled, loaded, and rotated. I checked my chute, then checked the oil in the engines and turned the props. I perused the landing gear and, finally, the tires.

There was more to it than that, but we split the duties amongst ourselves for preflight and each guy checked each thing while the pilot did what he had to do. Each of us reported back to him that we were a go. We even went over each other's work with our secondary duties. No stone was unturned. It was out of the norm for procedural standards, but we agreed to be extra diligent. We wanted this.

"Crew!" Rogers called out from the cockpit once we were ready. "We need a smooth run, no issues. Full communication with all stations, got it? There's a chance we can encounter enemy planes and we all need to be at our best. Once the Army sends us to a permanent base, we have thirty missions to get through before we can go home and see our families. Pretend this is mission one."

"Yes, sir!" the crew answered in unison.

I knew what was at stake. I had a pregnant wife at home that I hadn't gotten to spend much time with and before I got home, I'd have a child that I'll have never met. No pressure. I watched as each man took their position and readied for flight. We'd had enough practice in this that we assembled and were ready in minimal time.

The engines roared to life, the vibrations rolling through our plane and then we taxied. We went speeding down the runway. The uneven ground was rough and making the plane vibrate and shake, the rattle almost deafening, and then it happened: the smooth liftoff! I loved that take-off feeling of knowing I wasn't on solid ground any longer. It was exhilarating. The only other time I felt like that was when I was sailing and the wind picked up. I glided over the top of the water faster than I could drive.

Navigation clocked our flight path at five hours and forty minutes. I watched rolling green hills pass, snowy peaks, bodies of water, clouds, and birds. Everything looked peaceful from this height until you flew over land that still smoked from dropped bombs.

It was a view forever etched in my mind. Being on the ground and confronted with it when you could touch it was different. Flying through the air and seeing the smoking remains of the structures, the craters in the earth, and the small fires that still burned left an impression on me. I would be doing this. I needed to learn to compartmentalize my feelings. I chose to do this, and we were in a war. It was my job.

When we returned to base, I saw my first enemy planes up close. There were three captured German planes. A JU-88, ME-110, and a ME-109.

The JU-88 was a Junker, a twin-engine combat plane. The lectures I'd attended informed me those planes were fast and used in various ways. It could be a bomber, a dive bomber, a night fighter, a torpedo bomber, a reconnaissance aircraft, or a heavy fighter, and when the plane was almost unfixable, the Germans used the plane as a bomb. I remembered the teacher had said these planes had a range of one thousand two hundred miles. It wasn't something to scoff at and we needed to watch out for these while flying.

The ME-110 was a Messerschmitt. It had twin engines, though the lecturer said it didn't have all the capabilities the Junker had. It didn't make it any less of a threat. The Germans used this plane as a destroyer, heavy fighter, and night fighter. It carried some heavy guns that could easily take us down. The plane had two 20MM cannons, four 7.92MM MG 17 machine guns, and one 7.92MM MG15 machine gun.

The ME-109 was the backbone of the German fighter force. It could achieve heights of twenty thousand feet and even go as high as thirty-three thousand feet. It flew at two hundred fifty miles per hour. It wasn't as maneuverable or flexible as other planes but still deadly. I was happy I'd paid attention during lectures.

I spent a few minutes examining each plane before heading into the office, where I signed my first payroll. I doubt I'd ever see a cent of it since they'll be moving us out of here soon. The Army owes me two months' base pay and three months' flying pay. If I ever get it, I'll send a bulk of it home to Alyse, my dear 'lil wife. She's the financier of our little outfit Suhm, Suhm, and Suhm. That's the name I gave our little family now.

I hoped I'd get paid. I'd heard horror stories from other soldiers about not receiving their pay for several months. I didn't know how they expected us to live on nothing. It weighed on my mind since Alyse was pregnant. It's my duty and honor to take care of her.

CHAPTER 19

January 30th, 1944

I received my first mail since deploying. Talk about excitement. Twenty-five letters all in one crack landed on my lap today. At least I'd be busy replying after reading them. It took me a good hour to get through them all.

A couple of the letters contained lousy news from home. Two of my buddies died in vehicle crashes. That disheartened me and brought my excitement at receiving mail down a notch. Moments like those made me take a minute to pause and think about life, how hard it was, and the choices we make that put us in situations where death could happen. I silently closed my eyes and said goodbye, hoping they didn't suffer.

It made me more aware that Alyse could receive one of these letters, and I'd never get to meet my baby. I snapped my mind out of those thoughts because thoughts and distractions like that could make it a reality. I looked at the letters in my hand again and re-read that my friend Ray died in Florida, and my friend Opie perished in Texas.

I said a little prayer for each of them and their families. Then I pulled out some paper and began replying to all the letters. I started each by telling them how happy receiving mail made me. I recounted some of our training flights and finished with achieving our hours and getting ready to go to our permanent base.

"Well?" Jones, Hausman, and Rogers dropped next to me. "Are you a dad yet?"

"Do you know how long pregnancies are?" I laughed at Jones. "We haven't been gone long enough for the baby to have arrived yet."

"I don't know!" Jones declared. "You could have knocked her up before getting married. For all I know, that's the reason you got married."

Rogers smacked Jones on the back of the head. "Have some respect."

"I didn't mean it badly," Jones argued. "Suhm gets all the ladies and I don't understand why."

"She's due in May." I shook my head and chuckled.

"What are you hoping for?" Rogers asked.

"I don't know," I hedged. "I've thought about it a lot, and it's hard. I think a boy would be easier and I'd have someone to teach everything I know. Yet, a little girl running around in frilly dresses and getting all dirty when she plays outside sounds good, too. The only part that makes me not want a girl is I'd have to kill anyone that tried to date her."

The guys laughed at me and Hausman looked thoughtful. He got that distant look in his eyes like he was trying to solve a puzzle, and his fingers tapped against his leg.

"Maybe you could have both worlds," Hausman finally said. "Have a boy first and teach him about getting all the ladies. Then he'll meet someone, marry her, and have a girl. Then you don't have to worry about raising a girl because it will be his problem, not yours."

"You could teach me how to get the ladies," Jones

offered. "I could knock someone up and have a girl and you could babysit. It would almost be the same."

"You sound utterly ridiculous," Hausman fired off at Jones. "Even if he taught you, you still wouldn't get the ladies because of your mouth. It never stops running."

I threw my pencil at Jones and shook my head again. Looking sheepish, he picked it up and handed it back to me. I finished my last letter, stuffed it in the envelope, and addressed it. I placed them all in a stack to take to the mailbag.

"What about all of you? Do you want kids?" I asked.

"I'd like to have some," Rogers stated. "Three or four, I think."

"I hope your wife likes you that much." Hausman laughed. "I'd settle for one. A boy. Girls would be scary to raise."

"That's why you'll get a girl." Jones smirked. "I don't know if I want any kids or not. I know I'm not ready now. I don't even want to settle down yet. Hell, I can't even think past the war. We have at least thirty missions to get through and haven't even started yet."

"That hit me the other day," Hausman admitted. "Our last training flight. We flew over the bomb site and I couldn't help thinking that we were going to be the cause of that for people. It was a heavy thought and made me nervous. Can I be that person?"

"We don't have much of a choice," Rogers said softly. "Somehow, we have to make it right in our heads. Remove our hearts from the situation and I'm not ashamed to say that I don't know how to do that. We are delivering death and it's our job."

"We might be delivering death," I jumped in, "but we

are also working to help end the war. That's what I keep telling myself. The sooner we can end it, the less death there will be."

"Do you ever wonder if we'll have to drop bombs on one of those camps?" Jones looked at Rogers and then at me. "I've thought about it. Half of me says it would be a blessing to those poor people, and the other half says there is no way I could do it. They've suffered enough."

I hadn't really considered the targets before now. I guess I assumed they would all be strategic military targets. I remembered the conversation I'd had with Alyse about the strafing of Japanese soldiers in the water. I hoped that it wouldn't come to something like that for us. Nevertheless, I knew if it did, I'd do what I needed to get the job done because that was my mindset. It bothered me, but that's how I functioned. I understood war meant death.

"Now that we are all thoroughly depressed, why don't we go play a game of baseball?" Hausman suggested. "We can use the field since there are no scheduled flights."

CHAPTER 20

February 8th, 1944

The day finally arrived for us to move to our permanent base. We loaded our footlockers on the trucks, said goodbye to our friends, and were on our way. We left the camp and transferred to our permanent base at Norwich. That would be the base from which we would fly all our missions. Horsham St. Faith was made available to the Eighth Air Force, and the USAAF designated it Station 123(HF). It sounded plain and clinical almost, and we would call it home for at least thirty missions. We didn't know how long that would take.

The city itself had seen heavy bombing early in the war and the destruction was terrible. The bombs took out several historical sights and residential streets. A thick coating of cement dust covered things, and red bricks lay strewn about amongst charred wood beams and burnt timber. It didn't appear that any military targets received bombs on their location. The papers back home didn't talk about this. It was the reality of war, not the glory of victories or the pretty words used to describe the atrocities happening to make them sound more appealing to the reader. To think, I'd be doing this to other cities.

I couldn't dwell on thoughts like that either. I had to

focus on the objective of war, which, when I thought about that, my mind spun out of control too. I was doing my job, earning my paycheck to take care of my growing family. Drop our payloads on the designated targets, take the enemy out of commission and get back to my base safely. Stop thoughts. If only it were that easy.

Barracks number thirteen was the assignment we received, and the beds that my crew and I now occupied used to be filled by a crew that blew up in the air. The base commander's aid relayed the news when he handed out the bunk assignments. Welcome to your new home; the former residents died so you could be here. It was a sobering thought, one of many I'd had since arriving here. It's become apparent that I'll be sweating out every mission I go on.

In the short time I've been here, I'd already seen quite a few of the aircraft come back from Germany full of holes. As I'd already learned and had someone point out a few minutes before, some don't return. Back at the training camp, they told us our missions would be easy. All I could think was that had to be a company line repeated to keep us raring to go. The crews here at Norwich told a different story. Our gung-ho attitudes dimmed a little.

One guy told us in passing that the Jerries toss up everything but the kitchen sink to bring us down now. I can't say it made me or anyone around me feel great, but it amped up our nervous energy and those of us who smoked started puffing like a volcano about to erupt.

Now we sat around here and waited for that first mission, our red-letter day, while we watched the other crews come in with limping planes, feathered engines, and bellies full of holes. I randomly thought they should teach us these skills with these shot-up planes so that crews understood what they were getting into.

"The guys in barracks eight are having a card game tonight," one of the guys from barracks ten told us as he walked by. "You should join us."

"Sounds good to me," I piped up. "The waiting game is awful."

"Tell me about it." The soldier laughed. "It drove us crazy. We've done two missions now. The first is an eye-opener."

"I figured it would be," Rogers told him. "We're still eager to get started."

"Come on over about seven," the guy told us. "You'll get lots of stories about what to expect."

We watched him go on his way and looked at each other. "No one has to go," Rogers finally told the crew. "If there's a chance that I can learn what to expect from pilots that have been out, it will be worth it."

"I want to go," I chimed in. "Fooling around with other crews is a good way to learn things and it gets our mind off sitting here and worrying. A little fun won't hurt."

The entire crew decided they would join us and things lightened up a bit afterward. We killed time by talking about the trouble we got into as kids. Jones was a born troublemaker, which didn't surprise me or anyone else.

Game time came and we joined the other crews for a big poker game. We heard planes taking off on a mission and silently wished it were us. These other two crews were happy it wasn't them. They told us their last mission was a hairy one.

"The flak was crazy," the pilot was telling Rogers. "The Jerries are getting nervous or more arrogant. I can't tell which. Neither is a good thing. Evasive maneuvers get hard when it's coming at you from all sides."

Jones changed the subject to women at that point. I think he didn't want to hear about how bad things were. He was one of those guys who would rather do the job and handle it as it came. Part of me admired that trait, but a more significant part wanted all the information I could get to know how to react and practice situations in my mind. I didn't want to miss something and have it cost me a crew.

Even so, I didn't ask any questions. I let the conversation go where it would, observed reactions, listened to the stories, laughed along with the men, and played cards. Sometimes, overthinking things got in my way, and that was when mistakes happened.

I also hadn't read a newspaper in a few months and wanted to know what was happening worldwide. We listened to the radio on occasion, though more often than not lately, we didn't. Hearing some of the stories these two crews told us let me know that things were rough in the world. Tomorrow, I'd look for a paper, I decided.

CHAPTER 21

February 20th, 1944

It was more of the hurry-up-and-wait game getting played. Every day, we watched crews come back, listened to the stories they told, and filed them away in our memory banks as things we could expect. We were hoping to encounter them sooner rather than later. Not that we wanted to be flying into a bad situation. We only wanted to be flying. Some of the missions the guys said were cake, and the crews returned triumphant and ready for the next.

Then you had the opposite happen. One of the fellows in our barracks, Higgins, returned from his second mission and appeared shaken and shell-shocked. His face was pale and his hair stood up like he'd been grabbing it with his fists and pulling.

"It's getting rough out there," Higgins said shakily. "We lost two planes. I sat there helplessly and watched them explode mid-air. Ten chutes came out between the two of them. All I can say is I hope they made it somewhere safe and didn't get captured. I hope the other ten didn't feel anything. Have you heard the things they are doing to prisoners of war?"

I had heard, and I numbly nodded in response. Word

spread rapidly about the torture prisoners received from their captors and subjected to. I don't know where the stories came from since the guys were still prisoners, yet they existed. Some guys ended up sent to camps like Auschwitz and Dachau or gassed if they weren't flat-out shot. Those stories were easier to understand. The stories where the prisoners became enslaved, starved, beaten, or used as test subjects for the Nazi's experiments were believable since that is what they were doing to the Jewish people, but more complicated to corroborate. One thing they constantly drilled into us during training: remember your escape route if you go down. Memorize it and don't get caught. The alternatives are worse than expected.

My nerves wound up and got strung tight. I was scared. I had no idea when I would pull my first mission and every time I saw a plane come back full of holes or heard the pilot feathering the engine so they didn't crash on landing, I wondered a little more. How much was what they told us in training was a lie? We heard all about easy missions, and only the instructor who tested us hinted that things were awful and our lives were at risk every moment we were in the air.

The wait for orders was driving all of us a little crazy. All we'd done since arriving was lectures and laying around the barracks. It'd been two weeks. Between doing nothing and hearing all the stories, we felt that ETO happy feeling. We wanted to get on with it. We were over waiting for it to happen. Set us free to blow some shit up, is how Jones put it. I was a man of action, not words.

Two days later, we were sitting in the mess hall eating lunch after another lecture when Rogers burst into the room waving a piece of paper. Something had lit his face in a way I hadn't seen in some time, and his wide grin split his face.

"We've got our alert!" Rogers shouted in victory. "As of March 1st, we are alerted for missions, gentlemen. We get to start kicking Jerries out of the sky and blowing them off the ground." The slang was unusual for Rogers and it got the crew excited.

I let out a whoop of excitement and clapped Hausman on the back. "You ready?"

"Oh, yeah." Hausman nodded. "It's about time. Hurry up and wait. That's all we've been doing and it's getting old. I'm ready to take a few Nazis off the map."

"That's no lie," I agreed wholeheartedly. "The Army rushes us through training now and then makes us wait. It sure felt like a long time, but compared to the stories we've heard from others, we got off easy on the lectures and whatnot."

"Man, I understand we are about to be in life and death situations; it's war. I don't understand why they didn't tell us half the things these crews coming back are saying. That's the truth we need to hear, not your missions will be easy," Jones griped around the food in his mouth. "Give me the bombs and a plane if it's that easy. The constant waiting tells me we are in for some danger. And right now, I want it."

"Gents, it's about to get as real as it gets." Rogers grinned, borrowing the Brit's slang. "Easy or not, we get to do our part for the cause and avenge the deaths of all our men at Pearl Harbor. The guys that went down in these planes are the ones the other crews talk about. Those captured fellow Americans. We are going up there for them, and we'll drop our payloads in their honor."

"We aren't bombing the Japs," I responded with a shake of my head. "I agree with what you meant, though. The Nazi party is shooting our guys out of the sky. It's our turn to return the favor. The more we take down, the better."

A general cheer went up through our crew after our mini speeches, even though we didn't have a date yet. We were now on the list and would be called to action soon. That was the news we'd been waiting all this time to receive. Now that we have it, the gung-ho ready-to-fight mentality was firmly back in place.

We finished our lunch with a pep in our spirit that was previously lacking. The extra energy had us out on a physical training run to try and burn some of it off before another lecture we needed to attend on night flying. It wasn't anything we hadn't been through yet and we didn't have a choice. I knew we could get through it now, knowing we'd be up in the air soon.

I couldn't wait to write Alyse and tell her the good news. She might not see it the same way we did. However, it would mean the countdown of thirty missions would start and then I'd get to go home.

CHAPTER 22

March 8th, 1944

Orders are in!" Jones rushed through the door of the barracks. "We go out this morning. Rogers is getting the details. Gear up, men! The briefing is in an hour."

I jumped off my cot. "Mission number one, guys. Twenty-nine more and we get to go home!"

"Isn't it a bit early to be thinking about going home already?" Hausman joked. "We haven't even started yet."

"No way, man. I have a baby due in two months. All this time we've been sitting here, we could have had five or more under our belts already," I told him as I grabbed my jacket. "Don't you want to marry your girl and get on with life? Have babies?"

"I'm already practicing, my friend." Hausman laughed as he joined me. "There have been no complaints in that department."

"You must not be very good at it if you need to keep practicing," I told him. "I'm pretty sure I hit the mark on my first try." I winked at Hausman so he knew I was ribbing him.

"There will be plenty of time for jokes later, men," Rogers told us as he met the crew at the plane. "Here's what our mission is: the Erkner Ball Bearing Plant, sixteen miles from Berlin. It will be a huge raid. We will be in the back half of it. We are joining around nine hundred other bombers and approximately one thousand five hundred fighters. Command wants that plant destroyed."

"Load her up, men!" Jones shouted, jumping around. Nervous energy rolled off him in waves.

"Who are you talking to?" I asked Jones. "The ground crew already has her loaded. Plus, we still have to attend the briefing."

"I'm talking to you slow pokes and your preflight checks. Get on with it so we can do our job," Jones smarted off to me with a grin. "I can't drop the bombs here."

Rogers playfully shoved Jones and we walked around our plane to visually check it over before the briefing. In my estimation, the aircraft was in good condition and we headed off to the briefing, which was thankfully short.

Upon returning to the airfield, I verified all the plane's mechanics again. I turned some propellors and checked the oil lines while everyone else ensured the bombs were loaded correctly and secured and Rogers went down his checklist. We were dropping incendiaries and demolition. The incendiaries were bombs specifically made to start fires or destroy the area dropped in. They didn't explode the way the demolition bombs did. The demolition munitions detonated on contact in theory. Securing them was important. Every fuse class I attended went through my mind. We had this down to a science and we were taxiing down the runway in no time flat at the tail end of the formation.

Rogers got our position in the formation locked down and my heart raced. I sat up in the turret and watched everything around us, keeping an eye out for enemies and our engines. I paid very little attention to the scenery or cloud formations as this was our first live mission and I wanted to remain prepared for anything.

Cutty was on the waist gun and watching our left side. I could barely hear what crew members said on the comms. The noise was deafening. It so happened that I hadn't plugged my comms in correctly. Jones smacked my leg to get my attention and pointed it out to me. Boy, did I ever feel foolish. We didn't spot anything on the way to the target; believe me, we focused intensely on the airspace around us.

We listened on the comms to information relayed and adjusted as directed. Rogers's voice was calm as could be, and it impressed me to no end. If I were the one sitting in that seat, I would be a nervous wreck.

Since we were in the back of the formation, we didn't get to see much of what was happening in the lead and by the time we arrived at the target, the other bombers had laid waste to it. Rogers banked the plane and we flew over Berlin instead since those were the secondary orders. It wasn't our target but we needed to drop the bombs. We couldn't land back at base with them loaded.

From my position, I could watch the bombs fall and I saw them land on some houses and the streets. Gads, it tore that street all to hell. Red-orange bursts of flame and shockwaves emanated from the detonation sites. Black smoke rose thick in the air, climbing higher with each second and in the back of my mind, the visuals of the places I'd seen where bombs fell rose to the surface. I knew this wasn't a military target and we weren't doing anything differently than the Germans had done to all the places they destroyed. It still felt strange to be a part of it. Dropping bombs was our job and I had to think about it that way.

The sound of the bombs detonating was something

else, too. It was different than I expected and I don't know how to describe it other than final. I can't imagine what it sounded like from the ground or what the ground felt like if one detonated near you. The shock waves were gigantic and just as deadly as the explosions.

We banked to the left and suddenly, flak was all around us. Small black clouds appeared all around us from the 88mm cannons the Germans loved to use. It was louder than I expected and a lot more deadly. My adrenaline spiked into high gear and instinct had me duck. If I hadn't, I would no longer have a head. The metal shrapnel came through the plane right where my head had occupied. Right behind that, I heard the shouts from Cutty as a piece of flak tore through the aircraft near his head—two extremely close calls.

Air rushed through the holes and the sound of shrieking metal filled the fuselage. Every man on that plane aimed their guns at the two screaming FW-190s that zipped around us, trying to shoot us out of the sky. Our guns rattled and left a sea of shells at the gunner's feet as they rotated and continued to shoot. There was no time to think about anything other than stopping those planes before they dropped us.

A skilled pilot flew the single-engine fighter plane, I had to admit. His shots were accurate, though he didn't down us. We were better, though he had more maneuverability and was much faster than we were. Rogers pointed our nose up and we rose. Those FW-190s were notoriously inaccurate at high altitudes.

They made two passes at us, and then we lost them. The flak that came through the fuselage had almost taken out Cutty, Ribbits, and me. That pilot peppered Our left side with holes, with some in the tail, left wing, bomb bays, and nose.

Young and Merrill felt shaken but reported all clear.

When we got back to base, I walked around to look at the damage and was thankful no one was hurt. Our girl had so many holes she could be Swiss cheese. That was an eye-opening experience for our first mission. No lectures could have prepared me for that. I patted our plane and headed in for our debrief.

The squad commander told us we'd go out again tomorrow after we debriefed. I hoped it wasn't Berlin. If we were going to get shot at, I'd like to see something of France instead to make it worthwhile. With jittery nerves, we headed back to the barracks to strip off some of this gear and eat.

CHAPTER 23

March 9th, 1944

Why was the mission scrubbed?" I asked Rogers as he came back into the barracks.

"They don't tell me that." Rogers shrugged at me. "We were a go five times between yesterday and today and scrubbed each time. Intel, maybe? Weather? You know what I know. I'm not keeping information from you guys."

"I didn't figure you were," I told him. "I was just hoping for some information. This back-and-forth is frustrating. Get ready, so we get ready, then abort the mission."

"I know." Rogers sighed and sat down. "Nothing we can do about it. I'm pretty sure we will have a couple of down days. Get ready for a whole lot of nothing."

"Again," I grumbled. "Communication in the military is something the Army needs to work on. Think about it. If the governments of all these countries simply told their people what Hitler was up to and that he wasn't their savior, we might not even have to be here. All those people who thought Hitler invaded their country to save them and give them a better life. If they had known that he was going to treat them as sub-human and turn around and kill them in the next breath, they might have fought back."

"What good would it have done them?" Rogers asked me, playing devil's advocate. "He'd already invaded and conquered. They were outnumbered, out gunned, out maneuvered."

"True, though they wouldn't have embraced his false statements or cheered for him," I argued. "He already thinks he's God. They don't need to reinforce it."

"Ah, but what if all that reinforcement, as you say, builds him up so much that he thinks he's impervious and makes mistakes," Rogers asked, enjoying the debate.

"It's possible." I shrugged. "Hitler already thinks no one can beat him, though. Stalin isn't any better but at least we are fighting the same monster. Not to mention Mussolini, and Hirohito. There isn't a room big enough to contain them and their egos."

"Well, now, that's true." Rogers chuckled.

"The truth is, we're never going to know what's going through their heads," I muttered. "Who thinks that experimentation on people is a good idea in the name of creating a master race? Isn't the fact that we are all human enough? Look at how far technology has come. We are flying. I know there's so much more, but now that we are talking about this, I can't think of anything other than Hilter needing removal."

Rogers laughed and smacked his hand on the table. "There is no argument there. I saw you got some mail. How are things at home?"

"Alyse is doing good with the pregnancy," I replied. "I feel guilty for missing all of it."

"Understandable," Rogers agreed. "I'd feel the same way. Find comfort in the fact that you are not the only one feeling that way. There are a lot of men over here who are missing out on that. Speaking of, did you see that one of the guys came back over here after already getting sent home? He signed on to do another thirty missions."

"Why? Did he go home and find out his wife replaced him?" I joked. It was the first thing that popped into my mind, probably because I'd be gone long enough to worry Alyse would do the same.

"Yes," Rogers answered, shocked. "You already heard?"

"That was a guess," I said, stunned. "That's what happened?"

"Sure is. One of the other guys said they think he has a death wish now." Rogers shook his head sadly. "I couldn't imagine coming home after this to find that out. I honestly don't know what I would do in that situation."

"Drink," I stated. "A lot."

"And after that?" Rogers laughed. "What then?"

I didn't have an answer. "I can't say that a similar thought hadn't crossed my mind. That Alyse would get tired of waiting around for me to come home and find herself another man."

"I don't think you have to worry about that," Rogers said bluntly. "All the available men are over here."

I couldn't help but laugh. The worry still existed in my mind and all Rogers did was point out that I was worrying for nothing. Alyse hadn't once hinted that she was unhappy with me over here. I knew she was concerned about my safety, though our feelings about the war were very much on the same page.

"Where did the rest of the guys go?" Rogers changed the subject.

"I think they went to start a baseball game until they heard from you. Should we go find them?" I wondered.

"No." Rogers shrugged. "Let them have some fun. We can sit here and enjoy the quiet. I was going to write a letter to my parents."

"I already wrote my letters," I mused. "I was thinking about writing about each of our missions. So forty years from now, I could look back on them and remember when I was young and idealistic."

"Idealistic?" Rogers laughed. "I think I'm borderline cynical now. It's not a bad idea. It might even be therapeutic and help relieve some of the stress that builds up after being in those situations where you don't know if you will make it or not."

"I know." I shook my head at him. "We've been on one mission and are already talking like this."

"Eh." Rogers shrugged. "That was some accurate flak and our plane didn't even get the worst of it. We're allowed to talk that way."

"You're the boss." I chuckled. "Go ahead, encourage bad attitudes and whining."

"Oh, no." Rogers stood up. "Whining isn't allowed. Not now, not ever. I'll tolerate some attitude but refuse to allow whining on my plane."

"Whoa," Jones bellowed as he walked in. "Suhm was whining? This I gotta hear. Spill it."

Jones grabbed a chair, swung it around, and leaned his arms across the back. Rogers burst out laughing and I rolled my eyes.

"Do you hear me whining?" I mocked Jones. "I hear that from you and your lack of finesse with the ladies."

CHAPTER 24

March 13th, 1944

Rogers telling me to get ready for nothing was correct. We sat there for a dull four days waiting for orders. Then, today, we got called for our first No Ball raid on Abbeville, France. Abbeville's location lies in the northern region on the river Somme.

No Ball was the codename for bombing sites suspected of manufacturing the German's V-weapons, the V1 and the V2. Those were the automated pilotless bombs that Germany made in the French countryside. That way, they didn't lose planes or men when they were already running low on each.

Our goal was to find and destroy these sites that were well hidden. Germany wanted to use these bombs on London, and they had, in hopes they would submit to the German war machine. The hillsides and locations of these targets were not always definite because of how well they blended with the trees or earth. Several of them used the prisoners in labor camps to tunnel into the hillsides so that nothing at all showed on top.

"I know we aren't going to know what to look for," Rogers began after the briefing. "We are going to follow the lead of the other planes. The other pilots stated that there are anomalies in the landscape to look for; sometimes it pans out, and more often than not, we drop the payload on the hillside and take everything out."

"In short, we just destroy the French coastline?" Jones asked.

"Essentially, yes," Carlson added.

"Sometimes we will know we are in the right place because the German fighters will show up and shoot at us," Rogers concluded. "Eyes sharp."

It didn't take long for clouds to roll in, and soon, all we saw was a sea of billowing white under us. Occasionally, an opening would appear and we could see the ground, though it didn't last. I hoped there would be a clearing by the time we arrived.

I was excited to fly over France. It was what I had hoped for. When we reached our target, we couldn't drop any of our bombs due to 10-10 cloud cover. That meant we couldn't see anything. Cloud cover was on a scale: 0 meant all clear, a 3 was primarily clear, 4-6 was partly cloudy, and 10 was terrible. We had clouds so thick we wouldn't know where we were dropping our eggs.

Some of the other groups on the raid lost some planes and flak damaged others over the areas they saw as targets of opportunity. Only seven planes dropped bombs, and none of them were us, and not any of them were over the target at all.

I imagined it was missions like this that the instructors declared as easy, though I disagreed. We were tense, waiting for flak to come bursting through our plane. We trained our eyes on the sky around us. There were no conversations other than Rogers relaying our position and listening as other planes came under fire.

Due to our position in the formation and the cloud cover, our crew were one of the lucky ones that didn't encounter any flak this time. We all were grateful for it, though we suffered disappointment in not completing the mission by our own standards.

Rogers turned us back, and when we got to base, the crew received a three-day pass and our pay. That was enough for us to change our attitudes. We grabbed them and most of us took off for Aylesbury as soon as possible. Hausman's girlfriend was near there, and we knew the town enough to know what we could get away with and what we could expect.

"Drinking tonight, Ralph?" Jones asked as we got into town.

"Perhaps," I told him. "Was thinking I'd look for a card game to see if I could make a little more money. I need to send some home and it doesn't leave me a lot to live on here."

"That's the truth," Rogers agreed. "They want us to throw ourselves in front of bullets but give us a pittance in return."

Rogers was still annoyed at the scrubbed missions and being unable to drop our payload on the No Ball targets. We all were irritated by that, mainly since seven other planes found somewhere to drop their eggs. I guessed that was a bonus to being in the front of the formations. I knew we'd get there eventually, but until it happened, it was our destiny to have missions like we had today.

"We've got three days to kill. Let's find some women and do things our mothers wouldn't be proud of," Cutty joined in the conversation.

I laughed and slapped him on the back. "I've got you beat there; I don't think my mom's ever been proud of anything I do. That leaves me a lot of options."

"You don't get to do that," Jones griped at me. "You are married. Leave the women to the rest of us poor single folk who want to have a good time."

"Wow, you are laying it on thick, Jones." Rogers shook his head. "When was the last time a woman paid attention to you?"

"Not in a long time if Suhm is around," Jones grumbled good-naturedly. "It would do a fellow wonders if he'd help in that department. My concentration might improve."

Cutty boomed out a laugh. "I doubt that."

Hausman was too busy looking around for Beverly to join in the conversation. At least I didn't have to worry about him blaming me for the lack of female attention. He'd found one without me that snared him like Alyse captured my attention. I didn't know much about the woman, but Hausman's smile said everything I needed to know.

"There she is!" Hausman shouted and pointed to Beverly standing outside the pub. "I get three whole days with her this time. I don't know what you poor saps will do, but I will be a happy man."

I figured there was enough to keep the rest of us occupied and able to find temporary happiness around town. Rogers and I went in one direction, Cutty, Ribbits, and Jones went in another, and Hausman went off with Beverly. We'd meet up again in a day or so.

CHAPTER 25

March 15th, 1944

No sooner than we returned to base, we were handed orders. This time, it was for a city called Friedrichshafen on the Swiss border of Germany. The briefing was short and to the point and we all headed out to the airfield to do our preflight checks.

We didn't say much to each other, seeming lost in our own thoughts. I focused on what I needed to do to ensure our plane was airworthy and the other guys had their lists. Each gave me the all-clear, and I gave Rogers the all-clear.

The city of Friedrichshafen's location was on the northern shoreline of a lake, and the route would take us near a mountain range. It was one aspect I actually looked forward to seeing. We lined up, and after take-off, we paid rapt attention to the skies around us for enemy craft and flak.

It seemed like a hush fell over the plane when the Alps came into view. I knew that wasn't what happened, but the beauty was enough to steal your breath from your lungs. Snow-capped peaks with snaking white veins down the slopes, trees peppered around, and a ridgeline stretching across the horizon. The serenity passed too soon, and our minds were back on the job.

The city itself was our target this time. Our third raid had us dropping incendiary bombs on the Friedrichshafen. We'd heard this place was essential to the German industrial sectors. I believed that the location was why the crew was so quiet this time around. We knew we were dropping our payloads on civilians and I don't think it set right with a lot of us. We had no choice in the matter, though our demeanor was different this time.

"Do you know why this place is a target?" Jones had asked us while the bombs were loaded. "I overheard some guys talking that the factories there use the slaves from the labor camps. Dachau."

"Is that true?" I looked at Rogers. We'd heard awful stories about people kept at that camp.

"I don't know. You know Jones, always hearing stuff." Rogers shrugged. "I do know there are supposed to be tunnels where some V-rockets are protected. We aren't the first to bomb this place. We probably won't be the last."

The conversation echoed in my mind as we flew. There were always rumors. No one knew how much of it was true and what was nothing more than stories to incite us, so we were excited about dropping the bombs. It was another of those things I didn't want to focus too much of my thoughts on. The only people innocent in the war were the unsuspecting civilians trying to live their lives. Bombing prisoners held in camps wasn't appealing. Perhaps less so than dropping our payload on civilians.

We received the command to release the bombs and Jones dropped the eggs. I tracked them as they fell and could swear that I saw each one detonate and start a fire that spread through all the structures below. I knew I couldn't at the altitude we were at. I imagined all the people trying to flee in panic. I had to shut the thoughts down.

As I watched the smoke rise thousands of feet in the air, towers of billowing black, I wondered if we hit any of those tunnels. If the Germans were using people from the camps, some of our prisoners of war might be down there trapped and suffocating. I shook it off because that wasn't a pleasant thought to have either. Compartmentalize, I reminded myself. Shove it in a box and close the lid.

On our return flight, we caught a little flak. The telltale black poofs popped up all around, though we spotted no enemy fighters. It was ground fire and nothing hit our plane. I don't know how because the flak clouds surrounded us. Some angels must have been watching over us for not one shot to hit.

Unfortunately, I saw tragedy, which wasn't something anyone expected. I supposed tragedy never was. It wasn't long after the flak that we caught sight of two B-24s that were headed right for each other. Something had to be wrong because there wasn't any chance that they didn't see each other.

"Pull up," Rogers demanded of the pilots. "Come on, pull up." His voice was deadly calm, as if he were talking to an insurance agent on the telephone. I know I voiced the same thoughts in my head repeatedly as I watched it unfold.

Then it happened: they smacked together in a heart-stopping moment of screeching metal, bounced apart as if made of rubber, and surprisingly didn't explode on contact. Both aircraft spun out of control and plummeted to the ground like rocks or the bombs we dropped.

Every one of us looked for chutes that told us the crew had escaped, yet we saw nothing. I watched them the whole way down; it didn't seem right for me to look away. Both planes exploded on impact and I figured one or both still had munitions on board they hadn't dropped. It was one of the most challenging things I'd had to witness yet, and as we flew past, I could only tip my head to the lost souls.

That's what the Army expected of us. It was our job. All in a day's work, as they say. Sometimes, all that was available was a tough break. Even then, the words weren't enough to convey all that was lost or how we felt about seeing it happen before our eyes. It sounded cold and detached, not the feelings inside me tearing me apart. Yet it was all I could come up with tough break.

"No chutes," Rogers confirmed through the comms, still with a calm voice. I could see his face, though, and it defied the tone. It appeared he had the compartmentalizing thing down.

CHAPTER 26

March 20th, 1944

Frankfort, Germany, gents," Rogers called out after the briefing. "We need to be ready to go up in fifteen!"

I jumped to my preflight tasks with no arguments or questions. It'd been a rough few days after watching our planes collide and I did everything I could to distract my mind and keep focused on what I needed to do to get back home. Never before had the words that one drill sergeant said stuck with me or hit harder than the ones that reminded me that not everyone would get home as they wanted.

I enjoyed the flying and the camaraderie our crew shared, though there was no denying that things were stressful. I think the crew felt the same way, and it seemed like we forced the joking the past couple of days. The humor was stiff and unnatural, not funny even though we laughed and carried on.

We'd played cards, drank, smoked, attended lectures, tinkered with our plane and passed the time. Frankfort would be our fourth mission. One more after that and we would all have our Air Medal. After five successful missions, aircrews received an air medal.

Frankfort was one of those cities that we loved to

bomb. The 8th plastered that place with bombs at every opportunity they had. Today would be more of that if all went to plan. There was a small part of me that would be happy bombing Germany after what I saw and yet I knew it wouldn't really make a difference. It was nothing more than revenge.

I was numb inside from feeling bad about it, and I wasn't sure if that meant life had no meaning or if it was a by-product of war. Perhaps it was both. Hausman started talking to me about something similar he felt but didn't get very far with it before he gave up and decided to write a letter home instead.

Maybe another mission was what we all needed to get back to feeling functional if that was even possible. Logically, I knew those wouldn't be the only planes I saw go down. Accepting it didn't mean I was okay with it happening.

"Ready." I checked in with Rogers after I finished my checklist and got the go-ahead from the rest of the crew. "All clear." I needed to be in the present. We all did. I didn't know if I was the only one brooding; I could only speak for myself.

One by one, the crew followed me and boarded the plane. We got settled with minimal conversation and were soon bumping and speeding down the runway. All situations normal, nothing happened. About twenty-five miles from the target, we received word the mission got scrubbed and we were to return to base. We banked and made the turn, heading back.

Fifteen minutes later, flak hit our plane. Shots were all around us; those black clouds polka-dotted the sky. We did everything we could to evade getting hit. Chaff got thrown like it was confetti in a parade.

Rogers somehow managed to stay in formation while keeping from taking damage. Those guardian angels must have been with us because we received no hits again. More than once, I thought for sure we were about to receive our fair share, yet none landed. Others in the mission weren't as lucky, though thankfully, I didn't witness anyone going down. I knew that thought was on more than my mind.

We landed safely back at base and carefully checked the plane before debriefing and returning to the barracks. There was sort of a feeling of letdown and relief mixed together. I wasn't sure how to describe it. We wanted vengeance for the planes that went down last time, were happy none did this time, and were amazed that we suffered no damage.

"Hey, guys," Rogers said as he entered the barracks. "It counts as a mission because we caught flak. It's not a total waste. We have one more under our belts."

I wasn't about to look a gift horse in the mouth. I'd take it. A few guys broke into grins, and the mood changed just like that. Chatter broke out among the crew. We discussed some of our close calls with the flak and praised Rogers for his flying.

Jokes rang out across the barracks. Cutty broke out a deck of cards and we began to play. Rogers came and sat next to me, keeping his voice low.

"Having a hard time after those planes went down?" he asked me, already knowing the answer.

"Yeah, aren't you?" I shot back.

"Of course I am," Rogers answered. "You can't see that and not be affected."

"How did you remain so calm during that?" I asked the question that had been burning in my mind since it happened.

"I have to," Rogers finally responded. "I wanted to scream through those comms for those guys to bail. Did you think I didn't care?"

"No," I told him honestly. "I knew that wasn't the case. I saw your expression. I guess that's why I wouldn't make a good pilot. The skills are there. The emotions are a different matter."

"You do it when you have no choice. My panicking wouldn't have helped anyone. More than anything, I wanted to land this plane with all of you in one piece and breathing." Rogers played his hand and slapped a false grin on his face. "I don't think I've even been that scared before in my life," he admitted to me in a whisper.

"I don't want to say I'm glad to hear that, but I am," I confessed. "I thought it was just me."

"Have you been feeling guilty?" Rogers wondered. "I have."

"Me too," I told him with a grim look. "That might be the hardest part for me. The horrible thoughts about how glad I was that it wasn't our plane."

"I'm happy you're human." Rogers gave me a genuine smile and clapped me on the back.

CHAPTER 27

March 22nd, 1944

Fifth mission," Hausman stated as we prepared to run down our checklists. "Twenty-five more after this, not that I'm counting. Who could possibly want to count this as work when we are having so much fun?"

I chuckled and wiped my hands over the legs of my uniform. "No sense counting. Let's just make it through this, get our first Air Medal and be happy with that."

"Basdorf." Jones stepped close to us. "Who doesn't enjoy Basdorf?"

"Watching it burn, you mean?" Cutty laughed bitterly. None of us had been there yet.

"I've seen a lot of Berlin," I said, shaking my head. "It hasn't gotten any prettier. I imagine Basdorf looks the same."

"Macabre humor," Rogers said, shaking his head at us but smiling. "Let's earn that medal."

Doolittle, a general of the 8th Air Force, implemented a strategic change in how the Americans fought with the Luftwaffe. We used to avoid combat with them. Now, with the new changes, we did anything we could to engage them and force them into battle. The result thus far had been a lot of lost planes on both sides but the reasoning stood. We replaced our losses. The Luftwaffe couldn't. It gave us an edge and made the raids on Berlin exciting at times. So, our fifth mission happening on the outskirts of Berlin, could earn us a medal for something other than our fifth mission. It was that opportunity that gave us something to look forward to.

The Army awarded the Air Medal with a score-card type of award system. Five missions earned us the medal, or if we brought down several enemy aircraft. I knew some folks who had taken advantage of that scoring system to get the medals, and while it wasn't right, I don't think many people other than aircrews knew what we encountered up in the air sometimes. Sure, there were easy missions, but in my estimation, nothing was easy if you were getting shot at.

There were far fewer of us in the air than on the ground. I wasn't calling the infantry or ground crews easy; the truth was they saw things we never would. They dealt with the fallout from our bombs, and we relied on them to help take out the anti-aircraft guns that tried to shoot us down.

The life expectancy of someone on an aircrew was twelve missions. The ground crew wasn't any better, but they had better numbers to pull from if they lost a squad. The number of planes versus the number of guns on the ground aiming at us was frighteningly low. Ground weaponry vastly outnumbered us.

Then there was the whole fact of not getting paid regularly to top off the near misses of bullets that tried to bring your craft to a fiery end. I don't think any of our crew reached that bitter stage of resentment for performing their duty, though we'd all seen it in others countless times. I figured our day for that was coming.

"Here we go," Rogers said through the comms and we took to the skies.

"Clear," I reported partway through our flight as a check-in.

"Clear," Young echoed from the tail.

There were no enemy planes in the sky and no resistance from the ground yet. Things were looking good, though no one let their guard down. The only things we spotted were some fluffy clouds.

"Release," Rogers commanded when he saw the other bombs fall. Jones released our cargo along with the rest of the planes.

We flew over our target and hundreds of bombs fell, crushing whatever part of the city they landed in. Basdorf, at twenty-thousand feet, looked the same as any other bombed city. It was still ugly. There was still life down there because they launched a counterattack.

"Incoming! Eleven o'clock!" Ribbits yelled, forgetting to remain calm.

Flak burst on both sides of the plane about a thousand feet out. Cutty was throwing chaff as fast as he could as a defensive measure. The flak wasn't accurate until a lucky shot hit the waist window on the plane, inches from where Ribbits was busy throwing out the chaff opposite of Cutty. The shell fragment whistled right by him, his eyes wide with terror.

Ribbits threw out more chaff with shaking hands to help deflect the flak. Chaff was small, thin pieces of aluminum or plastic that interfered with their radar. We threw it off the plane to form a cloud that would jam up the radars, throw off the aim, and confuse the enemies trying to knock us out of the sky.

Movements were hurried and frantic, with adrenaline pumping on high. My eyes scanned the sky in rapid movements, watching for enemy planes. I tried to see through the little black clouds of smoke left by the exploding flak. There was so much I couldn't spot anything until we cleared the area.

We made it back to base without any casualties and only minor repairs needed to the plane. I think Ribbits had a new look at life after his close call. At least we earned an air medal for the effort and had a successful mission.

"Small blessings." I clapped Ribbits on the back.

"I almost needed a change of pants," Ribbits breathed out. "I've almost gotten hit twice. It doesn't get easier because I know my luck will run out at some point."

"Don't even think that way." Rogers came up beside us. "Keep thinking that we will be fine and we will be, I say. There's no room for doubt up there. We make a call, stick to it, and change course if needed. We can't do any more than that. You didn't falter in your job once, Ribbits. Take pride in that."

"The fear didn't stop you," I pointed out. "Doesn't that mean anything?"

"I guess." Ribbits slowed and glanced at Rogers, then me. "I wanted to drop to the floor and cower like a scared child."

"But you didn't," I reminded him. "Fear is okay as long as we don't let it win. You did what you needed to do to help keep the plane in the air and all of us alive. We each play a part and you didn't fail."

CHAPTER 28

March 23rd, 1944

Handorf," I repeated. "Why does that stand out to me?"

"It's outside of Munster. Wehrmacht HQ," Rogers reminded me as we reviewed the mission brief. "I know we are all tired and high-strung, but we signed up for this when we joined. Not only is Munster the home of the Wehrmacht, but we also have a Panzer base, and there's the guy who's the Bishop of Munster. Munster controls a lot of heavily garrisoned bases. We aren't point on this, but hitting the targets is no less important."

"Tired?" Cutty remarked, looking half alive. "This is our fourth mission in a week. Attempted murder takes a lot out of a man."

"Attempted murder." I chuckled. I agreed that the strain on us was getting heavy. However, I also agreed with Rogers that we signed up to do it. A break would be nice since the enemy liked to shoot at us and came uncomfortably close to hitting their mark. I looked down at the map placed in front of us and narrowed my gaze on Munster.

"Northwestern Germany. Anything else we need to be aware of before we go?" I asked the crew. We'd had our briefing already. This conversation was just a chance for our crew to voice their concerns before we loaded up. We'd heard of other crews that did this and they felt it helped increase their survival rate if everything was on the table before they took off. "Any rumors?" I looked directly at Jones.

"Not that I heard," Jones confirmed.

"Let's go then." Rogers clapped his hands and grabbed the papers from the small table.

The plane was loaded, the preflight finished, and we took our place in line. Off we went when we were up. The weather was colder than usual, and I was thankful this mission, if all went well, would only take about six hours of flying time.

"In the distance," Young shouted through the comms. He was too on edge to remain calm. "Five o'clock."

I swiveled my head to see two Junkers. They flew by awfully close and were going in the same direction we were. I kept my eyes glued to them in case they banked and came at us, but it didn't happen. Two against sixty bombers weren't great odds, so they made the right choice. A sentiment echoed through our comms from other crews. It didn't mean they couldn't warn ground gunners that we were coming.

We didn't experience any flak on our approach, which was more than a little surprising given our fly-by earlier. I tried not to take it as a bad omen or a good omen. It was nothing more than an anomaly.

"Open doors," Rogers commanded through the comms. "On my mark," he waited until he heard the command from the other crews, "release!" Our target was in sight and the bomb doors opened entirely on all the planes around us. We delivered our payload.

The sounds of the bombs detonating were music to our ears. A small cheer went up through the plane before

Jones closed the bomb bay doors to nothing but a crack. It meant there were fewer people, machines, and weapons to come after us. We banked and flew back toward home base, still in our formation. We saw flak exploding around some of the aircraft in front of us. The loud, small explosions kept our eyes sharp and on the skies around us, though nothing came close to hitting us.

Cutty and Ribbits threw out chaff as countermeasures and we made it home unscathed, to our relief. We watched some planes head to the mechanical hangars for repairs, but no one got shot down. I think the mission was a resounding success due to that alone. I quickly checked the fluid levels in our plane with hands that felt like ice cubes. I knew the ground crew would do it, but I liked to have my own hands on our aircraft to make sure that things were at my level of expectations.

"Suhm, go to medical and get checked," Rogers told me, tapping his cheek. I wiped my hands on my flight uniform and nodded resolutely.

I didn't feel anything but did as told by my commanding officer, who only had my interest at heart. I sat and waited while other guys got treated for various injuries and kept my patience. Since I was still cold, I jammed my hands under my legs to warm them up. I waited about thirty minutes before the nurse called me, and they'd warmed minimally.

The nurse saw my movements, grabbed my hands and checked them for signs of frostbite. She then gave me a warm cup of coffee to hold while the doctor examined my face. The heat was almost painful, yet I couldn't be more grateful as my hands started to thaw and slowly warm. I think my face was even colder than my hands were.

"There's a touch of frostbite here on your left cheek." The doctor tapped next to it. "Nothing severe. You might want to think about taking a warm shower to warm your core up. The temp you experienced up there was about forty degrees below zero," he explained. "If you notice anything else, come back and let me know."

If a touch of frostbite was the worst that would happen to me, I was okay with that. I wasn't worried about it, but warming up would be nice. I left medical and returned to the barracks to get warm and rest. Rogers said we pulled another mission the next day.

"You are otherwise okay?" Rogers confirmed as I wrapped a blanket around me.

"Just a small spot of frostbite," I relayed.

"Go take a hot shower. I need you on these missions," Rogers told me with a solemn face. "I can't have anything happen to you."

"Yes, sir," I replied with a deadpan expression. I got up to take as hot a shower as possible.

CHAPTER 29

March 24th, 1944

Rise and shine!" Hausman's voice barked out at one in the morning.

I jolted out of a deep sleep, the first I'd had in a couple of days. I'd gotten about five hours of sleep, which wasn't nearly enough. We were on an early morning mission today, and Hausman was the first to wake up. It would be our seventh one overall, but fifth in as many days. It was wearing on us all. If we continued at this rate, we'd finish our missions in a month. I threw my feet over the side of my cot and stretched, noting the frigid air and wondered how cold it would be at twenty-thousand feet. I didn't want more frostbite.

"Stop your hollering," I barked at Hausman. "Is there food?"

"Yes, there is." Hausman grinned. He was far too awake and cheery to tolerate. "We've got a hundred crews going out. What do you think?"

"I think you are obnoxious and I need coffee," Jones grumbled as he stomped out the barracks.

The general consensus was to toss Hausman in a bag and stow him on the plane until we were all functioning enough to deal with him. Even Rogers looked like he wanted to silence the man. I finished dressing, shoved my feet into my boots, and followed the rest to the mess hall to eat and fuel our bodies. We'd need it to retain body heat and not choke Hausman.

"Don't forget, we got a general riding along with us today," Cutty told me as we pushed the door open.

The aroma of coffee hit, and we headed immediately for the dark brew that would shock our bodies awake and warm us up. I downed a full cup before refilling and joining the line for breakfast before leaving.

Hausman was chatting away and I wondered if the man had slept at all or if he was on his second wind. He wasn't typically a morning person like that. I mostly tuned him out, ate fast, refilled my coffee again, and sat back down.

"You know about St. Nazaire?" Cutty asked me after my third refill of coffee.

The edges of sleep were fading from my mind. "I know it's in France. Are you asking me about this mission? Because we know the same information."

"No, the attack that happened there." Cutty scowled at me. "You're a grouch this morning."

"Not enough sleep," I answered automatically without apologizing. "No, I don't think I know about earlier attacks on the place. Is it relevant?"

"I don't know." Cutty shrugged. "It's elaborate and what has kept that city on the bombing map."

"Then fill me in," I replied. I sipped more of the caffeinated drink and leaned my elbow on the table.

"It's a port town in France and the Germans control it. Its location is perfect for the damaged ships to pull into dry dock and get repaired. It fits the big ships, like the Bizmark,"

Cutty explained. "The Brits did this whole secret operation to take out the dry dock. I think we even helped. They called it the greatest raid of all. The whole thing was brilliant. They used a decommissioned destroyer, outfitted the hull with delayed action explosives, lined it with steel and concrete, and hid commandos on board. They rammed that ship into the dock, and everyone started fighting. The Brits lost a lot of guys, but so did the Germans. The ship detonated after the troops were off and it destroyed the dock. The German ships in need of repair had to go somewhere else and it forced them into the English Channel to get there."

"That is brilliant," I agreed. "Did the Brits take control of the area? Because if they did, why are we bombing it?"

"No, the Germans still occupy it," Cutty replied with a mouthful of food. "That's why we still bomb it. To keep it a non-functioning dry dock and pretty much useless city in the scheme of the war. It's on the bombing schedule regularly."

I nodded my understanding. Hearing the history of the site helped me actually understand the objective more. I stood up again to refill my coffee and noticed people heading out. I quickly filled my coffee, drank it, and put my dirty cup in the bin.

Rogers stood, nodded the rest of us to follow and we joined the line of streaming soldiers out the doors to the airfield. It was just after two in the morning and I was thankful that the planes had been loaded with munitions while we slept. We still had to review our checklists and ensure everything was secured and flight-ready.

Our efficiency was noteworthy, and I was sure it had something to do with the general who would be on the mission with us. No one wanted a mark on their file. It was almost comical how well-behaved we were.

This mission had approximately one hundred Liberators, B-24s, that would drop their eggs on the airfield in St. Nazaire. It was inoperable for ships, and we would do the same for air support. The mission was solid and straightforward. It ran like a textbook.

We arrived before the sun rose in the sky. There was enough light for us to see where the bombs hit but not much else. The explosions were like fireworks and illuminated the areas around where they fell. We obliterated that airfield.

I watched one of our bombs smack into some small buildings on the side of the airfield and blew them all to pieces. There was hardly a building standing by the time we left the target. The Jerries wouldn't be using that field anytime soon. As we flew away, we saw flames and smoke billowing into the sky. This mission was an astounding success and our visiting general seemed pleased.

There was no small talk or joking among the crew with the general on board. We communicated flawlessly and ran like a well-oiled machine. I didn't see one snag in our group or how they performed. It's the same with the plane. Our girl was the best she'd ever been.

Our return flight took us near Paris and I observed the scenery pass below. Mist covered most of the city, but in the distance, I finally saw the Eiffel Tower sticking up through the fog, reaching for the sun. I smiled at the sight and felt grateful for the view of something so marvelous. I'd have to write a letter home letting them know I finally saw Paris and the Eiffel Tower, even if only for minutes and shrouded in fog.

Upon return to base, we received some much-needed rest. There wasn't one of us who didn't go right back to bed to try and catch up on sleep. Having the general onboard wore us out. We weren't used to behaving like professionals on display.

I didn't think he was there to judge us; I believed it was to see the mission play out before him and see how all the planes worked together. With his position in the rear of the formation, he could see all the rest. Regardless, it felt like final exams. Now we needed naps.

CHAPTER 30

March 26th, 1944

"Suhm, how much sleep did you get?" Jones slapped me on the back.

"Enough that I have plenty of energy to smack you around if you keep hitting me," I replied, giving him a dark look. I laughed when Jones frowned, thinking I was serious. "About twenty-four hours. Did you get any?"

"Oh, I got some." Jones burst out laughing. "Her name was Maria."

I rolled my eyes at him. "Where are we headed today?" It would be our eighth mission, yet it seemed like so much more than eight.

"Siracourt, France," Rogers answered, walking up on my left. "There's supposed to be a V-1 bunker there. Briefing is in an hour."

"Isn't that by where we went the last time?" I wondered aloud.

"Sure is." Rogers handed me a map. "The whole Nord-Pas-de-Calais area is rumored to be littered with these bunkers."

"There's so many trees," Jones grumbled. "I don't know where they are getting their intel from because I can't see shit from the sky."

"If they made them visible, there really wouldn't be a point to having a hidden bunker, now would there?" I mouthed off to my crewmate. Rogers chuckled and walked away, snatching the map from my hand.

"You need a woman." Jones scowled at me.

"I have one. Alyse's due to have my baby soon, remember?" I rolled my eyes at Jones again and began my preflight check. Maybe my attitude would improve if I got an early start on it. I don't even know why I had one, to begin with; I only knew I woke up feeling off-kilter.

Attitudes among the crew were pretty good after a little break and downtime. Many of the guys went to town and found fun with women and ale. This time, I stayed back and slept as much as possible. Dreams woke me up frequently and I needed my head back in place before we went up again. It might have been the wisest decision I'd made yet.

My body felt physically better than it had the past week, and I wasn't feeling as much pressure as before, even though I still felt not quite myself. It was to the benefit of us all to have me on my best foot when we headed out. Not that I didn't understand the other's need for a bit of fun because I did. I just needed to snap out of the mood I was in.

I tinkered with the plane to kill time until the briefing. I already knew the aircraft was in great shape. Nothing more than familiar movements to help put my mind in a better place. Even better was that it worked. When the briefing came, I felt like myself again and grinned at the rest of the crew to let them know I was back.

Our target area would be a large section near where we dropped bombs the week before. Those sites would be markers for some of us, and we would take out the hillside, so if there were an underground bunker, there wouldn't be one when we finished. Our plane's target for this mission was a parts factory and airfield a few miles from that hillside. Take out the hill and the field where they could receive support. Simple enough to accomplish.

"Suhm, I know you did a lot of the preflight before the briefing," Rogers started as we approached the plane, "do you mind if we take the guys through it again?"

"Not at all," I replied. "I wasn't quite in the right frame of mind and there could be something I missed." I didn't, but I wasn't going to challenge Rogers on it, and the guys needed to check their own stuff for their peace of mind.

"All-clear," the guys called out one by one.

"Load up," Rogers ordered with a smile.

We took our positions with a few jabs at each other and settled in for our mission. The weather was good, with no genuine cloud cover, though we all knew how quickly that could change. Oftentimes, it changed to our detriment. We kept our fingers crossed and our eyes peeled.

Our flight time wasn't super long, though it was still bitterly cold. It was not frostbite cold, just enough to notice my hands stiffening. I cupped them over my mouth and huffed some breath into them to try and warm them up when we got the ready call. I fisted them up and wiggled my fingers to keep the blood flowing through the extremities.

I put my hands back on the gun and watched out the window as the Liberators in front of us destroyed the hillside. We went a few miles further and dropped our eggs all over that factory. Of course, we were successful, and all that was left was smoke that climbed into pillars in the sky. It was an obvious sign that we'd been there for those who hadn't heard our planes approach or the bombs fall.

We turned and followed the formation back to the home base when we had fighters come upon us. "Three o'clock, enemy craft," I radioed through our comms with a level voice. I swung my gun and began to fire, shells pooling at my feet. I didn't let up, and I couldn't tell if I got a hit or not.

Cutty and Jones threw chaff while Rogers navigated us through. Nothing had hit near us, but I watched as a B-17 took a hit and exploded mid-air. There were no chutes. No one got out. For only a second, I let my chin hit my chest before I put my head back in the game.

"No survivors," Rogers communicated to the other crews.

"Tough break," I voiced the utterly terrible words.

"Tough break," echoed the crew.

We made it back to base in one piece and silently walked to the debrief with a weight on our shoulders that hadn't been there before.

CHAPTER 31

March 27th, 1944

Do you like my baguette?" Cutty called out to me with a smirk plastered on his face.

I glanced over to see he'd painted a bomb to look like a loaf of bread. Our ninth mission would be over France again. The mission brief said we'd be going to an airfield, this time in Pau; The Pau Pont Airfield, to be exact. It was some thirty miles from the Spanish border at the base of the Pyrenees Mountains. It would be a long flight.

I planned to study those mountains closely when we got close as that was our escape route if we were to get shot down over France or Germany. It wasn't likely that crossing a mountain range would be easy, but nonetheless, I wanted a peak at them.

"You're going to deliver a baguette to the Germans at the airfield?" Jones asked. "That's awfully nice of you to share food with them when everything is so rationed."

I laughed. "Bend over, Jerries, we've got something for you."

"I'm a swell guy." Cutty winked. "Suhm, that was just mean. What did those murdering Nazi bastards ever do to you?"

"Save it for later." Rogers ushered us to the plane with an eye roll. "We've got work to do. Load that last baguette, Cutty."

Cutty raced off with a chuckle to find a willing ground crew member to help him load the decorated bomb on the plane while the rest of us ran through our preflight checks. It was routine, and that was comfortable. The part that wasn't comfortable was knowing what we would encounter on the mission. Would it be one of the lucky days? Or would we scrape by with the skin of our teeth? The unknown is also what made it exciting. It was a dichotomy.

It was nine-thirty in the morning when we left. We were somewhere in the middle of the formation this time. Not at the end as we usually were. I wondered if that meant we were moving up in the hierarchy or that we'd lost that many planes. It was another one of those unhelpful thoughts that I had to stem from turning into a substantial internal dialog that would distract me from my job.

The flight over was uncomplicated, which was a blessing. Save for some random clouds, the skies were clear. Comms were quiet until we received the command to drop, and we did. We dropped all our munitions on the target and watched it burn as we circled and turned back toward base.

"Enemies at our four!" Warren yelled frantically, the silence broke. I heard the rat-a-tat-tat of our tail and belly guns firing while Ribbits and Cutty threw chaff like they were possessed marionettes doing a synchronized dance. I swiveled my gun to watch our side, fingers on the triggers. Rogers dodged enemy fire and tossed the plane around to keep us safe. It felt like we were in a small boat on an angry sea.

One of the planes behind us wasn't so lucky. "Craft at our five hit," Young relayed. I saw the flak hit the B-24 and smoke billowed out from her side. She spun into a death roll and I could tell the pilot was trying to recover, but it was useless. The plane was going down.

"Bail." Rogers urged through the comms. "Bail and live."

Nine chutes came out before it blew. I counted as each chute caught the air, its rider dangling below as they descended into enemy territory. It wasn't ideal, and I figured some chance was better than blowing up and having none.

"Nine chutes," Rogers relayed to the squads in front of us. "Visual confirmation on the nine."

"Tough break," I responded solemnly.

"Tough break," the crew echoed. It seemed to have caught on as our way of tipping our hats to those who didn't return to base with the formation.

This job wasn't for the weak. We all said a prayer for the soldiers who had to bail that they had landed safely and found a way out before getting captured. No one wanted our guys captured. They didn't deserve the punishment they'd get for being American soldiers. Neither did we want to see them blow up with the plane.

Moods were somber as we flew back. We had to divert to an RAF base due to weather closing in at the home base and it was seven-thirty at night when we landed. We'd flown a ten-hour day. It was a significant change from our routine. It was just for the night, but man, the Limey lugs live a life of leisure. It was a slap in the face after watching our plane go down.

The Brits only pull about two missions a week, they have girls waiting on them, and they eat and sleep like kings and then bitch about the hard life they lead. It's no wonder we had to be over here fighting for them. It didn't feel good to think that way since everyone lost something in this war. *It's all in a day's work,* we tell ourselves.

It wasn't like they enjoyed our company any more than we were pleased with theirs. All of us were feeling a little bitter about our loss and the Limey's living it up as they accused us of always doing didn't help matters.

We found places to bunk down for the night and tried to sleep as much as possible. It didn't seem likely we'd get leave when we returned. The losses always seemed to put a kink in our mental armor, and it took us a few days to hammer back out. The Army didn't afford us the time to do that, and while some of us learned quicker, some of us felt the loss more personally, even if we didn't know the crew.

We flew back to home base in the morning and received a week and a half of rest. Color me surprised. I was sure we'd be sent right back out on another mission. It was ridiculous how much we needed it, that rest period. We weren't even at the halfway point yet and already felt like we'd run through hell and back.

CHAPTER 32

March 31st, 1944

One of my pals showed up out of the blue at my barracks while we were resting. The only one who left base was Hausman so he could see his girl, Beverly. It was a pleasant surprise to see Norman's mug again. We spent hours discussing everything that's happened to us since we parted ways after training camp.

We traded the successes and things we saw as failures. The horror stories of missions came after that and those brought our jubilant moods down a notch. We switched subjects and talked about the letters from home we received.

Then, I found out he was only stationed twenty miles away in Attlebridge. That sealed that deal for me. April 2nd, I made my way over to see him there. Several men from the old outfit were there and we had a blast. We drank, danced, played cards, made our way through town and kicked up our heels.

It was what the doctor ordered. Relaxation, catching up with friends, sharing meals and drinks and reminiscing about the good times. There were sad moments when we talked about someone we knew who didn't make it out of a mission. We did our best to keep those moments to a minimum because all of us were desperate for downtime.

Some of us returned to Attlebridge to have a little fun before I headed back to my base. A local band was going to play some live music at one of the pubs and a group of us wanted to catch the act. I think it was a way to feel closer to home and the parties we all attended back in the States. There wasn't much happening in these towns here unless it was an American GI club.

There was a train that took me directly from there back to Norwich. It was such an easy trip to make for some rest and relaxation. It made me wonder where the others were; if they were as close as this, and we missed opportunities to stay in touch.

I knew it was a by-product of war, and with us being in the Air Corps and our life expectancy so short, any missed opportunity could be our last chance—dark thoughts to have after such a fun time with friends. I wrote a letter home as I rode the train back to Norwich.

I hadn't written to Alyse in a few days because of our many back-to-back missions. When I returned to base from the mission, we ate and went to sleep. It was all we could do to keep our heads where they needed to be for survival. You wouldn't know it to look at any of us.

I asked after the baby and how Alyse was faring with it all. I expressed my sorrow for not being there to be a part of it with her. Even as I wrote the words, I knew I intended to be sincere, though it didn't come across to me that way.

I missed Alyse. There was no doubt about that in my mind. Yet everything I'd been through here told me I was better off alone, not living with anyone. I couldn't pinpoint why I felt that way, but the thought hovered. I did want to be a part of the child that Alyse carried. I wanted to be there to hold the baby after it was born. Despite those yearnings, I also wanted to be right where I was doing what I was doing.

I didn't know if that made me a bad husband or not. I knew it made me feel guilty and that I wasn't worthy to be a parent to an innocent child. The flip side of that coin was that there were so many things I could teach a child.

I stuffed those thoughts in one of the recesses in my mind and told Alyse about meeting up with friends from training camp and rehashing missions with them without telling her anything about things happening here.

The Army cautioned us about giving too many details. Instead, I wrote those in my personal journal and told Alyse about close calls and little things that wouldn't get me in trouble. I told stories about the guys and the jokes we told. I also mentioned how much I missed reading newspapers.

A couple floated around the base, but someone else grabbed it whenever I went to find one, and it never resurfaced. I talked about feeling disconnected from the events because I hadn't gotten to read anything, and all I lived was the base life and the war. It was tedious.

After I finished that, I wrote a quick letter to Alicia and one to my parents. Those would go in the same envelope to save me from buying more. I stashed them in my bag and pulled out the journal to catch up. I knew there were things that I wouldn't remember from the last missions unless I wrote them down.

During the rest of the train ride back, my mind overflowed with quiet thoughts about the war, things I didn't like, and things I did. It sounded strange to hear myself think there were things I liked about war since it was generally bad.

I liked that I was fighting for other people's rights and protecting people back in America. I liked the closeness I shared with my crew and the friends I made over here. I knew those friendships would last me the rest of my life, even if I never saw them again. I liked facing the danger and coming out on top.

The other side of that was that I didn't particularly appreciate getting shot at or seeing other people hurt, and at times, I hated being the one who injured others. I was not too fond of the political games and having no freedom since the Army owned my life right now.

Despite that, I still wanted to be right where I was. I accepted the fact that it probably made me less desirable as a husband.

CHAPTER 33

April 8th, 1944

We should get a cluster this time, correct?" Jones asked me as we taxied down the runway.

"It's our tenth mission, so we should," I confirmed. I hadn't even thought about it until Jones mentioned it. "Looking to add to your decorations in hopes that some girl will find it impressive?"

"I don't need medals to be impressive," Jones scoffed. "I just need to say I'm your friend. Then, when they use me to get close to you, I spring that you are married and I swoop in for the prize."

Hausman laughed. "I feel sorry for whoever marries you."

The cluster Jones mentioned was an addition to our Air Medal in the form of a small bronze twig with four oak leaves and three acorns. It meant a second award of the same medal, in this case, the Air Medal.

Brunswick was our target this time. It was the Lower Saxony area near the North Sea. There was a ME-110 factory there that we were going to take out. Our group consisted of about two hundred aircraft from the 8th. It was a detrimental mission to aid the war effort. That was the line they told us.

I didn't doubt that taking out a manufacturing facility would put a crimp in Hilter's plans, though he always came up with some way to find more. Or he utilized whatever country he took over to make more. I didn't know. He was the parasite that wouldn't die.

More and more crews were painting their bombs to deliver messages that would never get to Hitler. He seemed to scoff in the face of our bombings and spread the word through his soldiers that Germany was winning. They were not winning, and I often wondered how many of his people believed the lies he spewed.

"On approach! Ready the eggs for release." Rogers radioed to the crew. I snapped back to attention. Our bomb doors opened, and then eggs fell out of the basket. I watched them fall and saw at least two if not more, hit the intended buildings and turn them into rubble. It was an incredible effort and successful to boot. I didn't dwell on the workers in the buildings or what it meant for those families. I couldn't.

"There's nothing left," Hausman called out. "They won't be making those planes there for a long while."

"Oh, shit! Incoming! One o'clock." Cutty screeched and we banked hard.

I swiveled my head and saw the fighters. The group in the lead encountered heavy resistance. Comms sprang to life with reports relayed between crews. Rogers maneuvered us to a position to help and our guns jumped to life. I did my best to shoot the enemy out of the sky, but I don't think we were much of a help as far back as we were. It didn't stop me from trying, though.

It was intense fighting and despite the cold air, I was sweating like crazy. My body was tense and it didn't relax even when I saw some of the enemy planes explode or go down in flames. It seemed like thousands of shells pooled at our feet while we held the triggers down, cramping our hands. There were over one hundred thirty enemy fighters attacking. My ears rang with the noise and I smelled nothing but gunpowder.

Each time a Liberator fell out of the sky, I wanted to scream out my rage. I counted no less than six that went down burning, very few of them with chutes deploying. There was too much smoke to see if chutes came out or not on some and we intently focused on aiming at the fighters.

"Die!" Cutty screamed as he pulled the trigger at a fighter that banked near our plane. I don't know if we got him or one of the other planes but it went down and blew up with the pilot inside. I didn't feel guilty for the vindication I felt.

One of the B-24s ahead of us exploded into a ball of flame that made Rogers jerk the plane to avoid debris taking out one of our engines. We did our best to keep our footing and eyes on the prize as every one of our gunners engaged in trying to help.

Miraculously, the only resistance we saw happened to the group of planes forward of our position. It played out before my eyes like a bad movie. Off to my three o'clock, I saw a P-38 take a hit and blow up five minutes after the B-24 took a hit. I was numb to it now. The number of planes I saw destroyed in this mission alone accomplished what the previous missions didn't. I detached from the pain of losing one of ours while flying. It might be different later, but for the moment, I remained focused.

We were taking heavy losses but it made me happy to see we were doing the same to the enemy. They weren't beating us and nor could I say we were winning. It wasn't enough on our side because we were still under fire and we continued to shoot and reload to fire more. We'd lost thirty-eight bombers by the time the air battle was over. Thirty-eight was a staggering number to me.

We needed to figure out which one of us had the guardian angel. It befuddled me how we took no damage. There was not one scratch on our girl or our crew. We landed, checked her over carefully, and found not one iota of damage. Given the sheer number of fighters we encountered, I didn't understand how that was possible.

"Count your blessings, men," I told them as we entered the barracks to drop gear before the debrief. "Someone up above is looking out for us."

"How do you figure that?" Cutty scoffed. "Did you see how many planes went down?"

"We didn't," Rogers pointed out. "I think that's what Suhm is referring to. With that many fighters attacking, how did we manage not to take one hit?"

CHAPTER 34

April 9th, 1944

N o rest for the wicked," I quipped. "War doesn't rest for Easter, though I wish it would."

"What would you have done instead?" Rogers asked as we took our seats on the plane for our eleventh mission. "It's not like we would get a delicious ham dinner here. Instead, we get to introduce Jesus to this FW-190 assembly plant and airfield."

"I don't think the Nazis believe in Jesus," I reminded him. "Hitler is their Jesus. Sad state of affairs, that."

"Focus, gents," Hausman interrupted us. "Let's be the Easter Bunny and deliver our eggs. We're going to Tutow, Germany, as they said in the briefing. A little history about the place: Allies bombed in 1943 and stalled the FW-190 production, but the production facility remained relatively intact. If we can be exact on our drops, we can make sure it gets hit this time. I'm getting to that point where I want out. I want to get married and have babies."

I laughed but sobered quickly. "Are the production facilities marked on that map?" I asked Rogers.

"Not specifically. Hausman, do you know which buildings they are and how do you know all this information?"

Rogers pulled the map out and handed it to Hausman.

"I listen," Hausman responded. He pointed out two buildings to Rogers. "Did you hear nothing at that briefing? These are the two we need to focus on. Look at the placement and size and think of the other airfields we've bombed and been at. It's not hard to figure out."

I raised my eyes at that comment but let it slide. We were all running on high emotions. Rogers didn't comment either, and from how he looked at the map, it appeared as though he was memorizing it. That was good enough for me.

The rest of the crew got to the plane and we began our preflight procedures. We gave the all-clear, loaded in, and got in line. Thirty-three other aircraft were in this raid along with us. Each plane carried twelve five-hundred-pound general-purpose bombs.

There were three groupings of planes, and we were in the third with about twelve heavy bombers. We caught word two groups had to turn back due to weather, but we didn't encounter the same problem.

There wasn't much talk on the way to Tutow. I figured after the attack yesterday, we were watching more carefully. Surprise attacks like that were a valuable learning lesson and it cost the base heavily. It wasn't fun to watch either, as any of us would confirm.

We arrived at the target without fanfare, dropped our Easter eggs and announced our presence loudly and boldly. I was happy to note that we succeeded where others failed, and those production facilities became rubble. Billowing smoke rose thousands of feet in the air, thick and black like a snake about to strike.

The sight was enough to make us cheer, though it was short-lived. As we left the target, we had the scare of our lives. We were flying into the sun and didn't see the thirty fighters that came out of nowhere and opened fire directly at us. They targeted the Liberators and as they shot, they flew directly through our formation while they fired and seemed to target more of the vulnerable bombers in the harder-to-defend positions. It didn't help that we had no fighter support.

It was why the instructors were so hard on us and tested us constantly. I had to swallow my heart to get it back into my chest. I held the gun in a death grip and opened fire almost at the same time as the other gunners. Rogers was cursing up a storm as he pitched the plane to avoid the bullets and crashing into an enemy. The formation broke apart as we engaged in battle.

One of the shots hit our number one engine cowling and lodged there. The fighters were a blur as they screamed past us with their guns blazing. I about broke into prayer when that was the only pass they made. We lucked out with only one bullet hit.

"Who else needs to change their drawers?" Hausman asked in a cautious tone.

Before anyone could answer, laugh, or agree, we saw one of the planes in our group get shot down by flak. The first shot fired from the ground was a direct hit. If I wasn't mistaken, the crew was on their last mission. My throat tightened painfully at the realization and I had to swallow a couple of times.

Eight chutes popped out of the plane and I expected it to spin down. Instead, it went end over end, and I wondered what got damaged to make that happen. I'd never seen a plane do that. My eyes tracked it to the ground, where it exploded on contact. The two that didn't make it out either died in the attack or on contact.

"God damn," Cutty yelled and thumped his fist into the side of the plane. "They were almost home free." His curse confirmed my suspicion of who they were.

"Safe landings," Hausman cried to the descending chutes as if they could hear him.

"Hoo-ah," came the simultaneous battle cry from all of us. A cry we hoped they felt as they landed in the enemy territory.

"Tough break," Jones said after they were no longer in sight. I was still too choked up to speak, so he said it.

"Tough break," the rest of the crew repeated. Perhaps one of the biggest understatements of the day. We lost ten planes and that didn't count the lost crew that no one heard from again after those eight crewmen landed in enemy territory.

Several crews wrote letters home after we returned, myself included. Sleep didn't come easy that night and throughout the barracks, we heard whispered prayers interrupted by nightmares and people gasping for air. It wasn't shocking, given what we'd seen.

CHAPTER 35

April 11th, 1944

Does it seem to you that each mission we go on, they get more difficult?" Cutty asked me.

"Sure does," I agreed. "I thought I was the only one that felt that way. Glad it's not just me."

"What did you think of the briefing?" Jones asked as we checked the bombs for a second time.

"Sometimes they give us a history lesson, and others it's like pulling teeth out of a fly." I shrugged. "I think they tell us what they think we want to hear. I don't know. That could be bitterness talking or lack of sleep."

"Probably both," Cutty added. "My feelings are similar to yours. Now that we are getting to our halfway mark, its as if they try to see what they can throw us into to see if we survive. It's rough watching those other planes going down and then feeling happy that it wasn't you."

"Yes, indeed. Talk about guilt." I shook my head and straightened. "That initial horror of seeing the plane hit, then the immediate feeling of joy that it wasn't you. It's shit." I didn't curse often but couldn't find another accurate word for the feeling.

"Don't dwell on it, guys." Rogers stepped close to us.

He looked no better than the rest of us with our dark circles under our eyes. "We've got all twelve loaded and secure?" Rogers gestured to the bombs. "Twelve bombs for our twelfth mission."

"Affirmative," Cutty answered before Jones could. "Time?" It wasn't our usual preflight routine and I think we all wanted to feel less alone.

"Yes. Oscherleben. An assembly plant and operational base, as they said. I would think that we could expect retaliation if it's operational. I like how they leave that part out of the briefing." Rogers changed his voice to mimic the guy who had given the briefing. "Soldiers, this will be an easy mission. Your goal is to bomb the assembly and base in Oscherleben. We have intel that makes this a high-priority target."

I chuckled and shook my head again. "You nailed it. Easy mission. The last one was supposed to be easy, too. I can probably name some guys who would disagree."

We took up our positions in the plane and then rolled into the line for takeoff. This factory made the bombers that Germany used and was one of their prime factories for the FW-190. If I had to guess, the area would be patrolled by several of the fighters—the same ones that tried to shoot us out of the sky last time.

I'd had plenty of experience learning how those planes maneuvered now that I'd seen them in action while they shot at us. I'd take one down, I vowed to myself, to avenge the planes I'd watched crash and explode.

The flight to the targets mainly was uneventful for each mission; it was after dropping the bombs that things tended to get hairy. That's when I needed to be at my most sharp and best. I learned more each time we went up and there were times it was hard not to get complacent and I had to work at it. Each mission might be the same in that we were dropping bombs, but nothing else was the same.

One could argue that getting shot at was the same; a bullet was a bullet. It wasn't true. A bullet that goes by you and doesn't touch you or the plane is just a bullet. But if it hits the plane, it could be a death warrant. Or if it goes through the plane and embeds in your body or through your body.

"Target in sight," Rogers called back. "Ready. Release."

We jumped into place, and our group dropped over a hundred bombs on the plant and base. Oily smoke rose in the air, obscuring our vision, and that's when the attack came. Eight ME-109s and FW-190s burst through the cloud of smoke and opened fire.

The sound of guns firing filled the air, and we wasted no time shooting back. The clink of shells hitting the plane floor was almost as loud as the firing of the guns. My heart hammered in my chest, almost in time with the bullets spewing from my gun. We yelled positions as loud as we could through comms to ensure the other guys heard where we were tracking and we answered each bullet they fired with four more. The smell of gunpowder was thick and mixed with the smoke from the bombs we had dropped.

The fighters tore through our formation, weaving in and out of Liberators, and the bastards managed to shoot down three of the bombers from our group. One of them held a crew that were all friends of mine. Guys that I hung out with and played cards with back on base. Fury rose in me so fast that I barely had time to react. Emotion took over.

Right after their plane went down, the pilot turned his guns to us. The square head made a mistake with that move. I was livid and I watched his every move. He buzzed our plane, got real close and I opened fire. I felt like I had nothing to lose, which wasn't the case.

The pilot approached us at a seven o'clock position and peeled off about three hundred yards away from me. I held that trigger down and didn't let up. I squeezed so hard that my hands turned white. I watched as pieces of his plane flew off and I didn't stop firing. He banked hard and slid down until the aircraft was standing on one wing, and then it went into a ninety-degree dive that he never came out of. I didn't let go of that trigger until he passed below the cloud line and I couldn't see him anymore.

"Yes! Nice shooting, Suhm!" Jones screamed, pumping his fists.

I'd gotten revenge for him killing my friends and some part of me was happy I'd shot him down. It battled with the sadness and was a strange paradox. I didn't have time to ponder all that it meant as we were still getting shot at by the enemy. I didn't have time to reflect on my emotions and wonder if I should feel bad for shooting another human out of the sky. I had a job to do and I was going to get it done by golly.

When we were back on base, I allowed myself to think about it. I went into the war office and made a claim on an enemy fighter for another cluster on my Air Medal. I told the story and had it corroborated by Rogers, Jones, Cutty, Hausman, Merrill, and Ribbits, who had all witnessed it. The officer told me I had an excellent claim and that he didn't see a problem with it going through. I'd have to wait for the official order on it, but I'd get my cluster, and every time I saw it, I'd remember my friends.

It appeared my old shooting eye still worked and was

in good shape. It didn't make up for the loss, but I did feel vindicated and like I'd done something that mattered. I lay on my cot and stared at the ceiling for a while. Today was my first claimed kill. The thought repeated and I didn't know if I should feel good about taking a life.

We'd already received orders for another mission tomorrow, our thirteenth. I wasn't sure I would come down before then but I knew I needed some sleep. I didn't eat with the rest of the crew. I lay there and tried not to think.

CHAPTER 36

April 12th, 1944

Our orders were for Laufen, Germany, and it would have been our thirteen mission. It got scrubbed part way through and we turned back to base. Rogers received word that we'd do it tomorrow instead. The command didn't give us a reason why, only to abort. Sometimes, we wondered how and why the calls got made, though none of us ever asked.

I wasn't naturally superstitious, though I felt them creep up on my brain anyway. Tomorrow was the thirteenth; it would be our thirteenth mission, and I lived in barracks number thirteen. The timing of it all was ironic.

We've had uncanny luck on our missions for all the talk about thirteen being an unlucky number and us being in that barracks. Yet that was an awful lot of thirteens to deal with and the anxiety was getting to me. Maybe they'd all cancel each other out. I'd never had an aversion to the number thirteen before and I can't say I liked growing one now, on the eve of the thirteenth.

I'd become the new owner of Salvo the Dog, his third new owner. He belonged to one of the crew that went down the other day. Before that, he was owned by one of the eight that went missing after bailing over enemy territory. I didn't want to make the poor guy have another new master if something happened to us out there with all those thirteens floating around.

Phew! The nerves this gave me were something else. Even my stomach felt upset and I was sure it was all in my mind. No one told me that war would have an effect like this on a person. Take someone with no anxieties or superstitious beliefs and then pile them on and expect us to be okay.

I doubted I would sleep much tonight, though I had to try. Going out on missions with no sleep was dangerous and stupid. I understood that it was sometimes necessary. However, being afraid of the number thirteen wasn't a good reason. I needed to get a grip. I popped up out of my cot.

"Who wants to play poker?" I asked the guys in the barracks. "I need distractions and writing a letter home right now probably wouldn't go well since I'd say nonsense and worry everyone."

"How about a run first?" Rogers suggested. "I've found that running is a great way to clear my mind because it focuses instead on putting one foot in front of the other so I don't fall on my face."

"He has a point," Merrill answered. "I'd be up for a run."

It wasn't what I wanted to do. Regardless, I was smart enough to admit it was what I needed to do. At least I'd get to play cards with a clear mind and possibly not lose as much as I would in my distracted state.

"Sure," I agreed and stretched.

"Fine." Jones sighed. "Want to bet on who will win?"

"Not a chance." Ribbits groaned. "Suhm has the longest stride out of all of us. I already lose to him too much at poker. No need to lose more."

"Point to Ribbits on that," Cutty agreed. "So, are we going to run as a crew?"

Carlson and Young stood up and nodded. Warren was already standing and we all headed outside after Rogers since it was his idea. The day was overcast and mild, so at least we wouldn't die of heatstroke under the summer sun.

Rogers set the pace fast enough to push us without killing us. We had to work to maintain it and after the first couple of miles, we all huffed from the effort. I hated to admit that it felt good and was working. By the fourth mile, my lungs were burning and my mind was clear. We completed the run after the fifth mile and sat outside to cool down.

"Okay, I admit it," Jones said, flopping on his back. "I feel better."

"I'll admit to being thirsty," Ribbits panted. Rogers threw a canteen at Ribbits and laughed.

"Suhm, what about you?" Rogers asked.

"I feel pretty good," I replied after sucking down half my canteen. "My mind is clear now and my muscles feel stretched out and used. Good call, boss."

"Still want to play poker?" Cutty asked me.

"I do," I answered with a grin. "After a shower. Some of you stink."

"And you are a bouquet of roses." Jones smirked. "Not that I am against a shower because it would feel great right now."

"Okay." I stood up. "Shower, food, then poker. How's that sound?"

"Deal." Rogers heaved himself to his feet. "Man, getting up was harder than it should be at this age."

"None of us are that old yet." Ribbits grinned as he quickly popped to his feet. "Food is always good. Sounds like a good plan to me."

That's what we did. It all seemed trite, but putting ourselves in a better frame of mind took creativity sometimes. While cards was an easy go-to for us, the exercise helped more than I think any of us thought it would. The little things like going out of our way to raise our spirits helped us cope with the war and the things we'd seen.

Remaining stuck in that gloomy place in our minds wasn't doing us any good. I wasn't advocating us to shove it down and ignore it, only for us not to dwell on it. We had a lot to process and every small act we could do to help was necessary. We all needed laughter.

"Okay," I said a few hours later. "Five card draw is the game, and sixes are wild. Who's ready to lose their money?"

"In your dreams, Suhm. Don't you remember last time when you lost all yours?" Cutty smirked.

"It's a new day, Cutty, and I'm feeling lucky." I grinned as I shuffled the cards.

CHAPTER 37

April 13th, 1944

Did anyone else realize the irony of today?" I asked the crew as we prepared for takeoff. "It's our thirteenth mission, on April 13th, and we live in the barracks thirteen." It obviously hadn't left my mind and I was grateful I'd gotten a little sleep despite that.

"Lucky thirteen," Hausman joked. "I jest, but we've been fortunate so far, so maybe it's our lucky number."

"You fools aren't superstitious, are you?" Rogers asked as he belted in. "And truthfully, that's a lot of thirteens for one day. Hell of a coincidence since yesterday was supposed to be our thirteenth. Maybe command has a sense of humor."

"Not likely." I laughed. Yet, I found myself wearing my parachute, my G.I. shoes, and had my knife on me and everything else I could think of to keep myself alive and safe. I wasn't trying to tempt the fates or whoever else was looking down on us and wondering how they day could be more exciting and challenging. Jones hadn't said a word, and I noticed he geared up like I did. At least it wasn't just me. That gave me a small measure of comfort.

"Okay, another airfield," Rogers told us as we taxied.

"We were all at the briefing. We know what we are up against. We've experienced many of these and are going south of Munich."

"Oberpfaffenhofen," I stated, stumbling over the name. It was a mouthful. "My gut tells me we'll encounter resistance."

"Mine's saying the same thing, Suhm," Rogers agreed, the comms a little staticky today. "I like that you have your chute on, and given our last experience, I'd suggest all of you get them on before we get in the air. We've been lax and seen too many planes go down as of late. If we prepare for the worst, then we are a step ahead."

"If you don't believe in superstition, why jinx us?" Hausman asked as he strapped his chute on. "Putting them on now when we've had such good luck seems like we are asking for trouble."

"Don't put it on then," I told Hausman. "I'm trusting my gut." It wasn't three minutes later and Hausman had his chute strapped on.

True to form, our flight to the target was uneventful and our bombs dropped with precision and accuracy. We destroyed the airfield. This place was the factory airfield of the Nazis and it didn't bother me one bit to watch it burn. That place was no longer in action and I smiled at the thought.

"Eight o'clock," Ribbits yelled, dropping chaff. Cutty joined in on the other window, both throwing chaff as if their lives depended on it, which they might. I swiveled and began firing and immediately noticed how much tighter my space was, which slightly threw my aim off. Despite that, I wasn't going to remove my chute.

Enemy fighters began shooting at the group and their aim was accurate this time. Our crew's guardian angels were with us because nothing hit our plane again—a miracle in and of itself. In fact, none of the group lost a plane. We watched as others took hits, though it was nothing that took them down. Clouds of black smoke filled the air around us, inhibiting our views.

I couldn't get any shots lined up without shooting through one of our own planes, which was frustrating, but our position was good in that we were protected along with the other planes. It was those on the outside of the formation that took the most damage, yet nothing critical.

I lost count of how many German planes I saw and not one available crack at them. I kept firing when they were within range, though I don't think I got any hits. Shells pooled around my feet, and I heard Warren and Young giving it their best efforts, too. It felt like hours but was nothing more than ten minutes. Getting shot at tended to distort time, I came to realize. When the battle ended, we remained vigilant and focused. We didn't want a repeat, especially with strung-tight nerves. I think we all felt like our luck would run out at some point.

After landing at the home base, the entire crew circled our plane at least twice, looking for a hole or some damage; there was not a single scratch. I lay my hand on the plane's side and paid her all the respect I had to give. She'd seen us through again.

"Debrief," Rogers reminded me gently. "I'm not normally superstitious, Suhm, but I am sure glad you showed the preparedness you did. That battle could have easily gone a different direction given that the inside planes didn't have clear shots."

"It's funny," I said as I fell in step with him. "I'm not superstitious either. I couldn't shake the feeling of needing that chute and thoughts of all those thirteens kept me from my normal sleep. It didn't hurt to be ready for anything. I don't normally wear my knife either. Yet I had that thing strapped on tight. Jones did, too."

"Maybe being in these conditions taps into those extra senses that some crews talk about," Rogers mused. "I can't say I'm a big believer of that either. We've all had instincts, and whether we chose to follow them or not, it led to things that might or might not be pleasant. I think here, it's more important we pay attention to those. It seems that those instincts get sharper with every mission, at least for me. If I didn't follow them, I believe we would have been damaged or downed by now."

Jones dropped back to walk with us. "What are you two looking so serious about?" he elbowed me in the side.

"Instincts," I supplied with a smug grin. "You know, those things that made you put all your gear on today."

"Couldn't hurt." Jones shrugged. "But I get it. There was something that felt like today would be a good day to wear. And look, nothing happened."

"Did it not happen because we prepared and the fates looked down from their perch and saw it and decided not today, they are ready for it? Or did it not happen because we are lucky?" I threw the questions out to the men.

Rogers chuckled and shrugged. "I have no answer for that."

Jones looked thoughtful for a second. "I wonder if the fates are single?"

CHAPTER 38

April 22nd, 1944

Listen up!" a general called out to the gathered crews for our briefing. The noise level died down and the crews all sat a little straighter and gave their undivided attention to the men at the front of the room.

I sat back in my chair and crossed my ankle over my knee. The space was cramped and my lanky frame took up much of it. It had been nine days since our last mission, which felt like a long time, though the first four days, I mostly slept, and soundly too. We flew a couple of times as support but not missions with an objective like the one we were about to be handed. I wasn't sure why those didn't count toward our total mission count, but they didn't.

"Your mission today will take you right over the Ruhr Valley. That knowledge is important for a variety of reasons. The first is that this is where the heaviest concentration of ground guns is located. I'm not sending any of you in that area blindly. Expect flak; expect to be hit. Be prepared. The second reason this is important is that the Germans will protect this valley to the death; this is where their coal mines are. The valley is not our target, but you have to fly over it," the general stated.

Could they not find any other route than sending us over the field of flak guns? I thought to myself. These missions were borderline insane. Yet I still wondered what it was like for our guys on the ground. *Was it a relief when they heard us overhead, or did they worry we'd miss and hit them? Did we create more chaos for them, or were we helping?* The questions were endless and I needed to focus.

"Today, your job is to drop your payload on the marshaling yards in Hamm." The general's voice snapped me back to the moment. "The marshaling yards are a strategic location for us because of the number of train cars in and out of this station, and we want to make sure their supply lines are interrupted. The Brits have targeted this several times, as have we. We keep at it to keep them down. Get to work, soldiers." The general shuffled his papers and stepped off to the side.

It wasn't much of a briefing, and I think it was more of a warning than anything else, which is more than we got for most missions. It was better than being told it would be an easy mission. I filed out the door with the rest of the crew and met up with Rogers, who was waiting for us.

"Number fourteen, fellas," Rogers said when we were all present. "Questions?"

No one answered. Of course, we all had questions, but no one had answers for them, so we kept them to ourselves. We reviewed safety routes, should we take damage, and alternate landing sites—same situation as always.

The difference this time was we were taking off in the afternoon at four-thirty instead of the early morning. Night raids had their good points. In this case, I believed they had us going at night to increase our odds of survivability. Flying over the Ruhr Valley in broad daylight was a suicide mission.

We had time to spare before we had to begin preflight procedures and we all separated to do whatever we wanted or needed to do. It was time to write letters home, knowing that the danger level of this mission was high before we even embarked on it. Young, Merrill, Carlson, Warren, and Rogers did the same. I didn't know where the others were.

I wrote my letters to Alyse, Alicia, and my parents and got them addressed and in the envelopes about the same time as Merrill. I offered to take his letter to the mailbag and he nodded his thanks. I walked out and saw the others engaged in a card game with another crew on the mission that night. After I dropped the letters, I joined them for a few hands for some relaxation before we took off for the flak-filled skies.

Rogers called us to gear up and we all got ready. There wasn't much talking or joking among us, more a quiet resignation of a difficult night. We filed out of the barracks behind Rogers and headed to the airfield with the other crews participating doing the same. We ran through preflight checks and boarded our girl, waiting for our position to taxi.

We went largely unnoticed on our flight to the target; there was very little flak. I expected more, given the location. Perhaps someone heard the drone of engines and sat out there all night until they heard us approach on the way back. Or it could be that our mostly successful bomb drops on the railways got their attention and they waited for our return, knowing the route we'd have to take. However, that wasn't entirely correct since we were under attack before all the bombs fell.

It wasn't much before we dropped, but it was there. I watched other planes take damage, though thankfully, none of it was critical, only superficial. It was enough to get our blood pumping through our bodies, though. We dropped our bombs successfully, hit the targets, and ensured we saw the destruction. We couldn't verify if all the buildings received damage because it was dark. Then we headed back to base.

I had never seen as much flak as I did that night. Rogers performed some beautiful, evasive flying, though it seemed a large portion of our luck ran out. We came under heavy fire, and I could barely hear the shouts of my crew through the comms over my ears as we did everything we could to fire back and get away. Between the plane's engines, guns firing, shells dropping, static on the comms, and the frantic voices reporting damage, I was shocked I could hear anything at all. To add to the noise was the sound of my rapid heartbeat, keeping time with the shots.

Well-aimed fire peppered the fuselage with holes and perforated our wings into sorry shape. Smoke filled the air outside and inside the plane. Not only that but our entire electrical system got shot out. I don't know how Rogers kept us in the air. I don't understand how none of us became a war statistic that night. Religious beliefs aside, every one of us men said more than one prayer that we made it back.

Explosions, shrieking metal, and the whining sound of bullets screaming through the air were audible over the sounds of guns firing. It felt like chaos and all we could do was aim our weapons at where the shots originated from and hope something hit the shooters to ease the firing at us.

There was no time for thoughts other than muttered prayers that we made it back alive. It was firing the guns, analyzing the damage as it happened, and watching our engines for smoke, damage, or worse, fire. We ducked when something sounded like it was heading for us and called out positions of guns firing at us. It lasted entirely too long.

Not only were we contending with the Germans, but when we crossed back over into British airspace, we were shot at by the damn Limeys. With the night as dark as it was, they couldn't tell we were the Allies, and they opened fire at the first sight of planes over their territory.

This time, I heard the cussing Rogers let loose and we had a more precarious situation than we did in Germany because of the lack of electrical systems. Rogers swiftly moved into evasive maneuvers but we didn't shoot back. It wouldn't be right even though we all wanted to. Adrenaline was high after we made it through that battle and our trigger fingers were itchy.

One of the Liberators banked out over the water to try and evade but got shot right out of the sky. It was too dark to see if anyone made it out alive before it exploded over the sea. It was disheartening and tragic. As much as I wanted to blame them or shoot back out of anger, I didn't. It was dark and we had Germans on our tails for most of the flight back. Young was having a hell of a time back there. I hated to admit it, but the mistake was easy to make in that situation.

"Tough break," I called out. The crew repeated it back with quiet reverence. We didn't know which plane it had been.

Once we arrived back at home base before landing, Jones realized we still had two bombs in our racks that didn't drop, and Rogers had to take us over the sea where we could manually drop them before landing. Jones and I struggled to free them. They were finally released and no more unexploded munitions remained. After sustaining the damage like we did, it wasn't safe to try and land with those on board. It could send us to our maker before we were ready.

When we got rid of those last two bombs and

returned to our airfield, we were shocked to see it on fire. We had no idea if that meant our base was under attack or not, so Rogers diverted us to Attlebridge. There wasn't one complaint among the crew about the decision.

Here's what I can say about Rogers: that man can fly. We had no landing lights, it was darker than dark outside, we sustained a lot of damage, and there were no runway lights. It's a miracle we survived any of it, and Rogers was a good reason we all lived. He landed us safely and we about kissed the ground when we jumped out of our plane. Our limbs shook from adrenaline and fear and it took us a few moments to gather our wits.

One of my buddies was on the ground crew and he brought us to the mess hall. His crew shared some much-needed booze with our crew. Even Rogers drank. We told them what happened and when they called us in to debrief, we found our nerves still strung tight.

We stayed the night while some of the mechanics worked on our plane. I didn't like that as I felt it should be me fixing our old girl since she'd seen us through. Rogers put his foot down and threatened to tie me to the cot if I didn't get some sleep.

When we left for home base the following day, a lot of work still needed to be completed, but the repair crew mostly restored the electrical system. We landed and went in for another debrief, and that's when we learned that the fire we saw resulted from two of our group crash-landing. One of the planes hit a radar shack and exploded, taking a couple of guys with it, though most were able to get out.

I didn't think any plane in that raid came through unscathed. Stories spread throughout the base on what we encountered, and it took us a couple of days to get our girl back in working order. She deserved all the tender, loving care we could give her. I was glad to do it, too.

After that mission, I wrote another letter home and told my wife I hoped we never had another like it. We never got told how many we lost that night, but I knew it was more than the two guys who didn't escape on the crash landing. Not with as many holes as I saw over the spread of planes on that raid, not to mention the aircraft shot down by friendly fire over the sea.

CHAPTER 39

April 25th, 1944

L ook here." Cutty pointed to the map handed to us. "Mannheim marshaling yard extends from here to here. These buildings here," he circled an area with his finger, "need to be hit." We'd already been in the briefing and received our mission orders. We couldn't help wanting a little more after the previous mission.

It was our fifteenth mission, and with the completion of this one, we'd received our second cluster to our Air Medal. This railway station was the second largest in Germany. Taking it out would be a boon to the Allies. We wouldn't be the first to bomb it, though keeping it out of commission was integral to the war effort to halt Germany. It was a line we heard often and were used to receiving.

"Let's look at the surrounding cities to see if anything about any of these places stands out to anyone," Rogers suggested, and we all studied the map closely and communicated what we knew if anything.

It wasn't futile, though it might seem that way to others. Rogers, myself included, believed that the more we knew, the better prepared we were for whatever may come our way. Granted, it was war, and what we might encounter was unpredictable. Knowledge was still crucial and the briefing didn't give us much.

"This marks our halfway point, guys," I reminded them after we loaded up and did our preflight checks. "Let's not get cocky or complacent. I want us all to get home."

Each of our crew put our hands together and did a quiet "Hoo-ah." Rogers started the plane and we took our place in line when it was our turn.

The weather changed while we were en route and when we finally arrived at our target, the cloud cover was too thick and heavy to see the yards. We didn't have a Pathfinder, otherwise known as PFF, along on this mission with us. Last minute decision was to go further. We dropped our bombs on a small town. A flurry of communication from the lead planes volleyed back and forth until they decided on where to release since these were bombs we couldn't return to home base with due to fuses.

It was the first place we came to that we could see the ground without the clouds, which happened to be right outside a town. We did nothing other than scare the hell out of a lot of civilians. The lead crew told the rest of the groups that we had permission to drop on a city as they wanted the Germans to experience the same as they did to others. I have to say that we didn't aim for houses. It wasn't our goal to randomly kill people, but we had to drop the load and the decision wasn't mine to make.

Without the PFF, hitting the yards accurately without taking out a passenger train, or something equally wrong, bombing the city was the best we could do. The PFFs were the planes that located and marked targets with flares, giving the bombers something to aim for, and it increased our accuracy and our successes on raids. It wasn't ideal to do a mission without one, yet it was becoming a regular thing lately.

I hated to call the mission easy; nonetheless, it was. Compared to the others we'd been on recently, it was simple. There were no enemy fighters spotted, and we encountered very little flak. The shots that came at us didn't hit anything. Not one plane received damage. Even the weather seemed warmer. It was only about twenty-five below zero this time. Balmy compared to forty below.

We landed and did our debrief. After that, there wasn't much to do. The quieter guys went to their cots and wrote letters home. I thought about it but I didn't have much to say. I felt restless and antsy. Roller skating would have been a perfect activity for me and that wasn't happening here. A dance would have sufficed but the Army didn't give us a pass.

I daydreamed about sailing and decided to sketch a new boat for me to build. I hadn't thought of being on the water in a while, and it suddenly tugged hard on my soul. I could almost feel the rolling waves beneath me as I drew. The salty air of the seas drifted past my nose, and the wind ruffled my hair. I could feel the fibers of the ropes for the sails grate against my palm as I positioned them where they needed to be to catch the air currents.

The sound of the water slicing against my hull lulled me even farther away from Norwich. I soon didn't remember the war, getting shot at, bombing cities, and worrying about making it back alive. I was on the water, flying across the waves in my boat, until the land masses became distant memories. It was nothing more than me and the water.

My pencil flew over the paper as I designed a new hull that incorporated some new lines on crafts I had seen since I left the States. I made the vessel a little longer and broader, added a mast, and sketched out a beauty of a boat. It would be big enough for a family.

I didn't know this drawing would become a reality, but I could dream. It would take me a couple of years to craft this. Alyse wasn't a big fan of sailing, but I could teach my child how to sail. We could do something together as they grew, a boy or a girl. I'd enjoy passing that knowledge on to the next generation. They could even help me build once they were old enough.

"Damn, Suhm," Hausman breathed out as he plopped down next to me. "I didn't know you were an artist."

The interruption jarred me and brought me back into the present. "I'm not," I replied, dropping the paper to the cot. "I build boats, though. Even won some races with one that I built."

"That's beautiful," Hausman stated as he picked up the paper and studied it. "Maybe I'll have you build me one after we leave this place. I don't know how to sail, but I could learn, right?"

"Of course," I answered with a smile. "I could even teach you."

CHAPTER 40

April 26th, 1944

After the afternoon of relaxing and designing a new boat, my mind felt different. I knew once I got home, I'd be doing some sailing. It was funny how much I didn't realize I missed it until I started to draw. The entire experience had become cathartic and soothing the more I did it. It was almost as much of an escape as actually sailing, given the circumstances of where I was.

"Don't you wish you could predict how a mission will go?" Jones asked the crew. We'd had our briefing, done our preflight, and were loaded on the plane waiting for our turn to taxi. Some sort of delay had happened, and we shut down while crews worked to resolve it. "It'd be nice to know if we could relax in the air."

Cutty rolled his eyes at the comment, though I halfway agreed. Prediction would be a valuable skill to have in these situations. Our sixteenth mission was to head to an airfield in Gutersloh, Germany. It was a Junker base.

"What's with this weather?" Hausman wondered. The weather was overcast more than usual, and it looked like a storm would roll in. The air grew chilled, wind speeds were picking up, and the darkness of the clouds was foreboding. It didn't mean there was weather over our target, though.

I was beginning to think the other five men on our crew never spoke. It was always the same five of us that had comments. However, it could be that we five were the ones closest outside of the plane, so we were more comfortable with each other. We did try to include them in our activities. Sometimes, they spoke, and I supposed our surprised turns of the head and how we stared when they did, didn't help the situation.

Young came up from the back of the plane and shook his head at me. "Milk run."

It was all he said before returning to his position and I repeated it to the other. A milk run was what we called a routine mission with very low danger. I was guessing that the changing of the season had something to do with the weather patterns we'd seen as of late.

"A milk run would be a nice change," I said with a shrug. "If we ever get off the ground."

"10-10 cloud cover." Rogers called it before we even took off. "Oh, here we go."

The crew took up our positions as we pulled over to the runway and taxied. The lift-off was bumpy due to unstable air currents, and I hoped it would even out. None of us liked the turbulence and it made our jobs more difficult.

We were over the coast of the enemy territory, loaded with bombs that we didn't drop. The call came in that the base scrubbed the mission due to the weather. The clouds had rolled in fast and heavy and there was no seeing through them. It was a churning sea of gray under us. I caught sight of some bursts of flak that broke through. It wasn't anywhere near us.

"Two o'clock, about a thousand yards," I warned

through the comms.

"Some square head must be bucking to make PFC," Cutty joked. "You see how bad that was?"

"He'll never get the rank shooting that way," I replied. "I don't mind if he doesn't get closer to us."

"No," Rogers agreed. "They can't see us. Guy is probably guessing where we are using the sound of our engines."

"Don't jinx us," Hausman turned to tell us. "I'm not in the mood for another battle with ground guns."

"Are you ever in the mood for that?" Carlson asked. "I'm not."

"Sometimes," Hausman confirmed. "It's a good way to relieve the stress that builds."

"You are crazy." Carlson laughed. "A five-mile run will do that and no one is shooting at you."

I nodded my head in agreement. "I'd rather run than get shot out of the sky. Good point, Carlson."

A few more flak explosions popped up in my view and I called those out, noting the position and approximate distance. They were still a way off from any of our planes. Considering the density of the clouds and no visibility, it seemed like a waste of ammunition. I couldn't blame them for trying, as I didn't know what the ground troops experienced.

Nothing else happened on the way back and we landed with no fanfare. We debriefed, were handed orders for the next day, and returned to the barracks. It wasn't quite time for dinner and no one was in the mood to play another card game. Neither did anyone suggest a run since the weather was dismal.

Instead, Young and Carlson came to ask me about the drawing of the boat I'd done since they heard Hausman talking to me about it. It turned out that Young had experience sailing, though not a lot. He wanted to learn more about the sport and we talked about it for a few hours until the dinner bell rang.

"That was unexpected," Rogers said as we exited the barracks. "It was good to see those guys interacting."

"It was, to both your points," I agreed. "Some guys are naturally quiet. I think both are uncomfortable being over here and in a war. I didn't ask them why they enlisted or if they had their number called. I have to remind myself that not everyone wants to be over here. The draft didn't give them a choice."

"You're right." Rogers looked at me in surprise. "I didn't even think of that. Thanks for the reminder, Suhm. You're a smart kid."

"Kid." I scoffed. "I'm married with a baby on the way. Germans have shot at me. I don't think the term kid applies anymore."

"Sadly, that's true for all of us regardless of age," Rogers stated, clapping me on the back.

CHAPTER 41

April 27th, 1944

"A nyone else tired?" I asked after the briefing. We had a couple of hours before we had to be in the sky. I sat on my cot, my mind wandering and feeling exhausted down to my bones.

"I think we all are," Rogers replied quietly. "It doesn't matter, though; we have our jobs to do. These raids for the V-rockets are difficult because intel is always sketchy."

"No Ball raids," I mumbled and shook my head. I still remember the rumors surrounding this area that they used slaves from the German camps for labor. "Anyone else counting?"

"Number seventeen," Jones answered. "I'm counting them all every time."

"Me too." I grinned. "I should have a baby any day now. Did I tell you guys that?"

"You did." Hausman jogged in place, trying to burn some extra energy off before being caged in a plane. "So, let's not do anything stupid so you get to meet the baby."

Rogers rolled his eyes at us. "Let's not do anything stupid regardless. I don't think Suhm would be happy if any of us didn't make it home because we did something dumb."

"That's right. Here's a thought for you to think about. By the time this war is over, there won't be anything left of Pas-de-Calais," I remarked. I'd needed to change the conversation so I didn't get stuck in the headspace of second-guessing myself to make sure I didn't do anything stupid. "With these gigantic bombs, it will be even worse. Four two-thousand-pound bombs. Have we ever had a payload this size?"

"Not that I can recall," Rogers confirmed, rolling with the change. "These are going to make a mess. I sincerely hope that no one is in that area. I can't even imagine the fallout."

While we killed time, we decided to do a sit-up contest to see who could do the most. Turns out Young held that record, with a second place to Carlson. My money had been on Jones, but those two surprised me. It got rid of a little pent-up energy and when the time rolled around for us to head out and start preflight checks, we were all in a better mood.

I got my first glimpse of the monster bombs and shook my head. These would leave craters, that's for sure. As each guy got on the plane, they cast looks over at the bombs with raised eyebrows. They weren't messing around with wanting this V-Rocket site gone and out of business.

"Those are big," Jones breathed out. "I'm happy there are only four. Fingers crossed none get stuck."

"I'll second that," Hausman joked. "Fingers crossed those drop and get off our girl."

Both Rogers and I rolled our eyes and got down to business. We were in the middle of the pack this time, so our wait for take-off wasn't too long. Our wheels left the ground and my eyes scanned the sky.

The weather wasn't against us this time; it was a

perfect flight. No bad weather, no enemies. There were about one hundred Liberators in our group with the big bombs. We were going to be seeing a whole lot of destruction. I had a pair of binoculars and watched as the bombs fell.

It was devastating when our usual five-hundred-pound bombs dropped and leveled buildings, streets, and anything in its path. Two thousand pounds was a terrifying sight to witness yet oddly beautiful at the same time. The patterns of explosions, shock waves that rippled across the earth, the color of the fires, and then the black pillars that rose like magic reaching for the sky all created a tapestry of destruction.

Our group hit the jackpot this time and we obliterated the site that held the gun emplacements. I watched through the binoculars as bombs hit and wiped them out of existence. There was nothing left but dust, rubble, and growing plumes of smoke. Cheers rose across the plane, even the five that never joined our banter.

"Targets hit," Rogers confirmed through comms. "Back to base."

We turned to head back to home base and we were suddenly under fire. Calls were rapid through the comms, with Rogers repeating what was said and radioing back our damage, position, and shooting position. It was the most accurate flak I'd seen yet. The orchestra of gunfire was underway. One piece came through my waist window, cut right through my coveralls over my right forearm and went out the other window without ever breaking my skin. It would have gone entirely through my forearm if it hadn't been at an angle.

"I might need a change of clothes after that one," I yelled, though I didn't think any of them could hear me over the whistling of air coming through the holes in our plane and the sound of flak hitting and bursting around us. There wasn't time to ruminate on the close call. I grabbed my gun and began to fire, swiveling to each position, calling out and holding the trigger down.

My hands were shaking and adrenaline raced through my body like there was a prize at the end of it. We kept our guns going until the battle was behind us, which took much longer than we wanted. We didn't have a chance to check with anyone else until we were back on the ground. Rogers radioed our damage when we reported a hit, and that was it. It appeared no one escaped the bullets this time.

There were no injuries, but our girl had to go to the subdepot to get repaired. She had so many holes in her she could have been Swiss cheese. I counted about thirty, but I only counted the sizable holes. I don't know how many she had altogether. True to form, she'd kept us alive and well. I patted her side and murmured my quiet thanks as if the plane could hear me. Without her skin, I wouldn't have any.

Thankfully, tomorrow, we'd get a day of rest. My plans included sleep—a lot of it. I felt like my nerves had taken heavy fire and I was exhausted mentally and physically. We all were. Rogers's eyes had a sunken appearance, and his face was pale. Carlson looked like he was going to drop where he stood.

We still had a debrief to get through, and then we all could drop like bombs. I figured Ribbits, Cutty, and Jones would head to town once they received their pass. I might after a day of sleep. Then again, I might stay on base and decompress.

CHAPTER 42

May 1st, 1944

W hat are we going to do when we hit thirty missions?" Jones asked. "The next one will be number eighteen."

"The next one is now." Rogers strode into the barracks and waved some papers around. "Briefing in thirty. Same place."

I finished my letter, sealed it, and addressed it. Jones groaned and shifted to pull his flight uniform on. I had to pull my shoes off first, so I started doing that when Hausman piped up.

"You aren't supposed to undress, Suhm," Ribbits joked. "Regulations require us to wear the uniform and not bare it all. It gets awfully cold up there."

"That's one way to scare the Germans." Cutty laughed and slapped his knee.

"Your luck, they'd like it and chase us just to see more," I replied and yanked my uniform on. "You're a disturbed fellow."

"You are all clowns," Rogers said, shaking his head yet smiling. "Guess that's one way to escape fitness training. Another mission to the same exact place."

"I think I'd rather run, do push-ups, play with weights,

and whatever else they had in store for us," I grumbled. "Less stress."

"I hate to say it, but I'm with you on that," Jones muttered. "And you all know how much I hate fitness training."

"Personally, I'd rather eat," Ribbits declared. "Where's the training on how to eat more without getting sick?"

"That's called marriage," Young joked in a rare moment of solidarity. "My dad says you grow as a person." Young stretched his arms out to either side of him. "In this direction."

We all laughed, breaking the tension of having another run four days after getting shot up in the area we'd be returning to. I guessed that meant we didn't get all the tunnels caved in and unusable or missed some gun emplacements.

We sat in the small briefing room on base for the briefing and managed to refrain from commenting on the location we were just at when we got shot up. It wasn't something I think any of us looked forward to. The memories of the last time were still fresh in our heads and even newer now that we were going back.

"No two missions are alike," I told the crew as we filed onto the airfield for our preflight check. It was more to boost my own spirit than anything else. I figured the rest could do with the reminder the same way I could. "This could end up being a walk in the park if the park held snipers."

"That's one way to look at it. Pas-de-Calais hasn't been overly friendly for us," Hausman said as he began his preflight duties.

"We haven't been friendly with the coast of France

either," I pointed out. "We aren't going there to plant trees."

"It's an egg drop, gentleman," Rogers stated calmly. "Late Easter present. We do our job, get back and add another mission to our bedpost. One closer to going home."

"I've got so many marks there already; I must be good," Ribbits told us as he made his way to the back. "Never had a complaint before. I'm going to run out of room to put notches."

"There can't be a complaint if there's never been a lady," I replied with a straight face.

That was the icebreaker that changed the mood on the plane. Score one for Young and one for me. Laughter rang out and smiles were all around. Hausman even slapped his knee; he laughed so hard. I felt like these guys were my family, my brothers, and it did my soul good to hear them all laughing. We were together all the time.

Our position in the formation was the middle again. I didn't mind being in the middle. Mostly, I was happy I wasn't in a fighter plane for these missions. Those men had stomachs of steel to fly the way they had to.

We took off and got into formation and once again, we were back on our way to France to ruin the coastline—the joys of No Ball raids. Very little communication took place on the way over, and we encountered no resistance. So far, so good.

The group dropped their bombs on the command and we watched them hit and kept our eyes peeled for flak and fighters. The lead crew called it a successful mission, and we saw very little flak and no enemy fighters. We did get peppered with some holes, so the flak that happened was accurate. The enemies hit nothing critical and we were still in the air.

It was a much better experience than our last time here. When we returned to the base, we checked our girl over and found only six holes. Compared to the previous time, it was nothing. She was getting to look like a patchwork quilt but flew as good as new. I'd try to patch her up if they didn't have something else lined up for us, like another mission or more training.

After we debriefed and rid ourselves of the flight uniform, we met back at the mess hall, got a meal, and talked about life in general. Carlson, Merrill, and Warren talked a bit more and we listened raptly to their views on the war and life back in the States. Then Young suggested naming our plane.

As a crew, we finally named her. We chose to call her Q-Bar Queenie. They nominated me to paint a Varga girl on her side, too. One of those pinup girls on our Queenie would make her that much more special and luckier. I was tasked with drawing her, getting the crew's approval, and then painting her on our girl.

That was the mission I needed to get my head back in place. In the recesses of my mind, I'd been thinking about Alyse and wondering if she'd had the baby yet and what it was. The thought was on permanent replay in my mind every time I had a down moment. Painting the plane was perfect to occupy my thoughts and as soon as we returned to the barracks, I grabbed a piece of paper and began to sketch.

CHAPTER 43

May 7th, 1944

Any word?" Ribbits asked as he walked in from showering. We'd had intense fitness training and a refresher course on fuses that morning. A couple of the newer crews were in it with us.

"On what?" I replied. "A mission?" I was getting ready to hit the showers next. I let the other guys go before me.

"On if you are a dad or not," Ribbits clarified with an eye roll. "Why would I ask about a mission? That's the reason we are here. I know those will come."

"Oh." I frowned. "No, no mail yet. Alyse was due around now. As slow as they are at getting us our letters, I probably won't know until the kid reaches high school." There might have been a bitterness to my tone. I tried hard to tone it down. It wasn't like I was the only person overseas experiencing being away from a pregnant spouse.

Rogers chuckled. "I hope to hell that we aren't here in eighteen years. Go shower."

I left the barracks and took a lukewarm shower, scrubbing the dried sweat from my body. I sent up at least sixteen prayers that Alyse and the baby were okay. The waiting was torture. I wrapped my towel around me to dry off and dressed while sitting on a bench. Other guys were in and out and all of them appeared to be in the same mood I was: worried and tired.

I'd just reached the barracks and was pulling on my shoes to check over Queenie to see if the patches I'd put on had stuck when an aide showed up inside the barracks.

"Briefing in ten," the soldier alerted us.

"Wow, ten whole minutes," Cutty griped. "Why the rush?"

"Who knows," Rogers mumbled.

We all got up and got ready, so there was no rush after we were briefed and went to listen to where our next destination was. This excursion would be our nineteenth mission and it felt like they were coming hot and heavy now. Maybe it only seemed that way because I wanted to go home and check on Alyse and the baby.

"Men, you'll be going into western Germany to a city called Osnabruck. You will have a PFF on the mission with you, so if weather moves in, you'll still be able to strike," the general told us. "Hit where the PFF marks and the mission will be a success. Takeoff is in two hours, pilots. Your positions are here. Dismissed." Short, though not very sweet. The general gave us very little information. Either intel was spotty, or this was nothing to worry about.

"Suhm, did you absorb all that information? We can't have you missing something." Jones elbowed me.

I snorted out a laugh and shook my head. Sometimes they were like that. I don't know who picked and assigned the targets or the logic behind them. Lately, it felt like covert things were going on and the secrecy was off the charts high.

"At least we get to eat before we leave," Ribbits added, heading straight for the mess hall. "I'm starving after all that training. I think I lost five pounds."

Ribbits was lanky like me, though the man could eat six times the amount of food I could. "We must fill all your hollow limbs," I agreed with Ribbits. "We don't need you wasting away into nothing. You'll have no hope of finding a girl if you look like a scarecrow that lost its hay."

"Why a scarecrow? Wasn't that the guy with no brain?" Ribbits shot me a look over his shoulder.

"Because I couldn't think of anything else that had stuffing that to lose to make a comparison to," I replied defensively. "Though, if the shoe fits," I drawled, my tone one of amusement so Ribbits knew I was joking.

Ribbits scowled at me, then laughed. "Food first, then retaliation, you bean pole."

We carried on some idle chit-chat while we ate and drank coffee, or what passed for it to fuel our bodies for the flight. We all noticed the other crews on this mission doing the same thing we were, so we stayed put until they started to head out.

We made our way to the airfield to make sure Queenie was loaded and got underway with our preflight duties. Finally, we were up in the air. There was less talk since we vigilantly watched for enemy craft. We'd had too many where we thought we would get lucky and encounter no one and ended up fighting for our lives.

Queenie took care of us like she always did and we dropped our payload over 10-10 cloud cover. However, the PFF ship marked our target and we released the bombs on the command from Rogers. We couldn't see to know if we aimed true or not. We all heard them detonate, though, loudly. As we pulled out and away to head back, we came under fire of heavy flak. It wasn't accurate due to that thick cloud cover. It was more than likely luck on their part. However, it was enough to raise my heart rate.

There were a few shots that found their way to our fuselage and I was grateful it was nothing more than superficial damage. We could hear the shots hit some of the other crews; from what I could see, it was still nothing significant.

The weather was colder than usual; it was thirty-seven below zero. My hands felt frozen to the gun, and Ribbits scored another spot of frostbite that got him sent to medical once we landed. Thankfully, no one had any major injuries, only the frostbite. If the truth be told, I was surprised that it hadn't found me either. Overall, it wasn't a terrible mission; it was on the simpler side of things. Queenie returned with no giant holes and no scratches. I'd say that was a good run.

"Nice work, guys," I congratulated them as we returned to the barracks after debriefing. "We made it through another mission and are all in the same condition as when we left. Except Ribbits, who has to be the odd man out and get frozen on the plane."

The guys laughed and commented on how cold they'd been. It wasn't an exaggeration. Frostbite was the most common injury we received, and I hoped it remained that way.

CHAPTER 44

May 9th, 1944

How does Belgium sound?" Jones asked while he rushed into our barracks. "I think we are about to pull our twentieth mission."

"Why do you say that?" I asked after finishing my letter home. We had already had breakfast, done physical training and a run, and then went to check on the repairs on Queenie. The other crew in our barracks were all napping, so those in here were doing quiet things so as not to disturb them.

"I overheard some generals talking on my way back here about some intel that they received

about some airfield there," Jones said in a rush of words. "Anyone know anything about Belgium?"

"I'll go make myself visible and see if I can figure anything out." Rogers stood up and walked out. I was under the impression he hadn't wanted a mission today and was hoping for a day off of flying.

"Ten left if we go out today. That could mean we have only two weeks left here," Housman pointed out, sounding awed. "Time flies when you are getting shot at by strangers that want you dead for no reason."

"Only if they sent us out ten days in a row," I reminded them. "They've rode us hard but not that many days in a row. Wishful thinking that I could get behind, though. I'd get to see my baby and learn how to be a dad. I don't know how good I'd be after seeing the shit we've seen." I ignored his time-flying comment as we were doing the same things the enemies were.

"Cut yourself some slack," Ribbits told me. "It's not like parenthood comes with a manual. Trial by fire, man."

"If we go out, this will be our third Oak Leaf cluster," Cutty remarked. "That's an accomplishment in itself, given the Army doesn't expect us to live past twelve missions. We showed them."

It was something we all knew, yet the reality of it sunk in as we sat there and waited for Rogers to return. It gave me time to reflect on times when I thought we wouldn't make it out alive. Yet I never gave voice to the thought, fearing my thoughts would make it a reality. There were more superstitions, but it wasn't unheard of for things like that to happen.

Our group was lucky, and of that, there was no doubt, but it didn't feel right to only credit luck. Our pilot was very skilled; me and the other gunners were sharp and accurate. It wasn't just luck; we'd had a pivotal role in our survival. I intended to make it home.

Rogers burst back. "It's true. Brief in two hours."

"Well, hell." Jones stood up. "Looks like we get that cluster after all." He did a few stretches, checked the time and grinned at us. "Ribbits, there's time for lunch before we head out."

"I'm in." Ribbits stood up. "I factually know that I can eat for two hours."

I laughed. "I think we all know the truth of that statement." I wasn't overly hungry but could graze to keep my energy up for a few hours. If there were any luck, I'd find a newspaper in the mess hall that someone left behind.

Luck wasn't on my side today. I saw nothing and grabbed some food to have in front of me to pick at while we waited. Another crew had returned from a mission and sat near us and told us of the resistance they encountered. Then we were trading stories of fighting. For a single moment, it felt like the war disappeared, even though that was the topic of conversation. It felt like a group of friends that met at a bar and just talked.

"Sorry to interrupt." Rogers tapped me on the shoulder. "We've got five minutes."

I made my apologies and stood, the rest of the crew following me. We dumped our trays in the bin and trailed after Rogers as he led us to the briefing. Three seconds after the last man entered, the briefing began and then promptly ended.

"The airfield in Florenne's south of Charleroie, that's your target today men," the general announced after all the crews sat down. "German fighters occupy this airfield. I don't think I need to tell you what a boon it would be to take this base out of commission. We believe you will encounter some resistance, though we don't think it will be much. German troops are diminishing."

"Famous last words," I mumbled with a frown. We were sitting in the back, so the only ones that heard me were Cutty and Rogers. "They sure haven't given us much information these past few briefings."

"I remember the last time they told us to expect resistance," Rogers replied softly. "We were lucky to land."

"We landed because of your skill," I reminded Rogers.

He nodded at me in acknowledgment of the compliment. There was a time and place for humility and keeping us all alive wasn't the right time. It could have been so much worse and we'd be going home in a different manner.

The general dismissed us and we filed out to prepare for the mission and complete preflight checks. I couldn't help but notice that someone in the chain of command was checking to see that we performed the checks.

Thirty-three minutes later, we were taking off. It was my first time flying over Belgium. I was at the point where everything looked the same from twenty thousand feet in the air—green ground, brown ground, and sometimes clouds or a body of water. I believe being here fundamentally changed something inside me. Often, my views were cynical, where they had once been positive and enthusiastic. I had good days. Just as often, we had days where we couldn't smile to save ourselves.

We encountered flak on our way to the target this time instead of on our way back to base. The first explosion caught us all off guard. Each of the gunners swiveled to find the direction the shot came from, and then it started all around us. Those friendly black clouds that signified someone trying to kill us popped up like a wall. None of it hit Queenie; Rogers and her got us through. However, we did have one plane go down over the channel with more than a couple of direct hits to their engines.

We all saw it, and the consensus was that one of our own shot it down accidentally. We'd been test-firing our tailguns simultaneously as a group to ensure everything worked well to prepare for more flak or resistance. A couple of the other crews had radioed their tailguns weren't working after we passed the flak. The plane had a position in front of us, so we knew it wasn't us who took it down, but it was still a shame. It was an unfortunate accident, though still an accident. They do happen and they are terrible for morale.

"Tough break," I said through the comms. I waited for the echo of the words from the crew and then tipped my head to the downed plane sadly. I hated missions where we lost a plane. It was now increasingly rare that we didn't lose at least one.

CHAPTER 45

May 10th – 18th, 1944

Furlough time. I knew they wouldn't give us more missions that close together. It was too convenient for them to string us along as long as they could since there were fewer aircrews than other types of troops. Ten missions didn't seem like it was very much. The other side of my brain told me ten missions could be a lifetime.

I did receive mail from home, which was very surprising. It was a cluster of letters that I tore into as if they were food and I was starving. The first one was from Alicia and she talked of movies and things going on in town. She asked after me and what other places I'd flown over and if I had seen anything exciting.

Then I read more of the same in a letter from some extended family members, enquiring about my health and giving me brief news of things back in the States. I set it off to the side and continued through my stack.

"I'm a dad!" I shouted to the crew in the barracks with me. "I have a little boy!" I clutched the small photograph of Alyse and the baby to my chest. My parents or Alyse's had to have had it done right after he was born because she was in a hospital bed. She looked tired but she was smiling.

"Yes!" Rogers crowed. "That's great news!" He was as excited as I was.

"Alyse is doing good; the baby is healthy and has a fantastic set of lungs, she says." I chuckled at that. "He was born on May 10th." I heaved out a happy sigh that they were all healthy. It felt like a weight lifted off my shoulders. "She named him after me." My eyes watered and I blinked back the tears. I had a baby boy named after me.

"That's swell," Cutty told me in a soft tone. "How does it feel to know he's here and everything is going well?"

"It's the best thing I've heard in a long time," I replied. "I'm beyond happy. Now, instead of feeling worried, I am scared out of my mind. I don't want Alyse getting one of those letters and me having never met baby Ralph."

The weight that lifted was now back on my shoulders. I wondered what the little boy would think of me and if I was good enough to be around him. This baby was an innocent life, and everything changed for me in a heartbeat.

"Well." Rogers moved to sit next to me. "I can tell you I will do my damn best to make sure that you return home. It's more than the letter, isn't it?" Rogers read me correctly, which didn't surprise me in the least.

"It is," I confirmed. "Remember how we talked about feeling different?" I waited for Rogers to nod his understanding before I continued. "It's that."

"You are doing your job," Rogers reminded me. "We all are. We don't get to decide where we go or what we do. Think of everything the people of these countries have lost. Remember, if we weren't doing our job, it would be worse for those people on the ground who are already suffering from unspeakable things."

I nodded. "That's what I've been telling myself. Now

that I know there's a little me back in the States, all that other stuff flooded to the surface. I felt guilty."

"We are on furlough." Cutty broke into our conversation. I knew he'd heard us; it was written all over his face, the same feelings I had. "Why don't we celebrate this happy news and forget the rest for now? A new life for our crew, even though no one has met him. He's a tiny little part of you, Suhm. I'd say that deserves a drink."

"I agree," Jones said, walking in mid-conversation. "What deserves a drink? Not that I need an excuse."

"Suhm's baby was born." Rogers grinned over at Jones. "Cutty suggested we celebrate."

Young, Carlson, Merrill, Warren, Cutty, and Jones crowded around me and thumped me on the back. Everyone one of them was willing to have a drink in little Ralph's honor. Jones tore off to find the others so it would be a crew event.

The news helped improve my overall demeanor, though it also made me want to go home even more than I had before. We took the time out to celebrate in town and did it quite well. Each crew member bought me drinks and I drank them all until I could barely stand up. At least we were celebrating new life and not drinking to avoid almost getting shot down. It was a nice change of pace. We toasted to Alyse and Ralph more than once.

We went to a few dances that week, watched a movie, and fooled around. Most importantly, we all got to rest. Thanks to baby Ralph, we all had rest that didn't feel forced. The little guy brought smiles and laughter to our entire crew, even though he was thousands of miles away in the States. I had the photo in the open so we could all see it. I'd also be taking it on our missions for good luck.

Our general had been kind enough to inform us that

big things were coming up and he needed us in tip-top shape. We'd never given him less than our best, in my opinion. The extra warning set off alarm bells in my mind and Rogers. We'd both heard whispers about something, though when we got close, the subject changed and we never really learned what it was. As the general had told us, we only suspected that it was something big.

We also received news that they decided to make us lead crew sometime during that furlough. We'd be in the front for the subsequent however many missions. While it was an honor, it was also nerve-wracking. We'd impressed someone enough that we got put to lead. The alternative thought was they lost enough aircrews that no one else had enough experience to lead. I stopped that one from taking root because I knew other crews on base were close to the end, the same as we were. I spent the last few days of rest trying to forget the stress of war before I was thrown right back into it. I stared at baby Ralph for hours.

CHAPTER 46

May 27th, 1944

"How many more practice bomb missions do we need?" Ribbits asked Rogers. "Don't they know we've been out on twenty missions dropping bombs already? This drill is frustrating."

"Obviously, they know that," I replied dryly. "Remember the general told us there was big stuff coming up? We're leading a group into Germany. I don't mind the practice, yet I wish we were just doing it and getting it done already. Plus, Jones, Hausman and you, Ribbits, are doing roles you haven't been doing on those missions. You are now on the radio and will send out the calls. Hausman will be navigating. Jones will be making calls on when to drop."

"Me too, for the getting it done and over with part," Hausman agreed. "I don't know if I like knowing something major is coming. It makes me nervous with the extra duties of being lead crew."

"You weren't nervous before that?" Jones asked as he dealt a round of cards. "I'm nervous every time."

"I like knowing." Rogers threw some cards down and held up two fingers to be dealt two cards. "It helps my mind stay sharp and not take anything for granted. We are in a war and should never let our guard down. Sometimes, we have one of those runs we could fall asleep on and be fine. Those are dangerous."

"It'd be perilous for all of us if you fell asleep," Cutty joked. "Let's not practice that."

"You all know that's not what I meant." Ribbits held up three fingers after he discarded. "I'm just saying, why did they make us lead crew if they think we still need to train."

"That's life," I countered. "We always need to be learning and bettering ourselves. If they thought we couldn't handle it, I don't think they would have made us lead crew."

"Yes." Rogers nodded his agreement. "Suhm had a point about your roles. Practice can't hurt. I'd rather you be entirely comfortable with those positions before we are thrown back into the ring and taking fire."

"Think of what a day that will be for us," I stated as we laid our cards down. "It's something to be proud of and I think we'll be great. Our first mission as lead crew."

"Look at you." Hausman grinned at me. "You have a baby and suddenly you are Mr. Optimism."

Rogers laughed and threw his cards at Hausman as he raked all the money he won over in front of him. "You could use some of that optimism. It's time to go practice. We can win our money back from this monkey after our flight."

"And we will win it back," I promised with a wink. "Optimism."

Hausman laughed as we all went to do our practice run. We worked well together as a team and I thought that was something the chain of command noticed. Our crew was close and in tune with each other. Ribbits was excellent on the radio, and Hausman and Jones performed beautifully.

When we landed and stowed our Queenie, brimming

with excitement over performing with high standards, we received a blow that knocked us down. The general's aide told us that the crew that shared our barracks, friends of mine, were shot down with no survivors. It was sobering and we all fell silent, our joking tossed aside as we processed the information. That crew had nineteen missions in; they hadn't been far behind us, and when we walked into the barracks and saw the ten empty beds, it was a shock. It didn't matter how often it happened. News like that didn't land any easier.

It wasn't like we could tell ourselves they were out on a mission because they wouldn't be coming back, and soon enough, those empty beds would get filled with a new crew coming into base. We'd all lost friends in this war, every one of us, though this was the first time we'd experienced it so close to where we stayed. The reminder the empty beds gave us was a cold slap of reality.

More than one of us pulled out our paper and wrote letters home. I began a letter to Alyse and every time I looked up, I saw one of those empty beds as my own. It made me wonder what my new son and wife would do if that had been me. I hadn't even gotten to meet him yet and it was in that moment that I realized how much they meant to me. I'd taken their presence for granted. I stared at the little photo of my family again and fought back a wave of panic at not seeing them again. I'd make it back, I told myself repeatedly.

Out of the ten crews I started with, only two remained. That statistic of a life expectancy of twelve missions crept up to haunt me again. Why had we been spared? Fate and God must work hand-in-hand and there had to be something down the road in store for us that they planned. We suffered a lot of losses and my fervent hope was that I lived long enough to meet my son and see my darling wife again. Those simple things would answer my prayers and I couldn't ask for more. I finished my letter before I reached the point I couldn't.

I sealed it up and walked out to put it in the mailbag. A breath of fresh air was needed and not having those empty cots staring at me was a momentary relief. I walked around the base for a while, just stretching my legs and working on clearing my mind. It wasn't as easy as I thought it would be, and I returned to the barracks.

The guys were all still in there, somber. "How about I win some of my lost money back?" I asked, forcing a jovial tone. "After all, I now have an extra mouth to feed and it isn't one of yours."

CHAPTER 47

May 29th, 1944

Twenty-first mission and we are lead crew," Ribbits crowed. We'd gotten orders the day before. I guessed that meant they thought we'd trained enough.

"We aren't going to be anything if we don't get our asses to the briefing," I replied with an eye roll. "Move it."

"Nervous, Suhm?" Cutty ribbed me.

"No more than usual," I answered him back. "Don't you want to pay attention so we get it right?"

"We always get it right," Cutty remarked.

"Now is not the time to get cocky." Rogers pushed him out of the way. "We need to focus."

I walked in behind Rogers and sat in the front next to him. We were the lead crew. It felt right to sit in the front for this briefing. Not to mention, those seats were open. Maybe I only acquainted the front as a place of honor and we'd finally earned our spot.

"The target today is the Politz oil plant. The location is on the Baltic Sea. The lead crew will cross the North Sea over Denmark, out over the Baltic, make a right turn, and into the target. You'll be near the Port of Stettin. There are over one hundred thirty-five labor camps in that area," the general explained. "That is nothing more than geographical information. You aren't hitting those. Taking the oil plant out is the objective, as that will harm the Germans the most. That plant accounts for ten percent of Germany's production. Questions?"

No one in the room had any. We left, prepared the plane, and took up our position in the lead group. "This is going to be a long one," I casually said while we waited for clearance. We watched as the Navigation crews and fighters took off; then it was our turn. The only sounds from the crew were the radioed positions, check-ins, and commands.

We caught a tailwind and were ahead of schedule. Things were looking good. Navigation was a full eight minutes ahead of us, and they dropped their marker. We had seen no signs of enemies, no communication that crews spotted enemies, and we dropped our payload right on top of the marker—precision at its finest.

I watched as the smoke crept up, thick and oily, telling us we hit our target. The smoke kept climbing, and it surpassed our altitude, which was twenty-one thousand five hundred feet. That's when communication happened, and our navigators were under attack. Twenty-five fighters came out of nowhere and flew through their formation.

Rogers immediately turned the plane. "Navigators under attack!" he stated in that calm voice that didn't seem right. He radioed the position to the rest of the group and that assistance was inbound.

We led our group to the navigators position. Once they were in sight, we opened fire on the fighters and chased them off. All the gunners in the group that followed us had their guns going. Some of the enemies went down, others escaped. Then another wave of them hit as if there were an endless supply waiting to attack. None of us saw where they came from. But we found ourselves in the same situation again.

Our guns ran full force, a sea of spent shells collecting on the floor of the plane as we chased them away and waited for the groups behind us to catch up as they still had their bombs to drop. We were breathing gunpowder. There were nine hundred ninety-three planes on this mission and we needed all the help we could get. My gut told me this wasn't over yet.

A third wave came and the navigation planes kept a tight formation. Our crew and the aircraft behind us formed up tight and opened fire. Rogers's tone remained flat and calm as he issued commands over the radio and dodged bullets shot at us. Thousands of hot bullets flew through the air and I knew someone on the ground had to be watching us and scrambling fighters to come after us. *How many planes did they have?* We needed to get out of this airspace.

I watched a crew that was friends of ours get shot down not long after they dropped their eggs and joined our battle. I wanted to scream my anger out over another loss but I didn't. It wouldn't do any good. I kept shooting. It was all I could do and I don't think I hit anything vital, much to my frustration.

Those guys that went down were on their last mission. The final one. That's what made it so tough and hard to bear. Only twenty-five of the one hundred fellows that came here with us remained. How did they expect us to function knowing things like that?

A few minutes later, we received communication that another Liberator's crew had to bail over enemy territory. The pilot counted seven chutes, giving us hope that maybe they'd make it out of there alive.

Nearly a hundred miles from our target, the battle was finally over, and I could still see the smoke from the destroyed oil factory in the air. It would make the general happy, and whoever gave orders to him to have us carry out. There were days it felt like the cost was too high and it put doubt in my mind that I'd get home. Doubt killed and I needed to vanquish it.

Once we landed back at home base, we received word that ground troops found seven bodies near the wreckage. The ground troops discovered the German home guard police had executed the three that no one saw bail while they attempted to escape their captors. It reiterated it in my mind that I was happy I wasn't on the ground.

That one mission cost us two planes and two crews. Twenty families were now without their sons, fathers, uncles, cousins, and whatever else they might have been. It was an awful feeling. I couldn't stop thinking about the numbers, either. Only twenty-five left that came with me. Seventy-five men killed and we hadn't been here a year. I knew the Army liked to put numbers to things and assign a value so they could figure out the cost of our losses. *How did they value a life? What was a person worth to them?*

That number said nothing about the ground troops or Navy troops on Queen Mary with me. It was staggering and unbelievable, and we had to keep going. We couldn't stop. We weren't finished with our missions yet. It was a numbers game, and we didn't fare so well from my perspective.

Yes, I was sure we were doing better than the Germans, but it didn't help to think that way either. We'd heard stories from people in town when we had a pass that a large number of the German troops didn't want to be fighting.

They weren't Nazis and didn't agree with Hitler or his thoughts. They didn't have a choice. Serve or die was the Nazi theme.

Nazis forced them to be where they were. No one forced me. I chose to do this, and there were days that I wished I hadn't. Today was one of those days. I was happy we completed our mission. That happiness battled with the heartbreak for those who didn't, given it was their last. Our first time as a lead crew, we lost two entire crews and their planes. *Did that make us a failure as lead crew?*

"Are you thinking too much again, Suhm?" Rogers came up from behind me. His tone was somber, and I didn't have to look at him to see his face mirror the bitter expression of my own.

"Hard not to, isn't it?" I answered the question with a question. "It doesn't get to you? That crew was done after today. Who says that won't be us?"

"No one," Rogers replied. "It gets to me too. I channel it back to myself to force myself to fly better so that none of our families receive that letter. It's the only thing I can do. Other than drink and gamble."

"I rarely see you drink." I narrowed my eyes at our pilot.

"Because if we get that call that we have an urgent mission, I can't be drunk. Do you want to get on a plane with a pilot that's been drinking?" Rogers pointedly asked.

"Then why let *us* drink?" I fired back. "You need us at top form as much as we need you."

"True. I don't control anyone other than myself. It's something the crew needs to figure out on their own. I don't see you drinking like some of them do," Rogers reminded me.

"I save it for the passes or furloughs," I responded

dully. "Same as you."

"It's tough. We must remember that we all handle it differently and that war changes you," Rogers said gently. "Neither of us are the same men we were when we started. Same with the other guys. All we can do is be better than we were last time and honor those that fell."

Surprisingly profound words from our pilot and I let them sink in and took them to heart. Yes, I'd lose sleep over everything we saw and heard today. However, I couldn't let it drag me down, or Alyse would get one of those dreaded letters. All I'd be able to do was look down on the son I'd never met and watch Ralph grow up to be someone I'd never get to meet.

CHAPTER 48

May 31st, 1944

There's a lot of clouds today," I remarked after our fitness training. It was humid, though the temperature wasn't high. "Do you think they'll send us out?"

"Who knows." Ribbits shrugged. "Sometimes I think they'd send us out directly into a hurricane. Then, once we arrived, they'd say never mind, abort the mission. It appears there is weather."

I chuckled at that, though I couldn't disagree. There wasn't logic to some of the things the Army asked us to do but we had to do it anyway. It seemed like a waste, especially when resources were so low and hard to come by.

I guzzled some water and kicked my feet up on a chair. It was still early morning and we had no scheduled training flights or missions yet, so it was nothing more than killing time.

"I think I'm going to ask my girl to marry me," Hausman informed us after he came back from showering.

"Wow. Do you think you are ready for that?" Jones jumped into the conversation. "I've thought about settling down and starting a family but I just don't know if I'm at that point."

"How can you be ready when you don't even have a girl?" I asked him point blank. "Hausman has one. You only have good times."

"That's what I don't know if I can give up." Jones grinned at me. "Things never get boring when it's a different girl every time. Oh, and if you tell them you are heading out onto a mission, some of them are willing to do some pretty fun stuff, which isn't boring."

"Come on." Ribbits shook his head. "Haven't you ever had one serious relationship?"

"I sure did," Jones confirmed. "My parents were all but planning a wedding for me before I left. I told them to stop that I didn't know if I wanted that, and that I might die over here."

"That's a hell of a way to get out of a marriage," I commented. "You could die back home, too."

"True, but it sounded more authentic to say I could die here, and look, we've come close," Jones argued. "It was one of those expected things. She lived next door; we dated all through school, and both our parents thought we should marry, have a lot of babies, and move into the same neighborhood as them. It was enough to make me join the Army. If I'm honest with myself, I don't think she wanted it either. Our goodbye wasn't all that emotional and it felt a little like she was pushing me out the door. I think she had her eye on some other fellow."

"I can understand where you are coming from with that," I told him. "I wasn't ready for a long time either. It was just one of those things that happened, and suddenly, you are ready, you find someone, and nature takes its course."

"Then you knock her up and ship off overseas." Jones quirked an eyebrow at me. "If that were me, I wouldn't have wanted to go."

"He didn't have a choice," Ribbits argued on my behalf. "He was already enlisted and given orders. Not going would have made him AWOL. They would have thrown him in jail somewhere, fined him, and either forced him to go or dishonorably discharged him. It wasn't like Suhm had good options at that point."

"I didn't, but even still, I would have come over here. It's what I wanted to do from the start," I explained. "I wanted to travel and see other places. Learn what life over here was like. I knew it was a war, and I knew it wouldn't be pretty. No one prepared me for the level of destruction I've seen or the amount of losses we suffered. Knowing I don't want my son to live like this keeps me here and in the game. If we take care of it, he can grow up without war. Not under a Nazi regime."

"War will always be something to contend with as long as there are humans." Rogers walked into the barracks. "There will always be a power-hungry warmonger in the group. What are you all talking about anyway?"

"Getting married, settling down, having babies," I told our pilot. "Hausman thinks he's ready to propose to his girl."

"You will make an honest woman out of her *after* you defiled her?" Rogers joked. "Good man. Have you talked with her about it? She's from here, right? Will you want to take her back to the States or move here?"

"We've only talked about it a little, but she did tell me that she was curious about the States and would love to live there," Hausman admitted. "I don't think I'd want to live here after seeing the destruction. Maybe once England rebuilds and life is easier and not war-torn."

One of the other pilots from the new crew in our

barracks entered and grabbed his flight jacket. "They are sending us up. Briefing is in fifteen minutes."

"Of course." Rogers shook his head. "Clouds be damned. Get ready, men. I'll meet you at the briefing."

I doubted we'd drop any eggs, but I grabbed the gear I thought I'd need and headed out. I took my place in the front, behind Rogers, and slouched in my chair. The rest of the crew filed in a few minutes later and we listened.

"Target is the marshaling yard at Lumes, France." The general wasted no time getting to business. "Take out the station and the tracks to put their trains out of business. There's a railroad bridge that needs a hit as well. You'll be without a PFF for this mission."

I did my best not to roll my eyes. At this juncture, France wouldn't have a coast at all. Since there would be no PFF, that meant if there were cloud cover there, we wouldn't be able to drop. We left the briefing, got down to business, readied Queenie and then lined up for takeoff.

"Mission twenty-two," Hausman declared happily. "We're getting closer, gentlemen."

"Yeah, yeah," Cutty smarted off. "Someone always says that each time and we end up in a world of hurt. Let's not invite trouble."

I silently agreed and kept watch for enemy fighters. The closer we got to the target, the worse the clouds became. They were thick with moisture and the higher we went we still weren't out of them. At twenty-thousand feet, the cloud ceiling was even higher. Above or below, it didn't matter. There was nothing but clouds.

"Man, these clouds are crazy!" Jones exclaimed in awe.

"They sure are beautiful, though," I replied. They

mesmerized me with the density, variety of colors, and the shapes they took on. Various patterns drew the eye with the ever-changing colors when the sun behind them moved positions. The clouds were a better sight than bombs hitting.

"I'm calling it," Rogers announced. He radioed the rest of the crews. "10-10 cloud cover. We're heading back."

It was as I expected. Rogers communicated the orders to turn back to the rest of the group and we turned. The mission still counted because we experienced some very inaccurate flak that came nowhere near any of our planes due to the clouds. We didn't even fire back because we couldn't see where to fire. I was okay with it; we deserved a run like that every once in a while.

CHAPTER 49

June 3rd, 1944

Have you heard of Overlord?" Rogers pulled me to the side and asked me. We'd just come from another training class.

"No," I responded slowly. "Care to explain?"

"It was one of those right time, right place situations where I overheard command talking about campaign Overlord. The Allies have some big plan in the works, and I think we'll be part of it," Rogers told me nervously. "It sounds like a massive raid, bigger than anything we've been a part of before."

"When?" I wondered aloud. "Wait, wasn't something big supposed to happen like that in May? Wasn't that the rumors that Jones was talking about?"

"I think so." Rogers nodded. "All these missions we've been on is to help take out those places near where the raid will happen. We are creating diversions."

"In France?" I frowned. "Why not Germany?"

"I don't know." Rogers gave me a strange look. "Germany is occupying France. It's a strategic foothold. If we can get it back, it advances our efforts that much more. But I think it's soon. Not today because there would be much more activity, but very soon. Write your letters home."

"Understood," I answered and went to grab some paper. I wrote to my sister, parents, Alyse, and an uncle who had been sending me letters. I couldn't say anything was going to happen or even what had happened, but I talked about life in the barracks and the guys. I mentioned inconsistent pay and rationing of food and fuel. Inane things that let them know I was alive.

With Alyse, I told her that I missed her and couldn't wait to see my son. I talked about wanting to come home and wondering what I would do for work after coming home. I told her I wanted to take her and our son sailing and roller skating. All fun and ordinary things that gave me something to look forward to after my experiences here.

I glanced up and saw some of the other guys writing letters, too, and caught Rogers's eye. He nodded at me, a subtle sign that he'd spread the word something was in the works. I finished my letters, addressed them, and put them in the outgoing mailbag.

Once a day, someone took them into town to get them sent off and pick up any that had arrived. Though there was mail that came every day, there were times it took over a month to get to us and it felt like we were missing time. By the time we read the letters, ten more important things had happened back at home and we wouldn't know about them for another month or so. Even still, it was a wonderful feeling when I got mail and opened it eagerly. I was surprised I'd received the mail about Ralph's birth as quickly as I did.

"Briefing at twelve-thirty," one of the other pilots told us and handed Rogers the orders.

I glanced at my watch and saw we still had over an hour before we learned of our twenty-third mission. There was nothing quite like sitting on nerves and waiting for whatever was about to land in our lap. I wondered if this was going to be another of the diversion missions.

The guys had plenty of time to finish their letters and started getting up to take them to the mailbag individually. Fifteen minutes before the briefing began, we all sat there and slowly got flight suits on before heading out to the briefing.

We purposely didn't sit up front this time but a few rows back. I followed Rogers's lead and worried that one of us would say something when they asked if we had questions. We were now the most senior crew of the bunch and seasoned well enough to read between the lines of what they didn't say.

There was a strange tension in the air and I was aware that I could be imagining it because of the information Rogers shared. However, the general looked more animated and sleepless than he usually did. He straightened his papers at least ten times before he began to speak.

"Soldiers, today your target is a gun emplacement along the coast of France at Berck-sur-mer. It's an artillery battery north of Normandy. This location is a heavily occupied area and it would be remiss of me not to tell you that you can expect resistance and flak. The battery sits on a cliff and is a part of the Atlantic Wall fortifications. It's of the utmost importance that you render these guns inoperable. Any questions?"

I held my breath, waiting for someone to speak up and no one did. I felt a little let down by that and had hoped that one of the other crews would question why these were so important. I guess they figured the fewer guns there were to shoot at us, the better off we were, which was true. It was a straightforward mission, so I couldn't fault anyone for not asking questions they didn't know they needed to ask.

We filed out and went to the airfield to prepare the planes for takeoff. Bombs were loaded and secured; we checked the chutes were loaded and packed, guns were oiled, and ammunition was loaded. It didn't take us any longer than usual, though it certainly felt like it. I couldn't put my finger on why, either.

Rogers taxied us out and soon we were in the air. "Eyes on the sky," I reminded the guys.

The weather wasn't perfect, though it wasn't terrible either. There wasn't a lot of cloud cover, which was great for the mission, but it made us a lot more visible than if there were clouds. The flight time was approximately three hours, maybe a few minutes more, right about average for our missions.

There was a little flak on the way to the target. Nothing was accurate, but it was enough to get our attention quickly and increase our heart rates. We fired back and it appeared we got a couple of hits in. Then, the artillery guns came into sight. Our bomb doors opened and we released at the perfect time on Jones's command.

I saw one bomb land directly on a gun and take it out. "The square heads won't use that gun again!" I shouted, not activating my comms.

After all our eggs dropped, we closed the bomb bay doors and banked to head back. I had a great view of the formation behind us. The sound of flak reached our ears right when a few holes tore through our Queenie. I turned my gun in the direction it had come from and opened fire. Young and Warren fired along with me. A steady stream of bullets raged from the plane back to the ground.

Ribbits was radioing the information back to the base and the other crews. Soon, the sound of heavy gunfire filled the air as multiple Liberators joined in to take out the ground artillery firing at us. Little black clouds popped up all around, and then a plume of smoke rose.

Flak peppered us with a series of pings and explosions as we took hits. Cutty began throwing chaff even faster. Rogers got us out of range as soon as possible, and we made it home without any losses. When we checked Queenie over, she had at least half a dozen large holes in her; not our worst day, nor ideal.

That night, we learned of Operation Overlord right down to the day of the attack. Some crews were still doing missions to keep up the level of distraction, though we'd been grounded and ordered to get Queenie in the best shape possible.

CHAPTER 50

June 6th, 1944

I ran to the bathroom for the sixth time. My stomach was in knots. I was about to be a part of one of the most historical days of this war. What a feeling it was, but I didn't say anything about my stomach cramps or nerves. We didn't do that. We bottled it up and made do.

It wasn't only me that was experiencing a case of nerves. It showed in various ways in the rest of the crew, from fidgeting to singing to themselves to jumping jacks and guzzling water. Even knowing what we were doing, I don't believe that there was one person on our crew that would change their part in it.

Our twenty-fourth mission was going to be in the history books. There was no question about that. The nervousness was unspoken though recognized, as was the pure excitement of embarking on the campaign.

Eisenhower was the supreme commander of the operation, which involved twelve other countries of the Allies. It was a massive effort, and yesterday's briefing was extraordinarily detailed and overwhelming. The whispers we'd heard had been accurate. This operation had been in the works for a long time.

The beaches of Normandy were our destination in that coastal area of France that we'd bombed several times. False information had gotten spread through radio communications that led Germany to believe we'd be attacking the channel of the Pas de Calais region, where we had been heavily bombing.

Eisenhower had received communication that most of the Panzer divisions had gotten diverted to that area. It was a brilliant move to play to Hitler's ego and belief that nothing could get by him. Obviously, the campaign needed the element of surprise to succeed. I could feel the success in my bones.

The surmounting challenges numbered higher than I could count. The Atlantic Wall was two thousand four hundred miles of obstacles created to keep the Allies out. Six and a half million mines, bunkers, artillery, and tank ditches stretched the distance. These informational numbers in the briefing gave us an idea of what we would face. The English Channel was known for its rough waters. Germany had the high ground. These were all things our combined forces would be facing. It was overwhelming.

I didn't want to be a ground troop for this. I was happy that we'd be above and try to clear the way for our soldiers and halt Germany from receiving reinforcements. We prayed for the weather to cooperate since it was notoriously bad in that area. We were all over the map with our nerves and overthinking on this mission. So many moving parts were at play it was difficult to keep them straight.

We'd be dropping bombs over the bridges, railroad lines, and other support avenues in the St. Lo area so that the

Germans couldn't receive reinforcements to the beaches. We'd been doing the same thing without knowing it was part of this campaign. With the knowledge the Army handed us, it felt like there was more pressure to perform the same missions as the ones we had previously completed. We were heading out just after midnight for our mission and in the early morning, the amphibious assault would begin.

From all accounts, it would be the most significant amphibious landing force ever assembled. That was where most of our troops would be, on those boats waiting to launch to begin the attack. That's why we all prayed for good weather.

I know what being on the sea in rough water felt like and if it wasn't something that a body experienced before, it could make you sicker than a dog after eating chocolate. I didn't envy the ground forces, especially with the Germans ditched into those cliffs waiting on high ground—something we'd all seen with our missions over the area.

"Everyone ready?" Rogers asked after the plane was loaded, checked, and declared ready for flight. "This is the big time. We won't be alone in the skies, but we won't have a PFF plane. Anyone with doubts, speak up now to address them before we are in the air."

"No doubts from me," I was quick to declare.

"Has anyone heard anything at all about the weather?" Jones wondered. "That area is always bad."

"Imagine being in one of those boats," Hausman replied caustically.

"It's approximately a three-hour flight," Rogers answered. "Even if we had a weather report, it could change before we get there."

"We are going in dark?" Ribbits asked. He meant no

running lights or something visible the enemy could target us with, not the time of day.

Rogers nodded at that and we all jumped in the plane. Chutes were ready and accessible and we all braced for the takeoff. Rogers blasted us down the runway and then we were airborne. There wasn't much nervous chatter or chatter in general. We were intent on our jobs and proud to participate in this operation.

The troops on all those boats depended on us to lay waste to the support structures in Normandy. The briefing told us that there would be something close to eleven thousand five hundred ninety planes in the air to support the landings.

It was by far the most extensive effort I had ever participated in, and those numbers were unbelievable to me. We'd been on some large raids, but eleven thousand planes in the sky simultaneously was something else entirely.

I hoped there were no accidental firings at other Allies, as we'd seen that happen more than once. With that much air support in the sky, it would be easy to do. I supposed that was why the briefing was so intense and filled with as much information as possible. It's almost too much for one mind to hold and process in that short of a time. I was still processing it.

It was too dark to see the weather from our position. We were above cloud cover for now, but several times, there were clearings and I could spot the lights on the ground. It gave me hope that we'd be able to perform as they expected.

"About an hour out," Rogers called out through the comms. "Weather is moving in quickly."

"I'm watching," I replied. It was looking nasty out there. Those weren't rain clouds; those were storm clouds, not a good omen for our mission. A few lightning strikes ribboned across the sky with a brilliant flash of light. Queenie bounced over turbulence due to the unstable air. I hoped that it would blow over soon.

"It's not looking good," Rogers communicated. We hit some more turbulence that had us gripping the plane where we could for stability.

I agreed with Rogers. It didn't look good. I held out hope that it would clear or there would be a clearing over the target. Thirty minutes later, Mother Nature dispelled that hope as the cloud cover was thick and not budging, at least over the land. The clouds were moving in from the coast.

"We can't drop without a PFF," Rogers radioed back.

I couldn't see the coast at all from our position. I couldn't even catch a glimpse of the coastline. However, we could see beyond the beach to the channel and the sea as the clouds moved. Gads! I have never seen so many ships, blimps, and planes in one place in my entire life. It was thrilling and terrifying.

The water looked like it was polka-dotted with thousands of ships from up here. It put the words told to us in the briefing into perspective. Those ships bobbed around in the choppy water as the storm moved over them and I could only imagine the state of the bottom of those boats. They probably smelled something awful and were covered in vomit.

"Received word we are not to head back yet," Rogers told us. "We are going up higher and going to circle."

"Got it!" I confirmed. Ribbits constantly communicated with the rest of the group and the base. His face was intent and focused.

Fighters were moving in and about an hour later, we saw the first ship shell the coast. The paratroopers were on the coast and the landing crafts were unloading in waves. After those first few shots from the ship, it was no longer a secret that the Allies were there.

Watching from the skies at six-thirty in the morning was surreal, and we would have to head back to home base soon. In the early morning light, we could see the swarms of naval and ground troops rushing as we passed over the six beaches.

Normandy and Utah looked not to be faring as well as the others, and return fire hit some of the landing craft near enough to cause significant issues. Even at twenty thousand feet, I could see the waters turn red.

That was the sight that we turned to go back home with, ordered to return to base, refuel, get a few hours rest, and get sent back out. It bothered me to see that, though I knew I should have expected it. The coast was under a constant stream of shells from the ships, and the sparks of gunfire from the beaches told me our guys weren't going down easy. I watched as we turned toward base and tried to guess which side the flashes of gunfire came from.

We left disappointed at not getting to do our part, though Rogers promised that we'd be back out soon. We also knew that we'd played a part before we even knew what was happening with the bombings we'd done on the railroads, gun emplacements, and airfields.

We got three hours of rest before they sent us back out. No one complained. We loaded, left, and continued our journey back to the coast of France. This time, we dropped our bombs, which was a relief, even if it wasn't part of the initial attack.

The air was thick with smoke, making it hard to tell our guys from the enemies. We dropped on our targets and joined the stream of planes clogging the sky and fighting as we turned to head back to base to reload and do it again. Ribbits was exhausted by the constant chatter of communication and keeping up on relaying information. I knew we were in for some crazy days of flying.

CHAPTER 51

June 7th, 1944

"A re you going to be okay?" Rogers asked us after we had less than an hour of downtime and immediately headed back out. It was enough time for a quick meal, Queenie to get reloaded with bombs, and a check-over by ground crews with minor repair work. We hadn't received any severe damage since the initial attack began.

Flak was fired relentlessly from the ground. Each time we flew over, we took some hits. I don't think the soldiers on the ground were aiming. I think they were firing out of pure reflex at the onslaught. None expected the Allies to barrel at them in the way it had.

"Exhausted," Cutty replied. "We'll do what we need to do."

We took turns sleeping for fifteen or twenty minutes while the others watched until we returned to the battle and dropped our eggs. It was the only relief we could get and it was perilous to have even one of us out of commission. We could still see troops launching to the beaches and more ships arriving to join the fighting.

Our reload time on base gave a few of a few moments for what we called cat naps. Nothing significant, and we stretched ourselves past our limits. The constant rotation of flying, bombing, returning, reloading, and starting all over was insane.

I tried to override that craziness with thoughts about feeling honored to be a part of something this significant, large, and essential, with us being the lead crew to boot. I was a part of the most important military campaign in history. It gave me enough adrenaline to keep going; that mindset and coffee. Each time we landed, I drank a pot of coffee. Rogers told the ground crew to get pots near where we'd land and be ready with it. It wasn't protocol, and I was shocked that one of the crew members did it. I was grateful beyond measure. All the crews appreciated the help.

It never ceased to amaze me to see the sight of all those ships that lined the channel and the sea. There was no chance Germans could get through that mass of warfare blocking the way. It's the same with the land and how we'd been dropping our payloads. Each return we made to Normandy was like I saw it for the first time. It was astounding.

We were too high in the air to see the bodies that littered the water and beaches, though the stories reached us when we were back on base loading up for another run. It sounded horrific. One guy told us that body parts littered the water and floated back up on the beach. Another talked about the launches picking up the bodies out of the water and bringing them back to boats while under fire.

The storm had blown some of the landing craft as much as one hundred yards off, and those troops' initial entry points were places they had no information on. They encountered mines and beach obstacles that kept them from gaining ground. We lost a lot of good men.

I felt guilty for feeling grateful I hadn't had to see that level of fighting or the bodies from our position. Alternatively, those stories are what kept us going on little to no sleep. We had a driving need to help as much as we could from the air, even under heavy attack from ground forces shooting their flak at us.

We fired our guns until we ran out of ammunition to take out the ground gunners that aimed at us. It was chaos and whirlwinds of activity. On each return, the ground crew scurried to reload bombs and ammunition to keep us alive. They patted us on the backs and gave us pep talks while we drooped and shoved coffee in our hands.

It wasn't any better for them, the difference being they weren't under heavy gunfire. They were run ragged, though, with as many planes coming and going. Even officers were out there helping to keep things going.

Conversations between us were stilted and infrequent so we could preserve what energy we had. We'd visually check each other over and resume our duties. On one of our reloads Jones said something that slightly brought me down.

"All these trips don't count as missions," Jones reminded us. "It's all part of the same one. Just think, with as many times as we've flown out, we could be going home."

"We're lucky we are making it back to the base," Carlson pointed out. "The flak is madness."

It was, I agreed. Now that it was daylight, we could see where it was coming from and aim at it as we approached. The problem was the enemy guns outnumbered ours. We'd take out one, and two more would be firing. I don't know where we found the will to keep going, but I was proud of us that we did.

CHAPTER 52

June 8th, 1944

I'd gotten a total of two hours of sleep over the past two days. We were all running on empty and unsure how long we could keep this up. The hard part was knowing it wasn't counting as another mission each time we went up. It was still our twenty-fourth. I didn't even remember how many times we'd landed and reloaded. I imagined the amount of fuel we'd used was astronomical.

I'd lost count of the number of bombs we'd dropped and the various holes we'd patched up in Queenie. She'd kept us alive, though, and had taken no critical damage that would keep us from landing safely. That was one point that each of us was more than grateful for these past few days.

Day and night, we'd been flying. On each return, we heard more stories, shoved food in our faces, and went back out. If we were lucky, there was a small break where we took thirty minutes to close our eyes. However, it wasn't often enough. We could feel the sleep deprivation taking effect on our minds and bodies. I knew how detrimental getting some rest was for all of us.

We needed to be on point when we were in the air. Ten lives and an airplane were at stake, and it was something

I'd heard Rogers mention more than once to officers who were on the ground when we landed to reload. He'd beg for a respite for even an hour to no avail.

It wasn't that the officers were being mean. They followed orders and had been working the ground crews while we flew. They were in the same predicament that we were. There wasn't one person on that base who wasn't scrambling to keep their wits about them as we battled through the start of campaign Overlord.

I started to worry about our reaction times and not being as aware as we could be while up there. Each time that popped into my head, we encountered something that got our adrenaline pumping and we got through it. Flak would burst through the side of Queenie, causing shouts of alarm as we struggled to find the direction to shoot, get rid of that obstacle, and check for vital damage.

The human spirit was a resilient thing. We pushed our bodies and minds past our limits and still fought. I imagined that every man on the ground was facing the same, if not worse. We needed to gain that foothold for things to calm down. We'd keep going until we had it, battered, bruised, and exhausted beyond measure.

The spirit of each of the men involved in the operation pushed forward through the losses witnessed, cherished the ground gained, and battled on regardless of their position on the ground, in the air, or on the water. In the moments I spared to think about everything that happened, I prayed to whoever was listening to get us through these unprecedented times.

We'd hear snippets of radio broadcasts with leaders back in the States cheering us on and I was too tired to think about how they would fare in these circumstances. Instead, we took the words of success to heart and funneled them to push us farther and do more. We'd grumble and complain about it later after resting and processing what we'd experienced.

Little did we know that would be our schedule for the next two days. We flew right past exhausted to dead on our feet. I honestly didn't know how we even managed to stand without falling over. Our limbs shook with pure exhaustion. Our body temperatures couldn't regulate, and our words slurred when we talked. Thoughts weren't connecting when we tried to do things. Our minds went on autopilot and I couldn't even begin to count the times I wondered what day it was, where we were, and which direction we were heading. I had to give credit to Hausman and his navigation.

When we finally got a break, we all passed out on top of our cots, fully clothed. I don't even remember the trek back to our barracks. My body shut down and told me absolutely no more. I remember the feel of the pillow under my head; after that, there was darkness.

CHAPTER 53

June 11th, 1944

I think I could use another six days of sleep," Cutty mumbled as he scrubbed his hands over his face.

"At least," I agreed. We all sported stubble and looked like pure hell. Cutty and I were in the process of shaving after finally showering. It revived me a little, though not quite enough. I figured I'd be better after coffee and some food.

"Hurry it up," Jones told us as he walked in. "The rest of us need to do the same. Maybe I'll feel human again if I do."

"Not likely," I replied. I wiped the shaving cream from my face, rinsed it, and moved to let Jones in. "I'm headed to the mess hall."

"Save some coffee for us!" Jones yelled after me.

That wasn't likely either. I was pretty sure that coffee ran through my veins by now with as much as I'd consumed since D-Day. I lucked out because a fresh pot had gotten put out only minutes before I walked in. I grabbed a plate of eggs, some toast, and coffee. I should have been hungrier than I was, and I only took the food so I didn't make myself sick. I knew I needed to fuel my body to keep going at the same pace. It didn't seem likely that things would slow down.

I finished the coffee before I took a bite and returned

to get more. A few more guys wandered in and loaded their plates chock full. None of the cooks complained and they looked to be in the same shape we were. We all looked terrible. The saving grace was we didn't smell and we were clean. It was the small blessings that got us through.

"Do you think they are going to send us back today?" Ribbits asked around his mouthful of food.

"Your guess is as good as mine," I responded, picking at my eggs. My appetite wasn't there.

"I can't believe the number of ships and blimps we saw," Hausman said as he sat down with his plate. "Ha, I rhymed."

I chuckled and rolled my eyes, forcing myself to eat. "We need more sleep if we find that funny."

"Give it up." Hausman elbowed me in the ribs. "I'm doing the best I can. It's not like we've seen much humor the past week."

"That's true. Eat your food and drink your coffee. Then find a better rhyme to entertain us with," I suggested and stood to get more coffee.

"You'll be sorry you told me that." Hausman laughed. He began to eat in earnest.

I probably would be but he was right; humor helped. I refilled my cup and picked up my toast. "Did you guys get any quality sleep?"

"No," Ribbits answered, pushing his plate away. "I had strange dreams. I got some solid hours in, though more would be nice. I think the solid hours happened right after my body hit the cot."

"Tell me about it," Cutty griped. "Anyone see Rogers yet?"

"He was just getting in the shower when I finished

shaving," Jones replied. "He looked like shit."

"We all do," I corrected him. "Imagine having to be the one to fly Queenie through all that mess. I'm surprised he's upright."

"It's astounding what the human mind and body can accomplish when we think we can't do anymore," Ribbits replied in a startlingly profound moment. "I've felt several times like I was going to collapse, and here I am, stuffing my face with pancakes and getting ready to do it all over again."

"Stuff your face, you mean?" Jones joked to lighten the mood.

Ribbits reached across the table and grabbed Jone's toast, eating it. "You know it."

"You guys are crazy." Hausman grinned. "I'll stab you if you try to take my food. Just giving you fair warning."

That comment made me laugh and the tension broke by the time that Rogers walked in. He sported a set of dark circles under his eyes, yet he gave us a genuine smile as he walked over to get food.

"See? The human spirit rebounds and finds reasons to smile," Ribbits reminded us before dropping the subject.

It was the subtle reminder we needed that despite rough things, we were still here and living to fight another day. It was something to be thankful for, even though I was sure our time here would leave scars that would last the rest of our lives.

Rogers walked up with his tray of food and sat beside me. "What's good?"

"Ribbits is stealing food off people's plates," I remarked with a wicked grin at Ribbits.

"Don't even try," Rogers warned. "I'll send you to medical so fast you won't realize there's a fork sticking out of your hand."

"That's the second time someone threatened him with a stabbing." Cutty laughed and shoved his tray away.

"He'll learn the lesson quickly." Rogers chuckled. "Don't come between a man and his food."

"Or his woman," Hausman added. "That might get you more than a stabbing."

"She might like it if I stab her," Ribbits cackled. "I'm joking, man, don't get all worked up. Have you popped the question yet?"

"No. We haven't had time. All we've been doing is flying. Remember? I don't think dropping a bomb near her with the words '*Will you marry me?*' painted on it would be the right way to propose."

"Correct." Rogers pointed his finger at Hausman and smiled. "When you screw it up, let Ribbits know so we can watch him try and fail. I want confirmation of his lack of style with the ladies."

I cracked up laughing. Rogers got two insults in with one statement. "Not only a master with a plane but with words."

"Bunch of jokers," Hausman mumbled good-naturedly. "On that note, I expect you all at my wedding and carrying expensive gifts for the trouble you've caused me."

That elicited a laugh from Rogers, and I again felt I was sitting here with family. We'd been through the wringer together and did our best to keep each other alive and well. It was the next best thing to having a wife and son at home waiting for my safe return.

"Any news?" Rogers asked after he finished eating.

"Just stories about Normandy, which is still going strong," Jones replied. "Those boys are doing some heavy fighting down there."

"Normandy will be burning for a while," I agreed. "What's on the agenda for today?"

Rogers shrugged wordlessly and got up to take his dishes back. He walked a little slower than usual and I wondered if some good old-fashioned physical training would do us some good. I was about to suggest it when two other pilots came in and looked around. They spotted Rogers and took off almost at a jog in his direction.

I figured that meant we would receive another mission. I assumed it would be Normandy and I motioned the guys to go and we walked back to the barracks to let Rogers have his conversation. It could be nothing more than him conversing with friends.

"Don't worry about it. If it's important, Rogers will let us know," I told them. "How do you guys feel about a run?"

"You want us to exercise?" Hausman looked at me incredulously. "After eating breakfast?"

"I figured the physical exertion would help us mentally." I shrugged. "Hey, I'm grasping at straws as much as you are."

"It's not a terrible idea," Jones replied slowly. "But we can wait until our food settles so we don't throw up."

They'd all eaten more than me, so it wasn't something I was overly worried about at the moment. I sat on my cot and leaned my elbows on my knees, hunching forward. I stretched my back lightly for a few minutes and then sat straight. Before I could make any other comments, Rogers walked into the barracks.

"Looks like we are going out today. The briefing is in an hour, so we have some time. Anyone want to lose some money playing a game of poker?" Rogers asked, sitting on his cot.

"I won't lose, but I'll play," I agreed, happy for something to do.

"I'm in," Cutty spoke up. "It's better than Suhm's suggestion of a run."

Rogers quirked an eyebrow at me. "You want to go on a run?"

"Not necessarily," I explained. "I was trying to think of something to do that would help us mentally. Physical exertion usually does that."

"True." Rogers gave a crooked grin. "Poker is more fun, though."

We played a couple of rounds before we had to go to the briefing and I was happy I hadn't lied. I didn't lose. I didn't win anything; I only broke even, but that was still better than losing. Cutty had no luck in that department today and we all ribbed him about it on our way to the briefing.

"Time to be serious." Jones poked Cutty in the ribs.

We walked in, took our seats, and listened as the general explained that our target was a bridge. I had to admit I spaced out on what bridge. I only recognized that we were going out to a place near Normandy. It was a bridge some sixty miles southwest of Normandy. A city called Tours.

I'm ashamed to say I heard nothing said in that briefing and I didn't know what was going on or what our objective was other than to take out a bridge. I suppose that was enough information for me to go on, and I could have asked, but I didn't want to disappoint Rogers. We were all still exhausted.

The bomb loaders had the plane ready to go when we arrived. We checked the plane over, rotated the propellors, and gave the payload a good once over. We got settled, put the headsets on, and took our place. I felt like a worn-out machine. This mission would be our twenty-fifth raid.

We took off and were quieter than usual, though we were intent on watching for enemies. Given the escalation of things in France with the invasion of Normandy, I believe we all expected a swarm of German fighters like angry bees after a kid knocked their hive over.

We didn't see anything the entire route over, not even flak, which was unusual, to say the least. Once we arrived near our target, we again had 10-10 cloud cover and no PFF ship to mark our location. We dropped our altitude to eight thousand feet but no soap.

Rogers radioed the information in and the mission got called off. We dropped no bombs. There was no flak and no trace of fighters. We returned to base with our bombs still secure and found out that we got credit for the mission anyway. Not one of us was going to argue that. Not after they told us to be up at twelve-thirty in the morning for another briefing.

We all went straight to sleep. We needed it.

CHAPTER 54

June 12th, 1944

This is rough!" I complained to no one in particular. "I don't think I sleep anymore."

"I know," Rogers grumbled along with me. "We're so close to going home though. Every time we pull another run with no rest, I keep telling myself that. It's a continuous chant in my head. You're almost done; you only have four more after this. Or whatever number it is. Today, it's four. Correct? I don't even know what day it is right now."

"It's June twelfth, Rogers," Hausman smarted off. "It's twelve thirty-eight in the morning on the twelfth."

"Thanks." Rogers shot Hausman a nasty look. "Rhetoric is lost on you, isn't it?"

"Only at twelve thirty-nine in the morning," Hausman fired back. "I'll be better at twelve-forty."

"I think the most sleep I've gotten in the past forty-eight hours is four hours," I kept on complaining. Maybe the sound of my voice would wake me up. "We're going up in the dark?"

"I think it will be light by the time we get to wherever we are going. Twilight, maybe," Cutty responded. "Maybe they are trying for the element of surprise again. That's the only reason they'd be getting us up this early to fly on no sleep with explosives."

Rogers chuckled as he pulled on his flight suit. "We fly with explosives and no sleep during the day, too. They don't care as long as the bombs get dropped on the target and we make it back with the plane."

"Hell, I don't care if we have the plane or not." Ribbits yawned. "I just want to make it back. I have a date tomorrow."

"How did you get a date with someone when we've been flying?" I wondered.

"Because I'm the man the ladies want. They come to me," Ribbits boasted.

"That probably means the poor lady was lost and blind," Jones commented. "If she wasn't, she was probably looking for me and you lied and said you were me. We all know I have all the luck when it comes to women."

The laughter got us moving and out the door for the briefing. Thankfully some considerate person made sure there was coffee there that we all pounced on and sucked down greedily. We had enough time to get a second cup before the general walked in and tapped his papers on the table to get our attention.

"Your target is an airfield at Conches. This airfield was of no interest to anyone until after 1943, when the Luftwaffe began to use it. There are three sections to this location and we need the airstrips unusable and the support buildings destroyed."

The general hung a map on the wall and pointed out the different sections. "There are station fuel tanks here," he tapped the map, "and flight control here. It's imperative those get damaged beyond repair. We've had other missions here that have left the runways with craters, but they are still using them somehow."

I tuned out after that because it was the same hype they always said, that we were aiding the war effort and turning the tides. It may be accurate, but this was our twenty-sixth mission and we'd heard it all before. It got old, and I wanted to get on with it so we could try to get a little rest.

Once the general dismissed us, we walked out to the airfield and began our preflight inspections with minimal talk. We were as run down as poor Queenie must have been after all these flights and getting shot up. I patted the side of her right under the girl I'd painted on Queenie. I did it for luck, believing she would see us through again. Each of the guys did the same thing. Our girl had been good to us and we needed to be good to her.

Rogers gave the all-clear and we taxied for takeoff. About thirty Liberators were on this mission and a PFF plane to boot. At least that way, we'd have a marker to hit if there were clouds. The ground crew loaded the aircraft with fifty-two one-hundred-pound bombs. Multiply that by thirty planes and you know that will leave a mark on that airfield.

"On approach," Rogers notified us so we could get ready. The bomb bay doors opened and the whoosh of air was loud and cold. "Visibility is good."

"Finally," I replied.

"Drop!" Jones commanded.

I watched them fall and saw at least two buildings get reduced to rubble and smoke billow up from one of the runways. Our aim was good and the bombs hit the target successfully. A cheer went up as the bay doors closed, and we turned right into some flak. It was the same story on a different day. The explosion caught me by surprise, and I swiveled around to find where the shots originated.

The first few shots missed, but then we got smacked hard. "Hydraulic line hit!" I called out through the comms. I could smell the fluid.

"Can you fix it?" Rogers asked.

"Negative," I called back.

"Shit," Rogers replied.

I kept my eyes glued to the engines for signs of smoke or fire. I wanted to chew on my fingernails just to keep my mind occupied and avoid going to the worst-case scenario every few seconds. I knew Rogers would get us down.

The entire flight back was sweat out by each of the crew as we hoped and prayed that the wheels would lock down or it would be a crash landing for us. I was reminded of when we had to divert to another base due to fires on the airfield. We'd be that fire if the wheels didn't engage. We were tense and quiet and each did everything we needed to do with careful precision to aid Rogers as much as possible.

When touchdown arrived, we were all strung tighter than a guitar string; no fiery endings for us yet. Queenie saw us through and we all let out a sigh of relief as we brought our girl to the depot to get repaired. We all kissed her side as we exited and said a silent thank you.

At the debriefing, we received a three-day pass. Sleep and drinking were on the agenda for each of us. Not necessarily in that order, either. The only thing I was sure of was those two things would happen.

CHAPTER 55

June 15th, 1944

Over the past couple of days, I went to town once with the guys and had a few drinks as a way to try and relax. Cutty and I shared a room. After a few drinks, I returned to the room and went to sleep. I was far too tired to do anything else. Maybe it was the alcohol but I actually slept like a rock.

In the morning, I went and got myself breakfast and ran into Hausman and his girl. She looked flushed and Hausman looked happy. I waved at them, and Hausman waved me over.

"Sit with us," Hausman told me. "We haven't ordered yet."

"I hear you are a father now," Beverly said to me as I pulled up a chair.

"I am. My wife Alyse had a son. She named him Ralph after me," I told her proudly. "I can't wait to see him."

"How exciting for you," Beverly crooned. "We are going to start a family, too," she added and giggled.

I looked back at Hausman and raised my eyebrows. "Anything else you want to share?"

"I asked Beverly to marry me last night." Hausman grinned at me. "We will look for a ring today to make it official. If I can find someone to take a picture of us, I'll send it back home so my parents at least know what she looks like."

"Well, congratulations to the happy couple," I said. "That's great news."

"I'm going to move to the States," Beverly informed me. She was giddy with excitement. "We will try and get all the details and marriage licenses sorted out today and have a chaplain on base perform the ceremony. Will you attend?"

"I'd be honored." I nodded at the woman.

"Did you guys have fun last night?" Hausman changed the subject.

"I went to bed early. I was so tired I could barely keep my eyes open. I couldn't even tell you when Cutty returned to the room," I admitted sheepishly.

The waitress chose that moment to come and take our orders and I kept it simple—eggs, ham, and toast. The happy couple ordered a considerable spread between them and I smiled and refrained from laughing. Alyse and I had done the same thing after we were married. We were ravenous.

We traded idle chit-chat while we waited for our food. Hausman spotted Cutty and Jones walking in and motioned them to the table beside us. They pulled the table closer to ours and Hausman shared his news. We all raised our water glasses to toast them. Then my food arrived.

I didn't waste time digging in, and neither did Beverly. If I had to guess, I'd say she was already pregnant, which was why Hausman looked like he was about to burst. I didn't voice my thoughts. If so, he'd tell us when he was ready. I figured they wanted to be married before announcing the news for propriety's sake and her parents.

It was still a reason to celebrate and we laughed it up and had a pleasant, relaxing morning breakfast with no talk of the war. It was a nice change of pace and I knew it would come to an end soon enough. Probably the moment we stepped foot on base.

After breakfast, we parted ways, and I wandered through a few local stores before returning to the base. The weather was agreeable and I wanted to get a run in because I felt good after doing that. I didn't necessarily like it, but it helped clear my mind and relieve stress.

I ran into Rogers in the barracks when I went to change into physical training clothing and he looked on the troubled side of things. I hesitated before asking what was wrong. Sometimes, I didn't want others intruding on my thoughts, which was the first thing that came to mind.

"Suhm," Rogers greeted me. "What brings you back early? I didn't expect anyone back until later."

"I wanted to get a run in while the weather was good," I told him with a shrug.

"Mind if I join you?" Rogers sat up and looked interested.

"Not at all," I replied. "I'd be happy for the company. Everything okay?"

"I don't know," Rogers told me honestly. "I think something is going on in my family, but they are afraid to tell me because of everything we experience over here. They don't want to burden or distract me. I don't think they realize that keeping secrets has the same outcome."

"Probably not," I agreed.

"So, let's run it out," Rogers suggested. "That was your idea, correct? Run to forget?"

"Essentially, yes." I chuckled. "It's not escapable but the physical release does me good. I don't care for running. I figured it was the lesser of the evils because if we pull orders,

I'll need my arms not to be tired."

"How true that is." Rogers nodded.

We did some light stretching and then let our feet pound the ground. We ran the base's perimeter on one side, watching for holes in the ground. That was the last thing we needed, to trip and break a leg. Our lungs heaved with the exertion, our arms pumped in time with our feet thudding into the ground, and sweat dripped down our bodies. By the time we got back, we'd run approximately five miles.

"Stretch," Rogers reminded me. "We don't need muscle cramps."

I followed his lead, and we both went inside to grab some clean clothes and shower. With an unspoken agreement, we returned to the barracks, lay on our cots, put hats over our faces, and napped.

It definitely wasn't the norm for me, but when the guys returned, Rogers and I had better attitudes and felt rested. My mind was lighter and I felt like I could face more of whatever was in store for us.

We joined the guys in the mess hall for supper and accepted another crew's invite for a game of poker. Cards and physical training seemed to be all we did. Right after we were dealt the second hand, we pulled orders, along with the crew playing cards with us.

"Briefing in an hour," the aide told us before delivering the rest of the orders.

"It will be our twenty-seventh mission," Cutty told one of the guys. "What number are you on?"

"Twelve," the kid responded. "It's scary out there. The Germans are getting desperate."

"They should be," Hausman told him. "We're winning."

I didn't know if we were, but we all liked to think we were. It helped us cope with the stress of war. We'd had a lot of good raids and the activity on June 6th showed massive effort on the Allies' part. The lot of us had seen Germany suffer several losses.

"Wonder where it will be this time," a young kid said as we walked by.

"France, somewhere," Rogers guessed. "We are trying to drive Germany out."

We finished our hands and then went our separate ways to prepare for what we assumed would be a departure right after the briefing. I shouldn't assume anything. Our orders were to return to the bridge in the Tours area that we couldn't hit the first time due to cloud cover.

Not only that, but it would be a night mission. The schedule had us leaving around twelve-thirty in the morning. We received the command to catch a couple of hours of sleep before we had to head out. The good thing I've learned about being in the Army was that it conditioned my body to sleep when it could. It probably wouldn't serve me all that well back in civilian life, but it sure did here.

Our alarms went off at eleven-thirty the night of the 14th, and we got ready for our mission. Shortly after the clock struck midnight and the calendar date turned to the 15th, we were taxiing down the runway loaded to the brim.

Queenie and the rest of the group carried twelve five-hundred-pound bombs. It was a lot of firepower for one bridge. Simultaneously, there were several other raids for heavy bombers to drop loads on other bridges across France. The overall goal was to shut down support routes and block the Germans.

Our route to the bridge took us back over the beaches

of Normandy and it appeared that our boys were doing alright. Even in the dark, we could see fires burning in the towns and telltale flashes of gunfire. Not that we could tell who was doing the firing. And by the light of the moon, we could see the boats all still cluttered around the channel; it made the sea look black there were so many.

We reached our destination and dropped our eggs on that bridge accurately. Our formation was perfect, and the bomb pattern was spot on. It felt good to complete a mission like that, and across France, Allied troops destroyed more than two bridges that night.

We saw a little flak coming at us from a distance, and Cutty dropped chaff. Ribbits radioed the position across the groups flying with us and we successfully avoided taking any fire. We brought our Queenie home with no damage. What a morning! I was happy to report that none of the flak hit us for once in the debrief. It felt great to deliver good news.

CHAPTER 56

June 18th, 1944

Thanks for being a part of my wedding," Hausman told the crew after walking in after a couple of days off. He used the time to get married, and the crew was right there with him. Our moods were upbeat and we were ready to get back out there and be done. Each of us was ready for the next phase of life: the after-war phase.

"Do you think it's because we are so close to going home that we feel like nothing can touch us?" Jones asked me.

"I don't think that's what's going on in my head," I replied. "I'm being extra careful and my nerves feel like they are stretched tight as guitar strings about to snap. I definitely don't feel like anything can touch us. I still have the feeling that luck will run out."

"Vigilance is the key, gentlemen," Ribbits told us. "We want to get home. We can't get lazy now that the end is near."

I pointed at Ribbits and nodded. "Yes. That's what I

think. It's easy to slack off and feel like thinking: okay, we've done our duty; we can relax. We can't. There's too much at stake. Whenever I feel like I am relaxing, I remember the crew on their last mission when they got shot down. I don't want that to be us. And no, I'm not saying they got shot down because they weren't paying attention. We weren't on that plane. We don't know what was happening. I'm just saying we can't back off now."

"No, we absolutely can't," Rogers joined the conversation. "These last missions are the most dangerous. I don't mean raids or targets, either. It's a mental mindset, as Suhm said."

"What's the first thing you will do when you get home?" Cutty asked, changing the subject to something lighter. I could tell he was bothered.

"Kiss my wife," I answered automatically. "Then, my son."

"I'm going to eat a giant steak." Rogers grinned, rolling with the change. "Good old-fashioned steak and potatoes. It's just not the same here as it is at home."

"You lived on a ranch. That's not fair," Ribbits argued. "The rest of us aren't from a farm with fresh meat. Maybe you should have us all over for a big dinner party with many steaks."

I laughed. "You men need a woman if food is your first priority."

"I got one now." Hausman winked. "We'll look for our own place when we get there."

"Will Beverly be able to leave when you do, or does she have a set time to serve like we do?" Jones wondered.

"Her time is up in about a month," Hausman told us. "If we finish before that, I'll wait here and then we'll arrange transportation home. Hopefully, better than sixteen thousand men crammed onto a ship going off to war."

"No enjoying married life for you if that's the case." I laughed. "There was no privacy on the Queen Mary when we came over."

"They'll fly us home, I think," Rogers stated. "We won't be on the next plane out after the thirty, though. We might be here a few more months but won't be on raids. We might get put on duty to teach some training classes. Remember the guy who taught us about fuses? I remember him telling me that's what happened to him."

"That's the part I'm looking forward to the most," Ribbits said. "No raids. I'm rather fond of not getting shot at."

I threw my pencil at Ribbits and laughed. Hausman's rushed wedding did us all some good. I thought again about how much I'd miss spending time with these guys but I was also anxious to get home. I wanted to see where my life went after this.

"Orders are in." An aide came into the barracks. "General wants to brief in forty-five minutes."

Rogers nodded his understanding and the aide scurried off to deliver the orders to the rest. "Twenty-eight, men. This flight will be our twenty-eighth mission. Can you believe it?"

"Sometimes it feels like we had our first one a lifetime ago, and then there are days when it feels like it was just yesterday. Time is a strange bedfellow," I commented. "We were so green and so ready to fight. I wanted to take on the world. We were kids, essentially, even though we were adults. Now I pray for no fighting and no flak."

"You should stop sleeping with father time," Jones joked. "Your wife might get jealous."

We all broke out into laughter. We joked around for a bit longer and then prepared for the briefing. It was humorous to me when we walked in that the seats in the front were left open for us like it was a reservation. I'd be happy to pass the baton on being lead crew.

I sat and kicked my feet out in front of me to stretch a little. My legs had that well-used feeling that came after physical training. It wasn't a bad feeling. However, I didn't want them to tighten up, especially since we were about to be crammed into our places on the plane.

"Target is Hamburg today, soldiers," the general droned on. "We want the usual targets bombed. The shipyards, U-boat pens, and oil refineries. We'll break you out into three groups, each dropping payloads on one of the targets." The general tacked a map that had the groupings listed out. "Any questions?"

Short and sweet, that was how I liked these briefings. "Looks like the shipyards for us," I told Rogers. "Any extra instructions?"

"Make sure we have plenty of chaff on board." Rogers stood and stretched. "Good idea on that run," he told me quietly. "I feel better."

"Me too," I agreed. "You want extra chaff because you expect flak?"

"Definitely expect it." Rogers nodded. "We're going back over Germany and they've got the hots for us now."

"Can you blame them? We are a good-looking crew," I bragged. "I'll double-check it when we get on Queenie."

We walked out to the airfield, and Cutty grabbed two extra containers of chaff. He nodded at me. "I got it."

"Perfect," I replied. "Let's see how much is already on board."

I climbed onto the plane and checked our supply, which looked fully stocked. Cutty followed and secured the extra and we went back out to do our preflight checks and spin the propellers. Everything looked tip-top, and we each gave our all clear to Rogers.

We boarded Queenie, every guy giving her a little love-tap as we got in, our silent way of asking her to keep us safe. We were first up and Rogers waited while our group lined up behind us. The formation planes took off and the fighters followed. Once we were good, we took off for Germany.

The flying was smooth once we rose to twenty-eight thousand five-hundred feet. It was higher than we'd ever gone to bomb, and we were curious as to why the extra distance. At first, the air currents were unstable. We learned that as Rogers radioed the position back. Once over Germany, it was to avoid flak. None of it came close to us at this altitude. He dropped lower when we opened the bay doors.

We dropped our payload and Rogers had to move into evasive actions almost immediately. We encountered a solid wall of flak and the extra altitude gave us a more considerable margin of safety. The air was black with the explosions and almost looked like a solid wall. It was beautiful flying, and we got only a few holes in Queenie before we rose back up into the sky. I didn't expend all my ammunition, either.

There were no enemy fighters, which we were all grateful for after that flak. The extra chaff was a good call because Cutty threw almost everything out the window. Nothing else eventful happened on the way back. I thought our twenty-eighth mission went well. Given what we'd encountered thus far, it could have been so much worse.

After debriefing, we received a leave pass. Instead of

staying on base, we all headed out to Aylesbury this time. It gave Hausman a chance to see his bride and an opportunity for us to let loose when we weren't in such a bad mental state, drinking purely to forget what we'd experienced. This time, it was just for fun.

CHAPTER 57

June 19th-23rd, 1944

I'd had a swell time on our leave. It was unanimous with all the guys. It was fantastic and what the doctor ordered. Monday night, we danced with some lovely ladies, drank, played cards, listened to live music, and ate well. It was a jovial atmosphere in the pub. We had no cares and no expectations. Our time here would soon be up, so we enjoyed it while we could.

Three other guys and I ended up in the back room of a pub we hadn't tried yet. We'd already danced and eaten and then received an invitation to play cards with some of the locals. Often, when we received invitations like that, the locals thought we'd be an easy mark. I had little to gamble with, so I wasn't worried about losing too much money. I'd pocket the extra winnings and continue with my original amount if I won. It was a good game plan.

A few of the Brits were hard to understand. Their accent was different than the London accent I'd gotten accustomed to. I don't know how Rogers understood them, but he translated when I didn't get it. These Limeys probably thought I was daft. I didn't mind because I won more hands than I lost and tripled my money. Rogers won, too. We both sported smug looks that probably annoyed some of the men.

I paid for a shared room with my winnings for Rogers and me. I had no complaints. A few gentlemen we played with weren't quite as pleased as I was. However, they should know how gambling worked by now; they weren't kids.

After cleaning up at cards, Rogers and I found a small café still open. We had ourselves a late-night dessert and then went to sleep. It was solid sleep and we got breakfast the next day before separating.

I headed to see my friends at Attlebridge, near where I was. I hoped that they were still there and lucked out. I spent time with them, and they were also close to being finished. We talked for hours before I left to return to Aylesbury that night.

We told the tales of our missions that aged us by a decade and shared the funny stories that helped bring us back into a good head space. We reminisced about training and shenanigans that we got into. Before I left, we exchanged home addresses to keep in touch. That was one of those things I didn't want to lose: contact with the people I spent time with.

The next day, I met up with Jones and we watched a movie and then danced with some ladies we met at the theater. For a few days, I felt like the person I used to be before the war. I knew it wasn't who I had become, but I was carefree and unburdened in those moments.

I felt awful thinking of my new family back home as a burden and didn't mean it negatively. It was more of a thought that I knew my life would change again drastically when I got home, just as it had when I arrived over here. It wasn't a bad thing. My fun free time with this pass was a last hurrah before a new reality sunk into my bones.

I spent the last day back on base resting and doing some physical training to get the booze out of my system. Rogers was back and joined me and we had long talks about what life would be like for us when we got home. I think the idea of civilian life scared us after everything we'd seen and experienced. Adjustment would be difficult.

When the rest of the crew trickled in, we traded stories of our leave, laughed, and then played some rounds of blackjack. We played for food snacks we brought back instead of money, mainly because many of us who went out had no money left after we returned.

The other crew in our barracks joined us and we were up far later than we should have been, yet none cared. In the back of our minds was the fact that we'd all be going home soon. This brotherhood wouldn't be an everyday thing for us anymore. While the situation wasn't ideal, we were here for the same reasons and banded together to make it through.

Everyone hoped they made their thirty missions. Every single person that came here wished that. Just as every man here had doubts that it would happen, it was hard not to when you heard, or worse, saw, your group's planes shot down. Or when you returned from a mission to find your barracks that held a crew of friends now empty. Thirty missions was a lifetime and a blink. I wanted to soak up the closeness I didn't have with friends back home. It was different here.

The other guys on base knew it as well as I did. No one was going to complain about us being loud after hours. Every crew on the base knew how close to thirty we were. They all wished they were in the same boat as we were.

CHAPTER 58

June 24th, 1944

W ake up," Jones called out early in the morning. "We've got work to do."

"It's too early," Cutty moaned.

"We've got orders," Jones kept on.

I was the next to groan but I threw my legs over the side of my cot and sat up. I rubbed the sleep from my eyes and glanced at the clock. It was barely five in the morning. I couldn't complain too badly since we just came off a pass where we all had fun. Perhaps too much fun the night before when we stayed up far later than usual.

"The aide said the briefing is in two hours." Jones laughed at our expressions. "Come on, we can take our time with breakfast and shower the stink off of us before heading out. It's our twenty-ninth mission."

"There are days I want to choke you," grumbled Hausman. "We could have slept another hour. And you *do* stink."

"This way, you'll be fresh, awake and ready for the mission," Jones went on as if no one were glaring at him.

I was sure he was doing it to annoy us at this point, and in some cases, it was working. Rogers just shook his head and got up. I did the same but shoved Jones as I walked past him. It was the only statement I needed to make.

"Bunch of grumpy Gus's." Jones laughed. "I'll grab us a table in the mess hall."

Jones would be lucky not to have food thrown at him. Cutty was giving him some baleful looks as he got dressed. I'd miss this when it was over. Not that I was about to tell Jones that after this stunt. I was dressed before the rest and headed to the mess hall and coffee.

"Look, Suhm, I even got a cup of coffee for you." Jones pointed to the table. "It's still hot."

"What did you do to it?" I asked as I sat across from him and inhaled the aroma.

"Nothing." Jones laughed and shook his head. "I don't have a death wish."

I chuckled and sipped at the brew. "What are you doing up this early anyway?"

"I heard people talking and it woke me up. I went outside to see who was out there at that hour and overheard the general talking to his aide. I didn't hide and stepped out and stretched like I was just out as I normally am and the aide gave me the orders and then rushed off like he was afraid of me," Jones explained. "I figure other crews will start coming in soon. Cook is just finishing up breakfast."

I smelled the sausage cooking and my stomach rumbled in response. I wasn't usually a big breakfast eater, but for some reason, this morning, I was famished. I wanted to eat everything. I was the first in line when the cook called out that food was ready. I took eggs, pancakes, fruit, sausage, juice, toast, potatoes, and cottage cheese. The rest of the crew gave me crazy looks because, typically, I was eggs and toast and nothing more.

"I'm hungry." I shrugged and returned to the table. I dug in and ate every last bite of it.

"It's all that extra running you've been doing," Cutty remarked as he sat down. "You're tall and skinny."

I shot him a frown and kept on eating. Yes, I was tall, but I wasn't skinny. I'd put on a lot of muscle since I've been overseas. I'd been skinny when I first arrived, but not now. I was lean. I'd probably gain ten pounds from this breakfast alone.

"Why don't you all stop talking and eat your food?" I grumbled.

"I can eat and make fun of you at the same time." Cutty grinned at me.

"Bunch of children." Hausman shook his head. "Speaking of children, Beverly is pregnant."

"Congratulations," I told Hausman. "Looks like you improved your aim."

Rogers burst out laughing and the rest of the crew followed. Hausman chuckled and threw a piece of toast at me. I caught it and ate it with a wink at him and a smug smile. Some of the guys ribbed him, but we all were happy.

We finished breakfast and returned to the barracks to kill some time before the briefing. It wasn't long before we were heading to hear where we were going next. Once again, the seats at the front were left open and we took our position.

"Target this morning is the Bretigny Airfield," the general told us. "It's a Luftwaffe base heavy on the Junkers. We've hit it several times and our goal is to keep it out of commission so the Germans can't scramble their planes."

It seemed simple enough to me. We hadn't gone there before now, so we weren't sure what to expect. We typically expected the worst and prepared for it. Maybe that was the key to our luck. Today was no different and we checked everything before issuing the all-clear to Rogers.

I thanked Queenie, patted her side and said my silent little prayer for her to keep us all safe and see us back. We took our places, waited for the okay to proceed, then took off. The weather in England was decent but as we approached France, the clouds grew.

When we reached our target of the airfield, we had 10-10 cloud cover and had to radio back the situation. They scratched the mission and gave the order to return to base. Rogers communicated the orders to the rest of the group and we went home. No guns had been fired by either side this time.

The dry runs were frustrating and none of us liked them. In some ways, it felt as though we failed. That wasn't the case, as the weather was something no one had control over. The saving grace was we encountered no enemy planes and no flak. We returned to base safely, intact, and with all our bombs.

When we debriefed, the officers told us the mission still counted toward our thirty and it was another thing for us to be thankful for at the end of the day. We returned to our barracks, shed our flight gear, and then lazed around. Not completing our objective was disappointing, but in the grand scheme, it wasn't a horrible day to have despite Jones waking us up before necessary.

CHAPTER 59

June 25th, 1944

What a glorious day!" Ribbits twirled around in a circle until he about fell over with dizziness. He was like a kid in the park on a sunny day.

"What are you talking about?" Hausman looked up from his letter.

"It's sunny outside, we are alive, and a girl wrote me a letter!" Ribbits crowed.

"What's wrong with her?" I asked with a smirk.

"She obviously has no taste," Jones answered with a smug grin.

"Is she real, or did you imagine her?" Rogers joined in the ribbing. "Human?"

I laughed and finished writing my letter home. With any luck, I'd beat the letter home and hand-deliver it from the mailbox. I doubted it, but it was still a nice thought. I addressed the envelope and sealed it shut.

"What a bunch of naysayers." Ribbits sat on his cot, though he smiled. "I met her the last leave we had. She's a beauty, too."

"Then what is she doing with an ugly mug like yours when she could have had this pretty one?" Jones waggled his eyebrows in jest.

"She wanted a real man," Ribbits replied. "I'm just the man for the job, too."

"In your dreams," Cutty joked. "I'll have to have a talk with her about her poor choices."

"Like hell," Ribbits smarted off, the letter clutched in his hand. "I'm writing her back now and getting myself a date."

"What will you do if we finish before she replies?" I asked, crossing my arms over my chest. "Think she'll make the trip over for a disappointing night?"

Rogers laughed. "You guys are terrible. I feel bad for all your women."

"To be fair, I think they all feel bad for themselves, too, with the lot of us," I commented. "It's odd seeing Ribbits acting all goofy before nine in the morning. It usually takes him at least three hours to figure out how to put pants on."

"Maybe the sight of you in G.I. underwear was uninspiring," Ribbits threw back at me.

"Oh, man." Jones laughed. "The crew is in rare form this morning."

"We should be," Rogers countered. "Look at how far we've come, as a team and individually. For example, did anyone here think Hausman would land a beauty like Beverly? Then actually get married and knock her up?"

Hausman laughed the hardest at that. It wasn't often Rogers joined in the ribbing and I was happy to see he was right there with us this time. The man was right; we'd all changed in so many ways since being here in the war, and I kept returning to that thought. I've been thinking about it in the past three weeks.

What if Alyse didn't like who I was now? Would she take my son and leave? Would who I am be attracted to Alyse now, or would I want to leave? That was the scariest part about going home. Would this new version of me be accepted? I did my best to shake it off, dwelling on the unknown and assuming the actions of others wouldn't get me far.

I was twenty-six and had my whole life in front of me. Some of these guys here were younger than I was. Rogers was the same age as me, and I think Warren was a couple of years older than us. He didn't engage often with this type of banter on or off the plane.

All I knew of him after seven months of serving on the same crew was that he was married, had two children, and taught math to high school kids back home. We asked him to join us all the time and he politely declined most of the time. He played cards with us sometimes but that was it. He rarely joined us in town; those were the best memories.

Carlson was quiet by nature, though he keenly listened to us and I think he wanted to join in our antics somewhere inside but was afraid to. I didn't believe his home life was good. He didn't talk about it when he did talk. He spoke about traveling when he got home—seeing new places and experiencing new things.

Young was just that. Nothing more than a kid. A smart one, too. He didn't join us on leave because he said his parents would disapprove. Like Warren, the rare times he did were the best. Cutty told him that his parents would never know unless he told them. Even when he did come out with us, he didn't drink, didn't dance, or flirt and kept to himself. But if there was a sign of trouble, he was up in a heartbeat and ready to stand with us.

Merrill was one of those men whose age or mood were hard to gauge. He had a poker face. He won a lot when he played cards with us because he could bluff like no one else. He joked around a few times when he got caught up in whatever antics we were up to, but he hung around Warren, Carlson, and Young more often than not. The rest were like siblings I'd grown up with; in a way, I guessed they were.

I'd still miss them when this was over. We'd become a family, even if it were a reluctant one on some of their parts. I got lost in thoughts swirling in my head for a moment until a hat smacked into me.

"Suhm! Are you still with us?" Jones called out to me. "I was talking to you and you just tuned out."

"I was thinking about how I would miss all of you when we went back home, though now I'm rethinking your part in that," I answered him with a smirk.

"You know I'm your favorite." Jones winked at me and did a little dance on the top of his cot.

That's what was happening when the general's aide walked in to deliver orders. He stood there for a full minute staring at the spectacle Jones made of himself before he shoved the paper at Rogers. "Orders for today. Briefing in an hour."

Jones jumped off his cot, his face reddening. "You jerks could have told me he was here. Now he will report back to the general that I'm off my rocker."

"This is our thirtieth mission." Rogers laughed. "The general already knows."

I stood up and stretched, my hands brushing the beams in the ceiling. "That's the truth, Jones. The general knows you are our resident jester in our royal court."

"Oh, now you're royal?" Jones mocked me.

"Not me, us." I gestured at Rogers, the quiet guys, and Hausman. "The rest of you are entertainment."

Rogers laughed and Hausman nodded and pointed at Jones. "Clown."

"Whatever." Jones took a bow. "I'm still the best. Your kid will have to settle with sub-par humor with you." Jones nodded at me.

"That's fine. I'll hire you to entertain Ralph's birthday parties. Don't forget to wear the red nose," I joked.

"We're lead again." Rogers looked up from the orders.

"I don't think this is our last mission," I replied in a softer tone. "My gut says otherwise. But this is our Distinguished Flying Cross flight."

"That's right!" Ribbits got animated. "That's amazing. We get a DFC. Is anyone else remembering the crew that got shot down on their last mission?" His abrupt change in topic caught me off guard and immediately sobered our antics.

"It's all I can think about," Merrill joined the conversation, startling us. "I'm trying not to because I don't want that to happen to us."

"It won't," Jones promised.

"You can't say that," Hausman added. "None of us can. We have an amazing pilot, and of course, me, so we'll get through it. Plus, as Suhm said, it might not be our last mission."

"We've already flown more than thirty," Cutty remarked. "I know that the flights around D-Day don't count as missions, but we were out a lot. Plus, the flights where we were support. Try and look at it that way. We've far surpassed thirty."

It was true, and Merrill relaxed a bit, at least in

appearance. Ribbits's comment about that crew got to all of us. If you looked closely enough, you could see the traces of it on their faces as they processed the memory. I remember returning to the barracks, looking at the empty beds, and feeling a hollow spot in my chest. It wouldn't be us, I silently vowed. Just like Jones, I held on to that belief.

"Let's go," Rogers told us, his tone neutral. "We have a job to do and will perform to our best."

We were the first crew to arrive and the general gave us a quick look as we took our seats and waited. He had to know it was our thirtieth mission. He held each of our gazes for a moment or two before returning to the papers in front of him.

Five minutes later, the crews started trickling in; only a few were in cheerful spirits. The rest looked a little bedraggled. Not that we weren't feeling the same way, but there was an end in sight for us. These other crews still had over half of their missions to complete. I felt for them.

"Attention," the general called out and the chatter stopped. "Today, you are going after a transmitter station. These drones are increasing their attacks on London. The quicker we can take them out, the better off we are at home in case Hitler turns his aim on the States. You will encounter resistance, and I want you at an elevated altitude for the heavy bombers."

The general showed us the map and pointed out the areas where intelligence reports showed active German troops, air and ground. They showed us routes for escape should we go down, then finally, the general tapped the map where the target was and looked up at Rogers and then each of our crew.

"There's a Distinguished Flying Cross for you at the

end of this. I want nothing more than each of you to come back. Men, the crew of the Queenie is flying their thirtieth mission today." The general ended the briefing. "Let's do our best to ensure each of you returns to base."

A few of the crews towards the back gave us a cheer, and then throughout the room, there was a general hoo-ah for everyone to have a safe journey. Some of the guys that walked by us thumped us on the backs as they passed and we began to smile.

The Distinguished Flying Cross was a medal for persons who acted in a single act of heroism or extraordinary achievement while participating in aerial flights that were not routine. Making thirty missions was extraordinary. Nothing about our missions was ordinary, despite them telling us they were easy missions. The ones they called out that way were anything but. The lifespan of an aircrew was incredibly short, and Queenie deserved that cross as much as we did.

After all our checks, we paid our homage to Queenie as we boarded and got ready. We were attached to our girl more now than ever. Rogers got us in position and waited for the okay to take off down the runway. Once given, we were underway.

Our formation was good, and I looked at the other planes, and once more, the thought that I would miss this hit me. I was a part of something so much bigger than I was and it was making a difference. That's all I craved, to make a difference, and I'd done it. We all had, and for whatever reasons, found others wanting to be a part of it all. They took the steps, and someone should acknowledge their bravery.

Seeing all the planes in the formation was a thing of beauty and each time we went up, I admired it. Today was no different, but it felt different. The weather was on our side and I was confident we wouldn't be returning with any of our bombs.

Rogers took us up higher when we were closer to the target. These drones, the V-1 rockets, were intentionally made for the bombings of London. More than one hundred were launched in a day at the city, making the transmitter stations for launch a priority target. We'd already heavily bombed the coast of France, where most of these had hidden locations.

They looked like flying bombs. When their engines stopped, the rocket fell out of the sky and exploded on contact. They left giant craters in the ground sixty to ninety feet wide. I couldn't imagine being on the ground when one of those landed.

Cutty began throwing chaff as we approached our target. The bomb bay doors opened, and we waited for the navigator's order. Hausman gave the commane, Jones got to work and bombs dropped. We were at twenty-five thousand feet in altitude, and I saw the flak coming.

"Flak, two o'clock," I radioed the warning to the crew. Ribbits passed the information to the rest of the group and we all fired back. Angry red bullets streaked through the air from several planes. The sounds of our guns mixed with the explosions of flak. We wouldn't go down without a fight.

The bomb bay doors were closing and I watched the planes around us get hit by flak. It was way too accurate today. Rogers began his evasive maneuvers, ordering the others to do the same. The formation changed and planes began banking and diving to avoid getting hit. Mayhem struck.

Smoke rose from the ground, gunpowder filled the air, and I tried to watch for flying torpedoes or enemy fighters. There was so much to lookout for now as technology advanced. It didn't matter how much experience you had when things were constantly changing before you could learn how to combat it while staying in the air. The sounds of heavy fire were deafening even with the comms on.

"Incoming!" Cutty screamed through the comms.

I jerked my head at his tone and saw a piece of flak strike our number one engine with the sound of an explosion way too close. "Fire on two!" I yelled as smoke billowed from the engine. Rogers immediately cut power to the affected engine and I watched for flames or sparks, but nothing came—just smoke.

It lessened as we flew and tried to dodge flak. We took some more hits, as did several other of the planes. My muscles were tense and I watched for anything I could shoot. "Smoke clear," I radioed to Rogers, who started engine two back up.

It appeared okay, but my thundering heart still doubted what my eyes saw. Thankfully, on the way back, we didn't encounter any enemy fighters or more flak to dodge. I watched that engine carefully, and when we began our descent, I smiled, seeing we still arrived back to base without having to feather any engines.

"Yes!" Jones screamed as we slowed.

I grinned and noted that my jaw felt tense. I guess I'd been clenching it the whole way back. I opened and closed my mouth to stretch out the muscles. I counted four holes in our girl and had no shame when I kissed the side of her after my feet hit the ground. She'd done it, along with the skills of our crew.

We went to the debrief and listened to the damage the other crews reported. I shook my head at how deadly accurate today's flak was. When Rogers conveyed ours, the general smiled, a sight we didn't see often.

"Rogers, your crew is the only crew in the 8th Heavy Bombardment Group to have returned from every mission without feathering an engine," the general told us. I think we all stood a bit straighter after that.

CHAPTER 60

June 26th-July 4th

My gut had been right that they wouldn't consider us done yet. There was talk of one more raid that they needed an experienced lead crew for and they asked before we left if we minded. It was nice of them to ask, though the way they did it couldn't really be considered a question. It was more of a telling than asking. The tone did not broker a response on our part.

With a week of fun before our truly last raid and mission, we didn't waste time. What better way to spend it than in London? We were on alert for V-rocket bombs and, luckily, didn't encounter any. Being on the ground for one of those wasn't something on my must-do list.

We caught the train to London. Most of us did. Carlson, Young, and Warren stayed back at base. We received a week's pass and wanted to celebrate the fourth with other Americans. Understandably, it wasn't a holiday that the Brits celebrated. I also didn't know what to do if we saw the rocket's red glares. It was a possibility we couldn't ignore. That's why we went back to London, to hang out in the Rainbow Room so we couldn't see the glares of rockets.

Hausman brought his wife, her first time at the club,

and Merrill joined us for once. It was his first time there, too. We would have to catch the last train out of London to make it back before our pass expired. Since the fourth was our last day on the pass, we toured around London the cheap way, by bus and subway, and stayed at small hotels outside the city with each of us sharing rooms. Anything we could do to save money and extend our time away from the base, we did.

Merrill hadn't explored London at all, and showing him some of the sights was just as fun as experiencing them the first time. We marveled at the palace guards and thanked our lucky stars that it wasn't our duty. Imagine having to stand there with bombs dropping nearby and not being able to react. Scary. I avoided taking him to the bombed parts of the city. We stuck to the palaces, abbey's, museums, and other tourist areas.

The Rainbow Room was hopping each time we went in and it had something for everyone. I did a lot of dancing and card playing. It seemed to be the same thing I always did on leave. However, this time was more remarkable because I knew it was my last time here. I didn't hold back. There was no point in being reserved at this stage of things.

At night, I danced until my legs wouldn't hold me up and then I played cards like there was no tomorrow. In the mornings, we caught a movie, whatever happened to be playing, or we explored more of London. Merrill was eager to see as much as we wanted to show him.

On the fourth, our last night, we all toasted each other, the States, our friendship, and life. I ate until my belly was going to burst and then slept the entire train ride back to the base. We arrived just after midnight and went straight to bed. We encountered no rockets, no one fought, and we all had fun. I threw caution to the wind and enjoyed my life in the moment. That was something I hadn't done in a while.

I did wish Alyse was with me. That was the thought I had before I fell asleep. She would have enjoyed London. She would have danced the night away with me kicking up her heels. Maybe, when I returned, we would take a night and do that together like we did before the war.

CHAPTER 61

July 5th, 1944

I woke up feeling like someone had thrown sand in my eyes. First, I needed a drink of water, followed by a shower. I smelled like a distillery. Rather, the barracks smelled like a distillery from all of us who had returned from London.

I rolled out of bed, grabbed my toothbrush, and beat feet for the showers. I didn't even wait for the water to warm. I just stepped under the icy spray and let the shock bring me to life. I brushed my teeth in the shower, washed up, and got out before the water warmed up.

Clothes and then coffee were next on my agenda. A few of the other guys were rousing when I walked back in to get dressed. The cold water helped wake me; now, I needed caffeine to finish the job. I nodded at the others and didn't have to tell them where I was going. They all knew. They'd all be right behind me.

I was on my third cup when Cutty came in. He went for the food, which I hadn't done yet. I was savoring the black tar of Army coffee on my tongue. The blacker, the better. I was probably one of the few of my crew who liked it.

"Did you save any of the brew for the rest of us?" Jones asked, sounding groggy.

"A cup or two, though I haven't finished drinking yet," I replied.

"What time is our briefing? Has anyone heard yet?" Hausman asked as he sat down with a tray of food.

"Probably ten," Rogers answered, sitting on his other side. "That's my best guess."

"It's as good as any," I told him. "Wonder where it will be?"

"France," Merrill responded. "I hear things too, even if I don't talk as much as Jones."

The expression on Jones's face is what got me to laugh. He looked as if he didn't know whether to be offended or laugh. I wasn't the only one to find it funny, either. Rogers and Cutty snickered as they ate their breakfast.

"Can you believe this will be our last?" Ribbits asked as he joined the crew. "It feels strange."

It did. It was almost bittersweet and I could see my emotions reflected in the faces of the crew around me. Yes, it would be nice not to fight or worry about getting shot down. There would be an adjustment to regular life after we got home, and I knew it would be harder for some.

Reality was setting its sharp teeth into each of us. While it wasn't bad, it was a change that would require us to adapt. After all of this, that wouldn't be easy. It would be hard for all of us, not just me.

"Let's focus on the here and now," Rogers suggested. "That way, we get through this mission and face whatever comes next. It's not like the move would be immediate. There are a lot of moving parts to consider."

"True," Merrill agreed. I found it funny that he decided to come out of his shell on the last few missions. I guess that could be why he chose to; he was anxious to get home.

The guys brought their trays back and we got our orders as we reached our barracks. "Briefing at nine," the aide told us.

"I was close." Rogers shrugged. "Still gives us an hour."

I figured I'd pack up as much stuff as possible, things that I didn't need daily to prepare for whenever they told me I was out of there. When I looked around, it seemed some of the others had the same idea.

"Gear up," Rogers announced about fifteen minutes before we were due at the briefing. Even that felt strange, knowing I wouldn't do that again after this. It was odd; I would suddenly miss the things that had become rituals that could potentially end our lives.

Even this melancholy mood was unusual for me. I wanted to go home. I wanted to see Alyse and my baby. Why was I so sad about leaving a war zone? I needed to snap out of it and focus on the job at hand. My time here wasn't up yet and I still needed to perform at maximum ability.

We filed into the briefing room and sat in the open seats. We had to wait for the general this time, and the room became standing room only. It appeared this would be a big mission. There weren't as many people here as there were for D-Day, but it wasn't far behind that.

"What's going on?" I whispered to Rogers.

"I don't know." Rogers looked down at the orders. "It doesn't say. All it says is strategic operation."

"They damn near have the whole 8th here," I pointed out.

"I see that." Rogers glanced around the room. "We'll be going out with a bang."

I winced at the wording. "Let's hope we don't go out with a bang, boom, or any other explosive word."

Rogers chuckled. "Bad word choice. You know what I meant, Suhm. Hey, do you have a job waiting for you back home? Something to go back to?"

"No," I responded. "I'm sure I could find something pretty easily. It's not something I'm worried about now that the depression is over. Are you nervous about that?"

"I am." Rogers nodded. "I can apply to be a commercial pilot, but what if I panic while flying and think someone is after me? I've heard of it happening to others."

I contemplated his statement carefully. I hadn't considered that. The changes inside weren't evident to others because they didn't always show. It honestly hadn't even occurred to me either. Great, another thing to worry about. I looked up as the general walked in and we all sat up.

"Soldiers, we have a multi-location operation today—a three-pronged attack. In total, we will have three hundred seventy-one bombers and four hundred forty-five fighters dispatching to three airfields in the Netherlands, two airfields in Belgium and a factory, and three V-weapon sites in France." The general got right down to business. "Here is the breakdown of the heavy bombers."

I let out a quiet sigh. This mission wasn't going to be an easy one. I felt reasonably confident that we would be going to France. We'd gone to the other locations before but were old hands in France.

"We have seventy-nine B-17s we will dispatch to the Netherlands. There, thirty-eight of you are going to hit Gilze-Rijen Airfield, twenty to Volkel Airfield, and nineteen are going to hit Noll," the general broke out into specifics. I was starting to see why the Army held us back for an extra mission.

"Next, two hundred twenty-one B-24s are being sent to these locations. Forty-three will target Bois de Cassen V-weapon site. Thirty-six are going to Le Coulet Airfield. Twenty-nine will target Foret de L'Isle Adam. Another twenty-nine will go to Mery-sur-Oise V-weapon sites, one of which will be our departing crew, headed by Rogers." The general called us out with a nod. "Thirteen are headed to Eindhoven Airfield. Five crews are going to Melsbroek Airfield, and two will target Tulemont Airfield. This operation is a coordinated effort and I want communication between all groups. One hundred eighty P-51s will escort these two missions. The remaining numbers will perform as back up and drop on any flak sites seen."

One of the other crews behind me spoke up to ask a question. "Can we expect resistance?"

There was always one that asked. I didn't think we'd be going out with these kinds of numbers if they expected an easy mission. Resistance was something we expected all the time, so this guy must be new.

"Yes," the general answered in an irritated tone. "We're at war. Now, pay attention. Here are your escape routes if you go down." The aide spread a map out over the wall and taped it up. "You'll fly out in a large group and remain together until you need to separate to go to your specified locations. Keep formations tight. If you let a fighter get in the middle of you, it won't be good."

The general then handed out assignments for locations. Since he called us out, we already knew, and we knew what to expect over that area of France. Rogers spoke to the other crews in our group as the lead and we all understood what was needed. Rogers conversed briefly with the fighters that would be with us and they reassured him they'd been over that area before.

It looked like we were all set, and we headed out to the airfield for preflight checks. My feet felt leaden, yet my heart was already racing in anticipation of things getting hairy up there. We all went carefully over the plane, almost robotically yet thoroughly.

"Listen up, guys," Rogers called out after receiving the last all-clear. "I know this is our last mission and probably the most important, not in targets, payload, strategy, or anything else. It's important because it's our last and we want to come back and prepare for whatever comes next for each of us. No slip-ups. I trust each of you with my life, as I know that you trust me with yours. I will never take that for granted. You have my word. No matter what, we are brothers for life, and I want to say thank you before we go up. It matters to me that you know I am grateful for each of you."

I snapped into a salute to Rogers, and the crew followed my lead. "It's your flying and our lady Queenie seeing us through some bad places. You have my utmost respect and are my brother."

I shook his hand, kissed my fingers, planted them on Queenie's side and climbed into the plane. I knew where Rogers was coming from, and he said the same things I'd been thinking. We couldn't afford to allow the feelings to get in the way of what we needed to do so we didn't lose anyone. I knew there wouldn't be time for banter between the crew today since there were many planes heading out and they'd be in constant communication with us and others.

"All-clear," Rogers radioed to the tower once we were ready. "Waiting on clearance."

We took our position behind several fighters waiting for the okay to take off, and it felt like a long time. It wasn't, but it felt that way because I wanted it to be over, yet I didn't want to miss anything. It was a conundrum going on in my head.

"Crew, you with me?" Rogers radioed to us, checking to see if our heads were in the right place.

"Yes, sir," I replied. One by one, each of the crew responded.

"Q-Bar," the tower broke in, "you have clearance."

Rogers pushed the engines and we roared down the runway, the plane shaking and bumping beneath us on the uneven ground. Our wheels lifted off the ground, the aircraft settled her shaking, and I became a different person than I was five minutes ago. There was no room for emotions up there, and Rogers was right. This flight was the most critical mission.

My eyes watched the skies around us, saw the massive number of planes, and smiled. It was a sight to behold. It gave me a sense of pride for my country and what we did to protect it and humanity. The fighters in front were radioing back and forth that nothing was in sight.

I watched while the other groups broke off and wished them well. There were so many new crews that I didn't know them all, yet I knew what they had in store as we'd already done it. I both envied them and felt terrible.

"Incoming flak, eleven o'clock," one of the lead fighters radioed. "Ready, chaff."

Cutty and Jones both snapped to attention and began throwing chaff. We were only halfway through our flight to the target and saw flak. I wasn't sure it was a bad omen, but it wasn't good either. Black cottonball-looking clouds peppered the sky. Only a few planes radioed in that they had taken fire but no vital damage.

We flew another thirty minutes before the next

transmission of activity happened. "Luftwaffe spotted," came the call. "Evasive maneuvers, fighters."

In our plane, the gunners went on alert and we focused intently on the skies. The fighters were sufficiently far enough ahead of us that we didn't see anything for another twenty or so minutes, and then we saw fighters engaged with the enemy.

I think the moment they caught sight of thirty bombers barreling toward them, they panicked. Four enemies peeled off and flew off into the distance. I aimed my gun and fired on the enemy that was trying to shoot one of our fighters out of the sky. I saw sparks and knew I'd landed some hits.

I was relieved when I saw him flee. I didn't think for a moment that they'd be gone the rest of the day. My guess was they were off to get more reinforcements. I hoped the group going to the airfield took care of that for us.

We approached the coordinates of the target and from our height, we could see a hillside that the Nazis were known for taking over and putting bunkers and underground storage facilities. The bomb bay doors opened while Rogers radioed back to the rest that the target was in sight.

"Flak, three o'clock!" I yelled, spotting the flames on the ground firing at us. I swiveled and began to fire back. I'm sure it was my imagination but the bullets seemed louder. I kept firing as Jones readied to drop our load.

The call to release the bombs came next and we dropped with success. That hillside took an incredible amount of damage. The flak kept coming, though, and we hit a wall of it. All guns were returning fire, the noise relentless. There was no way around it and Merrill called out that our hydraulics took a hit. We didn't stop shooting, and Rogers didn't stop flying.

I groaned because that meant a scary landing for us. Hopefully, nothing else would happen. Rogers was flying beautifully to keep us from taking more damage, though we saw Queenie sprout some new holes.

Noise filled the headsets we all wore that kept us communicating with the others. Planes were taking a lot of damage, some critical. We had to get out of there fast. The fighters dove at the ground and opened fire. The air lit with bullets, tracers, billowing smoke, and fighting like I'd never seen.

More enemy planes came screaming in and engaged the fighters as they apparently saw them as the more significant threats. It wasn't only me that got them in my sights and opened fire. Our group wasn't taking it; they fought back ferociously. I saw at least two enemy planes go down and didn't know who could claim the victory.

It didn't make up for each of our bombers taking damage, but none of us were shot down, at least not in our group. The chatter that Rogers was relaying to us from the others sounded like we lost some planes and pilots, fighters, and that one crew member on a bomber was wounded. The battle raged on around us.

The Nazis were fighting like they had nothing to lose and we knew that wasn't true. They'd taken severe losses since D-Day and even before. There was no question that they would lose the war, yet they didn't stop coming at us. Their numbers were dwindling, as well as their resources.

We'd gotten word that a lot of the German forces were starving, defecting, and just flat-out going AWOL. I'd even heard that they didn't believe in the Nazi's cause; they had no choice but to join and fight even though they didn't want to.

Rogers got us out of the flak zone, and the enemy planes disengaged finally, allowing our fighters to rejoin us. Just like with our aircraft, you could see the holes that peppered their planes. I couldn't imagine how frightening that would be, given that most were one or two-person crews. At least we had a large plane with several people for backup.

We made it back to base with no further damage, and we all began sweating when we tried to get the landing gear down. It finally locked into place; there was barely enough pressure, but Rogers brought Queenie and us down safely for the last time.

Only then did we let out a huge cheer. We'd done it! We flew our last mission and brought our girl back in one piece with all her engines still working. Elation swept through the crew as we got out. Cutty and Jones dropped to the ground and kissed it before hopping up and plastering kisses all over the side of Queenie.

Rogers held his hands up and laughed as they charged at him. A few of the other crews wandered our way and congratulated us on a successful mission, and it was our last. My chest swelled with pride for our crew and our plane. I walked over, stroked a hand down Queenie's side and thanked her profusely. Our old girl had been through hell and back and kept each of us uninjured save for some frostbite.

"Overwhelmed now?" Rogers asked, having evaded the lips of Cutty and Jones.

"Strangely, yes," I replied.

Rogers put his hand on Queenie and bowed his head. "I thought we were going down," he admitted. "That was a solid wall of flak and I don't know how the hydraulics and these few holes are all we got. I'm not that good, Suhm. It's improbable, yet here we are."

"You are that good, Rogers. I know Queenie is metal, yet this girl has a fighting spirit and she kept us safe. She watched out for us," I told him truthfully. "You did some masterful flying up there every time. Don't brush it off, Rogers. Look at how many crews we've seen go down, and you kept us up. Nine of us owe you."

"No one owes me," Rogers corrected. "You can buy me a drink but don't owe me. I did my job just as you did yours. You brought enemies down, Suhm, keeping them off me so I could get us home. That's not nothing."

I nodded and accepted the compliment. "We all had a part to play and despite our cavalier attitudes, we did what we needed to do. We had no slackers, and I'm thankful for the crew we were."

"Well said." Rogers put his hand on my shoulder. "Let's debrief and celebrate. I believe I might make the girl I left back home a proposal and settle down."

"No shit." I breathed out a laugh. "You've got a girl at home?"

"No. I left one, telling her I wouldn't hold her to me while I was here. Anything could happen, and I didn't want to put her through that. I said that if she were still available when I came back if I did, that we'd see how she still felt about me," Rogers explained. "I know I'm not the same guy who came over with expectations of ending the war with my skills."

I laughed because I think we all thought that way at first. "She'd be lucky to have you." We started walking back. "I worry that Alyse won't like who I am now."

"Don't worry so much, Suhm." Rogers waved off the comment. "She's just going to be happy to have someone else to look after your little guy so she can sleep."

I chuckled and kept walking. "Just wait. You'll have one and then you can toss comments like that. Neither of us knows how to be a parent."

"That's true," Rogers agreed. "But we know what not to do. That's what matters."

"Maybe," I replied. I wasn't sure about that. I needed something that I lost along the way. Time would tell. "When do you think they'll release us?"

"I wish I had an answer for that." Rogers sighed. "A month? Two? I don't think it will be less. They might break us apart and send us to other bases. I've heard they put us into positions of training the greenies."

I could live with that. It might do me some good to knock some of the cocky attitudes down before it got one of them killed. Not that I'd been any different than them, but at least I quickly learned I wasn't anything compared to the seasoned pilots who flew in combat zones. All that sitting around in training didn't help.

Walking into the debrief, the general gave us a respectful nod before we ran through the mission with him. At the end, he looked at each of us individually, holding our gazes for several moments.

"Congratulations, you are Lucky Bastards."

CHAPTER 62

July 6th, 1944

Cutty, you and Suhm will remain here on base," the general told us. "We are trying to organize when people will head out. It could be soon, but plan for at least two more months here. I'm going to have you both in the gunnery office. We need some instructors for the new boys joining us. You two would excel there, showing them what they need to know."

It wasn't the best news, but Rogers had warned me this would happen. "Yes, sir," I saluted the general before walking out.

"It's not bad," Cutty replied with a tone that said otherwise. "A couple of months though?"

"It could be sooner. He said that," I reminded Cutty. "Look at it this way: we get to shape the next generation of crews coming to finish up the mess we left out there."

Cutty laughed. "I could definitely boss these kids around."

"It's not all bad," I agreed. "We do what we need to and bide our time until our ticket home gets handed to us. There will be less pressure on us to be in top shape since they won't call us for missions."

"True," Cutty agreed. "That means we can go to town and get the last partying out of us before home responsibility takes the place of fighting in a war."

"Do you think of anything else?" I laughed. "I thought you had a girl now?"

"Well, how do you think I will get any further with her if I don't go to town to meet up with her?" Cutty elbowed me in the side. "She needs to see me cooking with gas."

"And you think partying and drinking is going to give her that idea?" I shook my head. "I'm not a fuddy-duddy, but I know that isn't the best way to land someone to start a future with."

"How was it you met your wife?" Cutty asked me.

"At a mixer." I laughed. "Point taken. However, we weren't drinking and carrying on. We caught movies, roller skated, danced."

"Maybe her peepers don't work and you were the best bet in town," Cutty joked.

I pushed him away from me and laughed it off. He wasn't being serious and I knew it. I did look different now. My body had changed, and I saw someone different when I looked in the mirror. It could all be in my mind and Alyse would see the same person in me she had when I left.

"Tomorrow is our first day on the instructor job," I told Cutty. "Want to hitch a ride to town and get a meal?"

"I'm always up for a gas," Cutty agreed. "Let's see who else is still here and see if we can get a group of us together for the last time."

We headed to the barracks and Rogers was still there. He was leaving in the morning for a different base in England to instruct pilots. He agreed to join us and Merrill, who was also going in the morning for a different base. The rest of the crew had already left. We'd said our goodbyes earlier that morning.

"We going to a pub?" Merrill asked as he pulled on his hat.

"Probably," Cutty responded. "At least, first. I'm going to meet my girl there. Maybe we can catch a play or a movie."

"You just want to be in the dark theater with your woman," Rogers joked. "We are going to sit right behind you, so you can't be improper with her in a public place."

"Geez, are you in cahoots with Suhm or something?" Cutty argued. "Bunch of Geezers."

"There might be a dance," Merrill suggested. I don't think he realized we were giving Cutty a bum rap.

"We can do it all." I shrugged. "You and Rogers leave in the morning. Cutty and I will be here."

"There's a plan," Rogers said. "Do it all. We'll see what's happening, and if there's nothing, maybe we can get something started."

"There's a brainchild." Cutty guffawed. "Let's get a buzz and cut a rug. Those we can do at the pub."

I laughed. Cutty was still young enough to have a good time. For that matter, we all were. The war aged us mentally and I needed to remember that I was still in my prime. So were all of us. Fun needed to happen because we'd be looking at a mountain of responsibility once we returned to the States.

We had to find jobs, take care of families and children, pay bills, and do the things that made us adults. Life was different overseas, and not just because of the war. We still had responsibilities, but the only people watching over us were the chain of command and each other.

Off to town we went, and we lucked out. We found a

card game at the pub, and Cutty and his girl danced while we played cards and won some extra money. We found a dance going on from there, though it was at the tail end, and we got a few dances with some ladies. Then we went to a late-night movie where we did indeed pester Cutty every time he got friendly with his lady. It was a great night and a swell way to say farewell to Rogers and Merrill.

We saw them off the following day before heading to our classroom to begin our lessons with the new kids. It wasn't rough; there were a few cocky ones that we needed to knock down a peg or two though it went well.

It was a different atmosphere than the rigid schedule of constantly flying. I supposed it was an excellent way to prepare us for the civilian life we would encounter back home—the regular hours of a typical job. I didn't know if that was for me, but I had to try. I owed it to Alyse and little Ralph.

This schedule became our daily routine; some nights, we went to town, and others, I just stayed on base while Cutty met with his girl. He didn't need me as a chaperone every time. I admitted to myself that I was ready for home now.

Cutty and I stuck together on the front of pestering the chain of command to see when we would get to leave. It finally paid off and we got our orders to head for home. The tentative date was August 13th, 1944. I read them three times before I was sure that's what they said and only then I allowed myself to smile.

CHAPTER 63

August 13th, 1944

French toast would be nice for once," Cutty whined at breakfast. "It's always the same thing. I might not ever eat eggs or pancakes again."

"Who are you trying to fool?" I chuckled. "You'll eat anything."

"Not quite," Cutty argued. "Aren't you tired of the same old thing every day?"

"I am," I agreed. "I'm grateful it's not some slop that tastes awful."

"Like the coffee?" Cutty pointed out.

"Yes," I conceded. "Though it's excellent at waking me up and filling me, so I don't want to eat much of the boring breakfast. Give and take, Cutty."

"The fuddy-duddy comes out," Cutty joked. "You think we'll actually get papers today?"

"Fingers crossed. I'm tired of trying to teach these kids that they can't blow up everything by pointing the guns. Some of them just don't get it," I complained.

"I think saying some is being generous," Cutty answered. "Some have their first mission coming up. If we are here, seeing what they say after that will be interesting."

"Fingers crossed that we aren't here," I countered. "Imagine their egos if they shoot a plane down."

Cutty laughed and nodded. "Good point."

"Look up." I elbowed Cutty. "The general's aide just walked in with some papers."

Cutty snapped his head up so fast I was surprised there wasn't a cracking sound. Sure enough, the aide walked right toward us. "Gentlemen, it's been a pleasure."

The aide lied smoothly, and my response was to smile in return. "Thank you, same to you." I took the papers and gave Cutty his.

Cutty had his opened before I did and he let out a whoop. He stood up and did a little dance while he waved the papers around. I tugged him back down and told him to be quiet. I quietly pulled my papers out and read that we would catch the one o'clock B-24 out to Hethel Army Air Base.

"It's real." I breathed a sigh of relief, placing the paper back in the envelope and tucked it into my pocket. "We'll still need to teach the morning class. It's a good thing we already packed."

"Nothing will keep me off that plane," Cutty declared earnestly.

"Not even the girl you've been seeing?" I ribbed him.

"No. She's not a long-term thing," Cutty replied. "She's interested in ticking off her parents by dating an American and having fun. In the last letter I received from home, my parents told me about the girl next door who expressed interest in me when they showed my letters to her and her parents."

I nodded my understanding. I'd heard a lot about that happening with other guys. Being a war veteran was apparently a big draw for women. Rogers said it was the uniform. Women loved men wearing a uniform. I couldn't say I disagreed, given how the ladies we encountered fell all over themselves around us. My ego wasn't so big that I thought myself so attractive.

"Then you have something to look forward to," I replied. "I'm looking forward to seeing Alyse and my son."

"Not your parents?" Cutty sounded surprised.

"I hope they are well, but my priority is my wife and son," I answered. I'd managed to go all this time without talking about what a disappointment I was to my mom, which bled over onto my dad. I'd received mail from my dad, who signed my mom's name. I assumed it was because she was too deep in a bottle to hold the pen.

"That makes sense." Cutty nodded. "Might want to see if you can find a babysitter so you can have some alone time with your woman."

"Ralph is a baby. He won't know what's happening." I winked at Cutty with a smug grin.

We got up to take our dirty dishes to the bin and head off for the classroom. It was our last session and I hoped to impart enough wisdom to keep them alive. That was the goal of each session. It was something the kids didn't understand because they were impatient to get out there and get on with it. I knew the feeling well because it wasn't so long ago that I was in their shoes and just as impatient to take to the skies as they were. It felt like another lifetime.

"Think they'll listen today?" Cutty asked.

"Who knows?" I shrugged. "All we can do is try."

"Will it matter?" Cutty sounded bitter.

"What would have made you listen when we were in their shoes?" I pushed Cutty. I was willing to follow other suggestions to help keep these guys alive.

"A naked woman." Cutty laughed. "In all seriousness, maybe a story about what happened to one of the crew while they were up. All we keep telling them is to watch."

I gnawed on that for a few minutes and decided we should do precisely that. "Then let's do that today. See if they can relate or if we can drill it in that we aren't here for fun."

"Which mission should we talk about?" Cutty wondered.

"One of the times we lost our hydraulics," I suggested. "Those were some horrifying moments. We heard so much about flak during our training, but nothing made sense until we experienced it."

"Yeah, okay," Cutty agreed slowly. "It's not like we have anything to lose."

"We might save someone," I told him. "The Germans are getting desperate and that kind of behavior will get someone killed."

"Let's hope the pilot is listening." Cutty looked up at the sky as a plane took off. "We lucked out with Rogers."

"You've got that right," I responded quickly. "Between Rogers and our Queenie, they had our hives covered."

"You could tell them about watching one of the other crews go down," Cutty told me softly, his voice low. "That type of thing stays with you."

"I know," I agreed. "I don't want to dishonor those we lost."

"We can't let their death be in vain either." Cutty turned serious. "I still see them. Each one."

"Me too, Cutty," I told him. "And the empty beds that one time we came back."

"Then that's what we tell them," Cutty decided. "We

give them the unvarnished truth about war and what to expect."

That's what we did, too exactly. We laid it bare for these kids: the feelings you get when you see a plane of your friends shot down and no chutes. A plane gets shot down, chutes come out over enemy territory and those friends are never heard from again. Having flak come through the plane and almost taking an arm off but missing you by centimeters. Electrical systems failed due to lucky enemy shots and an aircraft landing with no hydraulics.

They listened. We didn't give them any of the propaganda the Army gave us. We told them our stories, the unvarnished truth. With any luck, it would save one of their lives. We dismissed the class at noon, shook each of their hands and went to grab our stuff.

"Now we get to fly on a B-24 without going to drop bombs," I told Cutty with a grin.

"To Liverpool of all places." Cutty groaned. "The most bombed city outside of London."

"They'll rebuild," I said quietly. "All of Europe will."

"Well, my fingers are crossed that we make it there and out without flak. God knows I've seen enough of that to last me a lifetime," Cutty remarked. "I know you feel the same."

I nodded because it was true. Now that it was time to go, my fear about returning home surfaced again. What if Alyse took off running like a tattooed Indian when she saw me? What would I do then? My darling wife had no idea I was coming home and I kept wavering whether surprising her was a wise choice.

At precisely one o'clock, our wheels lifted from the runway at Norwich for the last time. I said goodbye under my breath and refused to look out the windows. I knew what the base looked like from the air; the sight was permanently etched in my mind. Cutty watched it fade away before he turned back around.

After the class and having rehashed our worst moments, I could clearly see the empty beds of barracks thirteen in my mind. There were things I would miss about being here, but my time with the guys on the crew was the most prominent. I'd also miss the laid-back days in town, the carefree dancing, card games, and the guys' banter. I patted my bag with their addresses and vowed to keep in touch.

We landed in Liverpool shortly after and got transported to Chorley Hall. It was something new, so I looked forward to that aspect. We had to wait for the next flight to take us to Scotland. Getting home was a lot more trouble than getting here, that was for sure.

I don't know how they picked who got to leave and when. We quickly learned it was more of the hurry-up-and-wait game we'd gotten so used to playing. It was a lottery system. The Red Cross Aero Club served us snacks and beverages and I had my first hot dog in a long time. It made me homesick, something fierce, and I don't think I've ever had a hot dog taste as good as that one did.

Cutty and I sat at one of the tables with other squadrons waiting to head home, too. At night, we stood in formation lines and saluted the flag as they lowered Old Glory and called it a day. Men were all around us wearing their decorated bomber jackets and I even saw one man who had sixty-five bombs on the back. Thirty-one missions about killed me. I couldn't imagine over twice that amount.

The next day, we waited around for the announcement that told the squadrons to check the "O" bulletin board to see if their name was on the list of those departing for home. Gad, did people ever run to that board. Neither Cutty nor I were on it that first day. We spent another day at the Aero Club and talked with other guys, trading stories. We were weary and anxious.

Some of the stories were downright terrible. I felt lucky in multiple ways and counted my blessings before falling asleep. The next day, both Cutty and I headed out. Next stop, Scotland.

CHAPTER 64

August 15th, 1944

Our next stop on the route home was an RAF airfield in Scotland. There wasn't much to do there. The food was lackluster and we had opportunities to talk with RAF crews and more guys headed back to the States. More importantly, every man we spoke to wanted the war to end. That was the theme from all countries represented in that group of people.

"How long do you think we'll be stuck here?" Cutty asked. Our first night there was cold and dreary even though it was the peak of summer. I imagined the place was stunningly beautiful on sunny days.

"Hard to say, Cutty," I told him.

We sat out by the airfield on a rock and watched the planes take off for home. We were sweating it out. No one called our names on the second day either and each time a plane left, it got harder and harder. It was worse than waiting on orders for our first mission. Patience was in short supply.

Our brains knew the end was in sight, just as they knew why we came here and were eager to get on with it. The bright side of the whole thing was that we were flying home instead of taking a boat. We'd get to New York in hours instead of days. That's what got me through the waiting. I didn't think I'd be able to tolerate a long boat ride home.

Scotland was beautiful, but I'd be happy to say goodbye. Our view of the sea was unbeatable, but we both wanted to lay eyes on our country, on our shores, not to mention lay our gazes on our families. I wouldn't have anyone waiting on me because I hadn't told anyone. Cutty had let his parents know ahead of time. I wasn't sure of my choice, yet I didn't change my mind either and send word back. Chances were, I was afraid and wouldn't admit it to myself.

I did a lot of jogging while we waited. I even got Cutty doing jumping jacks with me to pass the time. It was getting depressing watching the planes depart and not being on them. Our moods had taken a turn and we got a bit surly with each other. We even got cards from someone leaving and played poker with some other guys. The hours during the day felt like weeks.

Finally, they called our names at seven on the third night there. We'd be on the next plane out. We grabbed our bags and foot lockers and sat on them, waiting until we could board. We weren't the only ones either. When the C-54 landed and received maintenance and fuel, we stood up and watched silently, knowing we'd soon be on our way.

Only forty-four of us got to leave at a time, less if there were stretchers or a large amount of cargo. The transport plane used to be a commercial plane until the war started. Then, the Army used it to ferry cargo, troops, and politicians back and forth when time was of the essence. The military repurposed it the same way Queen Mary had been.

"Load 'em up, men," one of the crew called out to us.

I was surprised that none of us ran like our lives depended on it. We calmly approached the plane and got on like we were leaving for vacation. It was finally happening; we were going home. Reality set in when the plane took off and Cutty gave me a nervous smile.

"Did you say goodbye?" he asked me after we were at altitude.

"Yes. Did you?" I turned to look at him.

"I did. I was sad and happy at the same time," Cutty remarked softly.

I nodded my understanding. Cutty didn't need my words to know I understood his feelings. We both fell asleep during the trip home, and I missed seeing the States come into view. Only the descent and the change of the engine's pitch woke me.

Home. I saw the landscape and felt heavy emotions prick the back of my eyes. There weren't people that wanted me dead here, not that I knew of anyway. No one was going to shoot me. I could go sailing and roller skating. I had a son. I would get to kiss my wife. I had a room that I wouldn't share with several other men. Was I ready for this?

Yes, I decided. I was. I still didn't know what I would do with my life, but I was happy to be back home. Something I didn't think I would be in the days leading up to our departure. I was delighted that I was wrong about it, too.

CHAPTER 65

August 20th, 1944

"One o'clock in the afternoon?" Cutty said groggily. "We lost a day. Damn, war is still taking things from us."

"We slept it away," I reminded him while we waited to get off the plane. "La Guardia airport. We're home, buddy."

I watched the sleep fade from Cutty's face and an excited smile take its place. "Are you going back to Milwaukee?" he asked me.

"No. Trenton. My parents moved to Jersey to be closer to Alyse and me," I told him. "I'll send my father a telegram after we get everything sorted out and let them know I'm back."

"You've got no one waiting for you?" Cutty looked taken aback.

"I want to make sure my head is where it needs to be first," I replied. "It felt like lifetimes passed while we were over there and I wanted to have my head firmly in place when I see my family. I wanted it to be a surprise for Alyse. I can only hope she will be happy."

"Why wouldn't she be happy to see you?" Cutty asked as we taxied off the runway.

"I've been gone a long time," I reminded him. "We

didn't have long together before I was shipped off and Alyse might have gotten used to living alone."

"Is she an independent woman?" Cutty grinned at me. "You might be sorry, then."

"She's a strong woman," I corrected him. "Stop your yapping and get up."

The plane had stopped and the doors opened. Our orders were to stay in New York City that night. Then, we'd head out to Camp Upton on Long Island. The Army had arranged our rooms already, and transport awaited us.

It was a bit surprising to see people waiting to welcome us home. The crowd cheered, clapped and waved as we departed the plane. We were lucky we weren't on the Queen Mary again; many troops returned that way. This arrival felt like we were royalty or at least someone important. It was our first step on US soil since December, and strangers greeted us like they'd missed our presence.

I wasn't ashamed to say there were tears on my face. There were tears on Cutty's face as he waved back at the people cheering for us. It was a wonderful welcome home, even if it were by strangers. I felt overcome with so many emotions that I numbly stood there waiting for our ride to the hotel. I was glad I hadn't told anyone I was arriving and my roller coaster emotions were the reason.

Once settled into the hotel, I sent a telegram to my father letting him know I had returned, and then Cutty and I ate a huge meal. We stumbled back to our room for more sleep. In the morning, we headed to Camp Upton. Once we arrived, aides shuffled us off to do a debriefing, get cleared of duty, turn in property, and collect our pay. Cutty and I parted ways with a hug, a handshake, and a promise to stay in touch.

"Suhm," one of the generals called out to me. "Can I

speak with you before you leave?"

"Yes, sir," I saluted and followed him to a private room.

"Do you have a job lined up?" the general asked me, getting right to the point.

"Not yet, sir. I have a wife and a baby I haven't seen yet. I planned to do that and get acquainted with them before I looked," I told him, confused at the conversation. I sincerely hoped he wasn't going to ask me to re-enlist. I didn't know if I could do that.

"There might be an opportunity for you to work for the government if that is something that might interest you," the general told me. "I don't have a lot of information. The Army tasked me with reviewing returning soldiers' files to see if any looked like a good fit. You, son, I think would be one of those people."

"Yes, sir, I am interested," I answered immediately. I didn't care if I didn't know what the job was. It was work, and I'd take it. Or I'd at least consider it.

"Here's an address in Washington, DC." The general handed me a piece of paper. "Take a few weeks at home, and then head out. I'll put your name on the list."

Stunned, I pocketed the paper and left the base to board a train bound for Trenton, New Jersey. The scenery passed by in a blur and my thoughts consumed me. Home. It was three-thirty in the afternoon, and the ride passed quickly. The train pulled into the station at seven o'clock at night and I grabbed my bag and stood there momentarily.

A man who worked in the ticket booth came out and asked if I was Ralph Suhm, and once I confirmed that, he handed me a telegram.

"Ralph, I've arranged a ride for you to shore. Father." I

pocketed the note.

I thanked the man and went around the front to see if someone was waiting for me. A man was holding a sign with my name and I threw my gear in and got in the car. It felt like all I was doing was traveling. I was tired. I was also nervous.

The entire ride out to Surf City felt like pins and needles were dancing over my skin. This place is where my family stayed during the summers. It would be where I met my son for the first time. It was home. The car pulled up in front of the house, and I stood there, soaking it in. I put my foot locker down and dropped my duffel on top of it.

Alyse must have heard the car because she came out of the house and stared at me, unbelieving. I think she thought I was a mirage because she didn't move. Oh, how I'd missed her face. It was funny that you don't recognize the emotion until it stares back at you. Her face slowly morphed to one of surprise as I walked up to her. For the first time since December, I pulled my darling wife into my arms and kissed her. I was home.

CHAPTER 66

After the War

I showed up at the address the general had given me. I checked it twice before entering the building. It said Army Corps of Engineers, which gave me a pause before I went in. I didn't want to be back in the Army. I wasn't exactly sure about this position when the general told me they had a job for me.

With a sigh, I straightened my jacket, walked into the building, and went to the desk with a young man behind it. The only way I'd find out was to walk in. "Hello, my name is Ralph Suhm. My old Army general told me to come to this address about a job. General Hanson is who referred me."

"Absolutely, sir," the kid told me respectfully. "Have a seat, and I'll let them know you are here."

I sat rigidly still on the chair. The world I came back to wasn't the one I left. I did my best not to fidget and look professional. I had my qualms about being here. However, I needed to follow through to ensure I had money coming in to take care of my family.

"Mr. Suhm," a stodgy old man called my name. He had the look of someone who served during the First World War. "Please, follow me."

I stood and followed the man back through a long hallway with several gray metal doors that were closed to what looked like a briefing room. I walked around the table and sat when the man gestured to me. I waited until he sat and lowered myself into the chair.

"I'm Howard Burns," he introduced himself. "I understand you have freshly returned to the States from your tour of duty. How was it?"

"Successful," I replied carefully. I didn't know what kind of answer Mr. Burns was looking for and I didn't know what I could get away with saying.

Mr. Burns laughed. "A safe answer. I served and don't find good answers to that question either." I nodded in response. "Do you know why you are here?"

"I don't, sir," I told him honestly. "General Hanson told me there might be a job here for me."

"That much is true." Mr. Burns nodded. "We don't know how long it will last. It depends on the war. Our funding for these jobs comes from the war effort. Will that present a problem for you?"

"Not until I don't have a job," I returned. "Will this give me extra skills or teach me something I can use to find a different position elsewhere after it's over?"

"Possibly." Mr. Burns nodded. "The other thing I need to get out in the open is that this position would require you to live nearby. I understand you have a new family. Are they willing to relocate?"

"That I couldn't answer without talking to my wife. I can tell you that I don't have a problem staying in the city during the week and going home on the weekends," I compromised. I was thinking fast and offering solutions to problems that I didn't know.

"That is also a possibility. It will require a flexible schedule and confidentiality," Mr. Burns continued. "Are you willing to sign papers promising not to discuss work performed here?"

I nodded in response and wondered what the pay would be. I'd have to pay for two residences, twice the amount of food and utilities, if Alyse didn't want to relocate. I didn't imagine that she did since she had a support system in place in Surf City.

"Sir, may I inquire about the pay? I'll need to know if it will be enough to support two households if my wife chooses not to move here," I told Mr. Burns before he went too much further into what the job entailed.

"I think we can work something out," Mr. Burns told me. "My records indicate that you excel at fixing and repairing things. Is this true?"

"Yes, sir," I replied.

"Do you have objections to looking at manufacturing plans and seeing if you can alter them to increase productivity or engineer at a lower cost?" Mr. Burns glanced at a paper he held in his hand.

"No, sir. No objections," I answered.

"Well, let's get down to crunching some numbers.

That was it. Mr. Burns said nothing more about the work I would be doing or anything. I signed papers that declared my silence on the matter, and we worked out a salary that I thought would be sufficient for two households. Mr. Burns told me of an apartment not far from there that was below the cost of others due to my position and sent me off to look at it and secure it for myself. They could change it to a smaller one if Alyse decided not to live in Washington, DC.

"I'm home," I called out, letting myself in the house. "Alyse?"

"Quiet," she ordered me as she came down the hall. "I just put Ralph down for a nap. He's been extra fussy today. What did you learn?"

"There's good and bad to it, but I took the job. Have a seat, Alyse." I sat on the sofa and patted the cushion beside me.

"That doesn't sound good, Ralph. Just spit it out," Alyse told me, but she sat. She folded her hands primly in her lap and pierced me with a stare I swore could see right through me.

"The job requires me to be in Washington, DC," I began. "They offered up an apartment that would house us both and Ralph. The other option is you stay here and I commute on weekends, schedule permitting."

"How would you support two households?" Alyse's hands twitched in her lap. It was the first sign she wasn't happy with what I told her.

"The salary offered would pay both rent and the mortgage here. It's a reduced rent in DC due to the position," I explained. "I can't tell you about the job other than I'd be fixing things. I had to sign papers saying I wouldn't talk about it, and it's conditional on the war. When the war is over, the job would be over."

"That doesn't sound like a good deal to me," Alyse stated plainly. "There's no stability."

We both remembered living through the depression and how tight things were for our parents and then ourselves. It was only when the war began in Europe that the economy in the States changed. It's ironic how the war machine funded things.

"There's always the chance it will lead to another job," I countered. "It's a good salary, and you can move there with me."

"I don't want to leave here," Alyse told me bluntly. "This is my home. We have family here."

"I figured that would be your response. I can commute," I replied with my compromise.

"So, we'll have a marriage on the weekends." Alyse's displeasure was obvious, but short of finding a menial job in the area, this was the better of the options.

"It's a government job, and here are the benefits I'll get while employed there." I reached into my pocket and handed her the list of paid holidays, healthcare options, and other perks that I was sure were more propaganda. I'd learned firsthand how good the government was at that.

"It sounds like you've already made up your mind and I don't really have a choice." Alyse handed me back the paper after a quick glance.

She didn't fool me. Alyse was as smart as a whip. I knew she'd read that entire piece of paper in the few seconds she'd held it. Her mind weighed the pros and cons and Alyse stared a hole through me. I knew that she was mentally preparing a budget and how to make the most of it.

I may have been gone for most of our marriage, but I knew my wife. She'd survived on my Army pay until now, even when I didn't get paid. Alyse could pinch a penny and receive change. It's one of the many things I admire about the woman. She made it work, no matter what.

It might not be an ideal situation, though it was the one that presented itself and my gut told me to go with it. The scenario might have intrigued me because I wanted to be married, but apart. I wanted a family, but I desired a job that would take me away from them. I couldn't help but think that I would have picked one or the other before the war. Now, I wanted both.

I was sure that it made me a less-than-stellar husband and that was something I would have to live with for the rest of my life. Maybe I was selfish. I didn't know. I loved Ralph, there was no question about that, just as I loved Alyse.

"Come on, wife." I stood and held out my hand. "Let's go roller skating."

"What about Ralph?" Alyse took my hand and pulled herself up.

"He can come with. He'll need to learn the sport anyway if he's a part of our family," I told her with a grin. "Just like he's going to learn how to sail."

"This came in the mail for you today." Alyse picked up an envelope I hadn't seen on the table and handed it to me. I opened it and saw the letter from Rogers. Queenie had gone down with her crew onboard on August 16th while flying a mission over Germany. That was while Cutty and I were waiting for a ride home in Scotland. My heart twisted in its chest for the crew and for our girl Queenie, who saw us through some tough spots. Maybe we wore the old girl out and she had nothing left to give.

Alyse frowned at me while I read. Nonetheless, she didn't argue with me about going skating. After a thoughtful frown at the letter, she left to get the sleeping baby. I folded the paper and fashioned a sling out of a blanket that we could wear around our necks. Maybe the activity would lighten her mood a bit and help her see that the job would be good for us. Roller skating would help me get my mind off of our lost plane.

CHAPTER 67

March 5th, 1946

R alph, you need to come home now." Alyse sounded frantic over the phone. "The baby is on its way."

"What?" I practically shouted. My feet were in motion before my brain processed the information. "I'm on my way."

I grabbed my keys, wallet, and jacket and flew to the door. I'd just gotten home from work and barely put down my things before the phone rang. I stopped and realized I needed to let my boss know what was happening. I quickly dialed his number and hoped he was still in the office. He usually worked long hours.

"Burns," came the gruff answer.

"Hello, Mr. Burns, it's Ralph Suhm. I wanted to let you know that I won't be in tomorrow. Alyse is having the baby. I'm leaving after I hang up with you," I told him in a rush.

"Take the week," Mr. Burns told me. "Then I need you back. I'm going to have to send you abroad for a week."

My shoulders slumped, and then I straightened. This work was the life I chose, I reminded myself. The pay was sufficient, the war was over, and I was still working. I couldn't ask for more. I would have to make do.

"Yes, sir. Thank you." I went to hang up and heard the

congratulations before the line disconnected.

I rushed out of the apartment, down the stairs and hopped in the car as fast as possible. Alyse hadn't gotten pregnant right away after I got home and I figured Ralph would be our only child. Then we got a surprise and were told we were having another. I missed the first one. I didn't want to miss this one too.

It was about a four-hour car drive from DC to Surf City. I was sweating, wondering whether I would make it in time, and said several little prayers that I did. I didn't think Alyse would forgive me if I weren't there. She carried so much of the burden of our family on her shoulders that I wasn't sure I would excuse myself if I didn't make it.

I drove faster than I should have. Thoughts and regrets battle for space in my mind the entire drive. I arrived home to find Alyse pacing the hallway with Ralph trailing behind her, thinking it was a game. I scooped Ralph up, kissed Alyse, and then grabbed her bag that she'd already packed.

"Off to the hospital we go," I sang to Ralph. He giggled like it was the most brilliant and funniest thing I'd ever said. "You are going to be a big brother, Ralph. What do you think of that?"

I plopped the toddler into the back seat with Alyse's bag and instructed him to be good and sit still. Alyse didn't look like she was having as good of a time as Ralph and I toned it down and helped her in the car.

I raced us to the hospital while I sang silly songs to Ralph to keep him happy when Alyse had contractions hit. I don't think he was too keen on seeing his mother in pain. I pulled into the parking lot and thanked my lucky stars that there was parking not too far from the door. I pulled the car into a spot and jumped out.

I grabbed the bag and Ralph and ran to the passenger door to help Alyse out. I was sure the staff at the hospital grew accustomed to seeing frantic dads run into the lobby with a pregnant wife waddling behind them, cursing because their husbands weren't helping them.

"My wife is having a baby," I told the lady at the counter.

"Where is your wife?" the woman pointedly asked me.

I cursed under my breath and ran back outside to help Alyse. "Papa is not so smart," I told Ralph. "Don't make my mistakes, son."

We got Alyse checked in. Ten minutes later, the nurse settled her into a bed. Ralph grew tired and cranky as the hours passed and Alyse was still in labor. I left her in the care of the nurses and took Ralph to the cafeteria to see about finding him something to snack on while we waited.

When I returned, I found that Alyse had been taken to delivery while we were gone. A nurse showed me to a different waiting room, where I sat with an anxious Ralph and waited. When he finally fell asleep, I paced and looked at my watch every few minutes. *Did it always take this long? Was Alyse alright?* I had a ton of questions and no answers.

I was about to fall asleep with Ralph three hours later when a nurse walked out carrying a tiny little bundle in a blue blanket. "Mr. Suhm? Congratulations, you have a baby boy."

I about tripped over my feet trying to get up and look at the baby. "A boy," I breathed out softly.

She held the blanket away from his little red, wrinkled face and my heart melted. I had another son. I gently touched his little cheek with my finger, afraid I would hurt him. He was so tiny.

"You can hold him," the nurse told me. "Cradle your

arms and I will set him there."

I did as she instructed and then the tiny baby was placed in my arms. This moment was what I'd missed with Ralph and I didn't think I could stop kicking myself for it. I swayed back and forth ever so slightly and watched the infant sleep. When he stirred and made some noises, I gave a panicked look to the nurse, who kindly hid her smile, and she took him back.

"Your wife is getting moved to a room," she told me. "Someone will come and get you shortly."

I nodded numbly, overwhelmed by the feelings holding a newborn baby brought out in me. I looked down at my sleeping son and wondered how Alyse might have felt after having him and being all alone. I didn't have much choice in the matter since the Army sent me overseas for war, but I couldn't be sorrier that I missed that and wasn't here to share in it with her.

"You have a baby brother," I told the sleeping toddler. Ralph didn't budge. I marveled at their ability to sleep soundly like that and smiled to myself. I had two sons. I'd need to write letters to the guys and let them know.

I nodded off and woke up about half an hour later when a hand shook my shoulder. "Mr. Suhm, we can take you to your wife's room now. We can put the little one in a bed."

I scooped up Ralph, who felt like a wet noodle when he slept. I followed the nurse down a series of hallways that felt like a maze, and then we arrived at Alyse's room. She was the only one in there, and she looked utterly exhausted.

"Hello, darling," I greeted her. I put Ralph down in the bed the nurse indicated and then walked over to kiss Alyse on the forehead. "I saw him. You did a marvelous job."

"What should we name him?" Alyse asked me, her

voice sleepy.

"How about James?" I asked.

"James," Alyse whispered. "I like it. James, it is." She then promptly fell asleep. I took her cue, sat down in the chair and followed suit.

The rest of the week flew by in the blink of an eye. Alyse spent three days in the hospital and then they sent her home. Ralph was fascinated with the baby, and I felt the same way. Alyse was naturally tired but took back over running the house like nothing happened. She was amazing.

I spent as much time as possible with the two boys and held James as much as possible. I didn't know much about newborns other than they were tiny and felt fragile. He seemed like a peaceful baby to me. Granted, I had no experience in that arena, but regardless, I was still smitten. I don't think I'd ever forget holding him right after he was born.

Before I realized it, I had to leave and return to work. I'd shared with Alyse they were sending me overseas again, yet I didn't know the location. It was never for more than a week, and the travel was as exhausting as was the work.

I don't know that my assurances that I didn't want to leave meant much to her, and the weariness on her face tugged at my heart. I needed to provide for them and kissed them each before I got in the car and returned to DC. They were my motivation. My family was the reason I pushed myself to work harder.

I played with the boys on my trips home and had fun the entire weekends I was there. I taught them about cars, took them sailing and fishing, and had them help me make another sailboat. They loved it and I cherished the time with them.

They were too young to remember anything, yet it was still fun for me.

My actions might have caused tension with Alyse since she didn't join me and she had to be both of us during the week. I knew I didn't spend as much time with her as I should and she felt slighted. I tried to make it up to her and it was my belief I fell short.

Alyse was the disciplinarian, nurturer, and sergeant of the household. I don't know how Ralph learned of the term and it amused me to no end that he called her that: Sergeant Mom. Alyse found it less funny. When I could find a babysitter, I took her ballroom roller skating. Those were the nights to remember. The fun we had was priceless.

CHAPTER 68

The world was rapidly evolving and in 1951, I found myself racing back home again for the birth of my third child. It was good that I was a mechanic and kept my vehicle in shape. I was sure I defied every traffic law that existed.

Ralph still called Alyse, Sergeant Mom, and when he called me to say that she was on the floor and hurting, I told him to call his grandpa and help get her to the hospital. All I could think about was the worst-case scenario, which didn't help my driving. I'd noticed myself jumping to those conclusions since I returned from war.

I wasn't an emotional man. My whole life, I learned men didn't show their feelings. Yet I wanted to express them the entire drive to the hospital. Not even overseas did we show our fear or sorrow when we saw horrible things. We swallowed it and said trite words to cover how much we were bothered. There wasn't time for anything else.

I arrived in time to have a nurse hand me a screaming, red-faced infant determined to show the world that he wasn't happy. I had a third son. Pride swelled in my heart and I cooed and swayed with the tiny baby, hoping to calm him. He wasn't having any of it, and I can't say it bothered me. He was alive and healthy by the sound of his lungs as he wailed.

I waited patiently with Ralph and James after their

grandfather left. It felt like hours and I had no idea how much time had passed before they came out to get me so we could see Alyse. Ralph was worried about her and it didn't occur to me until later that it must have been scary for him to see his mother in that kind of pain.

When the nurse opened the door, Ralph ran right to her and James wasn't far behind. Alyse cautioned both boys to stay quiet and not wake the sleeping baby in that no-nonsense tone she had. The newborn was in a wheeled bed near Alyse and finally sleeping.

I bent over to kiss her on the forehead, and she gave me a small, tired smile. Ralph and James studied the sleeping baby with the unrelenting curiosity only children seemed to have. It was endearing. Alyse stared at me, her face heavy with exhaustion.

"What should we name him?" she asked me.

I looked back at my wife and, for the life of me, couldn't think of a single name. "I don't know, what do you think?" I hated throwing it back on her like that. On the other hand, she did all the work to bring him into the world. Why shouldn't she get to pick his name?

"Wayne," she told me and glanced over at the baby.

"Wayne." I tried it out. It sounded good to me. "I like it." I leaned over and kissed her. "Boys, that is your little brother Wayne. You will help your mother take good care of him, right?"

Ralph looked back at me with a serious expression and nodded firmly. James just copied what his big brother did, his usual reaction. I couldn't help but smile. I motioned them over to me and told them to kiss their mother goodbye.

"I know you need to rest and it won't be possible with them here. I'll take them home with me and we'll return in the morning," I told my wife.

Alyse gave me another tired smile and nodded. She said goodbye to the boys and closed her eyes to sleep after she pulled the rolling crib closer to her bed. I loved her fiercely and wished I could show it better.

I taught Ralph and James how to sail on Lady Luck. Alyse wasn't too fond of the idea but I felt it was something both boys needed to learn how to do. Plus, it got them out from under her feet. Wayne was a fussy baby and only seemed to relax with his mother. He wanted nothing to do with me yet.

The boys took to sailing like naturals. We had so much fun on the water that we spent whole days there. I packed a picnic lunch Alyse made for us on sailing days, took it with me, and we had a gas. They were eager beavers when I taught them things and they cracked me up with their antics.

I was home almost every weekend during those first few months of Wayne's life. Ralph and James loved it. Alyse bonded with Wayne and it became evident that he was her favorite, even though she said she didn't have one.

I'd received a letter from Cutty that told me he'd had another child, this time a girl. I didn't envy him that as I figured boys were more manageable. I was happy that he was doing well. He'd gotten a job at a manufacturing plant and had worked himself into a management position. He said it was the simplest job he'd ever had.

Rogers married the girl he'd told me about and had a parcel of kids. I'd heard from him three months ago and they'd just had their fifth, also a girl. He now had three boys and two girls. He became a pilot for a commercial airline and was doing quite well for himself.

Jones had finally married and had one kid on the way.

He'd become a teacher of all things. I figured that was why he'd waited so long to have his own children. He spent his days dealing with other people's kids.

Ribbits hadn't married, much to his parent's chagrin. However, he was dating a woman now that he thought he wanted to settle down with and perhaps start a family. He had a good job selling cars and was the manager of a car lot owned by the father of the woman he dated.

I hadn't heard from the other guys in a while and hoped that life treated them well. I still wrote to all of them. Out of all of us, I was the only one who worked for the government, and I didn't know if that made me bright or not. Life wasn't easy. Nevertheless, I did my darndest to make the most of it.

My time spent with the boys made those hard days worth the extra effort when I came home and saw the smiles light up their faces. Alyse smiled a little less and I vowed to spend more time with her. Then it ran out before I could.

I'd planned to take her out on the town the following weekend I was home and I'd already arranged a babysitter for the kids. It would be our anniversary and she had no idea I had anything planned. She wasn't used to overly romantic gestures from me, nor was I accustomed to supplying them.

I planned take her to dinner, then out to a play I had gotten tickets for, and then we'd hit the roller rink for some ballroom skating. She really enjoyed it when we got to do that. It was the only time I saw her let loose and have fun. It didn't seem like enough. I wanted to show her that her efforts at caring for the family and the house weren't unnoticed or appreciated. I was simply poor at communicating it for the last ten years.

In 1961, Kennedy started a program called USAID. It was the United States Agency for International Development. Word came down through the channels that they were recruiting and someone in the Corps had submitted my name and file.

Before I knew it, I had another job. The salary was better though the travel and the hours appeared to be much the same as what I worked previously. I still had to stay in Washington, DC, but they offered me better benefits and pay. I could also talk about this job.

I'd become a master mechanic and they would send me all over the place to fix vehicles when they needed maintenance and before sending them overseas. It wasn't anything I wasn't familiar with and it seemed to be a good job; not easier, just better pay.

Alyse was happy with the salary but not that I couldn't come home and spend more time with her and the kids. It grated on me a little, though not as much as I had expected. I had gotten used to this way of life, and in my mind, I had separated work and family.

Sergeant Mom was the same as ever. However, with Ralph now an adult and branching out onto his own, she had one less person to care for in the house. Ralph was going to follow in my footsteps and join the military. It made me prouder than I knew how to tell him. I didn't even give voice to the thought that I was elated that there wasn't a world war going on. I didn't want to tell him my stories and dissuade him from his decision. We could talk about those later in life.

Sometimes, I looked back and remembered the fun kid I used to be and missed him. I loved hanging out with friends, dancing, meeting new people, telling jokes, and goofing around. I wondered where that kid went and what he would be today had a war not happened.

I'd come a long way from that boy I was and I had to admit that I was leading a good life. I loved Alyse and probably didn't tell her enough. The bond I had with my boys was something I wouldn't trade for the world. I even liked my job, though it was exhausting and often hard on my body.

I thought it was safe to say I was a happy man. I made a difference, which was what I had set out to do all those years ago. I was part of something I couldn't have imagined, and while it changed me, I wasn't disappointed with the man I became. I admitted to being more detached but challenged anyone who saw what we did over there to say that there wasn't a part of them that became that way after living through the war. I had time to make things up to Alyse and I would do my best to do that.

CHAPTER 69

Present Day

Lisa set the stack of papers aside, picked up her phone and checked the time. She'd been sitting on the floor reading for over three hours; no wonder she felt so stiff. She pushed to her feet and did a slow stretch while she processed the information about her grandfather that she'd read.

He'd left so much of his life out of that summary he'd taken the time to write. It was apparent that Nana was the one who typed it; even still, he'd taken the time to write it down. He didn't talk about teaching all of his *grandkids* how to work on their vehicles or the time he spent playing games with them and entertaining them. He didn't mention the natural bond with children he had at all. He didn't mention Nana's sass and sharp tongue, her sense of humor, or how much fun they had together.

He stopped writing before he got sick with cancer and overcame it. There was no mention of the roller-skating balls he went to with Nana or the sailing he did with his kids and their kids. There was no talk of the competitions won and no word about the cancer coming back. Regardless, Lisa still felt like parts of her grandpa were a stranger to her.

There was a whole lot in those papers that she never

knew. She didn't recognize the man he was back then. It didn't change how she felt about him; her respect grew, as did her family pride. She also understood more about her grandmother and why she was so strict in some aspects. Yet she couldn't deny that her grandparents had been in love and with each other. It was something Lisa witnessed frequently.

Lisa pinned the stack of papers together so they didn't get put out of order and set them off to the side. She picked up each item in that chest, examined it, placed it mentally in the date he'd most likely used it from the papers she'd read, and carefully put it down to look at the next one. She did this until the chest was empty, save for a stack of photos she'd saved for last.

She spent extra time on the bomber jacket that had the same girl her grandfather had painted on his plane. The same plane that was lost over Germany days after he began his journey home. How easily that could have been her grandpa on that plane. She would have never gotten to meet him, and she wouldn't have uncles.

She ran her fingers lightly over the original painting as she mulled over the man he was before she knew him. What a thing to have lived through. The Depression, and being sent off to a world war. She marveled at the fact that they lived through some of their missions and never crashed.

She found pictures of the sailboats her grandpa made and sailed before going overseas, photos of some of his crewmates, pictures of him in uniform, and painting the plane. She smiled and touched her fingers to the image. So much made sense to her now.

She missed him, bringing her back to why she was here and how she found the chest in the first place. Her father was gone now, and that pain crippled her. It was weird how she felt like she got to know her grandpa and then lost him, too. It was almost too much to bear. She became overwhelmed, not knowing how to express her emotions. Grief was a beast that she couldn't beat. It reminded her she no longer had her dad to discuss it with.

There had to be something she could do to honor her grandpa. Her dad would have loved it. He idolized his father and researched so much of what he did while over in the war. Lisa thought she should have listened to more of the stories her father told her. Too many thoughts flew through Lisa's mind to process the enormity of the information she'd learned about her grandpa. She didn't know much about the Second World War, yet she felt like she'd ingested a ton of knowledge.

Lisa wondered what life was like for her grandma and even anyone during that time. She gingerly packed all the items back in the chest and tried to figure out how to secure it so she could send the foot locker back home. She didn't even want it out of her sight. It was a precious memento and a piece of living history.

Perhaps there was a museum that would be interested in some of these things. There was a lot of history packed in such a small packet of papers, not to mention the chest, which was also original. Lisa closed the chest and sat on it briefly before getting up to continue packing her father's house. If she stopped now, she wouldn't finish and had a plane to catch to return home.

The entire time, the chest sat in the front of her mind and the living room while she moved around it. There was no question it would come home with her, but what about after? She couldn't get the thought out of her head.

Lisa sat back down on the floor and opened the chest

again. She went through the stack of papers once more to see if she had missed something, and she came across the certificate for something called Lucky Bastard Club. She'd seen something to that effect in her Nana's house and remembered the plaque that listed each of the missions in a frame.

Lisa didn't remember why it hadn't connected before now, but she knew she'd heard Lucky Bastard Club from her grandpa before but didn't know what it was. She grabbed her phone out of her pocket and began to search.

After reading several articles online, she understood the certificate and summary much better. With her phone in her hand, she dialed a friend she knew that wrote stories.

"Hey, it's Lisa," she said when Michelle picked up the phone. "You're still writing, correct?"

"Yeah, what's going on?" Michelle asked. "Are you okay?"

"I'm tired and overwhelmed, but okay," Lisa told her. "I'm in Florida right now trying to pack my dad's house up so I can put it on the market. But I came across something unique and wanted to know if you would be interested in doing a story on my grandpa?"

"I can try," Michelle hedged. "What are you looking for?"

"He was a member of the Lucky Bastard Club. I came across his actual Army-issued chest that he had used overseas during World War II. All his original flight gear and a summary of each mission he flew are in there. I was looking for a way to honor him and my dad."

"What does your dad have to do with telling a story about your grandpa?" Michelle asked curiously.

"My dad was infatuated with my grandpa's service

and did a ton of research on the places he's been and things he saw while over there. It would make him happy to know that someone told his dad's story," Lisa explained. "Have you heard of the Lucky Bastard Club?" Lisa asked.

"No, I sure haven't," Michelle answered, her tone now interested. "What is it?"

"He flew over thirty missions in German-occupied territory and didn't get shot down," Lisa explained. "I even have his original bomber jacket."

"That's cool," Michelle exclaimed. "I love reading historical fiction. I could try to do a novel of my own about that. I love that it's something I've never heard of before. I'll do it."

"Cool. Thank you," Lisa breathed. "I'll call you when I get home and we can discuss it."

"Sounds good," Michelle told her. "Be safe."

Lisa hung up and felt better about having a plan in place about how to honor her dad and grandpa. That enabled her to get more of the house packed up. She figured out how to secure the chest and looked forward to what would happen next regarding getting his story out.

"Okay, Grandpa, Dad." Lisa looked toward the sky as she stepped outside. "I'm going to tell your story, Grandpa, and all your research won't have been in vain, Dad. Lucky Bastard Club, let's make it known. I hope I have your blessing."

*The following pages are
some of the photos
from Ralph's footlocker.
We don't know the names of the people,
or the locations of the images,
or who took them.*

B-24 LIBERATOR IN FLIGHT OVER EUROPE (ABOVE)

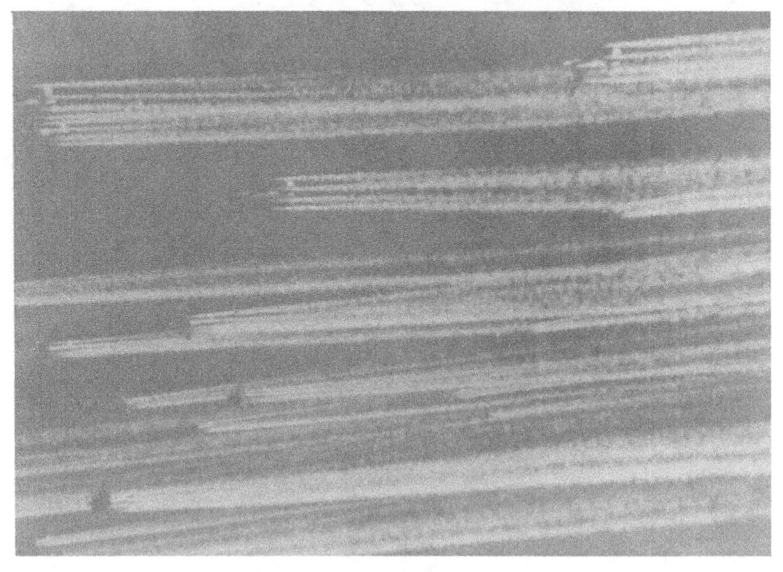

FORMATION OF B-24 LIBERATORS (ABOVE)
B-24 LIBERATOR (BELOW)

RALPH'S PLANE, Q-BAR QUEENIE (BELOW)

RALPH AND HIS CREW. RALPH SUHM, BOTTOM LEFT (ABOVE)
RALPH, ON THE RIGHT, AND FRIEND (BELOW)

RALPH WITH SALVO AS A PUPPY (ABOVE)
RALPH WITH SALVO (BELOW)

RALPH IN FULL FLIGHT GEAR (ABOVE)
RALPH PAINTING MISSION BOMBS ON QUEENIE (BELOW)

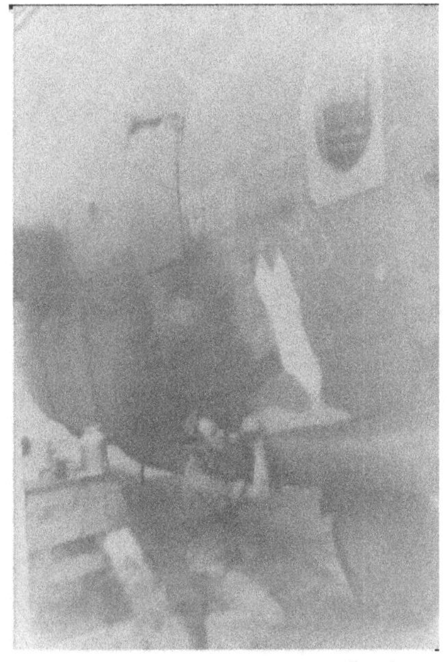

RALPH PAINTING THE VARGA GIRL ON QUEENIE (ABOVE)
TAIL OF QUEENIE AFTER RECEIVING HER NAME (BELOW)

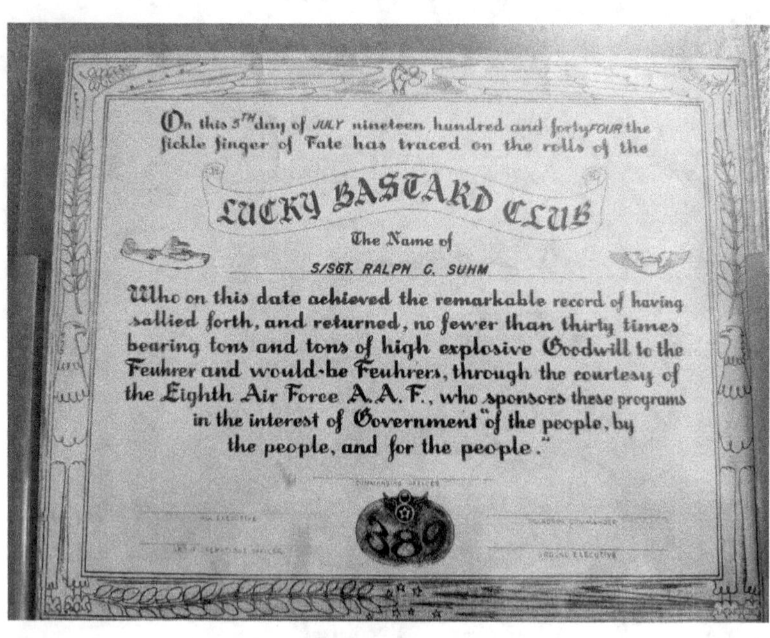

On this 5TH day of JULY nineteen hundred and fortyFOUR the
sickle finger of Fate has traced on the rolls of the

LUCKY BASTARD CLUB

The Name of

S/SGT. RALPH C. SUHM

Who on this date achieved the remarkable record of having
sallied forth, and returned, no fewer than thirty times
bearing tons and tons of high explosive Goodwill to the
Feuhrer and would-be Feuhrers, through the courtesy of
the Eighth Air Force A.A.F., who sponsors these programs
in the interest of Government "of the people, by
the people, and for the people."

THE FOLLOWING IS A LIST OF THE BOMBING MISSIONS WHICH THIS "LUCKY BASTARD"
COMPLETED, WITH HONORS TO HIS COUNTRY, COMRADES AND HIMSELF, OVER ENEMY
TERRITORY:

Date	Target	Country
8/MARCH/44	BERLIN	GERMANY
13/MARCH/44	NO BALL	FRANCE
18/MARCH/44	FRIEDRICHSHAFEN	GERMANY
20/MARCH/44	FRANKFURT	GERMANY
22/MARCH/44	BASDORF	GERMANY
23/MARCH/44	HANDORF	GERMANY
24/MARCH/44	NANCY	FRANCE
26/MARCH/44	NO BALL	FRANCE
27/MARCH/44	PAU	FRANCE
8/APRIL/44	BRUNSWICK	GERMANY
9/APRIL/44	TUTOW	GERMANY
11/APRIL/44	OSCHERLEBEN	GERMANY
13/APRIL/44	OBERPFAFFENHOFEN	GERMANY
22/APRIL/44	HAMM	GERMANY
25/APRIL/44	MANNHEIM	GERMANY
26/APRIL/44	GUTERSLOH	GERMANY
27/APRIL/44	NO BALL	FRANCE
1/MAY/44	NO BALL	FRANCE
7/MAY/44	OSNABRUCK	GERMANY
9/MAY/44	FLORENNES	BELGIUM
29/MAY/44	POLITZ	GERMANY
31/MAY/44	LUMES	FRANCE
3/JUNE/44	BERCK	FRANCE
6/JUNE/44	ST. LO	FRANCE
11/JUNE/44	TACTICAL	FRANCE
12/JUNE/44	CONCHES	FRANCE
15/JUNE/44	TOURS AREA	FRANCE
18/JUNE/44	HAMBURG	GERMANY
24/JUNE/44	BRETIGNY	FRANCE
25/JUNE/44	NO BALL	FRANCE
5/JULY/44	MERY-SUR-OISE	FRANCE

CERTIFICATE RECEIVED AFTER HITTING 30 MISSIONS (ABOVE)

AFTERWORD

While this novel is a work of fiction, Ralph Suhm was real. The missions listed in the book are those that Ralph participated in with Q-Bar Queenie, the actual name of the B-24 Ralph flew on. The dates and locations are factual to the best of my abilities. Enlistment, activation, and discharge dates were pulled from the paperwork found in Ralph's chest. The crew that Ralph worked with are fictional and creative license was used with their personalities and most activities.

Lisa is Ralph's granddaughter and one of my friends. She discovered the foot locker at her father's house after he passed away. Lisa's father, Ralph Jr., wanted nothing more than to honor his father, Ralph, and the service he performed for his country. After she found the foot locker and brought it home, I met with her and looked at all the items.

I saw the photographs of Ralph's sailboat, his trophies, the medals earned, and the countless pictures of his time in service. Reading Ralph's summary of his missions drove home how much these soldiers simply held back their feelings to survive their time overseas. The understated way they spoke of encounters I could never imagine being a part of and the horrors they witnessed was astounding.

It was nothing short of amazing to see firsthand the gear used by airmen from World War II and be able to hold it in my hand. That was when I was sure I had to write this story for Lisa, her father, and her grandfather. This book was by far the most challenging novel I've ever written, and I can't thank Lisa enough for the opportunity.

These men are heroes. There is no better way to word it. Ralph, the crew he worked with, and all the others who fought in World War II have my utmost respect and admiration.

ACKNOWLEDGMENTS

I want to take a moment to thank Lisa for digging through all her grandfather's belongings to get me the documents needed to write this story. She is the entire reason for it.

I have several people to thank. I didn't write this story without the help and expertise of others. It didn't take me long to learn how much goes into writing a historical book based on fact. I had wonderful help along the way. It took a village of encouragement at times and I am so grateful to have the people I do in my life.

Stacy: for his help digging through documents, helping research World War II history, and answering military questions along the way. I should also mention the patience he had with me during the writing of this novel. Thank you for your service to your country.

My parents: for giving me ideas of historical events to include and for reading the story. Dad, thank you for your service to your country.

Jonielle: for her help researching and bouncing ideas off constantly.

John: for helping me with historical facts, talking me through the time period, answering all my questions, and having the patience to do so. Your students are lucky to have you.

Carrie: for helping me get through the edits with her encouragement and support.

Chad: for beta reading and helping me edit. Thank you for your service to your country.

It is not my intention to leave anyone out. My sincere gratitude goes out to everyone who helps me, supports me, and encourages me through the process. I wouldn't get through it without all of you.